Praise for *Deadly Games*

"*Deadly Games* is a spine-tingling, thrilling ride that readers will devour in one sitting. Ms. Clark adds another layer to her ongoing saga about the Kinncaid brothers in *Deadly Games*. This is Ian's story, and what a story it is."

— *Romance Reviews Today*

". . . I found myself unable to put it down. *Deadly Games* by Jaycee Clark is one book that you don't want to miss if you like suspense."

— *Romance Junkies*

"Fast pacing and a well-developed plot make this an intriguing book . . . well detailed and well written . . ."

— *Romantic Times*

"Ian's story is well worth the wait. This suspenseful, action-packed, and thrilling story kept me on the edge of my seat. Another excellent romantic suspense from Jaycee Clark."

— *Joyfully Reviewed*

Books by Jaycee Clark

Angel Eyes
Firebird
Talons (coauthored with Shannon Stacey, Mandy Roth, Michelle
      Pillow, and Sydney Somers)
Black Aura
Ghost Cats (coauthored with Mandy Roth and Michelle Pillow)
Ghost Cats: Revenge
The Dream
Deadly Shadows
Deadly Ties
Deadly Obsession
Deadly Games
Deadly Secrets
Phoenix Rising II (coauthored with Donna Grant and Mandy Roth)
Ghost Cats 2 (coauthored with Mandy Roth and Michelle Pillow)
Hunted

Deadly Games

Jaycee Clark

BEYOND THE PAGE
PUBLISHING

Beyond the Page Books
are published by
Beyond the Page Publishing
www.beyondthepagepub.com

First digital edition copyright © 2004 by Jaycee Clark
First print edition copyright © 2004 by Jaycee Clark
Second digital edition copyright © 2011 by Jaycee Clark
Beyond the Page print edition copyright © 2013 by Jaycee Clark
Material excerpted from *Deadly Secrets* copyright © 2013 by Jaycee
Clark
Cover design and illustration by Dar Albert, Wicked Smart Designs

ISBN: 978-1-937349-74-5

Acknowledgments

This book would not have been possible without the unwavering support of friends and wonderful readers. Thank you all. Ian might still be in the murky part, his story only half done, if the call for him had not been what it was.

To Gail and Shalon, thanks for reading through another Kinncaid story. A big thanks to Val, who took the Texas out of Rori and made her more British, and to A., who pointed out things I never would have caught.

I have to give a special thanks to Mandy. Thanks for all the phone conversations, for saying, "Oh my God, you can't do that," or "Just write the damn thing." Thanks for all the help, all the links, all the ideas bounced back and forth. But mostly, thanks for the friendship. Hugs.

Oh, and I have to give one more special thanks to Kenneth—the strange one—who told me which guns my characters simply could not use and set me straight.

As always, thanks to my family, who still loves me even after writing this book. :)

Hugs and thanks to you all,

Jaycee

*I dedicate this book to the outcasts, the different,
the weird, and to those who love them —
life would be boring if all were the same*

Prologue

"What the hell do you mean you're not going to marry her?"

"Exactly what I said. I won't marry Brice Carlisle."

Ian Kinncaid sprawled in the chair in front of his father's desk. The dark wood gleamed as it always did, and what was normally a relaxed atmosphere was thick with tension.

His father rose and walked to look out the tall windows. As a child this room held the balance of fun and apprehension. He and his brothers were either in here playing or they were being called to account for some trouble. And Jock Kinncaid had never been one to let things slide. Not in business, not in life, and sure as hell not in family. You screwed up, you paid the price. Period.

Which was why they were both sitting in here now, though Ian couldn't figure out what the damn deal was, but the itchy feeling he wasn't going to like it crawled under his skin.

"Why?" his father asked quietly. The calm voice before the storm. His father's face was flushed, never a good sign.

Ian studied him. It had been a while since he'd seen his father this mad. And when had Dad started to get old? Still tall, strong and fit, but now there was more gray in his black hair and the wrinkles seemed deeper.

"Why? Why what?" Ian sat still. His father raged and he'd always waited. He was used to this game. They'd argue, yell a bit, not talk for a while, and then things would get back to normal. Same old, same old.

Jock Kinncaid turned from the window and speared Ian with a look that had him shifting in the chair. "I want to know why my son refuses to marry his fiancée."

Ian bit down on his own temper. "For the tenth time, she's not my damn fiancée."

"You should have thought about that before you got her pregnant."

What? *What?* So that was the game she chose this time. Ian took a deep breath. "First off, Brice Carlisle is not, nor has she ever been, nor will she ever *be*, my fiancée. Second, *if*, and I'm betting that's a damn big if, she's pregnant, it sure as hell isn't mine."

1

His father stared at him a while longer then huffed out a breath, walked to the desk, and sank down in the chair. "Look, this may not be the way you planned things, but you have to do the right thing. My God. I refuse to have my first grandchild born out of wedlock." He leveled another look, those blue eyes sharp as spears. "You'll marry her."

Ian stared his father down. "Are you listening to me at all?"

"You might not want to get married yet, but things change."

Ian stood. "I'll be damned if I'm getting married now and I won't get married tomorrow."

"I didn't say that damn soon."

Ian took a deep breath. "Look. I know this must seem like a perfect opportunity to you . . ."

That sound his father made in the back of his throat, somewhere between a scoff and a growl, had him stopping.

"Perfect opportunity?" His father stood with his hands flat on the desk.

Great.

"Perfect opportunity." Jock waggled a finger at him. "Let me tell you something, boyo. Neither I, Edward Carlisle, nor your mother — who, by the mercy of God, doesn't know yet — sees this as the perfect opportunity."

Ian rolled his eyes and stalked to the fireplace. "Please. You've been trying to get one of us with Eddie's oldest daughter for years. The problem is, she's known it, expects to become a Kinncaid, and none of us can stand her cold, selfish ass."

When his father opened his mouth, he plowed on. "Oh, she's pretty to look at. Brice has a great body, perfect posture, and the schooling to be a mate to a wealthy Kinncaid heir." He walked back and planted his hands on his father's desk. "But I'll bet my inheritance she's not pregnant."

"Then you'd lose." His father opened the desk drawer and took out a folded document, tossing it on the desk.

"What the hell is this?" Ian snatched it up and opened it. The checkmarks on the neat form. Blood work, pelvic exam, hCG levels. He flipped to the next page and the bottom dropped out of his stomach.

Pregnancy confirmed. He sat back in the chair.

Holy shit. His mind scrambled. Valentine's Day he'd been in and they'd met at the hotel. The round of sweaty sex ended in a fight that broke them up. Or rather, the fight ended the bout of sex short of his orgasm. Thanks to Brice calling out a name, and it sure as hell hadn't been his.

Ian took a deep breath, huffed it out and scanned down the sheet. Flipped it back to the doctor's form to read the handwriting at the bottom.

Patient eight weeks gestation.

It was currently the end of May . . . which would mean she was pregnant the end of March.

Thank you, God.

"It's not mine," he strangled out.

"What? Brice told Eddie the baby was yours."

His heart slammed in his chest but he bit down. "She's lying. The last time we were together was at Valentine's and the job was somewhat . . ." Ian looked up at his father before continuing, "unfulfilled, if you get my drift, Dad."

Jock rubbed his forehead. "She said you would deny it. Said you didn't want to marry her. But I didn't believe it. Never believed it," he muttered.

"Well, believe it. I'm not marrying her." Ian threw the papers back on the desk and leaned back, wanting to get up and pace.

Jock, his brow crinkled, his brows low over his eyes, said, "You were in for spring break. Down from Harvard. You and Brice went out then."

So they had. He'd had too much to drink, but had already spilled his guts to his brother earlier that afternoon about how he was going to have to talk to Brice again because she wasn't getting the point they were over. Aiden had agreed. Apparently the woman had told all and sundry they were still together.

"Nothing happened." Ian stood and rubbed the back of his neck. "Yeah, I drank a bit, but when she tried to kiss me I told her to forget it. It was over."

They'd been down at the lake. He still remembered how pissed she'd gotten, the way she'd tried to tackle him down, all joking, but there had been a determined glint in her eye. The way she crooned she could make it good for him. Now he understood it. She'd known then and she'd needed them to have sex. Lucky as hell for him that his brother Aiden had walked up.

Ian started to tell his father that, but no. This was his mess, he wasn't about to drag Aiden in on it.

Instead he turned and looked at his father.

"I'm sorry, the baby isn't mine. There is simply no way."

"There's all kinds of ways. You said yourself you'd been drinking." Those eyes already told Ian what his father thought.

"You think I'm lying."

Jock opened his mouth, then snapped it shut. He pointed his finger at Ian. "You're going to do the right thing. I didn't raise you any other way."

Ian could only stare at his father. "I'm not marrying her. Period."

"Yes, you are."

Rage quickly roiled through him, but he'd learned long ago he and his father were way too damn much alike. Calm. Calm. Calm. He took another deep breath.

"Tell her to set up a paternity test."

The incredulous look on his father's face might have been humorous at any other time.

Knowing Brice could weasel around that, Ian added, "And let Mom set it up with a doctor she knows and trusts."

The red crept up his father's face. "You're going to marry her."

"No." He walked back to the desk and leaned across it, looking his father in the eye. Why didn't the old man trust him?

"No son of mine will turn his back on his baby and the woman carrying it."

Ian straightened. "What?"

"You heard me."

"Repeat it."

Jock swallowed, his face twisted and furious. "Your mother and I raised you better. You *will* do the right thing."

Ian waited a beat and bit down. "And if I don't do what you *think* is the right thing?"

"Then you can leave." He threw up a hand. "Kinncaids don't . . ."

"Shirk their responsibilities," Ian finished with him.

Their eyes locked and clashed, their breaths both heavy, fueled with anger.

"I won't marry her. Not now, not tomorrow. If I did find out she carried my child, I'd petition the courts for it. But that woman will never be Mrs. Ian Kinncaid."

"Get out," his father whispered.

Ian's heart thrummed in his chest, faster and faster. "You're going to regret this. I'm your son and you sided with that whoring bitch."

He never saw his father's fist coming. The force to his jaw knocked him back several steps. Ian reached up and touched his jaw, moved it out and in. He didn't even bother to make a fist, didn't bother with anything. If the old man wanted to believe the worst of him, fine.

Jock stood on the other side of the desk looking as shocked and angry as Ian felt.

Ian nodded to him, turned on his heel and strode to the door. He reached out and grabbed the handle, then looked over his shoulder at his father.

"One day you'll wake up and see the woman she really is, but it'll never be as my wife. And I hope for my brothers' sakes she won't be one of theirs. Good-bye, Jock."

He slammed the door behind him and hurried upstairs. He shoved clothes into his bag, glanced around his room, and grabbed the photo of him and Aiden, another family photo, and the one of his mother. Rage and a good damn dose of fear pounded inside him. Ignoring the fact his hands were shaking, he snatched up his jacket, took a look around his bedroom, and walked out and right into Becky, the housekeeper.

"Here now, what's going on, then?" Her rotund figure was as familiar to him as the rest of the house. "Everyone gone but you and your father and you're yelling loud enough to wake the dead, ye are."

Instead of answering, he hugged her hard and said, "I have to go. Tell everyone bye for me." Then he looked into her eyes. "Tell Mom . . . Tell her . . . Give her a hug for me and tell her I love her."

She sputtered questions as he hurried down the hall and down the wide curving staircase. His father stood pacing in the foyer. Ian paused on the stairs for just an instant before continuing.

His father stepped in front of him, those blue eyes, so like his own, still blazing. In a low voice he said, "We're not done."

"Yeah, we are. You've made up your mind." He took a deep breath. "And I've made up mine."

"You leave this house, don't come back. Don't call asking for money either."

So that's the way of it. Fine.

A muscle bunched in his jaw. He could only shake his head. At the door he stopped again and said, "I'll leave the car with Aiden. I'd hate to get pulled over because you reported it stolen."

Childish? Probably. But damn it. He whirled, the short leash he'd kept on his anger snapped.

"You know, I was never the perfect kid. Aiden and I got in plenty of trouble. Gavin and Bray too. You want to throw me out, fine. Disown me?" Ian paused, noting his father didn't deny it. He bit down and nodded. "Fine. Disown me. Flesh and blood and the Kinncaid line of bullshit you always fed us, is just that, isn't it? Bullshit. Because when it comes right down to it, Jock Kinncaid doesn't stand with his own. Instead he believes the worst and disowns them. You're a goddamn hypocrite."

Ian slammed the door shut, threw his bag into the passenger seat of his convertible and roared out of the driveway, gravel spitting in the air even as his Porsche left black marks.

All he could hear over the thundering of his own heart was his father's words . . .

Don't come back . . .

Chapter 1

Thirteen years later
Czech Republic
October 28, 10:00 p.m.

The Prague club roared with the sounds of vices better left unknown, but too tempting for most. This Czech city was Janas-faced. Two faces of the same coin, its beauty and old world for the discerning tourists, but flipped, the red-light districts rivaled those in Amsterdam or the worst hells on earth. An evil, black and thick, rolled through the Prague underground, plumping its greedy fist from those who sought pleasure in unconventional ways.

So much for a quiet evening at home. Though quiet might not be found for a couple more days. Most residents were out celebrating — this was, after all, Czech Independence Day. The pop of fireworks burst through the air, laughter rang out and motorists zoomed by. Tonight was full of revelry. Fireworks still shot from Prazsky hrad, bursting the castle walls with color, and people still gathered in Stare Mesto.

Dimitri Petrolov, also referred to as the Reaper, strode to the front of Nero's Nightclub. Ivan, the bouncer, only nodded to him and let him pass. But then Dimitri really hadn't expected anyone to try and stop him. There was, after all, a good reason for his nickname. He was Viktor Hellinski's enforcer. And everyone who was anyone knew Hellinski was not a man to cross.

The club pulsed. Rammstein beat against the smoked tinged air from hidden speakers. Strobe lights flashed through the darkness, and dancers, revelers, drug users alike took on a macabre glow. The club was painted black, with the only relief burning murals on the walls that seemed to glow and flicker in the black lights.

"Hey, Dimitri, baby," a sultry voice called.

He looked to his right, where one of the night waitresses weaved between bodies with a platter of empty glasses. Debromil. Or was it her twin, Elsa? They were both blonde and stacked like Viking goddesses. Hopefully, they would simply remain waitresses and not wind up in Hellinski's other jobs. He merely smiled at her. Her silicone breasts, all but bursting from the corset she wore, didn't move as she gyrated to the music, her platter of empty drinks never wavering.

Dimitri wove his way to the staircase at the back of the club. Women, men, college kids moved out of his way. He ignored the drugs, probably ecstasy, being passed between two girls. Another couple kissed openmouthed. His foot on the bottom step, he heard the sounds of an argument between a man and woman, but ignored them. At the top landing he looked below at the strobing spandex- and leather-clad figures, dark in the shadows of flickering bright lights. The smell of cigarette smoke and the tinge of stronger chemicals mixed and melded with too many perfumes on too many bodies, and glossing it all was the permanent smell of alcohol. It was the fragrance of greed and vice. Well, one he associated anyway. Most here tonight were simply out for a good time. At least this was Nero's and not one of the other clubs.

He closed his eyes for a moment before turning to the hallway, guarded by two men he personally thought of as Pit and Bull. Their jackets did little to cover the holsters or the semiautomatic weapons harnessed there. But who the hell was he to raise a brow at a weapon. His SIG Sauer P226 was in his own shoulder holster beneath his suit jacket.

His skin itched with the knowledge that something was up. He didn't even look at them as he walked down the hallway. The black door at the end was marked *Private*.

Dimitri ignored this and shoved the door open, walking into the dark office. A low light spilled from a lamp on the desk. The tall leather chair was turned away from him, facing the large picture window that overlooked the floor of the club below.

"What took so long?" Viktor asked, not turning.

"I was otherwise . . ." Dimitri paused, "engaged."

Viktor scoffed. "Were you? Hope she gave you a good time, my friend."

Dimitri chose not to answer. Instead, he walked to stand at the edge of the window looking at the melee below. They reminded him of chaotic ants. Too much confusion.

"Nice profit tonight."

"Yes," Dimitri answered, not bothering to look at his boss. The man was reflected in the glass. No one could see them. To a viewer below, it looked like a giant wall of mirrors that only reflected the dancing blinking scene back to the revelers. He studied the man sitting in the chair, his hands resting on the arms, a glass of vodka in his hand.

They both stared out at the scene below them. Dimitri waited. He never pressed for details, never asked. Questioning, in his opinion, led to others questioning him. Questions often gave more away than silence. And silence, he had learned, afforded him more.

He watched as one man and woman screwed against the wall in the shadows. The bouncers and guards didn't notice, and if they had, nothing would have been done.

People gyrated on the dance floor; to him, they all looked the same. A sea of black ants. Drugs, sex, booze—just a good time, they'd say.

If they only knew.

"I have a job for you," Hellinski said.

Music from below barely pulsed through the floor or walls, there was a soft vibration from the base, but that was it. Dimitri knew these rooms were soundproof.

As was the rest of the building.

People came to play downstairs and some went upstairs and to the adjoining building for a different taste in entertainment that had little to do with dancing on the dance floor. It was only one of the many businesses that Dimitri helped his boss oversee.

These days he was gone more than here, only called in for specific jobs.

Dimitri waited in silence again.

"'Tis annoying habit you have, Dimitri. Silence. I don't like silence. I've killed others for their arrogance, you know."

"Yes, I know." And he had been the one to put the bullet in many of them.

"I'm also aware I'm not the only one who gives you orders."

He kept looking at the dancers and partygoers below. He saw a group of young men slip something—probably roofies—into the drinks of their dates.

"No, sir. You told me when I was brought in that I would answer to Elianya as well as to you."

The older man grunted and Dimitri turned to study him. Viktor did his Slavic ancestors proud. Wide slanted eyes, like those of a lion, watched him from their amber depths. Viktor's nose was slightly crooked, broken God only knows how many times. Scars slashed across the right side of his elongated face. The ash-blond hair was pulled back in a queue. The man was one of the most feared in the Prague underground, and in time, Dimitri knew, he himself would be on Viktor's hit list. It was simply the way the game was played.

Those amber eyes narrowed on him, even as Viktor straightened in his chair and pulled at the maroon silk shirt he wore. "Tell me what you would do if I ordered you to kill someone you might not want to."

Dimitri merely arched a brow. What game was the man setting into motion now?

He walked to the sideboard, reached into the small refrigerator, and pulled out a frozen glass. The vodka poured in smoothly. He set the decanter aside and turned back to his boss, sipping the clear liquid.

"When do I learn the name of this . . . problem?" Someone *he* wouldn't want to kill? His pulse sped. No way the man could know. Dimitri glanced at him as he sat in the chair to the side of the desk, his back against the wall, facing the rest of the room.

Viktor frowned and propped his left ankle on his right knee, his foot bouncing.

"Perhaps," Dimitri ventured, "the person is not one whom *I* might have a problem eliminating?"

Those eyes snapped back to him. Silence settled between them. "Perhaps."

Dimitri nodded. And waited.

With a curse, muttering of whores, Viktor stood, his hands clasped behind his back as he stared again out the window.

Apparently someone had angered Mr. Hellinski. Not wise, but then who was he to complain. This was what he did.

On a deep breath, the other man shook his head. "Come back tomorrow night. I will give you a name then. I want it done as soon as possible."

It was Dimitri's turn to frown. Why the hesitancy?

"Hellinski." When the man faced him, he said, "You're a hard man, with a business to oversee and protect, and as far as friends go,

I consider you one."

Viktor smiled, his scarred face more distorted. "And I you, Dimitri. And I you."

"You don't like people to cross you." Dimitri stared at him. "And you have no mercy for those who betray you."

Viktor inclined his head.

"I'm of the same mind." Dimitri stood, set the glass down.

Viktor's eyes widened in shock. "You think I would betray you?"

Dimitri smiled. "For enough money, yes."

Viktor laughed, but they both knew the words to be true.

"I'll be back tomorrow night."

Viktor nodded. "You're right on what you said of betrayal. I'll give you the name the night after tomorrow, as I just recalled I have a prior engagement. I do want the job finished within the next week."

Dimitri strode out of the office, seemingly not paying any more attention to anyone than when he walked in.

He slapped Ivan on the arm as he walked out of the club and put his head down against the cold autumn wind. He waited for a cab, noted that Ivan took out a cell phone and made a call.

• • •

She set the phone aside and bit on her thumbnail. Now what? Damn it all to hell. She had not worked this hard to see it all go up in flames. Not now.

One stupid mistake.

But she held the cards. She knew, she held the winning hand.

Kill someone whom Dimitri might object to?

She chuckled. For all the hard-won reputation, for all the crimes the man had committed, all the lives he had taken, she knew Mr. Petrolov for what he really was.

A savior of the weak, a champion of the downtrodden.

The Reaper? More like the Saint.

Oh, he killed all right. And Elianya Hellinski had no doubt that when her brother ordered her hit, Dimitri Petrolov—or so he was called—would not hesitate in carrying out his order. And probably enjoy doing it.

Things had not ended well with them. Damn the man, they could have ruled and created their own dynasty if he'd only listened to her.

But no. Elianya was a good fuck, but nothing more. Fine. She'd had others turn her down. Of course they were all dead. He would be as well. Pity though, the man was the best lover she'd ever had. But a woman had to do what a woman had to do. If the bastard didn't want her, that would be his loss. No man, no matter how much he amused her, would reject her. Period. She simply didn't allow that.

Besides, if he lived, he might be a problem. Might? She sighed. If Dimitri Petrolov was anything—it was a threat. She knew without a doubt Mr. Petrolov would kill her in a split second if he found out what she was really doing. For all his darkness and fear, the man was one of the most honorable she'd ever met. It was very sad. Honor was well and good in certain aspects—business, business where millions could be made, no. She had no use for such as the likes of him. Besides, she'd given the man his chance and he'd turned her down.

Ball-less wonders. Women were, without a doubt, the stronger, more driven sex. Men waited on orders, let too many things tie their damn hands.

No one tied her hands. No one. Not Dimitri, not Viktor, not any man.

Her heels clicked as she paced her office, the hardwood floors gleaming.

Stopping, she looked out the window, over the inky black waters of the Vltava River. She loved the nights. The night was the only time the truth shone in this world.

People hid behind daylight.

She grinned. And in daylight she would make certain it happened.

Walking back to her mahogany desk, she sat down and clicked on the address she'd paid dearly for. If this failed, there was always a backup. One should always be prepared.

Time to hire her own enforcer and make certain at the end of the night she was the one left standing.

• • •

New York, New York

The Raven clicked her way through wasting time as she waited on her plane, reading headlines via the Internet.

Her heart still slammed against her chest, but she knew enough to go slowly, to stay calm.

The last job went smooth as butter, and all the better for it.

Her eyes skimmed down the page, reading the weather reports. Good thing she was leaving New York and flying back home to Dublin. A storm was blowing in and she had no wish to stay here longer than necessary; already her flight was delayed. It would be early tomorrow morning when she arrived. She sighed.

An icon popped on-screen for Raven. Three messages.

She wanted to open it, but it was hardly safe. Not here. There were high-powered cameras all over airports these days. Though perhaps many would call her paranoid, she preferred the term cautious. Caution had saved her life more times than she cared to count and she wouldn't toss it aside now.

Once on the plane, however, she pulled the computer back out and clicked on her mailbox. The return address was probably as bogus as the one she herself created, but it served its purpose.

B-Widow only had one thing to say.

I've a job for you.

Raven closed her eyes and leaned back against the soft, plush, first-class seats. The black Atlantic thousands of feet below did not soothe her.

Nothing soothed her these days.

Nothing.

She took a drink of her ginger ale.

Perhaps it was time to call it quits.

God knew she had enough bloody money that she never had to do another thing in her life again.

And yet . . .

She was good at what she did. Never one to mince words, she knew she was damn good.

But she rarely took jobs back-to-back. Not wise.

And yet . . .

Something called to her.

Since the fiasco two years ago, she demanded names and information, gathering her own before she ever agreed to take on a mark.

A little unorthodox to some, especially to her trainer, Nikko.

But it was what she did and the way she preferred doing things.

After all, she didn't want some innocent man to die just because an ex-wife was pissed at him. She might kill for a living, but she had her own code of ethics, though most would never see them.

What the hell.

She set the glass aside and typed a reply back to B-Widow, wondering who, wondering what, how much, and wondering what excitement this next job would bring her.

Chapter 2

Elianya paced the confines of her office. She could hear the girls chattering out in the studio. With a glance she doubled back. Knocking, she motioned to the photographer to get on with it. She wasn't paying him to stand still. He had a job to do.

One girl, her bright red hair pulled in tight braids, stood sucking a lollipop. The new fluffer. Elianya sighed. She paced, waiting for the call to come through, and it damn well better. She had yet to hear anything.

A tingle of apprehension made her pause and look out the window. Warehouses surrounded her, some old and dilapidated; several had newer façades and housed who knew what. She'd been told to leave Dimitri Petrolov alone.

"He's to be left as is. You take him out and all hell will break loose."

"You're to make certain that doesn't happen."

Silence answered her. "It might be possible." Another pause. "Do not act until I give you the go-ahead. Understand?"

"Of course," she lied.

She would do what she had to, regardless of what her contact thought or wanted. Elianya wasn't stupid, the contact was merely covering their own ass. She checked her email once more to see if Raven had answered her, but as yet, her box sat empty. Damn. Elianya tapped her nails against her teeth. No matter. If Raven didn't get back to her, she'd just get Ivan to carry out her order.

Sighing and wishing she could find someone who actually did what they were hired to do, she walked out of her office and into the studio.

Girls of various ages and looks stood dressed in their costumes. Perfectly legal to photograph a layout for a new costume pattern company.

And even if it wasn't, this was Prague. Anything could be bought.

The music, normally a white noise, screeched against her nerves. She walked over to the large boom box and shut it off. Looking at the clock, she saw the time.

"Let me see what you have so far, Leos," she told the photographer.

He motioned her over to the computer set in the corner and said to the girls, "Do not go anywhere. We're not finished. I want more of the schoolgirl shots, and Rada, stay in the nurse costume. Someone is coming by later."

Elianya looked at Leos and wondered again if the man were gay or if he just wasn't interested in her. She'd never pushed it. It was so hard to find a great photographer who didn't go off into artistic flights.

He sat behind the desk, popped his camera in a base and tapped his long white fingers over keys. His hair was trimmed short, his triangular face devoid of mustache or beard. A diamond winked from his right earlobe and gold linked across his almost fragile wrists.

Unlike her last photographer, Leos was so clean he could have been religious. Hell, maybe he was. She'd never seen him drink, he allowed no drugs on set, and if a girl was too high to perform, he sent her home.

Leos was not only her photographer for their little side venture, he was also the studio's legitimate photographer for both the ad layouts and other modeling agencies. He was talented and driven—a damn genius. Two reasons Elianya saw to keep him on.

She watched the photos pop up on-screen. Leaning down, her arm against the back of his chair, her hand splayed on the desktop, she caught his stolen glance down her cleavage.

Elianya turned to him and grinned. Let him look, she'd paid enough for these babies. Well, technically, Viktor had paid for them.

She focused on the photos, nixed the ones she didn't care for, told him some changes to make in positions. While his fingers tapped the keys and he moved the mouse, she leaned down and whispered in his ear.

"I have another job for you. Are you interested?"

His fingers paused over the keys. "Perhaps. What job?"

She thought about what to tell him. He probably wouldn't do it. For a man who thought of photography as an art, Leos was undeniably stiff. Even if he did film porns on the side.

"I've some new clients and girls I'd like to shoot."

He looked at her and asked, "How old?"

She let her gaze roam over the gaggle of women and young ladies here. She knew most of them were college age; some didn't care and only wanted the money. A few worked in the public clubs that were aboveground for the most part. But two, two were in the corner and very quiet. Those two were hers. They spoke to no one and merely sat staring at the wall.

"Younger than anything here," she whispered.

"No."

Elianya laughed and ruffled his short graying hair. "You are almost boring."

He tapped again on the keys and picked up his camera.

Damn it, she wanted him to shoot the scenes. "I'll pay you double what you normally make here in three hours."

Knowing his fees, she assumed he'd jump on that offer.

"No."

"Over a grand an hour, Leos?" She raked her nails over his shoulder, but he shook her off and stood. "You need to let loose some of those morals, my friend."

His eyes didn't stray from hers. "No, Elianya. Find another. I do this"—he motioned to the girls sitting around props, two on the bed, another on the silk draped floor—"but I draw the line at younger. Period."

She huffed out a sigh. "Please, Leos?" She ran a finger up the front of his white pullover.

"No."

Damn. Elianya tapped her spiked heel against the floor. "It's merely photos, Leos. A click of the camera."

He huffed out a breath, but he didn't say no.

"I'll add another five hundred an hour. That's two g's. Where the hell else can you make that kind of money an hour, Leos?"

His shoulders dropped. "When?"

She smiled. "I'll let you know tomorrow night. Probably, we shoot early on the thirty-first, no? No, that's tomorrow, isn't it? Then on the first." Elianya whispered, her lips brushing Leos's ear, "It's merely a few photos, Leos. Don't put me in a bind. I might have to find another photographer. Then what would you do?"

He huffed a sigh out, glared at her and finally said, "What am I to do?"

"Take pictures and keep your mouth shut."

Leos watched her; she saw the indecisiveness in his eyes, the shame. Poor ball-less wonder.

"Leave me, I have work to finish here," he said, shoving back from the computer.

• • •

She went by Raven, though her passport said something different. Her hotel room was one of the nicer ones in Prague. She'd arrived yesterday and had been reacquainting herself with the old European cultural city. She only went for the best when she was on vacation. Work, unless her cover demanded it, didn't need to be top-of-the-line. Then again, she wasn't staying in a backpacker's hovel either. Her digital camera sat beside her laptop, the memory card having already downloaded the photo of the possible target.

He was in three-quarter profile, looking out over the busy street as he climbed into a sleek black BMW sedan with dark windows.

Dimitri Petrolov. Right-hand man of one Viktor Hellinski, brothel owner, minor crime boss, and God only knew what else. She pulled up a photo of Hellinski in another window. Wanting to know everything about these two. Some marks were easy. People rarely went for revenge anymore. She frowned and rubbed the back of her neck. These days few knew how to successfully operate under true vengeance. People not of Hellinski's ilk. Hellinski was the type who had contacts, and he was, she realized as she read further, rather high up in the whole criminal ring. Which meant his best mate was right beside him. If she took out Mr. Petrolov, she'd have to make bloody certain no one could connect her. The backlash itself would more than likely be her head on a platter handed to Hellinski himself.

She studied Dimitri's picture again, wondered if that were his real name. He didn't look like a Dimitri. He was too . . . something. His dark hair was a little too long, as if he didn't have time to cut it, his hairline receding to an M across his forehead. Dark eyes—blue? Black? Brown? They didn't appear green. Man probably hit six feet, not too muscular, but not lanky. Lithe, like the snap of a whip—lethal. And since the streets had dubbed him the Reaper, she supposed lethal fit.

Fine, he was a murderer, but then, technically so was she.

Cheekbones and jawline were harsh and unrelieved, his lips neither too full nor thin. His could have been the face of a fallen angel. A dark shadow, well past five o'clock, but not quite a beard and mustache, lined his jaw and upper lip. Something was arresting about his face, yet if she saw him in a crowd, she wondered if she would have looked at him again.

Her? Probably, but then she wasn't exactly normal, now was she?

She picked up her pen and jotted notes down on a legal pad. One she would destroy as she always did. There was no way anything would be traced back to her. Though in this day and age, that was iffy, and depended on luck — whether hers or the ones investigating was a matter of perception.

Petrolov worked for Hellinski, but she was finding out that Hellinski wasn't easily reached or found and owned several pieces of legitimate real estate. Must keep an excuse as to the money income, yes? Then there was the restaurant and several nightclubs here in Prague. Brothels in the hell-town of Cheb. And there was a woman.

Raven cropped and enlarged the photo of the blonde woman standing between Hellinski and Dimitri. She was without question beautiful and had the same shape of eyes as Hellinski . . . Ah. Sister. Miss Elianya Hellinski.

Did she know what her brother did?

Raven studied those eyes staring out from the photo — bloody right the woman knew. Something in those cold eyes calculated.

Digging deeper in her search, she was surprised to find Dimitri Petrolov had only worked with Hellinski for a few years. About five. Moved up those ranks quickly, did he?

So where had the man been before then? Men who went by the name Reaper did not just drop onto the organized crime circuit. Where did he come from?

She looked for another hour. Frowning, she read the flat report of one Dimitri Petrolov, who hailed from Russia. But where? Russia was a big bloody country. Family? None. Age? N/A. Raven scratched her cheek.

No one just jumped onto the scene. Was he educated? Or just a lackey?

Raven discarded that idea. A lackey didn't join Hellinski and within two years become his hit man, only to gain more power and the boss's confidence in the next three years.

She narrowed her eyes on Dimitri's photo.

And why would someone want to get rid of him?

Hellinski would have his own men to take him out. Keep it in the family. That man, with his pale hair and amber, tilted eyes, did not look like one to hire a female assassin and certainly not by the contact of *B-Widow*.

Definitely a woman.

So who? A jilted lover?

Digging lower she read the material on what was known of the Reaper, who enforced Hellinski's hold and power. Maybe an escaped prostitute who fled out of the stranglehold of those in charge of her?

The Reaper.

No one went against him. He took care of, cleanly and efficiently, any problems that arose.

In the photo he was dressed in a gray pullover, black jacket, trench coat, and pants. Man apparently liked dark colors. But then they blended well with the shadows.

Unease crawled under her skin.

Why?

He was just a mark. But reading the reports, she wondered. Something didn't add up. He should have worked for the boss longer to be this high up in power.

She wanted to know more about Hellinski. Her gut tugged as it did when she knew things were off.

What?

No real information on Petrolov — though that wasn't too surprising — quick move up, no friends, no associates, no family.

An idea zapped in her brain.

No, surely not.

But she'd worked both MI5 and MI6 long enough to spot the signs . . .

Was Dimitri Petrolov working both sides? Who the hell was he working for?

MI6? Interpol? The Americans? But if a Yank, then who the hell did he work for? They had more agencies than Britain had historical sights. FBI? CIA? NSA? INS? DOD?

No, the thought was ludicrous.

Raven stood and paced. Pacing cleared her head and focused things for her, it always had. Nothing in this whole bloody picture was clear. She'd learned the hard way to garner as much information as possible before the job so no complications arose.

And Dimitri Petrolov could be one hell of a complication. She wasn't stupid or psychic, but something told her to watch her step with the man.

To hell with it. Stalking back to her laptop, she hacked into her old system and saw a file on Hellinski. Skin trafficking, drug trafficking, arms dealer. Well, he was just a dream-filled bloke, wasn't he?

She read more until her eyes started to hurt. Looking out the window at the night, she decided to go out.

After a quick shower, she rubbed some lotion on and tried to decide on the short black dress . . . but then she'd have to wear the heels, which made her legs look great, but she could hardly run in the bloody things. Boots. And if she went with the boots, then she'd wear the black pants. Slinky lavender sweater, or as Nikko told her, slag sweater. So it drooped low enough anyone could see she had no real cleavage, but it bagged enough in the back and at the waist she could easily carry a weapon—and that was all that mattered.

She shook her short, short hair dry—and decided she loved her new style. At her scalp, she didn't have to do anything. No styling, no drying. She looked one way then the other. Bloody hell, it was short. Her face appeared even slimmer, her neck longer. She smiled and slapped on enough makeup that she'd fit into the club crowd. Not that she'd visited either Nero's or Babylon's, but she'd been in enough clubs over the years to know how to dress like she wanted to be there either with someone or by herself.

Studying herself in the mirror with a critical eye, she made certain her gun wasn't noticeable. Her skin reflected her mixed race, as did her black hair and pale green eyes. She'd always thought her mouth a bit too lush and wide, but she knew she was pretty. Men were rarely suspicious of a pretty woman. They saw what they wanted to see. And it had aided her enough, she wouldn't ignore her looks. Without a doubt, she knew her eyes were her best feature; long lashes and the jade color contrasted glaringly with her darkened skin tone. She had aristocratic features, as Nikko had told her time and again. A gentle curve of jaw, high cheekbones, and straight slender nose. She was tall. But pretty or not, she stayed in shape. Her muscles were not because of the latest bloody fashion or health craze that gripped the masses. She'd learned long ago to protect herself. Her stint as a constable and then in MI5 and MI6 only honed her muscles and her skills.

Knowing she'd do, she grabbed her long coat, made certain she had anything she'd need. Passport, room key, phone, cash, and her trusty little tool that would open any new computerized lock or start a car. Lovely little bit of technology and a birthday gift from Nikko.

Raven left the hotel, deciding to walk a while before hailing a cab. It was important to always know your location. A quick escape had saved her ass more times than she cared to count.

Prague was a beautiful city. From here she could see the old town square, glowing eerily green in the nightlights aimed at its medieval stone walls. The damp air promised cold and wafted with the smells of people dining at the local restaurants. She heard German as she passed a quaint little café. She thought she discerned Russian at a couple of places as people waited to be seated. English caught her ear time and again. Overall, it was a fairly quiet night with the exception of the two pickpockets, who easily made their marks and success-fully lifted a purse and a man's wallet.

Her phone rang.

"You taking the job?" asked a male voice, smooth and Italian as a dark rich wine.

"Nikko, luv, always so articulate."

He didn't answer her.

She shook her head. "I'm still deciding."

The answering silence told her more than his words would. The man knew she didn't make rash decisions, but neither did she nor-mally take so long to either accept or reject a job.

"Problems?"

"Problems?" Hmm . . . "Not so much problems, no. At least I don't believe so. Call it more a gut feeling."

He muttered something she couldn't hear. "Tell me of this prob-lem."

"It's not a problem." Not yet anyway.

"Tell me, *cara*."

She debated. Normally, Nikko knew very little of her jobs unless she wanted him to. Or she at least convinced herself he knew very little. But truth be known, everything she knew, everything she did, most of it, she learned from Nikko.

"*Cara* . . ."

She sighed. "I just have a feeling the mark isn't what he appears."

"Is anyone?"

"I get a feeling, just a feeling, that it's deeper than him working for his boss." There, she'd said it.

"What was the name again?"

"I didn't give it to you." Even as much as she trusted Nikko, she never gave him a mark's name. Who knew how small the world could be, and she didn't want complications. Number one rule—no complications.

This time he sighed. "You know, you're supposed to mellow with age."

She watched her surroundings, noted the group of co-eds in front of her. The guys were watching over the girls closely, except the one joker who seemed to be telling the girls how they could dress sexier. She smiled when the blond turned around and punched Mr. Laughs in the gut.

"Age? That would be you. Not me."

"I'm relieved this is your last assignment. I'm ready for . . ."

"Stop. Not the man and marriage act, Nikko. Grandbabies and the like. I don't want to hear it."

"Who said it was an act?"

Instead of replying, she hung up on him. The man might know lots of things, but some even Nikko didn't know, and if he did, well . . . She simply didn't need the hassle right now.

She hailed a black cab and climbed in.

"Do you speak English?" she asked the cabby, then thought of the phrase in Czech. "*Mluvíte anglicky?*"

He turned around. "Yes."

"Good," she said and smiled. "How about the club Nero's or Babylon's Sins?"

He narrowed his eyes, and ran a quick gaze over her.

She arched a brow. She'd heard about the taxi drivers in Prague.

"Nice lady like you might not want to visit such a club, no? More like Sunsets? Or perhaps Roxy? Roxy is the best nightclub in Prague."

Keeping her smile, she only said, "Nero's."

He shook his bald head, the lights from outside shining off it. "You pay, lady."

"*Děkuji.*" Then she added, "But don't try to overcharge or keep me in the cab. I know where the clubs are from here and you really don't want to test me." She met his eyes in the mirror. "Understood?"

He nodded and pulled away from the curb.

She watched the landmarks, noted the times they turned and where. Not that she didn't already have a map in her head of where she wanted to go and how to get there. The narrow medieval streets gave way to the wider modern roads, old world charm to modern ramshackle warehouses and buildings lining the waterfront of the Vlatva River. She wondered if she would meet Mr. Petrolov tonight. It was time to learn his habits if he was to be her mark, and if not . . .

Up to this point, if she declined a job, she simply declined the job. Something told her this might be different.

The cab pulled up in front of a club, and the red and orange lights outside gave an eerie glow. A queue of people snaked down the side of the building, and bulging men in tight shirts walked the edge. How many. She ran her gaze over them. One at the door, two more on patrol. Looking up, she searched for . . . There, just there, she saw the small black box of a security camera mounted on the light pole. Strange. Gadgets were getting smaller and smaller. No use in advertising you were watching people. Then again, most didn't look for the cameras and the smaller, less visible cameras were more expensive. And probably used indoors.

The driver pulled up to the front door and she got out.

Now she wished she'd worn her slapper heels. They'd get her in faster. Bugger it.

Climbing from the cab, she overpaid the driver and told him to keep the tip because as she figured it, he hadn't overcharged her, nor had he been stupid enough to try and lock her in the cab.

The chilled, late October wind bit through her small coat. She pulled it tighter and looked up. A whistle drew her attention to the bouncer. He raised a brow and jerked his head to the front door. She looked down the queue, then behind her. Finally, feigning innocence, she studied the bouncer. "Me?" she asked.

He grinned, a flash of crooked white teeth and dimples. He carried a firearm, the bulge under his jacket gave him away. She smiled back and walked up to him.

He lifted the rope and let her in. "First time at Nero's?"

"First time in Prague. Is this bloody marvelous or what?"

He laughed, his eyes appreciating her.

Men. With a forced giggle, she muttered thanks and walked past him, blocking out the mutters and curses of the people directly in front whom she'd just cut. Life was rarely fair, chickies.

Chapter 3

Dimitri sipped the wine and observed the nightlife of Prague. Headlights and taillights winked, like teasing young co-eds. He took another sip, the glass not much more empty than when he poured it over half an hour ago. He was to meet Viktor this evening and it looked like he just might be late.

There was a time he wouldn't have dared to insult Viktor Hellinski, but those days were long past. He glanced around the expensively furnished loft with its sleek, modern and very empty lines. There was nothing of him here.

Or perhaps that was all there was of him anymore . . . Nothing.

The only mirror in the entire apartment was in the bathroom. To look in the mirror was to see one's self and all he saw anymore was a lie. Someone who didn't know who they were any more than the people he was acting to deceive.

He set the wine aside and rubbed a hand over his face, scratching the stubble he kept short along his jaw and lip.

How the hell did he get to this point?

The bullets and blades were headed his way if any knew the Reaper was a farce . . . a complete farce . . . well, not entirely. It wasn't like he'd never killed anyone, but his marks had usually deserved it, and those he was ordered to kill he simply didn't think about. The target was an order to be followed. Period.

The end was coming for his tour and he wasn't about to let them decide when he finished. He'd be damned if he turned into one of those rogues who had to be put down like a rabid dog.

Shaking off the anxiety and fatigue, he stood, rubbed his hands over his face again.

The triple chirp from his cell had him reaching for the little silver piece of technology. The LCD screen showed him who it was.

"What do you want?" he asked without preamble. He patted his pocket for a cigarette.

"This phone still secure?" John asked, his British accent clipping the words.

"As secure as I can make it. Why?" Damn it, he was out of cigarettes. He took a deep breath and wondered how he'd missed that one.

"We've picked up chatter."

"What would the intelligence communities do without chatter?" he muttered.

For a moment the man on the other end was silent. Then, "Something happen?"

"No, why do you ask?" Dimitri rummaged through one of the kitchen drawers where he also kept an extra pack, relieved to see he hadn't even opened that one yet. One thing about Europeans, they weren't as health crazed as Americans.

He ripped the package open and shook a cigarette out, reached into his pocket and pulled out his silver lighter. The click echoed over the line.

"You were supposed to quit that disgusting habit."

"If you called to tell me the important chatter is the fact I'm still smoking, then I do believe your boys need some updated equipment." The nicotine hit his system on his first deep drag. "Or perhaps you need new boys."

"You're even more caustic tonight than normal. What happened? Did you kill a defenseless animal?"

Dimitri ignored the remark from one of the few men he honestly considered a friend and trusted with not only his life, but that of his family.

"What do you want, Johnno?" he asked, using the nickname John Brasher hated.

"What the hell is going on?"

"Why"

"Who are you about to take out?"

Dimitri frowned, took another drag and studied the cigarette as the paper slowly disintegrated from the burning tip. On a deep breath, he asked, "Who says I'm marking anyone?"

"Sources."

"And those would be?"

John's chuckle grated on his nerves. "Look, our bosses both want to know who the mark is and . . ."

"And?"

"And we believe the Raven has been sent after you."

That was news. The Raven. Dimitri smiled. He was marked? Wasn't that refreshing? And he knew ahead of time.

"Well . . ."

"The powers that be are not pleased. One, they hear you're marking someone, and then that you've been marked. Now, me—I don't think you've marked yourself."

"Yes, that's always a concern, isn't it?" Idiots.

"Who's your mark?" John asked.

"We don't discuss that, you know."

"Yes, but some are worried."

He leaned up and stabbed the cigarette out in the ashtray on his glass coffee table. Dimitri sighed and leaned back, closing his eyes and pinching the bridge of his nose. "Johnno, I have no idea who my damn mark is. Hellinski hasn't told me yet. I'm to meet the man tonight to find out."

Neither man said a word for a bit.

John cleared his throat. "Any ideas?"

"Yeah, Elianya."

This time John's silence was filled with more than quiet. Dimitri knew what the man wanted, and had vowed to give it to him.

"When?" Rage snapped the word over the phone.

He sighed. "I don't know. I don't know for a fact that it's her, Johnno, and . . ."

"You swore to me, Ian. You swore and if you take this from me—"

"Do you honest to God think I'd do that?" Anger sharpened his own words. He knew Elianya's name sent his friend into a black rage. The fact John had used *his* real name, Ian, was evidence of just how far the woman still pushed Mr. Brasher.

He could hear John grinding his teeth. "She's mine."

"You don't need to remind me."

Something on the other end crashed.

He patiently waited. "Look, Johnno, it's only a feeling I have. When I know for certain, I'll let you know."

"She's mine."

Again, he pinched the bridge of his nose. "I will never dispute that fact."

"But some things are out of your control, aren't they?" John asked, tired.

He stood and walked to the window. "If, and that's a damn big if, Johnno. Then she's yours. Somehow she'll escape or . . ." God, he was so fucking tired. "I don't know. We'll come up with something."

"I should have just killed the bitch years ago," John snarled.

"Yes, but then you'd be behind bars. Sanctioned marks are one thing. Vendettas are equivalent to murder, my friend."

"Bullocks, that. And you bloody well know it. As if you've kept the lines separate."

True. He twisted his wrist, pushed the sleeve of his shirt up to check the time. "I'm late, Johnno, and since you've informed me that I'm marked, I'd rather get my meeting with Hellinski over with, if it's all the same to you."

Again the silence stretched. "I'm in Prague at the safe house. When we heard you were marked, I was sent down here. I think they're going to take you out soon."

"Cheery fucking thought, eh?"

The line went dead.

• • •

10:30 p.m.

Dimitri realized how rattled John had been to use his real name. No one called him Ian anymore. No one but Johnno, Pete, and his brothers — when he actually saw them. Which was rare, though more so in the last couple of years than in the dozen since he left the family. Last he knew, everyone was faring well. But then he hadn't checked in the last couple of months. Things had been too hectic and dangerous here and he wanted no one, no one connecting Dimitri Petrolov, the Reaper, to anyone remotely connected to Ian Kinncaid.

He'd taken chances when the need arose and there were more of those than he'd cared to feel comfortable with. He'd had to use Johnno twice. Once to help him out in Colorado and again last year when a bastard congressman had been after Brayden's wife, Christian. Only his brothers had ever realized who he was and that he was helping, and even then he'd been in disguise.

His sleek BMW cut through the late-night traffic as he made his way to Nero's. The noises from outside were muffled through his car.

He rarely listened to music—music lulled and he could never afford to be lulled.

Constant watch. Constant guard. If he was a civilian, he'd be neurotic. But as it were, this was all part of the job. Focused attention, a gun in his shoulder holster, an extra 9-millimeter under his seat and a couple of cans of tear gas in the console.

He was thirty-six years old, trusted very few men and knew he'd probably die as alone as he'd been forced to live for the last few years.

He vaguely wondered if the Raven were successful and blew his head off, if anyone would notify his family. On that realistic but macabre thought, he picked his phone back up and redialed Johnno, who answered on the first ring.

"What?"

"If Raven's successful, I need you to do something for me."

Silence. Then, "She won't be."

"She's good or she wouldn't have been hired and you know it."

"What is going on with you?"

Dimitri sighed. How to explain that he'd lived so long playing this game, had taken so many out that he knew his time was up? "Just listen. If she succeeds, I need you to notify . . ." He trailed off. Last time he checked, his car was bug-free, but then he hadn't checked in a couple of days.

"I understand. You concentrate on your end and I'll look for her."

He hung up and pulled into his parking space in front of the club. Alighting quickly, he ignored the swarm of people out front and cut through them, heading for the door. He narrowed his gaze at Ivan. "Problems tonight?"

Ivan smirked, but the smile slipped and he looked away as Dimitri continued to stare at him . . .

"Problems?" Dimitri repeated.

Ivan shook his head. "No, Mr. Petrolov. No problems."

Dimitri watched him and leaned close. "How many pretties have you let in tonight, Ivan?"

The man actually blushed. Would wonders never cease. "Three. No, four. Wait." His eyes got big. "Five. It was five, no?"

Dimitri slapped him on the shoulder and walked inside. One of the men at the front of the line muttered about cutting and going to the end of the line.

From under his brows, Dimitri merely stared at the brash, rude college kid. The kid, blond, blue-eyed and maybe twenty-one, gulped and stumbled back a step.

Knowing he sufficiently put fear into the brat, he turned to Ivan and said loudly, "Ivan, have this person removed from the premises. I find he offends me."

Ivan nodded and moved to do his bidding. "Y-yes, sir, Mr. Petrolov."

The air from the club hit him as it always did, thick and sweet with pumping music and fogging smoke from too many cigarettes and enough recreational drugs that a patron could get high simply standing in the doorway.

Dimitri made his way through the throng of bodies.

"Hey, sweet thing," one of the regular girls said to him.

"Olga."

"When you going to ask for a massage that will take you to Heaven?"

He flashed her a smile. "Not tonight. I have a meeting with the boss man."

"Pity."

"Isn't it though."

As he wove through the people dancing, laughing and talking, to the band screeching on the stage, a tingle prickled up the back of his neck.

Slowly, he put his right hand on the butt of his SIG and made it to the staircase. She wouldn't hit him here in the middle of a club. Too crowded, though if memory served, Raven preferred crowds—was it crowded streets or parties? He'd have to look her up as soon as he returned home. Walking up the stairs he scanned the crowd. A woman. She never disguised herself as a man. Rumor had it she was beautiful.

And with her profession, she wouldn't be drinking or getting high. At least not staking out a mark.

Damn it.

There were four women watching him. A blonde with another guy over in the corner. From her glazed eyes, she probably wasn't it, and unless he was mistaken, the man was giving her a nice little present under the cover of the table. Give them a couple more hours and people would be fucking against the wall.

Two redheads were candidates, but red hair was memorable. And they were too . . . something. Too flighty, happy. Not his image of the elusive Raven.

Maybe that one. Over at the bar, trying to ignore the man beside her. She had short black hair and skin the color of a frothy café mocha. From here he could see the muscles of her shoulder as the sweater dipped off one. Looking down he noticed she was wearing boots. Not lace up to the thigh boots, like many in here, not even platform boots. No, unless he was mistaken, the woman was wearing very practical boots. He ran his gaze back up her, watched as she crossed those long legs and wondered what her calves and thighs looked like. Her eyes did surprise him. With her coloring, he'd assumed they'd be brown, but even from here he could see they were light. A blue? Or gray maybe? Green. Interesting. Soft jawline, straight nose, arched brows. Rather beautiful actually.

He narrowed his eyes and smiled at her.

Something in him clicked and he knew, knew the woman at the bar was Raven. Perhaps it was the awareness that tingled like a quick jolt of electricity through him. Whatever it was, he would almost bet she was his assassin. Almost.

If she was, he wanted to know who the hell had hired her. And if she wasn't . . .

He grinned wider as he walked up the rest of the stairs. Time to see who Viktor wanted him to kill.

● ● ●

Raven watched the man walk up the stairs and had to admit he was even more handsome in person than he was in his photographs. Must be his shadowed beard. Or the eyes.

And in that one quick assessment he'd given her, she'd gotten the feeling he knew who she was and why she was here.

Which was bloody stupid, but there it was. She still hadn't accepted the job, but she decided she would. Probably.

Whether or not she would kill him would depend on him and what he was really doing. If she was right and he was something other than he appeared, then she'd cross that bridge when she got there, but . . .

But if he was only the Reaper, a cold-blooded assassin who worked for one of the most brutal crime bosses in Europe, then she'd happily take him out without a second thought.

Then again, he might not be so easy to take out . . . She had the distinct impression she might have finally met her match.

Just her luck, the last assignment she accepted would kill her. Maybe she waited too long to get out. Probably. Maybe she never should have started on this career path, but that was beside the bloody point and freaking pointless.

"Come dance with me," the man beside her asked yet again.

Raising a brow, she only looked down at the hand he'd placed on top of hers.

"Luv, you really want to move your hand."

He quickly snatched his hand back. "You don't have to get testy. A dance isn't a reason to be rude."

She stood, grabbed her drink and walked away. She found a quiet place—as quiet as she could in a raving club—and watched the wall of mirrors above the stairs.

Just who was Mr. Dimitri Petrolov?

She should just kill him and be done with it, take the money and retire. But something stayed her, and if she'd learned anything at all, she knew to follow her instincts. Where they were concerned, she wondered if she'd kill the man at all.

• • •

Dimitri stood at the wall of mirrors and looked out onto the club below. Again it was packed, bodies so close together that Hellinski would have even the bribed police all over him if a fire ever broke out. But Hellinski was never one to worry about such things. He scanned the crowd again and saw the woman had moved from her perch on the bar stool. Methodically, he glanced over the occupants below.

There she was, leaning against the wall, taking another sip of the drink, but the amount of pink confection stayed the same.

Nice front, love, but you need to actually drink a bit.

Her eyes rose to the windows, and again their light stare caught him off guard.

"I can't believe I'm asking you this," Viktor said for the third time

Dimitri sighed, kept his hands loosely at his sides. "Who? It's a name, Viktor, just a name."

Viktor's dark blasphemy made him turn from his study of the mysterious woman below and study his boss. Viktor was pale, dark circles under his eyes, eyes normally as cold and unfeeling as the devil's heart. But now, they were worried, creased. The man sat on the couch and leaned up on his knees. Dimitri merely waited, knowing there was no rushing his boss.

Viktor's shoulders rose and fell as he clasped and unclasped his hands. In a low voice, he said, "Elianya. I need . . ."

Dimitri's eyes slid closed. Taking a deep breath, he said quietly, "I understand."

Viktor's head whipped up, sharp and predatory, his slanted eyes as threatening as a wolf's. "No, you don't. She's . . . She's not . . . I thought as she grew older." Viktor thumped his fist on his thigh and stood. "Damn it all. What I do is one thing. Business is business, but Elianya . . ." He shook his head and raked a hand over his queued hair. "Children, now, Dimitri. The stupid bitch will be the death of me. She's pimping out children and God only knows what else."

For a moment, Dimitri could only stare at the man who, if he was ordered, he'd have to kill. Viktor Hellinski wasn't by any stretch of the imagination a nice man, but even the crime boss apparently had his limits.

"I heard she was opening up negotiations behind my back to the American bosses as well."

"The deal you nixed last December?" Dimitri asked.

Viktor nodded and paced. Dimitri waited.

"Stupid. So damn stupid. I knew something was wrong with her. Even the doctors she saw as a child warned me she was dangerous, but I never wanted to . . ." Viktor looked at him, his face stamped with pain. "I thought I could help her."

The woman had been raised in a world where vice and crime were a normal means, brutal as it was, and she learned she liked the nice things that benefited her from others' pain. Of course other crime bosses were married, had sisters or daughters, and Dimitri had never met anyone as wicked and depraved as Elianya. No matter her upbringing, something was twisted within her.

Dimitri shrugged and decided to be honest. "I've never cared for your sister."

Viktor glared at him. "You liked her enough to fuck her."

He didn't deny it. "Some things one learns one can live without. No man needs a blow job that badly."

"You think I don't know that? She asked me to have you castrated when you turned her down and told her to leave your apartments."

Dimitri almost crossed his legs. "Thank you for not following through on her request."

Viktor shook his head. "Children, Dimitri. Interpol will be all the fuck over us. You take care of this. Clean it up. Her photographer called me. Leos. He is a good man. I don't want him hurt." Those slanted, amber eyes pierced him again. "I mean it. The man is decent and talented and I can use him."

Dimitri shuffled through his memory of Elianya's entourage and clicked on the neatly trimmed man with the ponytail. Quiet, but temperamental, always behind a camera or computer. New age porn producer . . .

"They are to meet tomorrow night for a session. I will find out where, and tell you. I want her . . ." He fisted his hands. "Just clean it up. I can't . . . I won't." Viktor raked his hands over his head, and a long blond strand fell to his shoulder. "I know some of the girls here are young, but damn it. I'm not a child molester for Christ's sake."

That might be debatable, but Dimitri didn't think Viktor wanted his opinion on the semantics of law and minors.

"Give me your word, Dimitri. Give it to me in blood that you'll handle this matter."

Shit.

Dimitri straightened from his perch against the desk, grabbed the wicked sharp letter opener off of Viktor's desk and pricked his finger. "I swear to you, Viktor, I will take care of the matter." He wiped the knife off on his pants leg, tossed it on the desk, then smeared his blood on Viktor's palm. "Contact me with a location."

"I should just let you take her out tonight, but I can't find her."

"Do you want her found tonight?" Dimitri asked.

Christ, kids. Why was it, just when he thought he was deep enough in the filth of society, he realized he could still sink deeper?

Viktor stood at the windows and waved him away. "I don't care what you do. Or when. I just want it done. Please, just . . ." His shoulders rose on an inhale. "Make it fast, clean."

Viktor's back was to him and Dimitri didn't know if he should pity the man or admire him. No way could he sanction the death of one of his siblings, but then his brothers were more white bread and butter than seedy underworld negotiators.

"Yes, sir." Dimitri turned and walked out of the office, his nose tingling with cigarette smoked laced with the sweet tang of hash.

Grow up in a world of drugs, prostitution, and kills and what the hell did Hellinski expect?

Time to contact Johnno, and he still had to find out who the hell the woman was downstairs.

Kids. Nausea twisted his stomach.

Chapter 4

11:16 p.m.

Raven watched the man leave the club. Carefully, she walked out behind him, weaving through the dancing people. One girl in a sequined top slammed into her and Raven tried not to throw the clearly drunk girl away. Instead, keeping her eyes on Dimitri, she turned the girl around and gave her a small push toward the dance floor.

Her eyes stung from the smoke and she had the impression her pulse matched the beat of the music pumping through the air. Dead good time everyone seemed to be having though.

At the doorway, Ivan asked, "Leaving so soon, babe?"

She only flashed him a smile and pointed to her mark. Dressed in dark clothing, a long black overcoat, he looked the part of a crime boss's hit man.

"Do you know him?"

Ivan's eyes widened as he watched Dimitri Petrolov stop by his car. Without warning he said loudly, "Mr. Petrolov! This fine lady here wants to know who you are."

The man paused and pierced her with eyes, a wicked blue, dark from here, but maybe cobalt? She wasn't certain. A muscle jumped in his jaw as he studied her and those eyes narrowed. Squinting slightly at the edges. His hair was a bit on the long side and his features appeared even more unforgiving than they had in the photograph she had of him. Her heart did a slow flip. He put his arm up on top of the car and continued to study her, one long languid gaze down her body and then back up to her eyes. One dark eyebrow cocked.

She notched her chin up and stepped closer.

His smile could coax angels to sin. "Does she?" As could his voice, gruff and deep, as if he smoked. He opened his door and gave her wink. "It seems you just informed her, Ivan."

With that, the man climbed into his sporty BMW and sat for a few moments before the engine purred to life.

She stood there and watched the car. To go back to the hotel or . . .

She turned to Ivan. "Where does Mr. Petrolov live?"

Ivan's eyes widened. Then his face creased in that same gap-toothed crooked smile he'd given her earlier. "You do not want to go to that man's place." He nodded. "Trust me."

She only raised a brow.

"Really, he's not a nice man. You don't cross him. No one cross him."

"His place?"

Ivan's eyes narrowed on her. Then he shrugged. "First off, I don't know. I don't even know if the boss knows." He shook his head. "But even if I did, I'd never tell anyone. I value my life way too the hell much to spread that sort of information. Even to a pretty little thing like you, yes." His gaze ran over her. "Now, you staying out here or going back in? I must know, people want in, lady."

She sighed and shook her head. "Let 'em in, Ivan. I believe I'll go back to my hotel."

Ivan's smile was one that would probably give children nightmares. "Where's your place?" He nodded to the black car that pulled away from the curb when the traffic let up. "Mr. Petrolov might call back and ask for it."

She gave him her own chilling smile and hailed a cab. Turning she said, "Nice try, Ivan, but I'm not that big an idiot." She hurried to the cab and climbed in.

"Can you follow that black BMW in front of us? But discreetly. Stay at least three cars behind." She flashed several extra koruna at him.

The cabbie stared at her for a moment, then nodded as he jerked away from the curb and cut off an oncoming car.

One thing was certain. Mr. Dimitri Petrolov was a . . . a . . . Bloody hell. He was dangerous. So was she taking him out or not?

That was the question. She kept thinking of him putting his arm on top of the car. What about . . . Something had been in his hand . . . What?

Bugger it.

The databases had yielded nothing on one Dimitri Petrolov, which she knew was just impossible. No one just appeared on the scene a grown man. She wondered if he'd ever been fingerprinted. A facial scan? She'd have to wait on that.

Chewing on her thumbnail she wondered . . .

The car turned left and her driver did as well. As they waited on traffic, she looked down the street and saw Dimitri's car was also waiting in the jam.

What was she doing? She'd probably turn the job down, so why was she following him? Well, if she took the job, or needed to know more information on the man, then she had it.

They made several more turns and she realized they were heading into a quieter part of town. Bloody great, he'd probably make them. The traffic would thin and then what?

She watched as he turned down another street, and told the driver to keep going straight. She glanced down the street he'd taken. His taillights came on as he braked. There was a building at the end of the street. She'd come back later. As the driver went past, she gave him the address to her hotel and watched the Prague nightlife blur by outside.

● ● ●

Dimitri drove through the streets without thought. He quickly dialed John.

"What?" John asked without preamble.

"Got a computer?"

"Does Britain still have a queen?"

"I'm sending you a photo." He blared his horn as he swerved around a car parked in the middle of the damn road.

"Of?"

"If I knew that I wouldn't be sending it to you. A woman I saw tonight in Nero's and then she followed me out. I want an I.D."

"I'm on it."

Silence stretched between them.

"Fuck it," he muttered. "Call me back in twenty. We need to discuss something."

With that he hung up. Taking a deep breath and maneuvering through the late-night traffic he wondered how he'd gotten caught up in all this shit. He came from a world of privilege, and though he knew his family knew of heartache and suffering . . . they had no idea how twisted things could truly become. How depraved some were.

He wished he didn't know.

He was tired. He hadn't been this tired since Green Hell. Twenty days with little sleep, long treks in the jungle, pouring rain, rationed food and evasion tactics. For whatever reason, since then, everything since, he'd always reminded himself he could have been back in that jungle with the boys wishing for the end of the damn training. It wasn't so much the training itself as the unknown. The mind games.

But here he was a world away and he'd almost trade places with one of those new Ranger recruits to be able to get out of this hell. God, how long had it been? He was too tired to think. He hadn't lasted too long with the Rangers. After a couple of missions brought him to the attention of a certain man, he retired and went to work for a different division of the government. And here he was. Still on missions, still evading. One jungle for another.

He shook off the thoughts and paid attention to the world around him.

October in Prague was quiet. The festival was already over, though the atmosphere of celebration still hung in the air as surely as the independence banners and posters reminding all of freedom.

Freedom. Was one ever truly free? He sure as hell wasn't. Half the people he dealt with weren't. He wondered vaguely when he'd become so cynical, so jaded. At the warehouse, he checked the mirrors again to ascertain he wasn't being tagged. He watched a cab continue on straight and felt a prickle along his neck. There had been two cabs that had followed him for a while, then again, maybe they weren't following him at all.

Paranoia was not always healthy, even if it did keep him alive.

He pushed the button and a door moved aside. He drove his car inside. Automatically reaching for his gun as he saw the man leaning against his other car.

John.

Well, hell.

He cut the engine and climbed out.

"Who's your target?" John asked, his arms crossed over his chest, his ankles crossed as if he didn't have a care in the world.

Dimitri knew better. John could sit for hours seemingly carefree and at ease and all the while devising ways to eliminate a target, carry out a mission, or simply coming up with an idea for a new lure. John Brasher was a man of many talents.

"We need to talk," he said, walking past John and pulling his pack of cigarettes out.

"Fuck."

"My sentiments exactly."

Once inside, he locked the door and ran a quick bug check. Switching on a portable jammer, he looked at his friend and said, "I'm so sick of this game, Johnno."

John's brown eyes narrowed. "We all are."

Dimitri shook off the thoughts and took a deep drag.

"Those will eventually kill you."

"If I die of lung cancer later in life, I'll count my blessings that it wasn't a bullet in some godforsaken jungle, desert, prison, or brothel."

"You left out backstreet alley."

"That too."

"Quit buggering around, and just say it straight, Ian." John walked to the window and looked out.

Ian—Dimitri—who the hell was he anymore? He watched his friend and couldn't imagine the hell John had gone through. Actually, he could. He'd seen it. Had picked John up and beat the shit out of him when he'd threatened suicide. But then, Ian couldn't really blame the man either.

Watching the man he loved as much as his brothers, he said, "Elianya Hellinski."

John, dressed in jeans and a dark blue sweater, barely nodded. Neither spoke for a long while. Dimitri finished his cigarette and stabbed the butt out in the ashtray. He sat in his chair, his temple on his fist as he rested his elbow on the arm of the chair.

John's shoulders were tight, the muscle in his jaw jumping and the pulse in his temple pounding. Sighing, Dimitri said, "I won't take this from you."

Slowly, John turned to him, his dark eyes black with memories. "No, you won't."

He remembered three years ago when he and John had worked together for Hellinski. They'd worked together before and their bosses apparently liked the way things went between them. They managed to keep things smooth without causing too many undo problems between their governments over petty issues of agents not working together when they were effectively on the same team. It wasn't a surprise to either of them when they learned they were assigned this operation. John had been higher up in the ranks, Ian coming in later from a stint in arms trafficking in Canada. John, straight as they came, also rejected Elianya, but she'd turned on him. When John returned to London on business — which was technically a leave so he could see his family — Elianya had somehow followed. They never knew since she'd been in Prague the whole time and no passports had her name or aliases on them sighted at any checkpoints. But then she could easily hire anyone she wanted, and apparently had. Two weeks later John's pregnant wife had climbed into his car with their three-year-old daughter, Bella, and John's world had ended in an explosion of mangled steel, burnt bodies, and shattered dreams.

The powers that be removed John, going by Jacob at the time, off the case and reported Mr. Jacob Angelovsky dead. He changed his last name and moved around after that. Hitting one bottom after another. The first year, Ian had worried John would do something stupid, and once he almost had. Ian reminded John that at the rate he was going, Elianya Hellinski would win. If John wanted vengeance then he'd better the hell stay alive long enough to see it through instead of fucking wimping out.

So John had gone back to work behind the scenes. The contact man for many of them. It kept him in the loop where they could watch him, where he still knew what the hell was going on. When Ian needed him to, John was there to help set things in motion so that when they were both of out this godforsaken job, they had something else to do that still exploited their skills. KB Securities served the high-end client with whatever they needed. Bodyguard, security system, secure transportation.

Ian Kinncaid couldn't wait to get back to the real world . . . or would that just be the civilian world? A world away from shadows and sanctioned killings would be nice. He'd settle for drug- and murder-free, but Utopia was a bit beyond most. Hell, he'd just settle to be Ian Kinncaid again.

"John." He stood and walked to the fridge, pulling out two bottles of water and tossing one to his partner. "Viktor wants it done as soon as possible."

John took a deep breath.

"What made the bastard finally turn on her?"

Ian took a drink and set the bottle very carefully on the counter. "The fact she went behind his back and opened up negotiations with the American ring he nixed last year."

"Woman was never one to back down."

"No, and apparently her new clients are of a special breed of depraved humans. She supplies them with children."

John, in the process of taking a drink, paused and then lowered the water bottle, his eyes weary. "Well, we both know she's not one to start up an adoption ring."

"No." He washed the sour taste out of his mouth with a slow drink of water and watched his friend.

"Son of a bitch."

"Yeah."

"You should have let me kill the woman years ago."

"Should have, but we'd both have been in a brig and you know it."

John shrugged. "We wouldn't have left any trace. She would have just disappeared."

Ian held up a hand. "I don't want to know anymore. You do what you have to, let me know how I need to help, but unless you really think I need to know, I'd rather not have the details."

John took a long drink of water before saying, "You mean like you kept the details from me of one Nina Fisher and of course our dearly loved Congressman Burbanks?"

Ian ignored the references to the times he helped rid his family of those who would have harmed them.

"When?" John asked.

Ian looked at his friend. "As soon as possible. I'm supposed to find her and get the deed done."

"Wonderful."

Ian thought about how to phrase his words. "I don't want to just take her out, John. If she's into kids, I want to know who, where, and when the hell she picked them up. I won't leave any child in the kind of hell Elianya would provide."

"Agreed." John took a deep breath, then sat and pinched the bridge of his nose. "I suppose now would be the time to inform you since it came up, I wasn't sent to just watch your back, there's more going on here. What exactly do you know about the child porn ring going on?"

Ian shook his head and stood, the water roiling in his stomach. "What ring? Or should I say which ring?" When he'd first come on this sting, he'd been opened to a world he'd rather have just heard about. Pornography in surplus in dark shadows better left alone, murder, enforced prostitution . . . He'd mentioned once to his superior how he didn't know how he was supposed to make a difference here. Pete had told him it wasn't about making a damn difference, but following orders and getting the job done. Mr. Dimitri Petrolov's job was to move up the ranks in one Viktor Hellinski's organization. No one cared about the girls, no one cared about the dark aspects. They were all worried that Mr. Hellinski was tied into fronting terrorists.

"What about the porn ring?" he asked with a sigh. "The one Viktor's just learned of and is so pissed about?"

"One that has a strong base of supplying here in Prague. We think the kids are being taken from low-income families, though that's still undecided. Some cop in your Connecticut stumbled upon a murder that apparently led to sex crimes. The victim had a computer and all sorts of info on the financial end of a child porn ring. Dots are leading back to here, but it's still sketchy. However, Interpol and boys from both our governments are wanting this one cracked."

"Of course they do." Child porn. Ian closed his eyes and shook his head, wishing the hot sickness would vanish. "You know where I want to be right now?"

John's chuckle grated across the space. "Anywhere but here?"

"Anywhere but here, any person but me."

John's eyes narrowed on him. "You know anything about this?"

Ian shook his head again. "No, but then we're just learning of it." How in the hell had he missed this? Was this Elianya's brainchild? Honestly, he wouldn't be surprised. He sniffed and looked out at the night. "What else do you know you're not telling me, John?"

"Well, apparently this is one of the largest, most lucrative rings the guys have ever uncovered. Everyone wants it stopped so they're tapping all their resources."

"And that includes me."

"That includes you."

John cleared his throat. "There is also the deal with the hit on you, and of course your mystery woman in the photograph."

God, he'd forgotten all about the woman. "And? You know who she is?"

John frowned and rubbed his forehead. "Where did you say you saw her again?"

He watched John carefully. "I told you, she was in Nero's tonight. I saw her watching me when I walked in. She watched for me while I met with Viktor and then followed me out. Asked Ivan who I was." He narrowed his gaze thinking about that cab.

John nodded and continued to rub his forehead, wrinkling the skin. His sigh slumped his shoulders. "I know her."

"What?"

"Right there in front of our fucking faces all this time and no one ever noticed. Never. I hope to God I'm wrong on this."

"I'm tired, I have to find Elianya tonight and I don't have time to figure out what the hell it is you're talking about."

John sat forward, his elbows on his knees, the blue sweater bunching. "The woman in that photo is a woman I once worked with. She did a stint in both MI5 and MI6 and she was bloody wicked."

"So what is she doing here?" he asked.

"I don't know, but I intend to find out."

"What do you hope you're wrong about, John? You think she's Raven?"

John shook his head. "Nothing is certain and I don't want you shooting her if I learn she's come back in to work, or even if she's investigating the porn rings from another angle."

He arched a brow. "So then she's perfectly harmless."

"There is nothing harmless about her. Watch your back."

• • •

Raven sat on the bed in her hotel, now in jeans and a black sweater. She knew where he lived, or had an idea. Why else would he drive all the way out there?

Girlfriend? From accounts he had none. A meeting? Probably not

45

in a residential section of the city. Then again, anything was possible.

So was she taking this job or not?

She sighed and nibbled on her thumbnail, listening to the traffic whir below.

Truth? She knew she was probably going to turn this job down. B-Widow had never given a reason for the hit and until she had it, there was no way Raven was just carrying it out. Which was dumb considering the fact the price had gone up to five million euros.

But if someone wanted him eliminated to that extent, one had to wonder why.

The hell of it was, she was too curious to just leave this alone. She knew. She had to find out what was going on, and if a hit had been put on one of the good guys she'd rather know and warn him. For now, she'd put B-Widow off again on the fact she was doing research and still deciding and wanting until the end of the week. Should be no problem.

Dimitri Petrolov was cocky, that was for certain, but if he'd taken her photo, then what? She knew he held something in his hand earlier that evening as he'd studied her. Everyone and their bloody grandmother could take a digital photo these days with nothing more than their mobile phone, or a camera that fit in their palm. It really complicated jobs like hers. If she hated anything it was a bleeding complication.

Sighing, she clicked on the email to answer B-Widow. Finishing that, she grabbed her leather jacket, her pack with all the essentials in it, and hurried out. Time to scout the last place she saw the BMW.

• • •

October 31, 12:20 a.m.

Elianya read the message on the computer. Damn. Why would the assassin take so long in deciding? She should have gone with a lesser known, someone more into the simple money, few would turn down a job for several thousands, let alone five million. And if Raven turned her down?

Anger licked quickly through her. Then Elianya would use a backup plan. Backups were wise, she knew. Anything could go wrong at any time, and at this point in the venture she couldn't afford for it to go wrong. Let her brother raise his empire on his old prostitutes, drugs, and occasional arms deal. She . . . she had other ties, other vices she'd exploit, and damn if she wasn't creating her own empire. She knew she was already as wealthy as her brother. While she'd acted the business minded sister who wanted to do nothing more than open her own boutiques, she'd been running another much more lucrative business.

And it was time to take out the competition. Checking her watch, she knew she'd have enough time to get done what she needed and head out to Kladno. She had clients coming in and wanted to make certain they received all they needed. Then it was to her house in Cheb, the lovely little Baroque town house she bought fully furnished. Then tomorrow night she was meeting Leos for a photo session at her other business studio in Cheb. Busy busy.

She clicked off the stereo, killing Mozart floating on the air. Quickly, she picked up her long white ermine coat and slipped it on, pulling her hair free.

Grabbing her briefcase, she left her office and hummed as she planned how to end the tension between herself and her brother.

Chapter 5

Elianya told her driver to wait and climbed out, hurrying into Nero's. Of course Viktor would be here at Nero's. Was it any wonder the man was falling behind? He'd become complacent.

She winked at Ivan with a smile she knew promised more—not that more would happen. He was a loose end she needed to tie off. Ivan had placed the bug in Viktor's office here, but his use was at an end. At least after tonight.

Inside, she walked straight to the staircase, cursing a young idiot who almost spilled a glass of red wine on her coat. Her heels clipped up the stairs. She ignored Viktor's two guards and stalked down the hallway.

How to play this? Staring at the door, she willed tears to her eyes. Blinking more moisture she opened the door. "Viktor?" She forced a tremor in her voice.

Her brother, his hair queued back, dressed immaculately as always, stood staring out the window on the floor below.

"Come in, Elianya." His voice was flat, but then why wouldn't it be? He was trying to kill her.

She started to cry. "Viktor, I n-need your help." Quickly, she shut the door behind her and locked it.

"What do you need help with?" Still he didn't turn around.

Would he kill her? Probably not. If he was going to, he would have done it himself and not asked Dimitri to do it for him.

She took off her coat. Didn't want to get it dirty now, did she? Very precisely she draped it over the leather chair by the door. Still she left the white leather gloves on.

"I've gotten . . ." She sniffed. "I've gotten into trouble, Viktor." She walked to his sideboard and thought about pouring herself a glass of cold vodka, but decided against it.

Obviously some would think she would have committed the deed, but then, she'd buy those off, or fuck them off. Either way, she'd do what she had to.

She turned and walked to his desk, as she had countless times, pouting as he turned around and letting the tears shimmer on her eyes.

Men were so easy.

His amber gaze, so like her own, studied her with a weariness that only stirred anger within her. He shook his head and sighed, sitting behind the desk.

"What, Elianya? What do you want now? What have you done now?"

She quivered her lip and chin. "I thought I could make us more money, Viktor. I only wanted to make you proud."

"So you always say." He tapped his fingers on his desk and watched her.

She picked up the letter open and put it down, picked up his pen and twirled it.

"I don't mean to cause you trouble, Viktor. Honestly, I don't. I only want to make you proud of me . . ." She let the last trail off in a quiver of fresh tears.

Again he sighed and put his hand on her knee. "Elianya, I know you don't mean trouble, but you always cause it. I love you and I'll always be proud of you." His mouth tilted down at the corner and his eyes narrowed. "I find I lack pride in many of your schemes."

The bastard was lying through his teeth. She hopped off his desk and leaned over to kiss his cheek, noting how he stiffened as she leaned close. "I love you too, brother. I am sorry I disappoint you, though."

She dropped the pen back to the desk and picked up the letter opener. As if not thinking, she fiddled with the object in her hand. Nice and sharp, wasn't it? But then she planned for it to be. She'd have only one chance. Some things one hired out for and others one carried out. This she would do all her own.

Elianya stood looking out at the crowd below, the few straggling up the staircase, those surrounding the small tables talking and laughing of whatever people talked and laughed about. Perhaps that table there was talking about their day, the group of ladies laughing about men? Though really, what was to laugh about men? Men were really such sad creatures.

Women, women were the strong ones and always had been. She knew that, hell, she proved it. The group of young boys pointed to the girls at the next table before leaning close to one another and laughing. Another man pinched a woman's ass.

Here it was almost midnight and the place was still on a good leg. Give it another hour and things would deteriorate. There had been sex under the stairs, she knew, she'd done it with several of Viktor's guards, heavy petting under a table, drugs passed as if they were candy.

To some it may seem wild and vice-ridden. She saw the potential for more. Prague was still such a simple city, its old world charm, friendly attitude, belied by the nightlife fun many could have, that many sought.

A shame she hadn't moved to Amsterdam years ago. But business was business and though she might better feel at home in the Netherlands city, she also knew the need would grow and spread. Why open shop when there were already plenty saturating the market? No, she waited. Waited here, learned her brother's contacts and used them when the time came.

She almost smiled.

Turning, she saw her brother watched her. "What?"

He tilted his head, his gaze running over her, his hands laced over his middle. "What happened to you? Where did I go wrong, Elianya?"

She frowned as if confused and cocked her head. "What are you talking about, Viktor?"

Stupid man.

She inched closer to him, and closer.

He shook his head. And she burst into tears.

"You think there is something wrong with me. I know it. I always knew it," she sobbed.

The look of confusion on his face, the wrinkled brow almost made her smile.

"I should just kill myself and save everyone the trouble," she muttered, pointing the blade at her wrist.

Viktor reached for the knife, and when he did, she grabbed hold of his hand and looked into his eyes. "Please, please help me, Viktor."

His eyes narrowed and she brought the knife up, plunged it into his gut. He gasped. She twisted the blade and shoved him back into his chair. Leaning close she whispered, "There is no helping me. I only want what you have, brother and *promiňte*," she said, apologizing. "But, I have to kill you. I'm sure you understand. It's just business after all, and be honest, you ordered my own kill."

His eyes widened and blood pooled at his mouth. He tried to reach out to his desk. She stabbed his arm, excitement coursing through her. Many believed stabbing was a man's sport, but she was finding she liked it.

Freud would undoubtedly argue, but really, what did a knife have to do with a penis. It was merely a weapon. One she found she liked.

"Now, now, you don't want it to end too soon. I have a present for you, after all." She turned his chair to face the computer, but left him away from the desk so he would not be able to hit the alarm he'd installed. With a few quick taps on the keys she opened her own file. "Now look here, Viktor. You remember that man you trust *so* much with all your business . . ." A photograph of Dimitri Petrolov popped on-screen. Then it faded into another photo of him but with different hair, then again into another man with a blond beard. The pictures changed from one to another until she clicked the cursor on her favorite.

She watched her brother blink, cough. "What . . . is . . . this?"

"This is my parting gift to you. You might not know these, all these are the same man. Can you guess who?" She glanced at him, saw more blood pooling at his mouth. "No, guess not. Mr. Petrolov, or whoever he claims to be, is a mirror." She walked behind his chair. The metallic scent of blood teased her nose. Leaning close, she said, "An illusion. My sources tell me he's with a government agency. Either the Americans or Brits. Very sketchy." She chuckled. "Of course, I plan to uncover all the truth." His complexion had gone white, and rage glittered in his eyes. She laughed. "You want another secret? Some of your hits he never even carried out. He faked them." She licked his ear, then whispered, "He lied to you and he *betrayed* you."

She straightened, saw the blood on her white gloves, and plunged the blade into the side of his neck while he was too busy studying the photo of the man in black fatigues with an assault rifle.

Standing behind and to the side of him, she jerked the letter opener free. Blood splattered across her white-gloved hand and shot in a stream across to their right, arcing across the wall. She tossed the letter opener into his lap, hurried around the desk, pulled off her stained leather gloves. Carefully, she dropped them into her purse and donned her white coat. Looking at her hands, she noted they were mostly clean, and with the sleeves of the coat, no one could see the sleeves of her suit. At the doorway she paused, checking her reflection in the mirror. Her braid was still in place. She pursed her lips and wiped a small red speckle off her cheek. She grinned and then chuckled.

In the mirror she could see her brother's body twitch. Stupid devil. His problem with her had been that he'd always underestimated her. The room reeked of blood and she turned.

The letter opener had slid in so easily after the first break of skin. She'd always loved the feel of a blade, the warmth of blood. A shiver danced down her back.

Shrugging, she walked to the corner of the room and pressed the hidden button in the light sconce. A small panel opened. She opened her purse, took out her key ring complete with the little flashlight attachment, and pressed the center, lighting the dark passage beyond. Elianya stepped through, pressed the switch on this side, the door swooshing shut behind her.

She walked down the hidden spiral staircase her brother had built into the wall in case the need ever arose, her heels clicking on the stairs. Place needed airing. Her nose tingled from the dust. The passage opened in an alcove in an employee area off the bar. The music thrummed through the air. She quickly closed the panel behind her and walked through the small room filled with boxes, bottles, and glasses. She pushed through the door as the bartender turned to shout at her before recognizing who it was. He nodded to her and she winked and smiled at him.

"Keep up at this pace and you'll draw a hefty wage in tips alone, my friend."

He grinned and set three glasses on the bar.

She strolled through the crowd without a care in the world.

Well, there was a care. His name was Dimitri Petrolov, or was at the moment.

Outside she leaned close and whispered to Ivan, "Tomorrow meet me at the regular spot."

He smiled slowly and nodded as she walked to her car, still

parked at the curb. Once inside she told her driver to head to her house in Kladno.

• • •

Raven sat in a car she stole from the car park of the hotel. It was a sporty little Audi, gray and loaded. The owner shouldn't miss it until morning, and if it was reported before then, well, a stolen car would be nothing new.

She wasn't about to have a cab sit here, rack up a price, and then have to explain as to *why* she wanted to sit here. Strangely enough people tended to remember things like that. Lights off, engine cut, she sipped the black coffee she'd picked up at a coffee bar.

She'd crossed the Vlatva River back into the Malá Strana, or Lesser Quarter. More open space and gardens over on this side. Old aristocratic homes lined the streets with the exception of a few modern additions, of which the warehouse-industrial building seemed to be. In her rearview mirror she could see the lighted walls of the castle.

There was no sign of a black BMW, but she waited anyway and was finally awarded because she'd been watching the second level.

Lights shone in the windows upstairs and shadows, silhouettes of at least two men, occasionally crossed in front of them. One she clearly recognized as Dimitri Petrolov's, whether from his profile or something in his carriage, she knew not. She only knew he was inside.

So with whom was he meeting?

There. He crossed from one window to the next, turned back and back again.

Pacing, was he? Then he stopped. He stood now, in the light of the window, looking out before turning back to his guest.

Five million?

Since when did anyone in their right mind turn down five million because of a bloody instinct?

But she knew if she took the job and the money and later things arose that told her she'd made a mistake, she didn't know if she could survive that a second time. She barely survived it the first time.

Her phone beeped. She glanced at it. Nikko.

She chose to ignore it.

Raven watched the shadows and wished she had a way of hearing what they were saying. At least she knew where to find the man.

Chapter 6

Dimitri and John climbed into his BMW after running a scanner over it. No bugs.

He opened the garage door and backed out.

As he drove away from his house, he asked, "Why Kladno?"

"I just remember a house there. A Renaissance residence she said one of her lovers had acquired for her. Since we can find no record of it, I decided we should check it out ourselves."

This was the first he was hearing about it. Several blocks later, he checked his mirrors and saw three cars following him. He took E48 northwest out of the city.

"Why do you think this is the place?" he asked.

Cars piled up behind him. In the dark it was hard to tell if any were following him or just heading out of Prague to home, to another city, or even into Germany.

Neither he nor John talked as they drove toward the old city. The expressway was busy tonight. Cars passed him, and several he guessed were driving under the influence, even though it was prohibited. He had his expressway pass, which he always kept current. Never knew when he'd need to take a trip such as this.

The town of Kladno came into view, its lights winking in the night. An old city, it boasted a population of about eighty thousand. A big center of industry, especially coal for the Czech Republic, he knew it was a quiet historical town few sought out. In fact, he'd never done more than drive through it. There were other towns he'd visited, and preferred. Kladno, though charming with its mixture of medieval and Renaissance melding with the modern factories, had never appealed to him.

He followed John's directions. Twice they took a wrong turn, but finally they arrived.

It was almost two in the morning when he pulled up in front of the large house on a quiet street. For all appearances, this was just the average historical town house, shaded a different color than the one next to it, but it was set behind its own iron fence and gate.

He looked around. "Does the house have a garage or a courtyard to park the car?"

A gray Audi drove passed them. He watched in the mirror as the car braked at the next intersection and turned right.

"I think there was a courtyard around back," John said.

"This it?"

"Yes."

"You're certain? I don't care to deal with the Kladno police because you think this might be the place."

John didn't answer as he climbed out of the car.

Dimitri looked up at the four-story house. He opened the door and climbed out of the car. Nothing moved. No one passed in front of the windows. The houses on either side were quiet and dark.

The air hung heavy with oncoming rains and the sharp smell of coal. He could hear the faint hum of the plants outside of town.

Their doors clicked in the night. He transferred his phone to vibration mode and watched as John did the same.

He pulled his SIG from his shoulder holster.

"Ready?" he asked John.

"I've been ready for three fucking years," John muttered.

• • •

Elianya shook her head, shocked at what had happened. Damn it. Damn it. Damn it.

With a curse at the guards who had heard nothing and had let the bastards leave—or so they said—she paced. What the hell did she do now?

"Madam?"

She stared at the body and wondered how the hell to get out of this mess. Leave it to men to fuck things up.

"What?" she snapped. They'd have to dispose of the body, well, bodies. She wasn't about to chance leaving the other one alive. And they had yet to find the other one.

"Explain to me again, what the hell happened?"

The guard shuffled his feet, and said, "We thought . . ." He cleared his throat.

"Yes?"

"That is, we were going to do a practice run, and —"

She held up her hand. "You wanted to make a bit of money on

the side." She pierced the idiot to the spot. "Don't lie to me. I'll always know. I detest liars, and lying." Well, she did. "Doing something is not nearly as grievous an offense as lying about it." She crossed her arms and tapped her fingernails atop her sleeves. "Remember that if you don't want me to end your career too soon."

She looked back to the body. Young. Too damn young to be dead, and this one would have made her so much money. Small for her teenage years, she was almost an exact replica of her much younger and alive — though hiding — sister.

So much for the shoot tonight. Damn idiots. "Do not ever again try a stunt like this."

The girl could easily have passed as twelve, and with some digital enhancements even younger. Shit. And the girls had been such a find — hell, even a bargain at the price she obtained them at from the greedy Ukrainian relative.

"There's someone coming, madam."

His words jerked her back. She whirled to the doorway where the guard stood. "Who? The police?"

He shook his head. "No, your brother's man. Petrolov."

Her mind racing, she realized this might not be so bad. "This might work. Kill him when he gets up here."

His eyes widened.

She walked to him, patted his cheek and said, "He's a loose end and it's not as if my brother will care." She laughed to herself. The guard, a remnant of Russia's once feared KGB, merely narrowed his green gaze at her. "Do you wish to take Petrolov's place?" she snapped. "I assure you, if he's here, he has an idea of what's going on, and he won't like it. That one will turn on those involved. You don't want him to see you. When you're done with him, find the other girl and bring her to me. We should probably just kill her. I want no loose ends." She shrugged. "No, let her live. But get this place cleaned. We have another appointment scheduled for tomorrow evening."

She grabbed the edge of the counterpane and tossed it over the girl. "Wrap the girl and bring her to my car. Quickly. We've got to get rid of her."

Hurrying out of the room, she turned on the next landing and motioned for her driver to follow her. To the other guard, she said,

"Grab videotapes and the folder and CPU sitting on the office desk. Get those in the car in back and be quick about it."

She looked over the balcony into the darkened entrance below. They'd enter the house at any moment.

Did Dimitri know his boss was dead yet?

Hurrying, she hoped they wouldn't discover her library. Damn it. With any luck, her Russian guard would follow through with his job and then she could come back here and oversee the cleanup. They all but ran down the old servants' stairs at the back of the hallway, down to the kitchens and out into the courtyard.

The cold night air hit her in the face, damper here than it had been in Prague. She watched her driver quietly shut the trunk lid. She slid in the backseat and told the guards to go back in and finish it.

The car started and pulled into the misty night. She watched out the back window, but no one followed. No shot fired. Nothing.

Chuckling, she smiled. So damn easy.

"I believe we should head down to Vienna. I'm in the mood for a spa. What do you think?"

"Yes, madam."

"Of course we must first dispose of some of our cargo."

"Yes, madam."

So easy.

• • •

October 31, 1:56 a.m.

Raven jogged through the night, watched as the men climbed over the gate. Two of them. She'd followed them all the way from Prague and just knew she'd been made several times, but apparently not.

Lights shone upstairs, creating halos in the gathering mist.

She should just stay out here.

From her point farther down from the house, she saw a car pull out into a back alley and drive in the opposite direction of the street they were all on.

She frowned.

No way they could have gotten inside and then driven away.

She should stay out here.

The darkness swallowed her black clothing and she put her hand on her gun under her jacket. Moving quickly, she climbed the black iron fence farther down from the gate. Perched precariously on the top, she scanned the ground and shadows. Nothing moved. She jumped, landed, rolled to her feet in one fluid motion, her gun out, scanning the area around her. Bloody trees cast some deep shadows.

She hurried to the side of the house, and decided on a darkened window.

Unzipping the pack on her back, she pulled out the suction cup and diamond bit. Contraption always reminded her of geometry class and those protractors that students could use as weapons if they so chose.

The glass cut quickly away, and she unlocked the window, swinging her leg up and listening before crawling in. Place smelled like a rose garden. She wrinkled her nose.

Showtime.

• • •

Dark. So dark.

She sucked her thumb, her heart thundering in her ears.

She saw what the men did. The mean, mean men. One of them hurt her. Hurt her bad. But she'd gotten away. She didn't like his hands.

She'd run.

And she'd heard her sister, Zoy, stop screaming. They'd held Zoy down, their hands at her throat . . .

She slapped her hands over her ears and tried to be quiet. Very, very quiet. They couldn't find her. She knew what would happen if they did. They'd made her watch. Told her it would be her turn soon.

Her sister had yelled at them, cursing the men who did this.

The house was so quiet.

She shivered and closed her eyes, curled tighter in her hiding place. What if they found her?

Should she leave the house? They might see and it was dark outside.

The monsters would get her if she left. And snakes.

She whimpered and wished Zoy would come for her.

The monsters would get her if she wasn't quiet.

Quiet, quiet. Like a shadow.

• • •

Dimitri slipped into the house first, John covering him and closing the door behind them both. They checked the downstairs rooms. Nothing. John took the second story, Dimitri decided on the third.

The thick carpet on the stairs swallowed his footfalls.

A sweet floral scent waved in the air. Nothing stirred in the house. He glanced behind him when he reached the top, thinking one of the shadows shifted, but no, nothing moved. He waited, staring at that space just to the bottom of the stairs.

Then he heard it. Just a whisper of a sound. Like a . . . whimper? Moan? He pulled back, aiming the gun at the floor as he hurried along the wall, checking first one room then another.

He heard nothing from John below stairs.

The room at the end of the corridor cast a soft glow into the darkened hallway. Thick carpets covered the floors. The walls were tasteful, with high-dollar art hanging on them. And unless he was mistaken, that one there was a Rembrandt.

Sculptures and plants filled alcoves.

Nothing moved, nothing stirred. He stepped closer to the room at the end of the hallway.

Nerves skittered along his skin. He knew, knew he wouldn't like what was in that room. And just like that, he felt it. The cold ice seeping down over him, slowing everything, focusing his senses. His heart thrummed against his chest.

He stood to the side of the door, heard a soft thump from below and started to call out to John, when he heard the moan again. He swung back to the room, his gun aimed.

With the toe of his boot, he pushed the door open the rest of the way. It swung open slowly. At first he saw nothing but a large room done in white lace and pale yellows, a fireplace, a seating area with wingback, yellow damasked chairs. Teddy bears and dolls scattered against one wall. A large dollhouse sat beneath a window.

But then he saw the camera equipment, black and gangly, almost alien in the room. The camera was aimed beyond his vision.

He stepped into the room.

The camera was aimed at the bed.

Jesus. He froze.

But the bed was empty.

He hurried into the room, scanned the area, noted the floor-to-ceiling mirror on one wall. The dolls and bears, the small white bed.

He glanced away, but a spot caught his attention.

He walked back to the bed.

A spot near a pillow, a smear on the sheet further down.

Sickness rolled through him.

Dolls. Bears. This was a child's room.

For show?

Or more?

Elianya was into child porn.

Christ.

His breathing quickened as he stared at the stains. He reached out and touched one, surprised when the spot left a damp red imprint on his finger.

Still fresh.

He looked back to the camera. One a digital. Expensive cameras, both digital and 35mm, sat on tripods. Lights glared down on the bed from their stands on their own tripods.

Then it clicked. His head jerked back to the cameras. A fucking set. Goddamn it. Quickly, he walked to the digital and saw the last picture. A man covering a girl.

A young girl.

Son of a *bitch!* Something inside him snapped. He heard it crack, break and shatter. He stood there, flexing his fingers over the butt of his gun. Flex. Flex. Flex.

A muscle jumped in his cheek and he bit down until he knew his teeth would shatter and pain shot up to his brain.

Flex. Flex. Flex.

All he saw was the girl, obscenely naked and being horribly abused.

Then he looked closer and jerked back.

Dead. Her eyes stared wide at the camera, glazed . . . but . . . He looked back at the bed. Then back to the camera. The man's hands were at her throat.

Ice trickled over his skin, the room around him blurring. The young girl's face on the camera shifted to others he hadn't been able to help. To others he had. To faces he wanted to forget and knew he never would . . .

He blinked and focused.

Rage hot and thick threatened to break through the ice.

He took a deep breath.

So small. She was so damn small with her cloud of black hair, pale face and blue, blue eyes pleading . . .

His heart hammered in his chest.

Flex. Flex. Flex.

A shot pinged across the room, an explosion in the silence. He whirled, kicked out, and brought his hand up, knocking the gun out of the man's hand. A useless move, for the man was already falling, even as the gun slammed into the wall. Dimitri aimed his SIG Sauer even as the man thumped dead to the floor.

A woman, dressed all in black, stood in the doorway, her gun still pointed in his direction. For just a moment, a split second, his finger tightened on the trigger as he thought it had been John, but no. The man dead at his feet, with half his head blown across the wall, wasn't John.

He and the woman stared at each other. He didn't take his eyes off her. And in that instant, the world shifted back.

She stood there, dressed in black — black pants, boots, a turtleneck and leather jacket — tall, athletic. Dark hair, mocha skin, and those icy green eyes. The woman from the bar.

"He had a gun aimed at the back of your head," she said softly. She had a British accent.

They still didn't lower their weapons.

"Didn't want him to take your mark?" he asked, his voice graveled more than normal.

She smiled, dimples winking at him. "Oh, I haven't marked you," she said, tilting her head, "yet."

He narrowed his gaze at her even as hers shifted beyond him to scan the room. He saw the color leave her cheeks. "Jesus, Mary and Joseph," she whispered. She licked her lips, swallowed. "Is this room what I think it is?"

Still staring at her, he shook his head. "Put your gun down."

"Are you going to shoot me?"

For one moment, she stared at him, then shrugged and lowered her weapon, still pale, her eyes darting this way, then that. "Fine, but I draw the line at handing it over to you." She shoved it into her pants.

"Who are you?" Dimitri asked.

"I think the more important question is who are *you*, Mr. Petrolov."

Again they stared at each other.

"Are you Raven?"

She grinned, but didn't answer his question. "I hear your partner coming up the stairs."

He listened and heard John's soft footsteps hushing along the carpets. Why hadn't he heard her?

"Where did you come from?" he asked.

"I followed you."

Of course she had. He motioned for her to come into the room. He felt his phone ring, but ignored it. John walked to the doorway. He took one look around, took a deep breath, another. "Christ. A bloody fucking porn set." Then he turned to the woman. "Hello, Lenora."

"Hello, John."

John looked from one to the other. "Which one of you killed this guard?"

"This guard?" Dimitri asked.

John jerked his head to the doorway. "Took out one downstairs in some sort of study."

"I did," the woman said. "Mr. Petrolov doesn't seem too impressed, even though the bleeding bugger had a gun aimed at the back of Mr. Petrolov's head."

John's gaze narrowed on his. "This true?"

Dimitri turned away from them and back to the camera, then glanced again at the bed. Still, like a broken doll, she lay in frame, but no longer in reality. Where the hell was the girl?

"I think someone died here," he said softly, glancing at the other camera.

He wanted to flip back through all the cameras. But at present, he knew he simply couldn't stomach what he'd see on them.

"What?" John asked.

He pointed. "Blood on the sheets." Then he pointed to the cameras. "From the last frame on this digital, I'd have to say our pedophile went a bit too far."

John and Lenora walked to stand behind him. John took another deep breath and started to flip through the digital shots. Dimitri ignored most of what he was seeing. Right now, he simply couldn't handle it. But then a flash of white at the edge of one frame caught his attention.

"Wait."

John looked at him, his face grim. "What?"

"Do the next one. I think there was another girl."

And there she was. At the edge of the screen, the same wide blue eyes — terror rounding them, cherub cheeks and long dark curly hair. One big man reached for her as she clearly ran.

"Did she get away?" the woman asked, her voice so low he barely caught it.

He shook his head, chills dancing over his arms. He had to get the hell out of here.

"I don't know, but I'm not leaving here until we know for certain."

John, studying him, grabbed his arm. "If anyone died, this is a crime scene."

He wretched his arm free. "I think even you can see that murder happened here and that may be, Johnno, but I'll not leave any child behind in this house."

He didn't need to look again at the cameras or in the room to know the exact location of everything, even down to the last music box set atop the mantel. The pink curtains in the dollhouse.

Out in the hallway, he closed his eyes, took a deep breath and then another.

He hated this fucking job. *Hated it.* He didn't care what he had to do. This was it. He was out.

She had looked so small, so damn small — but then had she really been? Was she older? He knew from living with the slime this long that things were rarely what they appeared, but regardless, she hadn't deserved death. She hadn't deserved whatever else had gone on here.

Who was she and who had hurt her?

If he'd gotten here sooner.

"Why the hell am I just now learning of Elianya's little side business?" he snapped out, his hands fisted on his hips, not turning back to the room.

His muscles tightened.

John sighed. "I was ordered not to tell you."

He glanced over his shoulder, piercing his friend with a look, but John didn't look away. "Why?"

John's brows rose. "I didn't ask why. You don't ask why. Christ." He raked a hand over his face. "I have to call this—" He broke off and answered his phone. "What?"

Damn bastards. He'd seen a lot and had been part of more, but by God, he'd never been a part of this. The fact that Viktor might have known for a while, the fact John *had* known for a while and hadn't told him . . .

He took a deep breath, closing his eyes.

Then they shot open. The other girl.

He didn't listen to John. Where the hell was she?

"Are those the only cameras?" he asked from the doorway.

Lenora hadn't walked far from the cameras. She still stood there, pale and studying one of the pictures. "Well, we know the digital is still working. And it appears the film may still be in the thirty-five millimeter." Her eyes rose to his and iced, mirroring his own rage. "If we look through all the frames, we might just have the bastards who did this."

"Thanks, I'll let him know," John said, his features hardening. "No, I'm with him. I'll make certain he gets to a safe house." John's eyes, bright with anger and something else, zeroed in on him. John flipped his phone shut. "It appears you're out of a job, and even if you weren't, your cover's been blown wide-ass open."

"What? When? How?"

"That was an informant we have inside the Prague police. Your boss was murdered, and whoever did it left images of your past aliases complete with names, or some of them, on Hellinski's computer."

The gravity of the situation here and as a whole clicked through him.

"We've got to get you out of here. Several people are going to want you dead. Word's already hit the streets you were undercover," John said, dialing his phone. "Hellinski's friends are not going to be happy."

"Who killed him?"

John's gray eyes narrowed on him. "Elianya, it appears. Went in, no one saw her leave, and then one of the guards went in to tell Mr. Hellinski he was late for a meeting."

"I'm not going anywhere just yet." He walked back into the room to see Lenora/Raven, whoever the hell she was, taking both cameras off their stands. For a moment he studied her.

Her head was bowed, but he noticed the tremor in her hands. Hell, his own were still shaking. Her shoulders rose on a deep breath then another. Without turning to him, she said, "I couldn't work vice. Never could do that. I can't stand sex crimes." She shrugged, turned to him, and he caught the haunted look that flashed in her eyes. "So I worked wherever else they needed me. Narcotics, scams, kidnappings, terrorism, homicide, wherever, however, just not something like . . . like . . ." She waved toward the bed. "No child should even know about such things, let alone experience them."

He almost didn't answer her, but then he did. "I couldn't agree more." Still studying her, he said, "I don't know if you're the elusive Raven who was offered a couple of mill to put a bullet in my brain or not, but—"

"It was actually five million." She sniffed and shrugged gain. "But who's counting."

With that she finally looked at him with those witch's eyes.

He didn't say anything; neither did she. Finally he nodded. "Thanks."

"For not killing you or saving your life?"

"Both."

For a moment they simply stared at each other and he felt it again, hot ice between his shoulder blades. He shifted and rolled his neck.

"We should check the rest of the house."

She nodded, glanced again around the room. "Yes. I'm betting there is a hidden video camera in here somewhere. Live action sells more on the market than frozen frames."

He agreed. "We'll look for the damn camera later. Now, I want to find a live girl."

She nodded and followed him from the room.

• • •

Voices filtered through the quiet. She heard the thumps and bumps. A shot.

She shivered. So cold. Why was she so cold?

Her thumb shook in her mouth.

Think of something else. She'd think of something else.

Back home. Back home before Papa and Mama went away.

But then they went away . . .

Her eyes shot open, but only a sliver of light showed around the edge of the door. She huddled tighter.

She'd pretend to be a shadow. No one looked for shadows. No one cared about shadows.

Shadows were silent. Shadows didn't get hurt.

She waited, heard them talking.

A man's voice.

A woman's.

She whimpered.

Please, not the monsters. Please not the monsters.

• • •

He raked a hand through his hair.

Shit. Cover was blown. Which meant he'd have more people after him. And here he was playing games. What the fuck?

"Hide and seek is never fun as an adult. Have you noticed that?" Lenora asked as they stepped into another room and flipped the lights on.

He ignored the fact she finished his thought.

Another room like the first. This one done in blues and grays. Sports paraphernalia on the mantel. Trains and action figures on the walls. Again, there was one large floor-to-ceiling mirror on one of the walls.

Rage licked hot through his veins.

"There are some things I could have lived without seeing," he muttered.

Determined, he walked to the bed, dropped down on one side. He wished he hadn't. Under the bed was an assortment of BDSM toys, chains, whips, boxes of things he didn't care to open.

Christ, how many others had there been?

He straightened, checked behind the curtains as the woman ripped through the closet and the armoire. "The longer I'm alive, even with all I've seen, I'm constantly reminded there is still a depth even the lowest haven't succumbed to."

He couldn't agree more.

He knelt in front of the fireplace.

They both heard steps coming down the hallway and pulled their guns as John walked around the door.

He shook his head and ignored them. "I've got a team cleaning your place in Prague and . . ." He frowned. "What the hell are you two doing?" John asked.

Then he heard it. A whisper of a moan.

"Shh," they both answered.

John continued. "I called this in, explained to my superior what the bloody hell was going on. And he said Pete's trying to get in contact with—"

"Shhh," the woman said again, her head tilting to the side. She strode to the mirror, tried to lift the gilded edge of the golden frame, but it didn't move. One eyebrow cocked at him. "Two way, perhaps?"

He pulled his gun free, but she only shook her head and pulled something hanging from her waist, beside her pack. It unfolded and she removed a suction cup from the center tube. "Always come prepared, boys."

Chapter 7

Prepared?

John's phone chirped and he answered it, still watching them.

The woman dangled the instrument from her hand and motioned him back. "Get out of my way." Taking a deep breath, she placed the suction cup on the mirror and widened the diameter. "So who are you? John said your cover was blown. What's your name? You already know mine."

True. Still he didn't say anything.

"Should I call you Dimitri Petrolov, then?" she asked.

If he wasn't Dimitri Petrolov, who the hell was he currently? Another alias?

Someone from his past covers?

The names all floated through his brain.

"Dimitri Petrolov no longer exists," he said, blinking as the shaded lies of five years blurred.

She paused and looked at him, her dark brow cocked.

Petrolov was no more. And . . .

"Ian. My name is Ian."

She smiled. "Nice to meet you, Ian." She quickly cut a large hole in the mirror. There was a slight grind as she lifted the cylindrical piece of glass away. "I'm glad you turned out to be a good guy. I'd hate to think I let you live if you were part of this. Of course, then I'd just hunt you down anyway."

"Still contemplating that five million?"

She shook her head. "No, it was the price that gave me pause. If they wanted you gone that badly, I had to ask myself why. And if I turned it down and found out you were party to the shit going down here," she said, winking at him, "I'd have gone after you pro bono, so to speak."

"Target practice."

"Some of us don't need target practice, luv." She frowned and looked into the hole. "Looks like we found the videos."

"Move," he told her.

John was still on the phone, barking orders to someone.

Ian walked up and she stepped back.

Ducking his head, he looked into the small enclosure behind the mirror. A video camera sat on a tripod. More sex toys hung from the wall. The more he saw the more angry he became. A voyeur's haven. A swing hung from the ceiling, manacles were chained along the wall, more whips and leather and velvets. He didn't care. What people wanted to do, what they liked, were their own business.

But this . . . This was Elianya's sick and twisted version.

"Check the other room, behind the mirror," he said, pulling back. "I'm betting the video camera is there as well."

"I'll just get right on that," she said, sarcasm heavy in her voice. "Since I work for you and all."

He ignored her and glanced around the room again.

A whimper.

A cherry armoire, at least eight feet high, stood in the corner.

Slowly he walked to it, noted one of the doors was slightly open, the dull metal handle not flat against the wood as the one on the left door.

He pulled his gun free.

The woman beside him did the same thing.

They aimed at the armoire; the thick carpet swallowed their footfalls.

Quickly he jerked the door open.

A breath of air whooshed out.

Nothing. It stood bare.

Then just a sigh.

He looked at the woman beside him, then back to the armoire.

Inside, there were shelves and two doors on each side at the very bottom. No more than eighteen inches high or so.

Squatting down and taking a deep breath, he pulled the right-side door open, just as the woman pulled hers.

For a second he glanced her way, but noted it was empty and looked back to his.

Inside sat a little girl, her black hair curly, her eyes wide and dark blue.

She looked just like the girl on the camera, on the bed.

Her eyes were wide and vacant, staring at nothing, pupils dilated. He watched as her chest rose and fell quickly. Dressed in a white eyelet, with her thumb firmly in her mouth, she was a white bundle in a small space.

He closed his eyes. Opening them he said, "Just a minute, baby. Hang on, we'll get you out." He leaned down further.

"How the hell did she get in here?" he asked. She was curled up in a little ball. Not even her toes peeked out.

"Poor kid," the woman muttered.

Turning to Lenora, he said, "Do you think she'd rather you go in there for her?"

Lenora only shook her head, straightening. "Sorry, I don't do kids in any way, shape, or form. If you need me to go in and get her I will, but I've never really . . ." She took a deep breath and he wondered if something else was going on here.

He focused on the small girl trying to hide. There wasn't even enough room to reach in and get her, unless he pulled her out by her feet. He really didn't want to force her to do anything. God only knew what she'd witnessed.

"*Máte přání?*" he asked her softly in Czech. When she continued to stare, he tried again, "*Jmenuji se Ian. Jak se jmenujete?*"

Not a flicker of recognition. Nothing. Just that fast panting, wide staring eyes as she sucked her thumb.

Damn it.

He wanted to coax her out.

He tried German. Then Russian next, "*Privet. Govorite li vy po angliyski?*"

Still nothing. All the while he wondered if he should just reach in and grab her. She sat unmoving, hardly blinking, her small face pale, her eyes . . . God, those eyes.

Gently, he reached in and felt her cheek. She was cold, and clammy. Just as easily, he took her wrist, red and abraded, to feel her pulse. He frowned at the fragile bones. There it thumped, a bit too quickly. How old was she? Four? Five? Six? Too damn young.

He told her again in different languages that he was going to give her his coat. "I'll take you out of here."

She didn't move, didn't blink, just stared ahead.

He shifted directly in front of her, shielding her as he stood and shucked off his long coat. He had no idea if she had any other injuries and didn't think this was the time to check them out. Being careful not to startle her, he reached inside, surprised there was more room in the cubby than he'd realized. He grasped her under the arms and pulled her toward him. When he had her out, he wrapped his coat around her and picked her up.

At first she was stiff, then she slumped against him, her head dropping on his shoulder. Her thumb still in her mouth, he felt the motion of her jaw as she suckled. Ian pulled her back far enough to see the eyes still stared past him to the room beyond. Covering her head, he stood.

"Come on," he told the woman, who was taking the video from the camera within the hidden chamber.

They walked out of the blue room and back down the hallway to the yellow room, where John stood pacing and barking into the phone.

The little girl roused in his arms, trying to get down and looking toward the bed.

She frowned and looked at him. Her eyes, God, those eyes. They weren't vacant now, but asking questions, confused and terrified.

Ian tightened his hold on her, even as her breathing quickened and whimpers crawled up her throat, squeezing inside him.

"I want those cameras," he said softly to Lenora.

She nodded and looked from him to the child in his arms.

Lenora, or Rori as her friends called her, stared at this man.

Earlier he'd been quick, fast as a striking snake, and now he was as gentle as a breeze. He held the little girl as if he were used to holding a child against him, wrapped in a coat, as he muttered soft things into her hair.

He walked into the hallway. She grabbed both cameras, staring at this room, the empty bed — and she remembered. That poor kid . . .

Rori muttered a prayer for the lost ones and turned her back, following Ian out into the hallway.

He and John Brasher were talking, the girl still squirming in Ian's coat.

Again he said something softly to her. She stilled in his arms.

John got his first look at the little girl and shook his head, his don't-screw-with-me face hardening even more into a mask that would send most running in the other direction. His flat gray eyes darkened.

And she knew if it was the last thing any of them did, they would find the buggering bastards who had committed this crime.

Ian shifted his gaze from his whispered conversation with John to her.

"We're leaving and you're coming with us," he said. His dark blue eyes dared her to object.

John looked quickly from Ian to her, then back to Ian. "I think we should discuss—"

"She's coming," Ian said, still not taking his gaze from her.

Rori returned his study, wondering what he wanted.

She shrugged. "What the hell, the car was nicked anyway."

Ian cocked one brow and John muttered something, drawing her attention to him.

What was John Brasher doing here? Just her luck, when she didn't take a bloody mark, she was made, and by none other than someone she had worked with.

Christ.

They all headed back downstairs.

Ian stopped in the entryway and said, "What if there are more locked here in the house? This wasn't a one-time affair, John."

Rori agreed. "It's probable she has them locked in here or nearby. They . . ." She cleared her throat and looked away, taking a deep breath.

"I've already taken care of it," John said. "Our first priority is to get you"—he pointed to Ian—"the hell out of here, and her." He motioned toward the little girl, who lay quietly in Ian's arms. "A team is on their way to tear this place apart. And find whatever evidence we can to dismantle this ring."

In the darkened entryway, the house was again silent. She glanced around at the prestige, the ornate house, the wealth, and thought what blackness it hid.

Shaking her head, she walked outside.

The temperature seemed to have dropped even further since they had been inside. She followed them to the black Beemer.

"Won't there be a bulletin out for your car?" she asked.

Ian didn't pause. "Probably." Then he looked to her. "Which is why we're taking your Audi. You were driving the Audi?"

She shook her head. "So much for my tailing skills."

He grinned. "At least you have something to practice on."

John opened the gate. "Will you both put a sock in it?" They walked through the gate, scanning the street.

"Did I mention a car pulled out into the back alley when you two were scaling the gate?" Her boots thumped along the sidewalk.

"Probably Elianya and that sad bastard driver of hers," John muttered. "Now, as I said, we don't have time to piss around, let's go." He held his hand out. "Give me your keys and follow me. We'll ditch your car somewhere other than here and strip it."

Ian shifted the girl, reached in his pants pocket and handed the keys to John.

They parted and Rori led him down the street to the car she'd parked in the shadow of some trees near the park.

The engine turned over as easily as it did the first time. She turned around and watched as Ian—what was the man's last name—buckled the child in the seat. Still she merely stared, didn't utter a word or a sound, but she did turn around and look back at the house.

Ian shut the back door and slid into the front seat beside her, double-checking his gun, and motioned for her to follow John.

Without a word, she pulled out and followed the car in front of her. Ian turned toward the backseat and checked the girl. "She's in shock."

"I would assume so, yes. Especially after all she's been through, and we both know they probably gave her something." She took a deep breath, wishing they could change the subject.

"She needs a bloody hospital," he said, his voice edged and ripe with fury.

"Probably." Glancing at him, she said, "We could just drop her off at one." What kind of man was he really?

His eyes glittered, hard and bright. "We're not *dropping her off* anywhere." He checked the side mirror and scanned the streets. "Someone else already did that. I'll be damned if I'm another that just says, 'poor thing,' and moves on my fucking way."

For a moment she didn't say anything.

She followed John to the outskirts of town, the old world dropping off into modern industry.

"Most would rescue her and move on," she said as she turned behind John, only to have another car turn from the opposite direction and follow them.

"I'm not most people," he said, shifting in his seat and watching the car as its headlights drew closer.

He could say that again. Mr. Ian was not like most men.

"So what are you going to do with her? She's not a bloody stray dog to just take with you." Rori frowned as the car sped quickly around them, the motor roaring.

"I'll run a trace on her." He frowned after the green Mercedes. "Get closer."

"I know that."

"And if no one claims her," he continued, rolling down the window, "then I'll take her home."

"Mr. Mystery Man has a home. Marvelous." She pressed the clutch and shifted again. "And I know how to keep up, thank you."

He speared her with a quick glance. "Good, because I have a feeling that car is about—"

They both saw the rapid-fire succession of bullets shatter the back of the BMW, peppering the boot of the car, the red taillights going dark.

"Damn it." He leaned out the window, firing off several rounds of his own, taking out the tires of the shooters' car. The Mercedes fishtailed, its back tires catching the edge of the road. In a scream of metal it rolled end over end.

Rori swerved to miss a piece of the car that rocketed across the pavement in front of them.

Bloody hell.

She jerked the wheel and almost overcorrected. They rocked and straightened back onto the road. Rori slammed on the breaks. Ian cursed again, and glared at her.

"Finish it," she said. "They would have."

"I don't need you," he said, emptying his clip into the windows and door panels of the car that now rested on its top, "to tell me how to finish a job."

That remained to be seen. He sat back in his seat and she drove on, noting John had turned off the road. He was leaning into the car, wiping it down.

"He'll never get everything," she muttered.

"The catch twenty-two for those of us in these games. With today's technology we can be found on both sides of the law."

She pulled up behind John. Ian looked at her and said, "Stay with her."

"I'm not a bloody dog either."

He gritted his teeth. "Please."

She smiled. "Bet that hurt."

He climbed out of the car without a word to her and she watched as he hurried to help John. What an interesting job this was turning out to be.

• • •

Ian took the electric drill gun he always carried out of the back of the car and went to work on the plates. He quickly unscrewed them as John transferred their stuff to the Audi. Both listened for any sign of traffic on the road.

The night was still and quiet. No one drove down the long lane they were now on. John walked up. "Can I ask why the hell you never took the GPS out of this bloody car?" He wiped at a trickle of blood that ran from the cut on his cheek. "Fucking bastards."

Ian looked at him. "You think I'd ever drive a vehicle that had an active GPS?"

John frowned. "No."

Ian pulled the lining of the trunk away, ignoring the bullet holes that now pierced the trunk lid. He'd raised the bottom of the trunk when he'd first purchased the car. Always paid to plan ahead. He quickly opened the compartment that had been hidden. He handed the four handguns, ammo and tear gas off to John, who only shook his head. "And to think I thought I could leave this business."

Next he grabbed the duffle bag that contained extra clothing, hair color, new passports and money. He double-checked the car, noting they'd taken everything traceable from it. He'd rubbed all the ID numbers off when he'd installed the compartment in the trunk.

Satisfied, he slung the duffle over his shoulder and walked back to the car. The woman, Lenora, could, without doubt, handle herself.

Now he needed to talk her into his next plan. Of course, that was all on the idea that the child had nowhere to go. Either way, he'd need her help and they had plenty of work to do before dawn.

• • •

She looked out at the night. Dark, dark was the night. She didn't like the dark. The dark held monsters. And monsters were bad. Monsters hurt. They had big hands, claws, and didn't care when you cried. They stuck you with their claws and then you went to the fog.

She didn't like the fog.

But this man didn't have claws. And he hadn't poked her arm.

So tired. Where was Zoy? She blinked and sucked her thumb.

Her head hurt.

Zoy?

The monsters.

She shivered again, cold. So cold. She pulled her legs up inside the big warm coat. Sucking her thumb, she fingered the ends of her hair.

The monsters were everywhere.

Maybe if she stayed really, really quiet, they'd leave her alone.

She closed her eyes. She wanted to be a bird.

A bird that could fly. Away. In the night. To the moon.

She opened her eyes and looked to the sky, but there was no moon. Did the monsters steal it too?

They took her sister.

No. No.

She shivered.

Where was Zoy?

The man, big, his eyes dark, his mouth mean, walked to the car. She shivered in the blanket. He'd picked her up. Let her out of the room.

Why didn't they take Zoy too?

Maybe they'd go back and get her sister.

She listened as they talked, but didn't understand them. He'd spoken to her. Told her hello and that he'd help her.

But he was big. And big people became monsters.

She closed her eyes and pretended to be a bird. Fly, fly away . . .

Chapter 8

Ian drove the car, talking to both John and Lenora as they decided their best bet was Karlovy Vary, the spa town of the Czechs. It would be dawn in a couple of hours and there wasn't much any of them could do about that.

The team called in to clean up his apartments in Prague had checked in. There had been two casualties, neither of which were Snake and Tanner. The two men Ian had worked with before. Gar was busy in Paris getting them a passport contact here.

To get into Germany, they needed passports. He had one, John was good, as was Lenora. The problem was the little girl. Without proper papers they'd never get her out of the country. By the time they could, he'd probably be dead, and so would the child.

At the edge of town, he pulled into an empty lot and got out.

John slid into the driver's seat and Ian climbed into the backseat, picking the little girl up and moving her between him and Lenora.

"This will never work," she said.

He tilted his head and slammed his door even as John pulled away. "Why not?"

Her brows rose and she shook her head. "Well, you are . . ." She motioned to him. "You."

"And?" He studied her, waited to see what she would say. For the most part, she'd been very quiet. He'd heard her from time to time whispering to the little girl, who still hadn't uttered a sound. Ian pulled his coat up a bit more around the little girl.

Lenora looked out the window. "Fine. Who am I to say if anyone will ask questions."

"Lenora—" he started.

"Rori. I really detest Lenora. So," she said and turned back to him, "if we're going to pull this off, call me Rori."

He ran his gaze over her angular face, the softened jaw, straight nose, arched brows and those wicked eyes. He nodded. "Fits you, I think."

She rolled those eyes and turned back to the window.

John muttered something as he drove the car up to the front of the Hotel Dvorak and parked. The valet came out. They all knew what to do. Ian and Rori stayed in the car as John climbed out, said something to the valet and nodded to the doorman.

"Do you realize the trouble if anyone asks questions."

He watched John, at the front desk, as he shook his head, nodded, then produced something from his pocket. Ian grinned. Poor night clerk.

"No one will ask questions other than perhaps what her name is." He glanced back at the little girl between them.

Her eyes were closed, long black lashes crescented against her pale cheeks.

Rage hissed through him again, but he ignored it and waited for John.

"Well, I've no idea what to call her," she said, her voice laced with confusion and indifference.

"We'll just ignore names for her until it's time to come up with a passport." If he didn't want to answer anyone's question, then he simply wouldn't. Period. It had worked for him thus far, he saw no reason it shouldn't now.

The child didn't stir even as he put his arm around her. So damn tiny. Her nose was still childlike, turned up at the end, her chin still stubbed. She had a round face that looked gaunt with dark circles under her eyes.

He fisted his hand, still studying the child. Who was she? Where the hell did she come from? Was there anyone searching for her? There better damn well be.

The lightest touch on his knuckles startled him, and he looked over her head to see Lenora — no, Rori — watching him.

"We'll find them."

He narrowed his gaze at her. "This is hardly your assignment."

One brow rose. "Neither is it yours."

"It is now."

John knocked on his window. Ian turned even as John opened his door. He gathered the sleeping child to him and climbed from the car. Rori slid out his side and both she and John gathered packs, bags, and tossed other cases to the bellhop who had appeared.

Waiting on Rori, they walked into the hotel, the trees along the River Tepla bare of leaves, their branches rattling in the chilling wind. He covered the little girl's head, tucking her against him as the warmth of the hotel washed over them all.

Inside, the hotel lobby was empty and silent. Ian walked straight to the bank of elevators, Rori on his heels as they all made their way up to the suite John had obtained.

The ride up was silent. Ian calculated they had a few hours here at the most. Someone checking into a hotel this late at night left an impression. But they didn't have a choice. They needed a place to stay. He wanted to make certain the little girl was only in shock. She hadn't uttered a single sound since they'd carried her from Elianya's almost two hours ago. The only noise had been the soft sound of her sucking her thumb.

At any other time, Ian might have enjoyed a stay in this high-class hotel, but as it was, he couldn't have cared less.

John and Rori secured the place while Ian laid the little girl on the bed, then ran a warm bath. She'd need clothes and an identity. They needed to print her and run her through Interpol to make certain there were no yellow notices on the girl. He knew there would soon be a black notice on the girl they'd had to leave behind. Well, if her body was ever discovered, there would be.

He shook his head, even as he cooled the water.

"She probably needs a doctor," John said.

Ian looked at him in the mirror. "Probably."

"Could just drop her off at the hospital. You need to get out of Europe as soon as possible."

"I could, I won't, and I already know that."

John tossed the bag onto the counter and walked out, saying over his shoulder, "Snake and Tanner should be here within the next hour or so and I've already got a contact for passports."

Ian frowned. "Snake was a medic, wasn't he?"

John didn't answer him as he walked into the room and on into the living room.

Ian stood, shut the water off, and wondered what the hell to do now. He looked into the darkened room to see the little girl still lay on her side where he'd put her. Her eyes weren't open, but her thumb was still firmly in her mouth, the sight sadly vulnerable. He strode across the room and felt her pulse. It was more normal, and she seemed a bit warmer.

He walked into the living room, grabbed the digital camera and returned to the room to snap a quick photo of the little girl. Again he could only stare down at her. Her image, her softly rising chest, lay over and under a more gruesome one he'd seen on a camera.

He shook his head.

"I'll admit I know very little about children, but considering, I'll bathe her," Rori said directly behind him. He hadn't heard her come in.

Ian ran his finger down the little girl's pale cheek, felt the slight movement as her jaw shifted with her sucking, wishing he could make things better for her. He set the camera aside and gently eased the coat away. Her eyes shot open and she shoved at him, bolting.

He raised his hand, speaking softly. Again in Czech, German, Russian, hoping she understood something.

She sat huddled on the bed, her hands fisted at her chest, her eyes wide and terrified.

"This is never going to work," Rori muttered.

He shot her a look over his shoulder.

"Now, if we gave her something, easy as pie."

"Someone already did give her something, unless I'm mistaken, and I'd rather not be mixing drugs in her system. God only knows what Elianya gave them."

Ian continued to speak softly to her, showed her the bathroom, laid a towel beside the tub, grabbed his own bag and walked out of the room, leaving the girl alone with Rori.

He had no idea what the hell else to do.

• • •

Rori sat on the windowsill and ignored the child. Ian thought he could put the girl at ease by talking to her.

She rolled her eyes. What the bloody hell did he know?

There was nothing that could put the child at ease after what she'd been through. Even if she'd only seen. Seeing left impressions that were often as terrifying as the experience itself. Fear led to complacency.

Rori glanced back over her shoulder, to see the little girl watching her. Rori smiled slightly and knew the best thing was silence and stillness.

It took another ten minutes, but finally, she heard the rustle of material, saw from the reflection in the window that the little girl slid off the bed and hurried to the loo. The lock clicked behind her.

She breathed a sigh of relief. Well, at least the child was feeling better. She could move. She could walk, and she understood she could go to the bathroom alone.

Progress often came in small increments.

Rori stood and walked into the lounge.

Ian didn't turn as he scanned the screen of his laptop. She wondered what he was looking at, but then saw the camera and knew he'd entered the photo of their mystery kid and was running it through Interpol.

"Anything?" she asked.

He typed on the keys, then paused. "What are you doing in here?"

She shrugged. "She's taking a bath. I guess. She locked herself in the bathroom."

He glared at her and stood. "And you just let her. My God, she's little more than a baby. Do you have any idea how many kids drown in the bathtub every year?"

She shook her head. "No, do you?"

He started toward the room. Then paused and raked his hand through his hair. "No, but that's beside the point." He whirled and pointed at her. "You're supposed to be watching her."

Rori strolled over to the table, where a platter of water bottles stood. She grabbed one and twisted the top off. "What? She's fine. Trust me. If she didn't want to go in there, she wouldn't have. Give her a few minutes and then I'll knock on the door." She drank deeply. "Do *you* have any idea what it's like to have no privacy when you really want it? To be so terrified that you distrust those who would help?"

His droll expression told her it was a stupid question.

She took another drink and glanced around the room. "Where's John?"

"Went out for a few things."

"Like?"

"Clothing. Unless I'm mistaken, you don't have any, nor does the child."

She shook her head. "You have inconspicuous down to an art."

He shrugged, glanced back into the darkened room, then turned back to her, but paced to the window, then back to the doorway of the room. "We needed a secure place to stay for a few hours and this was the best we could do under the circumstances. Until you both have passports, she can't leave the country. You know as well as I do that if I left the country with the child alone, that would raise suspicion. And we can hardly take her photo or drag her through Germany wearing an eyelet nightgown and my coat."

He stalked to the table, ripped the zipper back and pulled his bag open. He quickly flipped through the passports, then grabbed one. She saw several stacks of bills and raised a brow. Man knew how to travel.

"What else have you got in your bag of transformation?"

He ignored her and sat again behind the computer.

"Aren't you a jolly conversationalist?" Rori went back to the room and listened at the door. Splashes and trickles echoed. The little girl was taking a bath. She grinned, turned and yelped.

Ian stood directly behind her, listening himself. She'd never heard him or felt him approach. She frowned.

He frowned.

"She's taking a bath," she told him.

"I can hear, thank you very much," he snapped, his arms crossing. A muscle flexed in his jaw. He rubbed a hand over his jaw, then the back of his neck. "What if she has injuries we're not even aware of? Was it only her sister they abused? Did they rape that little girl before she got away? How the hell long was she . . . was she . . ."

"Held prisoner?" Rori asked.

He raked a hand through his hair, the long strands sliding back down on either side of his forehead to hang to his chin.

She noticed as he talked, his voice lowered, softened. Where most would yell, she could see his rage left a frozen wake. His tone, bladed to a point, could slice even as his eyes all but burned.

"She'll be all right," she heard herself say.

"How would you know?" He looked again at the door.

Rori looked away, walked to the window, and cursed the fact her pulse leapt at his simple question. No cars moved below. No people strolled along. The only movement was the black snake of the River

Tepla as is meandered through the town.

"Who hired you and why didn't you kill me?" he asked.

She didn't turn; like the child earlier, she could see his reflection in the window.

Rori waited, not knowing how exactly to answer him. "The contact was bogus. I've tried running it."

"You do that to all your . . . clients?"

She shrugged. "Those that are a bit too secretive, yes. I like to know everything I can about any job."

He nodded and paced away from his stance by the bathroom door. "Less complications that way."

"Exactly." She sighed. "And after a botched job a couple years ago, I learned to rely more on instinct than what a computer might say." She turned to him then. "Besides, the fact the computer had very little to say about Dimitri Petrolov, there was something about the whole situation that didn't fit."

"Lucky me."

"Yes, you're just a jammy bugger." She heard the slip of skin squeak on the marble tub. "Now, I have a feeling your ward will be coming out and I'd rather her not dart back in and relock the door."

He took the hint and walked out of the room. She sat back on the windowsill and waited.

She heard the rustle of things in the bathroom. Heard a whispered something, but couldn't make it out.

Then the click of a lock and a crack of the door.

Silently, she waited.

• • •

The room was dark. Monsters were in the dark. But they were in light too.

She reached up, stood on her tiptoes and flicked the light off.

Her breath panted out and she waited. Was anyone here?

What about the lady?

The man?

Would they hurt her as well? The others had hurt her.

She looked at her arm where the spots itched. The spots where they put the long silver needle in. She shivered.

No. No. She'd think of something else.

Her stomach rumbled and she was thirsty. Maybe they had some juice.

She pulled the door open a little more. Nothing moved and her toes were cold. The air was cold against her wet skin and hair. Water trickled down her back from the wet strands.

Her teeth chattered.

Maybe if she was really good, they'd go back and get Zoy.

She wanted Zoy.

She opened the door wider and stepped into the cool room, pulling the towel tighter against her.

The woman still sat at the window. Slowly the woman turned.

She stopped by the bed and looked to the doorway of the room. She could run. Maybe she'd get away.

But if she left, the snakes would eat her. That's what the other lady had told her. If they ran away from the adults snakes would eat them. And spiders. The lady said spiders too.

She didn't like snakes or spiders.

The deep rumble of voices floated from the other room and through the door she saw the man . . . the man who helped her.

He hadn't hurt her. He gave her his coat and he spoke to her. Telling her she didn't have to be afraid, that no one would hurt her. But he still looked mean. Maybe he could scare away monsters, snakes *and* spiders. He looked like he could. She nodded to herself. He would. Spiders would run away from him and he could probably shoot a snake.

He walked back in front of the door, talking to the other man.

She looked over at the woman.

Carefully, to see if the woman jumped at her, she stepped toward the doorway.

There, she saw the man again. He glanced up and stopped, then he smiled.

Pulling the towel tighter, she darted a look around the room, saw the other man. And behind them was water. On the table.

She swallowed. She'd sipped some of the water in the bathtub, but it tasted like soap.

Would they let her have any? The other people wouldn't let them. She stared at the water.

The nice man picked up a bottle and held it out to her. She didn't understand what he was saying.

She stared at him and he squatted down, holding the bottle out to her and talking softly. His voice rumbled over her and reminded her of her papa's.

But Papa went to Heaven. She knew that. But still, this man hadn't hurt her. He'd helped her. Even if he did look mean.

Still, she watched him, kept the towel held tightly to her. Watching him, she scratched again at the red dots on the inside of her arm.

Then he spoke and she understood him.

"U tyebya vsyo v aryadke?"

She stopped, snatched the bottle from him, trying to open it. Slowly, he put his hands on top of hers. She froze, her heart kicking against her chest, holding her breath. He twisted the cap.

His eyes were nice. Very dark blue . . . like hers. And Zoy's.

He smiled at her and asked the question again. *"U tyebya vsyo v aryadke?"*

She shrugged her shoulders. She didn't feel okay. She was tired and hungry and wanted Zoy.

His eyes might be blue like hers, but they were hard. But he hadn't hurt her, so maybe he would help her. And since he'd picked her up, he'd kept the monsters and snakes and spiders away.

Chapter 9

Pink-fingered and yawning, dawn crept over the night sky. Elianya sat in her car, parked down the street, watching all the activity of her town house.

Rage flowed thin and quick through her, a fast striking adder.

Damn the man. Damn him to everlasting hell.

They had dumped the body near the first stream they'd come to. When her guards had not checked in, she'd finally had her driver turn around so that she could check things out for herself.

Her driver said nothing. There were six police cars, their yellow and blue lights flashing in the early morning. Men in nylon coats and others in long dark trenches walked in and out of the front door. She looked up, saw people in the upper levels as they stalked back and forth in front of the windows.

She closed her eyes and took a deep breath. She was glad she'd told the driver to turn around.

"We should go if we're going to make Austria at a decent hour." She didn't look at her driver. "You called in the reservations?"

"Yes, madam."

She nodded. Now what to do? She had another passport, complete with another identity in case this little eventuality ever arose. Elianya sniffed, she was not about to spend any time in jail. She pulled her white fur tighter around her.

The problem was that if they found the cache of videotapes, which she was certain they would, and some of the paper files, then the authorities would know most of the places she would go.

Of course, they probably wouldn't know them all. They couldn't know them all. Not all were on file, or even operating yet. She could drive up to Cheb, but that was dangerous. Too many of her brother's people up there. Too many bosses and enforcers who would love to make her pay.

She sighed. That had not been planned well. She should have made it look as though Viktor had been killed in an accident, or at the very least by his own enforcer. Then the bosses would be helping her and aiding in trying to kill one Dimitri Petrolov. Of course, they would undoubtedly be looking for him regardless. He knew too many of their secrets. Too many shipment dates, too many meeting places, too many names.

She grinned.

All men.

She should have planned to just take them *all* out, but this worked as well. There had been an opportunity and she'd taken it. She just needed a bit of time. She had enough money in her Swiss and Cayman accounts already under another name.

Now it was simply time to become someone else.

She sighed again. "Go." She sat back as he pulled away from the curb and drove in the opposite direction of the chaos behind her.

Overall, it wouldn't matter. She still had the main client list on her CPU in the back of the car. She still had account numbers. All she needed to do was find someplace to download it all onto her laptop and then back it up on disk.

Her phone rang.

"Yes?" she asked.

"You idiot!" the voice said.

She waited.

"What in the hell have you started now?"

"You told me to leave Petrolov alone and I haven't even touched him."

"No, you blew his damn cover. Do you have *any* idea the amount of manpower you just put on this damn case? Everything will be blown way the hell open. Fuck."

She tsked. "You worry too much, my friend." She picked at the fur. "Perhaps I rushed things with Viktor, but—"

"Perhaps. We've now got a vacuum there. You know as well as I do, there will be war over who gets his holdings." The other person muttered something she didn't catch. "And since you decided to leave the guards alive, they know who killed Viktor Hellinski. The guards knew he was alive before you went in. Then he's dead. Not real bright."

She frowned. "I saw no reason to kill them. It will work out. I've money, and connections. If they want to fight over my brother's holdings, let them. I have my own."

A sigh answered her. "You may now. Tomorrow who's to say?"

Elianya knew she'd make it through this. She had undoubtedly rushed Viktor's demise, but he was gone, she was moving on. And to better things.

But there was one thing, one she would take care of before she completely turned her back on the past.

"What of Petrolov?" she asked.

"He's our problem now. Your little stunt has alerted everyone to the fact we have a mole. Whether or not Petrolov dies is moot. The problem is much bigger than him now."

Not the way she saw it. Perhaps the powers that be would figure out who their snitch was, maybe she would help them there.

But no matter what, Petrolov—until she learned his real name—would remain foremost in her mind.

"I'll contact you later," she said.

"Don't. I shouldn't—"

Elianya hung up and cut her phone off. She didn't care to talk to the informant. She looked at the small piece of technology and realized how stupid she was. They could trace her by her cell phone. At the first opportunity she would destroy it. It was tempting to simply toss it out the window. But that would be stupid.

She took a deep breath and wondered how to find out Petrolov's real name. She would. The contact had to know it, and she would obtain it.

Elianya was not above blackmail and obviously her contact was worried. They should be, she could ruin them. She would unless they told her what she wanted to know.

And what she wanted was very simple.

A name.

His name.

Not just another alias.

Petrolov's true identity.

• • •

The sun over the city glinted a dark silver off the river, mirroring the glass windows across the way. The men behind him talked in low voices. Rori stood behind the minibar cutting up fruit room service had delivered. Cinnamon and baked pastries filled the air from the streusel and kolaches brought up, coffee swirled within the scents of the baked goods, reminding him he'd had nothing to eat since lunch yesterday.

Snake, a medium-sized Latino, originally from New Mexico, had looked over the little girl, noted her eyes were still a bit glazed from drugs or shock, and decided against giving her anything else. Though cautious, the child moved with ease, belying any injuries she might have. She sat quiet and still now, sucking her thumb. So, Snake, ever the efficient man, had gently placed his hand on her neck and squeezed a pressure point until she merely slumped to the side on the couch cushions.

Ian bit down. "Was that necessary?"

Snake, his dark eyes narrowed, stared at him. "Probably not, but it was a hell of a lot quicker than waiting for her to go to sleep or waiting until whatever drugs are in her system to work their way out."

Snake started to reach down and lift the child, but Ian stepped forward and mumbled, "I'll do it." He scooped her up, ignoring the stares the others threw him. "Where do you want her."

They went back to the bedroom and he laid her gently on the bed.

"She'll be out for a few minutes, and considering what you've told me, I'd rather not have her come to while we're examining her," Snake muttered, pulling out a stethoscope, some vials, a blood pressure gauge.

Ian stood at the foot of the bed, thrumming his fingers against his thigh as Snake quickly checked her heart, her pulse.

The harsh bruises on the back of the girl's neck yelled at him from her pale skin. And as Snake quickly undressed her, more bruises and injuries made themselves known.

Ian fisted his hands, cursing, "Son of a bitch."

Snake's head whipped up. "Wait in the other room."

He started to. God help him, he almost turned around. Instead he swallowed, walked to the window and sat on the sill, looking out at the morning activity—at people who may or may not have a care in the world.

Not like the poor soul on the bed.

Christ. He closed his eyes, took another deep breath and wished again he was anywhere but here.

Snake tended to whisper to himself, muttering as he examined, and Ian ignored him, or tried to. He didn't even turn around when he heard Snake's oath, and wasn't surprised when the man softened his voice, as if calming the little girl who couldn't hear him.

"Well," Snake's voice didn't pull his attention from the street below, "she's been bound, given injections in the arm, from the needle marks. Not too many, so I would have to say they didn't have her too long, as the last one is still somewhat fresh. Probably last night's. I'm taking some blood samples to see what she's been given."

He closed his eyes, thinking of the evidence he'd knowingly washed down the drain. "She took a bath."

"I know, but from what I can tell it doesn't matter. She wasn't sexually abused from what I can tell. Of course, where she was, what she saw . . ." He trailed off. "As for suffering as the poor girl on the video, no. This one here's still a virgin, no bruising, no tearing, no signs of any sexual assault."

Thank God.

Ian turned, breathing deep, controlling the rage that had roared up in him through the last few minutes. He cleared his throat. "When will you have the results back on her blood work?" He walked to the bed, sat on the other side, reaching out and grazing his finger down her pale cheek.

"Hard to say. Probably in a few days." Snake tossed his stuff back into the bag, carefully set the vials into a small tray and placed the tray in a miniature cooler. He quickly zipped all the compartments shut.

Voices floated in from the other room.

"Poor kid. Bastards," Snake said, taking her pulse again.

Without taking his eyes off of her, he reached out, took her other hand and said, "How old do you think she is?"

Snake laid her hand gently on her chest and pulled the covers up. "Hard to say. Some kids are really small for their age, malnutrition, genes, whatever, others larger. But going on average, I'd say probably five. But she could be four or even six." He shrugged, grabbed the discarded shirt and pulled it back over the girl's head. Ian helped him put her arms into the garment.

He rubbed his hands over his face. "How much longer will she be out?"

Snake straightened, twisted, his back crackling. "A few more minutes, why?"

Ian stood, walked into the living room and asked for a printing kit. Tanner, shoving pastry into his mouth, reached over, grabbed a kit out of his bag and handed it to Ian.

Back in the room, he eased her fingers onto the pad, then onto the paper, printing each digit. Her palm was warm against his own fingers. In the bathroom, he wet a washcloth, then quickly cleaned her fingers off. He didn't want her sucking on the ink.

Probably wouldn't hurt her, but still.

When he was finished, he tossed the washcloth into the wastebasket, where they were tossing all their towels. He knew when they left here, they'd also clean the room, strip it of linens, crammed in a bag, and someone would toss it below themselves — preferably in the incinerator.

Leave nothing behind.

That was the motto.

He leaned his arms onto the counter and looked at himself in the mirror. His shadow was practically a beard. His hair long.

He only saw the man he'd been for the last five years. One Dimitri Petrolov, who had saved girls, helped men and killed some he wished he could forget.

"You look tired," Rori's quiet voice said behind him.

He shifted his gaze to her in the mirror and didn't say anything for a moment. Was she here only because he'd ordered her to be? Was it more? Did she still plan on taking him out? He didn't trust her. Not really, yet something about her pulled at him.

Her head tilted to the side, her eyes narrowed. "What?"

For a moment they just stared at each other. Ian's muscles tightened, his gut squeezed and all he saw was her, and those wicked green eyes.

The woman tries to kill him and he finds her attractive.

A slow grin lifted her lips, dimpling into a smile. "I'd love to know what's going on in that mind of yours."

He blinked, then looked at himself again in the mirror. Turning his head one way then another. "I was thinking it was time for a trim."

"And a shave?" Her eyes twinkled. "Do I get the honors?"

Should he go blond? "I wouldn't let you near me with a razor."

Her chuckle danced between them and sunk straight to his groin. He shifted.

"Darling, if I wanted to kill you, I wouldn't use a razor."

He needed his bag. He turned, but she blocked the doorway.

They both stood there, staring at each other. Ian inhaled deeply and caught a whiff of something floral, jasmine and spice? His eyes ran down her. Still dressed in her turtleneck, the sweater clung to her curves. Trim belly, a rather flat chest and muscled arms. Her legs were long. Her neck graceful, seemingly longer than he remembered from her provocative sweater earlier last night. Her lips were lush, full, and that straight-lined nose tilted up just so at the end, making her almost vulnerable somehow. He stepped closer.

She didn't move, only continued to stare at him.

"Why didn't you mark me?" he asked, his voice low. He put one arm up on the other side of the door facing so she'd have to duck and go under to leave. Her eyes were wickedly pale, and this close he saw they weren't just green, but also dusted with golden flecks.

Her lashes swept down. "It didn't feel right."

"You always do what you feel is right?" He leaned a bit closer, and noticed her shoulder muscles tighten. Definitely jasmine.

She licked her lips, looked at him from under her lashes. "Mostly."

Ian leaned closer. "Good. So do I."

To hell with it. He leaned in and she met him halfway.

Her lips were as soft as he thought they would be. Neither of them touched except with their lips. He shifted, standing a bit closer, just a bit more and their chests would be touching.

She tilted her head, angling, and bit his lip. Ian sucked in his breath, his eyes darting open. Her eyes watched his and she slowly licked the spot where her teeth had nipped, her tongue warm and wet.

He felt her smile before she ended the kiss and pulled back. One brow cocked, she said, "And I never do anything I don't want to do."

As she watched, he licked his lip at the same spot she had only moments before. "That makes two of us."

He didn't move as she walked away and across the dark room, back into the living room.

John stood in the living room, looking into the bedroom, a

straight line to the bathroom. His eyes met Ian's and John only shook his head.

What the hell was he doing? Ian hurried into the living room, grabbed his bag up and turned to head back to the bathroom.

"The passports should be here within the hour. I need to take your photos," Tanner said.

Ian nodded to him and kept walking. Too much to do, too little time.

So what the hell was he doing kissing the woman who had been hired to kill him?

Shit.

He was losing his mind. That was all it was. Had to be it.

As he walked through the bedroom he glanced at the bed, saw the girl was awake and watching him. He slowed, but didn't stop near the bed as she tensed. Ian gave her a smile and walked on.

He set his bag down, and almost shut the bathroom door. Instead, he left it open so he could see into the room. He pulled his shirt off, draped a towel in the sink, and pulled the scissors out of the bag. Wetting his hair, he combed it. It was longer than he realized, almost to his shoulders.

The scissors clicked, echoing in the tiled bathroom as dark locks of his hair fell into his hand. He dropped the pieces into the towel. Snip. Snip. Snip. It took several minutes, but he had most of it off.

He heard her voice before he saw her appear in the mirror again. He paused. "What?"

"You want to look like you cut that yourself?" She stepped up behind him. "Here, give me those."

His eyes met hers in the mirror and she grinned.

"Stabbing's really not my thing. Incredibly messy. I'd rather a gun any day." She held her hand out. "And besides, your blokes in there would have my neck broke before you even bled out. So give over."

Ian slapped the scissors in her hands.

"You'll have to get down a bit, I'm tall but not that bloody tall."

Ian knelt down. "Why do I get the feeling you enjoy this?"

"Yes, having a man on his knees before me is rather nice." She continued to snip his hair. She paused and both their eyes shifted in the mirror to the doorway, where the girl stood, wearing a too large

T-shirt of his. Her thumb firmly in her mouth.

Her eyes only stared, she barely moved.

Ian didn't know how the hell to put her at ease or even how to communicate with her.

Rori jerked his hair, yanking his attention back.

"You keep moving and I won't be responsible if you get a bad trim." Snip. Snip. Snip.

He kept his head straight, but his eyes on the little girl. She came a bit closer. Then a bit closer, but never completely into the bathroom.

Ian grinned at her again, hoping to put her at ease.

"There," Rori said, rolling her fingers into the towel. "You've a head of hair on you, but I think that'll do, no?"

He turned his head one way, then the other. It was short, almost a crew cut, but he didn't care. He would probably shave it off when they switched identities again anyway. He nodded. "It'll definitely do." His eyes met hers. "Thanks."

Smiling ruefully, she handed him back the scissors. "Now, if you could just find a razor, we might be ready by the time your friends arrive."

With that, she walked out of the bathroom, and the little girl hurried out of her way, hiding around the doorway.

Rori stopped, asked the little girl if she was hungry, and made motions to her mouth as if eating. Then motioned for her to follow.

The little girl looked from him to Rori. Deciding to help out. He smiled again, pointed to Rori and then gently closed the door. He wrapped the towel up, tossed it into the wastebasket and wiped the counter clean.

Stripping, he quickly climbed into the shower and washed the last of the hair off. He shaved, redressed. Making certain the bathroom was as clean as he could get it, the tub and drain free of hair, he nodded. He opened the bathroom door, steam billowing out into the cool room.

He almost stepped on her.

The little girl sat on the floor, in his T-shirt, her spindly legs and bare feet straight out in front of her, pastry crumbs all over the shirt, and what looked like a bit of poppyseed filling on the top of her lip.

"Looks as if you've eaten," he said, squatting down.

She placed the kolache on the white plate beside her and wiped her hands on her shirt.

He didn't move.

She stared at him, in that straight silent way she did, the dark blue eyes wide and curious.

Then ever so slowly, she stood, her head tilting to the side. Her little hand reached out and touched his cheek, rubbing the now smooth skin.

He smiled at her.

"Looks like you're charming all the ladies," John said from the doorway.

The little girl quickly jerked her hand behind her back.

Ian reached out and rubbed her arm, smiling. "Yeah," he answered John. "If I could only charm this one into speaking."

Chapter 10

She clutched the teddy bear to her as the man tightened the belt across her lap. The seat was big.

They were on a plane. He said he was taking her someplace safe. The lady was still with them.

Where was Zoy? Didn't Zoy get to come? She clutched the black bear tighter to her as he settled back into his seat and patted her hand. Telling her it would be all right.

Earlier that day, they left the hotel and she had new clothes. A blue pantsuit with fat white buttons and a white collar. He even gave her a black coat that went to her knees. She wasn't cold anymore.

Where were they taking her? She'd tried to ask him, but her voice wouldn't work.

The man knew she spoke because he'd asked if she was hungry earlier and she nodded. He'd smiled then and called her Darya.

Why did he call her Darya?

Zoy had called her Ayrena.

But the man called her Darya and he gave her the soft black bear.

She buried her face in the fur and held on tight. They were going on a trip, he'd told her as they walked into the building with all the people. They'd been in a car all day, driving and driving. She wondered where they were going when they'd come here. Planes took off and zoomed away. Big and heavy as smooth painted metal birds.

The man carried her onto one, telling her she was going to be like a bird and they were going to fly.

She wondered if she'd see Zoy. Maybe someone else was bringing her sister. The man sat on one side of her, on the aisle, and the lady sat on the other side beside a little window. The man and lady had argued, or she thought so. Apparently they'd both wanted to sit on the outside.

But the man was sitting there now, watching her, watching the lady, watching everyone. He always seemed to be watching everyone.

Was he looking for her sister too?

He looked at her and ran his hand over her hair, which the lady had braided. She waited. He seemed nice, but you never knew.

Sometimes nice became mean.

Like the other . . .

No. No. She shook her head and put her thumb in her mouth. He frowned for a minute and she noticed his eyes darkened. He looked different with his hair cut and his smooth face. And the glasses. She liked his face smooth, it didn't scratch her forehead or cheek when he held her.

And for some reason, when he held her, she felt safe.

She looked at him again. He'd keep the monsters away.

Please let him keep the monsters away.

The plane jerked as it moved. She looked out the window and saw the buildings going by faster, faster, faster. She squeezed the bear to her chest, scared.

Her tummy tickled and she was pushed back into her seat. She held the bear tighter as she saw the tops of the buildings out of the window, and then the blue sky. She couldn't hear. A loud hum filled her ears, her head.

Her heart fluttered and she turned to the man, scared that they'd fall.

He smiled and patted her hand. She sucked harder on her thumb and held her bear even tighter.

Would they all turn into birds?

• • •

Rori watched the scenery whir by below. Frankfurt fell away and the German countryside below was dotted and squared in greens, browns, and grays.

They'd left the Czech Republic that morning via Cheb and into Dresden, Germany. A few hours on the autobahn put them into Frankfurt in time to catch British Airways flight 905 that afternoon.

She sighed and leaned back against the seat.

That morning, a man, nameless, stopped at the hotel, dropped off a packet, taking a wad of money, and was gone. One of the men, Tanner, tall, blond brown hair, dark eyes and squared features, had gone downstairs to a shop inside the hotel and purchased them clothing. So that her passport didn't look the same as what she was wearing that day, she put on one of Ian's white T-shirts and her jacket. Quick snap of the digital, a few computer strokes, a bit of finessing and voila, new passports.

She was listed as Lori Hightower, wife of Evan Hightower, businessman. They'd just adopted their daughter from an orphanage in Russia. They had all the papers to prove little Darya was theirs. The new family was flying home to London.

Ian . . . no, Evan watched her. She didn't have to look to see that, she could feel his gaze. She knew the second those dark blue eyes of his landed on her. It was a static shock. Out of the corner of her eye, she glanced at him. Clean shaven, his hair cut short, the British persona he had taken on as Hightower somehow made him appear a bit softer, more crisp instead of the sharp-edged and shifting Petrolov. He even added small wire-rimmed glasses. It was he who now wore the turtleneck, a dark plum one, black Armani pants, loafers and the gold watch.

Amazingly it wasn't even the visual disguise so much as this aura that seemed to surround him. The man didn't just look different from Dimitri Petrolov, he *was* different. The way he sat, the way his head tilted, the way he spoke.

Glancing at him occasionally, she couldn't help but wonder who he really was. Was Ian his real name or just another alias?

To be honest, if not for the eyes, she wondered if she'd even recognize him. Actually, she probably wouldn't, because she'd only see the glasses.

People saw what they wanted to see.

The secret to a successful disguise was to tell them what they wanted to see.

The little girl, dressed in a little navy and white pantsuit with a black peacoat, looked the part of a newly adopted daughter.

Clearing her throat, Rori said softly, knowing no one could hear her, "You know, with her dark hair and those blue eyes, little Darya could easily be Mr. Evan Hightower's daughter."

"She *is* my daughter," he said, his words short and clipped, and undeniably British. "More importantly, darling, she's *our* daughter." His eyes bore into hers.

Rori—Lori only nodded and gently brushed a wayward curl back off Darya's forehead. A black teddy bear, *Mr. Bear*, bought in the gift shop on their way out of the hotel early that morning, was clutched to her chest. From the moment he'd given her the gift, she hadn't relaxed her hold on it.

Her thumb was again in her mouth. She had heard the men talking that morning, knew the girl had not been abused, and felt more for the child than she cared to. Thank God.

Rori didn't want to feel anything for the child, yet couldn't help it. The thought of what she went through, of what still lay ahead, greased old memories and nausea through her. As hard a woman as she was, she wouldn't wish that fate on her worst enemy. Locked away. Men with big hands, drunken laugher and . . .

She shook her head.

Every now and then Darya craned her neck to look out the window, but then she'd sit back and silently stare, rubbing the teddy bear.

Mr. Hightower spoke softly to her. She wondered what he was saying to the child as she didn't understand them.

The child didn't answer. They knew she spoke Russian because he'd asked Darya if she was hungry earlier and the child looked at him and nodded.

He'd grinned. "Ah, so it is Russian, little one."

Since then, he'd been telling Darya one thing or another, and the child was glued to him.

Rori remembered that too. Finally finding someone you wanted to trust, but were afraid to. Someone who seemed to care and you were too bloody afraid not to hold on to them, terrified they'd leave you behind and just as scared to get too close lest they turned on you.

God she was tired. Wishing she had her laptop out of the overhead luggage compartment, she leaned her head back and closed her eyes. If nothing else, she could get a few minutes' rest. Just a few . . .

As the hum of the engines filled her head, the rumble relaxing her, she dropped off into sleep.

And into memories better left forgotten.

She'd hidden in the closet. If she was very, very quiet, he wouldn't find her. He couldn't find her if she was quiet.

She hurt. He'd made her do things she didn't want to think about. Things that hurt, things that she knew were wrong.

She was gangly, taller than most girls her age, and wished, wished with everything in her that she had the courage to run away.

But he'd told her, warned her that the coppers would get her and bring her back, and when they did, she'd wish she were dead.

She already wished that.

She listened very carefully, fear trickling through her as surely as the blood from her nose where he'd slapped her.

The sound of doors opening and slamming, mixed with his yells.

"Come out you, lit'l slut! I'll find you, I will." Slam.

She covered her ears. And waited. He would find her and she trembled knowing it. She shook her head. Please . . .

Her hands scrambled along the bottom of the closet and she felt the weight on the floor, circular and cold against her hand.

It was heavy. Slam. He was coming closer.

She picked it up . . .

Please . . . She whimpered.

• • •

He watched the girl, her eyes closed, her cheeks moving with the slight movement of her thumb. His nerves were strung tight, but so far, so good. If they could get to his place once they landed, everything just might work.

Darya's fingers were white-knuckled on the damn bear he'd bought her. Poor kid. First thing he'd do is buy her some toys. She deserved some things to play with.

Maybe a doll?

What did little girls play with? He frowned.

She twitched in her sleep, her smooth brow furrowing, and whimpered. Bastards. One day . . .

Gently, he leaned down and whispered in her ear that she was safe. She twitched again and again he shushed her. She finally settled, and he pulled her against him, letting her head rest on his arm. She smelled of soap and some indefinable fragrance that always made him think of children.

What the hell had happened to his life?

If anyone had asked him a week ago what he'd be doing now, his answer would have been working.

Working for Viktor Hellinski.

Working for the agency and international task force trying to find out which brothels and bosses fronted terror networks. Period.

Finding criminals even as he himself posed as one.

Now?

Now someone was trying to kill him. His cover had been blown, so more were trying to kill him, a woman he'd never met before was his wife, and they had a daughter.

Chaotic. It was utterly chaotic and out of control.

He hated things to be out of control.

Strangely enough, he felt a bit of peace he hadn't felt in a long damn time. Why? He had no idea and he didn't want to know at present.

The feeling was so vague and rare, he figured he'd best appreciate it and try to figure out what the hell they were all going to do next.

First priority was Darya's safety. For him, Britain was still too close to those who had hurt her, to Elianya, who wouldn't think twice about eliminating a child.

But Darya might not be his to protect. What would he do if he found she had a family somewhere?

He shifted in the seat and took a deep breath. He'd make damn certain it was a safe environment to return her to. She and her sister hadn't just appeared in Elianya's porn enterprise. He knew, knew from firsthand experience that families in dire straits often did unspeakable things.

Like sell their souls, sell their children. He'd tried not to judge, but damn it. How could any human being sell their child into the sex ring. He knew, as Dimitri, that many had not known, had believed their daughter or occasionally son was going to work. But just as many *had* known that their child was going to be lost in a world of sex and vice and they simply hadn't given a damn.

If Darya's family was of the last, he'd simply kill them and be done with it.

Rage flowed through him, a slow river of lava. He shifted again.

And all this anger wasn't doing him a bit of good. God, he'd love a cigarette—or as Mr. Hightower might think, a fag. But Brit or not, Hightower wasn't the type of man to smoke, so the nicotine would just have to wait. Damn it.

The voice in the back of his head asked what he was going to do with the little girl if she had no one else to go to.

Giving up, he opened his eyes and stared at the overhead air vent.

He had no idea.

Turning, he looked down on Darya's dark head.

An innocent child.

What the hell did he know about innocence or children?

They should be protected.

He'd stayed in this fucking game too damn long. He wanted out, out to have a real life.

Like photographs in his mind, he saw his brothers and their families. Wives, children. The smiles, the laughter. Things he remembered from his own childhood. Not that he'd ever planned to have a family. Families were tools that could effectively be used against him. A wife and children could be exploited, harmed, even killed to teach lessons.

He'd never thought about it until John had lost his family. Then he'd seen what his friend had gone through and vowed he would never, *never* put anyone in that type of jeopardy.

Children should know safety. Know love.

And where did that leave him? Or Darya?

He didn't have a fucking clue.

Mr. Evan Hightower closed his eyes and still his mind wouldn't settle.

He glanced at the woman posing as his wife.

Lori. She was asleep, or at least resting. Her hand lay on the armrest, long-fingered, free from rings, and short buffed nails. Her cheeks were smooth and the pulse in her neck jumped against the white collar of her shirt. The dark purple jacket she wore brought out a blush in her cheeks. Her dark brows, arched and high, made him want to smooth his finger over them. That ridiculously short hair made him want to run his hand over her scalp.

She frowned, her head jerking to the side. He looked at her face, still smooth. Settling back he tried to think. He looked at Rori again. Her hand fisted on the armrest.

He reached over Darya, who was slumping down partially into his lap, and put his hand atop Rori's, rubbing the back of her fist. He could see the line of vein running along the back of her hand, felt the ridge where the blood flowed.

Her muscles tensed in her arm.

He frowned again. Shifting, he gently shook her shoulder. She tried to pull away and he tightened his hold, shaking a bit harder.

Her eyes shot open and she jerked in the seat.

He studied her. "Easy," he said. "You were dreaming." And from the looks of it, not a pleasant one.

Her eyes wide, she glanced at him, then at the little girl between them. She took a deep breath, her chest rising on her inhale, and barely shook her head.

His hand lay again atop hers, hoping to calm her, to take that haunted look from her eyes. A look he'd never seen in those icy eyes, a shadow he didn't *like* seeing there.

He felt the tremor even before her hand turned and her fingers laced with his. She didn't say a word, just stared out the window. He looked at their hands, his dark and tanned, hers long-fingered and elegant, her nails trimmed short, practical. Her fingers were white-knuckled.

He rubbed his thumb across the back of her hand, still staring at their joined hands.

The woman didn't look at him again; the pulse pounded in her neck and sweat beaded on her forehead.

Some dream.

Still rubbing her hand, he leaned his head back and closed his eyes, the warmth of the child nestled up against his side.

What did he honestly know of family?

Chapter 11

Rori looked out at the pine-covered slope. Loch Affric, dull and gray, in the late afternoon light, shone through the trees.

They had been here for a week.

The lake — loch — would be beautiful in the summer months. She was in bloody Scotland. How in the hell did she end up here? She was still trying to figure that one out, as she had been for almost a week.

They'd landed in London and spent two days in different hotels, while Ian had changed his identity yet again.

No more Evan and Lori Hightower. Now they were Ian and Rori Kinncaid. Ian Kinncaid. Kinncaid. She'd run a search on the name after they arrived here and found several lists. Granted, this was Scotland, Kinncaids everywhere. But with that spelling, there was a branch in America and a family in particular who owned hotels. Was he part of them? Not that she'd been able to find thus far. So was Ian Kinncaid simply another alias or not?

Their current residence was an old Georgian manor house, built after the uprising of '45, or so she was told. History had never really been her thing. She saw no reason why people felt they had to know every little date that ever happened in past lives. She didn't care. Now was all that was important, and how one went about spending it, dealing with it and living it. Tomorrow would come, and depending on whether or not you buggered the day would affect the next day.

She looked out the window; the pines and bare trees obscured a clear view of Loch Affric. The day was cold, the clouds low, hiding the mountains that surrounded them.

The place made her twitchy, out in the middle of bloody nowhere. The only sound, the birds. Not that it was a bad place, she rather liked the quiet, but even her place in County Waterford wasn't this remote. She thought she'd lived in the country, but this . . . this was almost desolate, lonely.

So why hadn't she left. She could have at any time, she knew. But there was Darya . . .

And she wanted the time away. No one demanded anything of her here. She didn't worry about the next job. There *wasn't* a next job. That made her smile.

So here she was in Scotland, dressed in jeans and a thick cable-knit sweater, trying to keep warm while a light snow dusted the ground.

A sound drew her attention and she turned, looking at the man who was talking on his mobile as he shuffled through some papers.

Heading to the study near the back of the house.

She looked around at the dark wooded antiques, crystal vases, and priceless works of art. There were no photos here. Not that she'd seen.

He'd hardly spoken to her all week. Men came and went. John Brasher, Tanner, Snake, who kept checking on the little girl, and Gar. She remembered Gar. A complete computer geek. Pushing away from the wall, she turned and followed Ian.

"I don't care. I want the tickets. This week. The sooner the better," he said into the phone.

Rori noticed his shadow trailed after him as she always did. The little girl was never far from him. And he seemed to be the only one that could calm her after her nightmares, of which there were plenty. Nightly, the girl visited demons and woke up screaming. Every night it broke Rori's heart and every night she couldn't make herself go to the girl, to see, to recognize and remember that pain.

The thick rugs hushed their footfalls in the hallway. Darya looked at Rori over her little shoulder. Dressed in an ivory sweater and jeans, her teddy bear clasped to her chest, she stopped, darted around Rori and ran down the hall toward the kitchen.

Gar the nerd was also an excellent cook, as was—surprisingly—Ian. There was a never-ending supply of biscuits. She didn't ask who made them, in fact, it would ruin her image of Ian if she found out he'd baked the chocolate chip ass-widening delicacies. Better to think of him as the badass assassin. Agent, covert operator, assassin, whichever. Semantics as far as she was concerned. She'd seen the man in action. She knew a fellow eliminator when she saw one.

She watched as the child disappeared around the far corner. This house was a child's hide-and-seek paradise or nightmare, depending on one's point of view.

Rori turned around and followed him to his study. The door was shut. To hell with this. She'd played nice for almost a week. She wasn't one to be put out. If he wanted her help, fine, but she could find something to do other than play shadow to Ian Kinncaid. And he could bloody well start talking to her.

Without knocking, she opened the door, then shut it behind her. He looked at her, the phone held between his shoulder and jaw as he flipped through the file in his hands.

She walked to the chair and flopped down, leaning back.

He frowned at her.

She frowned back.

"Yeah," he said. "Who was she? Yes? Yes? Get me a name. Thanks." He flipped the phone shut and clipped it to his belt to hang with the other three he had.

She herself had two. One for personal use and one for work.

Nikko had called so many times she'd lost count. On both phones, she simply wasn't ready to talk to him yet. Though she should probably ring him back soon before he started his own search for her.

"What?" he asked, walking around the desk to lean back against it. Today he wore his normal black trousers, matching black sweater, the sleeves pushed up to his elbows.

She could see just a bit of black hair peeking out of the vee of his sweater.

"I would like to know what the hell is going on. I'm not one of your lackeys or followers or — "

"Employees?" he supplied, crossing his feet.

"Employees?"

"As co-owner of KB Securities I would have employees," he said, one side of his mouth kicking up on a grin.

"KB?" she asked.

"Kinncaid-Brasher."

"Should have chosen another name," she muttered. Sounded like a jolly toy shop.

His expression didn't change at all. Still a smirk, those dark blue eyes holding a question — what question she wasn't certain, nor did she want to know.

"I'm not a bloody employee, thank you."

He scratched the side of his mouth. "Yes, I wanted to talk to you about that. Any ideas yet on who hired you to off me?"

"Off?"

His gaze didn't change.

"No. *B-Widow* hasn't contacted me since before all hell broke loose."

"Well," he said and waved a hand. "We've enough people working on the threat as it is. Doesn't matter. What matters now is my family."

The way he said it. *My* family. So definite. So bloody real. For a moment she wondered what it must be like to be considered that possessed. That taken, that owned.

Owned?

Family.

What the hell did she know about family, then? Family to her was either buggered or Nikko. She preferred Nikko.

Nikko. Perhaps she did know about family. Ties that held people together weren't always forged in blood.

"And then you'll get to meet them," he said.

His words pulled her back. She frowned.

"As my wife you wouldn't want to seem not to know a thing about them, and I believe I should show you something."

"What? What are you talking about?"

He sighed as if annoyed. "My family. You're to meet them. As my wife."

"Like bloody hell." She shook her head and wanted to stand, but didn't. She tapped her foot. "Do you really think it necessary?"

"If I didn't, I wouldn't have mentioned it."

She frowned and watched him thrum his fingers on his thigh.

"Do you think it wise?"

"What?"

"Well, you've people out looking for you who, I'm quite certain, would love to put a bullet in you. Why would you go to your family?"

He took a deep breath and ran a hand over his hair. "One, I don't *want* to lead anyone to my family. But, they have no idea about any of this, any of what I do. The least I *have* to do is make certain they are safe and things are as they should be. And two, Darya." His eyes narrowed on hers. "I know this is all . . ."

"Buggered?" she supplied.

"British euphemism. Yeah, buggered." He sighed and watched her. "If you have something else, other plans already in place, let me know and I'll figure something out. But I need to know that if anything happens to me, Darya has a place to go. A safe and secure place where she will be loved without question." Those eyes hardened, burned a cold fire. "She's been through too damn much to deserve otherwise. So we could use your help in carrying off this cover. If you're interested."

She thought about it, tapped her finger on her thigh and watched him. "How long?"

He shook his head. "Not a clue."

"Basically, I play the little wife indefinitely. Why doesn't that appeal to me?" Nikko would have a fit, probably laughing his arse off.

"I could keep Darya safe," she heard herself say.

He nodded. "Undoubtedly. But she needs more than safety and I don't know that either of us can effectively give it to her."

She studied him for a moment and felt again his loneliness brush momentarily against hers.

"We're very fucked-up creatures, you and I," she muttered.

He half laughed, half grunted. Instead of answering he walked to the door and through it. She waited in the chair until he came back and looked back around the doorway.

"You coming?" His hand slapped the door facing.

She stood and rolled her neck. "I need a workout," she muttered.

The smirk widened.

"Not that." She took a deep breath and stretched her right arm by crossing it over her chest and pulling it to her by the elbow with her left hand. "I'd love to take your arse to the floor." Damn the man and . . . "You practice any hand-to-hand combat? Martial arts?" She stopped, realizing how the entire exchange could be construed into sex.

His grin might be deadly if she cared. And of course, she didn't. He was just . . . a man . . . His gaze raked over her. Maybe a really handsome, lickilicious type of man. A slow rainy day, make love in the bed all day kind of man, but still . . . A man all the same.

"Want to find out?" He smiled even more, those brows rising.

She shook her head and stretched her other arm.

He just stared at her, his head tilting slightly. "Yeah, I think it would," he said softly.

"What would what?"

His eyes narrowed a wee bit. "I'll show you later."

She only cocked a brow at him and motioned for him to go as she joined him in the hallway.

Again they walked down the long corridor. Such a lovely, filled . . . house. Big, wealthy house. An aced des res. She couldn't live here, but it was without question fabulous.

"You bring lots of rescued kids, people, whatever here?"

He kept walking. "I've never brought anyone here. John knows it exists, but that was all."

"Oh."

The feeling that the house somehow reflected the owner wouldn't leave her. Here he was, all shades of any man he wished to become, and his home could have been anyone's.

Upstairs the soft winter light did little to brighten the darkened antique-lined hallway. They walked passed Darya's room, then passed her own room to the master's suite at the end of the hallway.

"The master's domain. Men are such insecure creatures," she muttered.

He didn't look at her as he opened the double doors and walked into the room.

She paused at the doorway.

What did the bloke think? "Look here, boyo."

He halted and turned. There it was, that wicked grin again. "I didn't ask you here to make love to you." Again his gaze ran over her, as caressing as a hand. "Though I'm quite certain it would be more than enjoyable." He shook his head, a chuckle gravelling out across the room. "I wanted to show you my family so that you would know who was who, what they do."

"A briefing." Of course that was it. Bloody hell. What was she anyway? A complete ditz? Not that the idea of his didn't have some lovely merit.

Then she actually looked around the room.

In dark blues and grays it could almost be dreary in such a setting, with the dark woods and clouded, fog-laden days, but here, it seemed to suit him somehow. Wealth, tangled with sensuality and the knowledge that this was his domain.

Where the rest of the house did little to let her see into this mysterious man, here things were different. The rest of the house was without a doubt a façade. Everywhere she had looked nothing was answered, no clues were given as to who he was.

Not so here.

Dark-canopied bed that she was sure very few could honestly afford, large enough for an orgy. Blinking, she looked around the rest of the room, two walls covered in windows letting in the soft afternoon light. Comfort and quiet wealth.

A fire burned in the fireplace and on the mantel were photographs. Rori walked over to study them.

Ian and another dark-headed man with a single dimple in his cheek. The two had their arms around each other and she could tell from the coloring and facial features they had to be related. Other photos of Ian and a redheaded woman, the woman and an older man with white hair and the same cobalt eyes as Ian. There were other people, twin men, candid photos, as if the photographed had no idea anyone was taking a picture. Photographs showing people's lives.

She looked around the rest of the room as she held a photo of the redheaded woman years ago holding a baby. Pictures were everywhere.

For some reason the site of all those framed photos on the mantel, on the dresser, the armoire, the side table, the end tables, on basically anything that stood still, left her feeling sorry for this man.

He picked up the first one she'd seen of him and another man, their arms thrown over each other's shoulders.

"This is my brother, Aiden."

He held the photo out to her and she looked from it to him, noting the way his features had changed. Not so much the face or the expression, but more an easing of tension that always surrounded him.

So alone.

She knew the world he lived in. A world of grays and shadows until everything was night and nothing seemed real. Deep crevices waiting to swallow souls and jagged mirrors that never really reflected the person within.

And here was yet another facet.

She took the small photo from him, her fingers brushing his on the wooden frame.

"Aiden," she repeated. "He looks a bit like you." Her gaze scanned some of the others. "Actually, most of the men do in some form or fashion."

"Family genetics." He grunted. "Aiden is the oldest, a year and a half older than me."

She studied the man, noted the shared features, the differences. Same coloring, different lines around the eyes, and Aiden had a dimple. Something different about the chin. "Aiden the oldest. Tell me about Mr. Aiden."

"He's the CEO of Kinncaid Enterprises."

"What does Kinncaid Enterprises do?"

He looked at her, his eyebrows rising. "They own hotels."

They, not we.

"Ah. A Kinncaid of those Kinncaids. So your brother owns the hotels."

"Brothers."

"They all own it?"

He shrugged. "It's a family business."

She set the photo back down and picked up another. "So if it's a family business, what are you doing working undercover as one of the most feared enforcers in Eastern Europe?"

He picked up another photo, running his fingers over the man's face. He set it back with the others.

"Aiden's wife's name is Jesslyn," he said, continuing as if she'd never asked a question.

Man didn't like to discuss some things apparently, but then she never discussed what led her to where she was, so that was fine with her.

"Jesslyn." Rori picked up the photo of Aiden with a blonde-haired woman. She was smiling, but there was something in her brown eyes. Worry? Pain? Something.

"They have two boys, twins. Ian and Alec."

"Awe. Named after his uncle, was he?" she asked, wrinkling her nose at the photo of two babies. Babies confused her. She had no idea what she would do with one should she ever have one. Which would never be an issue with her, so it hardly mattered.

The next photograph showed the couple in a garden, or as the Yanks called them, yard, with the twins now walking. A two-story house with a deep porch. Nice. "Proverbial suburban family?"

He chuckled. "That would depend on your definition of suburban." He tapped the woman's face. "Jesslyn isn't the normal society wife. Widowed from a car accident that also claimed the lives of her children, she wasn't really interested in my brother at first. Then there was this . . . problem." He frowned. "But it was straightened out and everyone lived. They decided to marry."

"And happily ever after?"

He shrugged. "As far as it goes, I suppose."

"Next?" She took a deep breath and for the first time smelled him. Sandalwood, or something like it. Not quite, much more subtle, maybe just soap. Whatever it was, it smelled bloody wicked.

"These are the twins." He pointed to two different photos. Though the men looked identical, there were subtle differences, hairstyles and expressions. One looked . . . jolly. The other more somber and serious.

"Brayden and Gavin. Gavin here is the family doctor. Obstetrics-gynecology. He married a social worker and adopted her adopted son, Ryan." He showed her another photo of a smiling family. A lovely woman with long red hair, freckles, and a son who smiled from ear to ear. He looked about nine or ten.

"What's their story?" she asked, looking at him.

His face hardened. "Found each other, went through hell, battled evil and are living their happily ever after."

"And that's the reason to look like you want to kill someone?"

A muscle ticked in his cheek. "No."

"What evil did they battle, then?" She set the photo she'd been holding back on the mantel, watching him.

His nostrils flared on his deep inhale. "The woman who gave birth to Ryan broke out of prison and came after him. Kidnapped him and my niece, Tori."

Oh, hell. She swallowed. "Did she hurt them?"

"She almost killed Taylor, Gavin's wife, who spent weeks in the hospital after taking a bullet to the lung. The woman roughed them up a bit, terrified the kids more than anything. Could have been worse."

Bitch.

"She won't be terrorizing anyone else," he said, his voice matter-of-fact, as if he merely spoke of the fact it was cool out.

"Good." Rori didn't need to ask to know the woman was dead.

A fleeting confusion flashed in his eyes as he looked at her. She stared back.

She finally broke their staring contest. It was either that or she might do something stupid, like stare longer, or kiss him, or who knew what. This was what happened when she thought about retiring — or had retired? Went barking mad.

He turned back to the photos. "And for the next lesson."

"What was the nephew's name again?"

"Gavin married Taylor and they adopted Ryan."

"Ryan. Got it."

He nodded. "We'll go over it again."

"How lovely."

"This is Brayden, antiques dealer, one daughter, Victoria, though family calls her Tori. Last year he married Christian." He pointed out photos of each person. The daughter had the same coloring as all the Kinncaid men. Dark hair, blue eyes, strong angles. Though she shared a dimple that Rori had seen in the oldest brother and in the matriarch. Christian looked quiet with her short dark hair and smoky gaze. Pale complexion and a seriousness from her that spoke even through the stillness of the photograph.

As Rori scanned, she saw the woman was in some of the other photographs. Not many. She was never posed in any that seemed to be professional photographs. Hers were candid, caught usually in the company of the little girl. "Brayden's Christian has been around for a while."

"Nanny."

She pulled back. "Your brother married his daughter's nanny?"

Doctors, hotel owners, antiquities dealers. Nannies. She'd come from . . . who the hell knew.

He arched one brow. "She's more our sister." He tilted his head. "Well, obviously not to Brayden." A small grin, as though he kept a secret, lifted the right side of his mouth.

"Fine, Mr. Antiquities marries his daughter's nanny."

"Yes, earlier this year, around Valentine's Day I do believe."

She got the impression he was leaving something out. "What are you not telling me?"

He shrugged. "There was also a problem for them."

"Problem as in Aiden and Jesslyn's problem, or more along the lines of the evil Gavin and Taylor battled."

"Both."

Damn. "You've an interesting family." She leaned back against the armoire. "So is their problem still living?"

"Whose?"

"Either."

"No."

She shook her head. "My, my, aren't we ever efficient. Your family is either very lucky or cursed."

He pointed to another photo of a man with the same features, angles of face, single dimple that Aiden and Tori had, but his coloring was that of the mother's. Brown hair, or dark red, green eyes. "The Changeling."

"Quinlan. The youngest, workaholic, family hotel business."

"Five boys."

"Yes."

"So what's his story?"

He shook his head. "Quinlan is easy. He's all work. Travels overseeing the overseas hotels and resorts, finds new buys to discuss with Aiden, and when at home, he lives in the hotel. He likes his coffee black, as religious in his workouts as he is about everything else."

"One of those, is he?"

He ran his finger over the frame.

"One of whats?"

She waved a hand. "Never notices the world around them, timetables and charts. Likes everything just so. No variation of the routine."

He pursed his lips. "Yes and no. He notices everything, that's why he's good at what he does, but he does like his punctuality."

She grinned. "So you're alike, are you then?"

"Hmm . . ."

He was looking at her again, that serious, straight-on way, as if trying to understand something.

"What?" She started to take a step back and realized she was against the armoire. That slow smile started to play across his lips, softening the strong jaw.

He took a step toward her, that tilting of lips still on his mouth. "I make you nervous."

She thought about lying.

"You keep shying from me and my family will think I'm mistreating you."

"No man will ever mistreat me," she said, and wished she had controlled the tone a bit more.

"There sounds like there's an 'again' at the end of that statement." He stepped even closer, his eyes running over her face, as if he were learning every line.

She wanted to look away, but she didn't.

"Why would you care what they think of me? Would the very proper Kinncaids of Kinncaid hotels not approve of a woman like me?" She motioned to the photos. "All perfectly Anglo-Saxon. They might take a care to a part-black woman in the family. I hear you Yanks take skin color rather seriously."

He shrugged and stepped close enough she smelled the clean scent of his soap and that other scent. Maybe his aftershave. Made her want to lean up and lick his jaw just to see. She took a deep breath.

"I really don't care what they think of you, if they do or don't approve. The fact I'll actually introduce you to them will make a huge impression." He notched his chin up, staring at her. "I don't care what color your skin or eyes are. You're just you," he said softly. "But I do have a confession to make about something I am biased about."

"What?"

"I have a big issue with the gun you use."

She frowned. "My gun?"

He grinned. "A SIG's better."

She blinked and shook her head. "Not bloody likely. You should really try my Walther."

"You'd let me shoot your Walther?" he asked, his voice low, his eyes intense on her even as he shifted closer. "Now I am turned on."

Nerves skittered up her back. She hated to be blocked in. Sliding to the side, she said, "Will you let me shoot your SIG?"

That grin flashed, his eyes narrowed and a bit of the devil dared her, even as his voice, husky and deep, said, "Depends on if you know how to handle it."

She stopped easing away. "There's not a gun on the market I can't handle, prefabbed or custom-made."

"Hmmm. We'll have to test that theory sometime."

Blimey the man could seduce with no more than his bloody voice, and she realized how far off topic they were. Rori took a deep breath and shook her head. Where the hell was her head?

"You didn't answer my question. And why should meeting me matter to them?" She pointed to the pictures. "You've obviously seen them often enough."

He shook his head. "No, several men have been to see them, to help them out, to take care of . . ."

"Problems?" she supplied.

He smiled. "Problems. But Mr. Ian Kinncaid hasn't been back in many, many years."

"Because?"

He stepped closer and she started to move to the side. His arms shot up on either side of her. "We're really going to have to work on this."

She swallowed and looked into his eyes. If she wanted to, she could make the man move, but then . . . She took a deep breath. She really didn't want to move him.

"Work on what?" she asked.

"You acting as if you're afraid of me."

It was her turn to arch her brow. "I'm not afraid of you."

He leaned in closer. "You're not?"

She licked her lips, watched as his eyes dropped to her mouth. "No, I'm not."

"Well, that is something then," he whispered, his eyes rising to meet hers, his breath warm on her face. "Isn't it?"

He closed the distance between them.

She'd kissed the man before and though it was nice . . .

Then his lips were on hers. He didn't touch her, except for his mouth. His tongue traced her lips, coaxed them open, his teeth gentle as they scraped over her full bottom lip.

Rori leaned back against the armoire and he shifted, his chest on hers, one leg between her own.

She sighed and opened her mouth as he swept in. His kiss demanded cooperation and she gave it, sparring with him, as his tongue licked the sensitive roof of her mouth.

The kiss set her blood to humming, speeding through her veins. She started to move her arms up, but his elbows came down on her arms, his own hands moving from flat against the armoire doors to frame her face.

God.

He pulled back a moment and shoved his hand into his pocket. He took a deep breath and frowned. "Better."

Bloody wonderful. Here she was thinking of them together and he pulled away. Better? Like it was a bloody lesson?

Rori took a deep breath.

His one hand still on her face, he said, "There's something else."

She cleared her throat before taking a calming breath. "What?"

His head tilted to the side. "This." He straightened and pulled her left hand to him.

She glanced down and blinked. "What are you about?" Freeing her hand from him proved useless. Finally, she looked up into his dark blue eyes.

Sometimes this man was so bloody intense. Those eyes were narrowed on her, the planes of his face seemed harsher than moments before. "We can't just say we're married. Rings, Rori."

Still she tried to pull her hand free. "Not everyone wears rings."

"My wife does." Those eyes challenged her.

Just like that. *My* wife.

A slight grin pulled one corner of his mouth. "There's that look."

"What bloody look?" she snapped.

The grin grew. "That look that says, 'What the bloody hell am I doing?' and 'Fuck off,' all at once."

Rori took a deep breath. "I don't think—"

Without another word, he slid the ring onto her finger. She stared at it. Nothing ordinary for this man. No plain gold band, no big flashy diamonds—not that she'd wear the latter anyway. No, this ring was wide, appeared old with the almost tarnished yet shimmering gold. Round stones so deep blue or green they appeared black were spaced and raised from the band. Deep grooves and swirls roped along the top and bottom of the ring. It looked old, pagan, Mediterranean. It was beautiful.

"You're not about to say something so clichéd as 'I couldn't possibly,' are you?" he asked, rubbing his thumb back and forth over the ring that fit perfectly on her finger.

She could only stare at it, and vainly liked the way the dim lights glinted on the gold and nearly black stones. Swallowing, she looked from the ring to him and said, "Of course not." The ring pulled her attention back to it. She shouldn't wear it. "Is this an heirloom? It appears old. I don't want it . . . That is." It was just a ring, and a beautiful one that he'd given her. "Never mind."

An inquisitive smile lightened his face. "No, it's not an heirloom. Or I suppose it might be, but I saw it in London and thought of you, so I got it. Simple."

She rolled the ring on her finger. "Right, then. Simple. Just to keep the cover complete."

He ran his tongue around his teeth. "Something like that." Ian reached into his pocket and pulled out a gold band with the same design inlaid within the smooth band. He handed it to her and smiled. "Do me the honor, dear?"

She rolled her eyes and grabbed the ring off his palm, noticing it was still warm from his body heat. "How long have you carried these around in your pocket?" She pushed the ring onto his long finger. His palm was warm where she held it. The band slid past his first knuckle. She ran her finger over the metal.

"This I'll defend," he muttered.

She looked at him. "What?"

Ian shook his head, his voice low. "You're wearing my ring."

She cocked her brow and leaned back, even as he moved in. "So?"

His hands ran from her hands, up her arms, over her shoulders, to her neck. "We're in Scotland," he said, his voice low, his lashes sweeping down to hide his eyes. "And you're claiming to be my wife. Do you know what that means?"

"Yeah, it's not forever," she said, her gaze locked on his lips.

Ian's thumbs gently stroked her jaw, back and forth, back and forth, his fingers playing at the nape of her neck. Tension swirled in her gut, made her breasts heavy and tickled down her backbone. She looked back up into his eyes, and her breath halted at the seriousness swirling in them. He leaned in closer and then closer.

Instead of replying to her comment, he whispered against her lips, "Have I told you how sexy I think you are?"

Her eyes closed, she just shook her head.

"You are," he muttered between nibbles on her lips. "Sexy and confident and that's a turn-on, babe."

He ran one hand over her short-cropped hair.

She kissed him back. "I hear husbands are supposed to tell their wives these things."

"Are they?" The other hand moved from her neck to her collarbone down to cup her breast. She pulled back out of the kiss to tell him . . .

His thumb stroked over the center of her breast.

To tell him . . .

He gently squeezed.

Her breath huffed out.

"I've thought about doing this since I saw you at Nero's wearing that lavender sweater that showed off your shoulder." He kissed her neck, his tongue trailing a path from her collarbone to her jaw to her earlobe.

She shivered.

"Oh, yeah, I've thought of doing this . . ." He kissed her mouth again, their bodies pressing against each other, then he whispered against her lips, "This and a hell of a lot more."

Chapter 12

Elianya looked out at the falling snow.

Damn it.

All her hard work had screeched to a halt.

There was still the shipment moving from the Caribbean, and tomorrow she'd be on a plane to Paris, then on to Miami. Hot sultry weather in November . . . Ah.

And once she was in the States, she'd simply contact the person who owed her. Then she'd learn Dimitri's real name. As of yet, there was no trace of him. But he wouldn't leave a trace, would he?

If she learned his real name, she'd know how to get to him.

If there was anyone she could use against him, she would. Nothing like loved ones to draw an enemy out.

Elianya smiled. He was one man she hated, almost as much as Jacob several years earlier. And she'd taken care of that man and his little family. Though she suspected his name had been something else, she'd never learned what it was.

She hadn't asked and hadn't cared. All she cared about was that the man she'd hired had done his job. He had followed one Jacob Angelovsky and then had gotten rid of him. Explosions were wonderful things. Not her personal favorite, but they always made such a statement. Personally, she'd have rather Jacob suffered a bit more, but done was done. As soon as the man had called her, she'd called her second contracted killer to take out the first. Neither man had a clue who she was, or who their mark was. They knew facts. They were hired to do a job and they completed it successfully.

A little bomb on the ignition and boom! Problem solved.

The man had had a family! A family, she had learned later! How could he do with her what he'd done and still have a family? He'd deserved to die. Of course, he'd deserved to die before that for rejecting her. To learn he'd had a family only served to put the icing on the cake.

No man made her the *other* woman. She was any man's *only* woman.

Now Dimitri—or whoever the hell he was. She had men looking for him.

So who was working with him? Who had the other man been that the Russian guard had spoken of? *Your brother's man and someone else* . . .

Who had the someone else been?

She ran a hand over her coiffed hair and checked the clock. It was almost time for her massage and last spa treatment. Who knew when she'd get back to Europe. New York had some good spas, but not like those here.

She was a European snob and she knew it. The Americans were capitalists and she would use that. Other than their use to her she had no need of them.

But she knew she could make a beautiful profit in the U.S. with her girls and she damn well would. Before long, she'd be someone the other bosses came to.

As she pulled on the thick white robe and grabbed her room key, she decided she needed to hire at least two more bodyguards. Her driver was loyal, but after her brother . . .

At least everyone would know she meant business.

Business was always important. A sharp head in business led to power. And power . . .

Well, there was nothing like power, was there?

She checked the mirror on her way out and decided she'd hire three bodyguards. Two men and a woman.

She liked diversity, after all.

• • •

November 13, 11:00 a.m.

Ian put the car in drive, ignoring the way Roth glared at him. He merged with the rest of the traffic from Dulles.

John, Tanner, and Snake were following in another vehicle. He could only shake his head at the black SUV following them. Leave it to one of the guys to rent the vehicles, and it looked like a damn fed convention coming to town.

"I wasn't in charge of the rentals," Roth said, straightening in his passenger seat. Roth, tall, short dark hair, a beard and built like a linebacker, was already helping in the area of protective services that KB Securities provided.

Ian shrugged. "It's fine."

"Jones probably would have arranged it anyway."

"True, along with several other details."

Roth only grunted. Roth was also a retired Ranger who went to work with the same agency that had recruited Ian. He was originally from the Midwest somewhere, not that Ian cared. Roth was good at what he did and that was all that mattered. People paid for protection, and for the price they paid, they got it.

"Exactly where are we going?" Rori asked from the backseat. From the set of her pale green eyes and the furrow between those perfectly arched brows, he could tell she was still pissed.

Not that she had to come along, but he was glad she had. All for the girl.

His gaze shifted to the little girl in the rearview mirror. Dressed in a blue sweater and jeans, little half boots on her feet, the black bear clutched in her lap, she appeared the normal little girl.

Except for those eyes.

He took another deep breath and paid attention to the road and the other drivers around him.

"I should be driving," Roth said. Again.

Ian only glanced at him, pulling his pack of cigarettes out of his pocket and shaking out one. He needed one. Long damn flight, and here he was in D.C.

"You pulled me off the detail in Boston for this. And what am I doing? Riding. The guard drives. The targets never—"

"I don't need a rundown on bodyguard and target marking procedures." He pressed the car lighter to the end of the cigarette and took a deep drag, shoving the lighter back into the slot and cracking the window.

"That will kill you," Roth muttered.

Ian ignored him.

"Well, I agree with him," Rori said from the backseat.

"I didn't ask you."

"No bloody kidding." Her eyes shot ice at him. "One more week. You should be able to find out in that amount of time if anyone is looking for her, if your family is safe and if you have to help with anything else. After that, Mr. I-don't-jolly-ask, you're on your own."

He wanted to smile at her. He didn't. He took another deep drag.

His eyes stayed on hers for another moment, and in that second he could all but taste what it felt like to kiss the woman senseless.

A week.

He sighed. He didn't know what the hell to do on that front. She was agreeing to pose as his wife.

Though he only planned to be here a couple of days and then they were getting out of this area. He didn't want anyone to link him to his family. But he hadn't lied to Rori before. There was simply no way he could not check on them, and if—God forbid—he ran into them, they had their story straight. Of course, if that happened, then he'd have to explain later how they divorced. Lie here, lie there. Lies were a pain in the ass.

He was out of this damn job as soon as this was finished. He finished off the cigarette and tossed the butt into the ashtray.

No fucking more.

He hated the fact he had to be here so close to his family to begin with, but he had to check on them himself. Pete had told him they were fine, but they weren't Pete's family.

If anything, he needed to warn them. He'd already hired his own men to oversee their protection, and to explain that he'd have to at least meet with Aiden. Some things he could probably get away with, but hiring several bodyguards for his family was not going to be one of the times he could merely shadow their lives unseen.

The plan was to arrive at the hotel, check it out, meet with Aiden and discreetly make certain the rest of the family was all right. Two days tops. With Aiden's help, they could create a story, or more accurately, he could create a story Aiden would likely go along with.

Maybe there had been a threat against the hotel . . .

Or maybe there was a threat against Jock and Mom. That would work. And so that they wouldn't worry, everyone else would go along with it. With the wealth that the Kinncaids had, they could be targets for any idiot wanting a buck. He'd probably go with that angle.

For any that needed to know, Rori was his wife and Darya was their daughter. More than likely he wouldn't even see anyone other than Aiden.

"You think they'll actually go for it?" Roth asked.

"For?"

Roth shook his head. "You haven't changed since the last time I worked a detail directly for you."

Ian didn't answer him.

"And here I thought I was the only one who was the recipient of his gracious communication skills," Rori said from the backseat. "He gives just enough information to get you to go along with crap, then has the annoying habit of telling you to be ready to go within the hour."

Ian shook his head, taking the exit he needed. "You were ready in ten minutes. You're just pissed because you didn't get to sleep late."

He noticed how late she slept every day. How the hell she did it, he had no idea.

"Two words, boyo."

He grinned. There were three cars following them down the ramp; one had started to follow them two miles from the airport. The blue Taurus.

"Roth, have someone tailing us?" he asked.

Roth didn't even move. "The blue car?" A smile lifted one edge of his mouth. "Probably. Been with us for ten minutes. Can't be sure, think it's G-tags."

Ian kept driving, weaving in and out of traffic, the black SUV behind keeping with them.

The blue car finally turned off two blocks from the hotel. He took a deep breath. Two days. He could handle two days.

He never knew if he liked being here or not. Normally, it was fine. But now he had that humming itch under his skin.

"Ready to get to a room?" he asked Darya in Russian.

As usual she didn't speak. She only looked at him, but the corners of her eyes softened.

Slow progress. He wanted to know more about her. What the hell did he actually do with the girl if there was no one for her?

One of his brothers? They were all married and had families. Aiden or Brayden would probably take her in. Then again, with Ryan's history of abuse, Gavin and Taylor might understand how to better handle her.

Rori leaned up in the backseat. "You and I are going to have one long chat when I get you alone."

Roth grinned.

"You promise?" Ian asked her.

She glared at him. "Why the hotel?" she asked him.

He sighed and pulled into the line that was driving up under the portico of the hotel. "Because I can check on what I need to without being readily seen. And I like my family's hotels."

"Why aren't you seeing your family? Why in the hell did I have to learn all their names and occupations if we're not going to see them?"

Another point of her aggravation, it seemed. "To avoid complications, which you know."

One perfect brow arched at him. The car slowly moved up. He turned in the seat to look at her.

"I don't want to draw attention to my family."

"In regards to you, yes. I remember saying the same damn thing." Her eyes narrowed. "Then why the bloody hell did you come here? And as Ian Kinncaid?"

He stared at her for a moment. Saw the confusion on her face. "As far as Ian Kinncaid? I used it because as far as anyone running a check is concerned, Mr. Ian Kinncaid is a businessman who has played the markets and recently opened a growing security firm. He resides in Scotland and is a rather quiet soul. I know all my other covers were blown. But only one man, well, a few more I trust, know that I am . . . well . . . me. Ian Kinncaid. Technically, for you and Darya, it's the safest identity I can use. Because that is the one name they may actually not have." He checked the mirrors. "As for the other part of your question, as to why I had to come, do you have any family?"

Something shifted in her eyes. "Why?"

So distrustful. A feeling he was rather familiar with. "You'd understand if you did."

She shrugged. "I suppose there is someone I'd risk it all to see safe."

Really? He'd love to know who that was. Instead he grinned and said, "Why, thank you, wife. Nice to know you love me that much."

Her look could have frozen hell.

"Won't someone recognize you?" she asked, her voice irritable as they waited on the line of cars.

"Maybe."

"Well, you're traveling as Ian Kinncaid, don't you think someone will alert someone in your family that you're here? None of this makes any sense."

"Probably, then again, the staff is known for its discretion."

"Of course they are." She shifted, her clothing hushing over the leather seats. "Until someone offers them enough money."

He ignored her. She was right . . . probably. Except for those that had been there so long they knew what to do and what not to do. Loyalty was of top priority. This allowed him to be close enough to check on his family without lots of undo travel between places that wasted time. He'd stayed here before, and it was time he came out as himself.

"What I don't understand," she said from the backseat, "is why you'd use your own name."

He drove up behind another car, only one more left before they could get out. He scanned the crowd, the cars, the motorcycle over to the right.

"Rori, I've been over this. Seeing as how I didn't know which aliases were blown, I figured why the hell not," he lied.

"Of course," she said.

Truth was, he wanted to use his real name. For Ian Kinncaid the businessman to be seen as Ian Kinncaid, the businessman with a group of his own security men, would only validate who he claimed to be. Of course, there was the issue of why they were with him. Which he would explain if the need arose.

"What if your family is here?" Roth asked.

Hell. "Then I'll deal with it. They probably won't recognize me anyway. It's been years since I've been home."

"Looking like that? And as Ian Kinncaid? Yeah," Roth said. "They'd never know who Douglas McGregor was or Marque. But well, you look . . . like you."

He only shot Roth a look and pulled the black car up to the curb, noting the young faces of the valets. Two, blond-headed.

"I want the names of all the valets and garage attendants," he said, getting out.

The blue-coated valet ran around the edge of the hood. "Welcome to the Highland Hotel."

Ian ignored him and waited for Rori and Darya as Roth scanned the traffic and waited for them.

To the valet he said, "Don't move the vehicle until I let you know."

"But it's against . . ."

Ian only looked at him.

His Adam's apple bobbed. Kid could only be maybe twenty. "Y-ye-yes, sir."

Ian picked Darya up, smelling her fruity shampoo when her hair tickled his jaw as she laid her head on his shoulder. He scanned the crowd, and held his hand out to Rori.

• • •

Jock Kinncaid looked across the conference table to his sons. Aiden and Quinlan were silent, but then they always were.

Gavin paced. Brayden lounged back in his chair tapping on one of those hand gadget things everyone seemed to have these days.

A phone rang and Quinlan pulled it from his breast pocket.

"Dad, we've acquired the castle, there's nothing left to say about it," Aiden said calmly.

"We don't need another location in Europe."

His oldest son didn't say a thing to him. Damn kids. He was retired, but that didn't mean he didn't have a blasted opinion on things.

The women were all in one of the ballrooms at Taylor's baby shower. She was due any day. Gavin was worse than Aiden had been when Jesslyn was pregnant. One would think their wives were the first women ever pregnant.

The men read books, for the love of God, on how to raise kids, and how to deal with babies. Had there been any books when he and Kaitie were having their sons? Hell, no. And they'd turned out all right.

Quinlan told whoever was on the phone to hang on and reached for the landline phone there in the conference room. Well, there was still time for that one.

At least the others were all settled with their own families.

He looked away toward the windows that bordered the street and watched the cars pulling into the hotel. Not even eleven in the morning and already they were seeing traffic. Some probably for the luncheon crowd, others as early arrivals, others meetings. Who the hell knew, it was all profit.

He took a deep breath and looked back at his oldest son. "Why did we purchase it?" He leaned up onto the table. "Just because I'm not in the office doesn't mean I don't want to know what the hell is going on with the company, damn it."

He might be getting older, but he wasn't in the grave yet.

Aiden closed his eyes.

Gavin turned. "Dad, would you relax. They'll make a profit. They always do. Even I, who has nothing to do with Kinncaid Enterprises, knows that. That's why I trust them. And so do you. You're so worried about the latest purchase, go see the thing. Take Mom on vacation. Just quit griping about it."

He sat back. "Excuse me?"

"You'll get yourself worked up, then Mom will have our asses." Gavin frowned.

Brayden said, "Gav, sit down and quit your pacing. You're making me twitchy."

"Sounds like a medical problem to me," Gavin answered.

"Dad, Gavin's right," Aiden interjected. "It's fine. The castle needs very little work, a facelift on the interiors, and we've already contacted the contractors for that. We'll be open in two months and we're already booked three weeks past opening."

Jock sat back. No one had told him that. He humphed. "I should have been told."

Aiden gave him a dubious look. "I thought you retired."

"I did, doesn't mean I don't want to know what the hell you boys are doing."

"Afraid we're going to—" Aiden frowned, looking out the window.

Jock turned, saw three black SUVs pull up. "Huh. We have any dignitaries staying with us?"

Gavin turned. "Probably a politician and some friends coming for lunch."

"Anything on the books?" Quinlan asked, already dialing his damn phone.

Brayden shook his head and rose. "It's a wonder you don't all have high blood pressure. Who the hell cares who it is. Can we order now? The shower will be over and then the women will want to *oooo* and *ahhh* over every little thing. Discuss birthing horrors and what all."

Aiden laughed, his attention turned. "Like that would matter to you. Christian pregnant yet?"

Jock watched Brayden out of the corner of his eyes. The door slammed open and Ryan, ten, and Tori, nine, came hurtling into the room.

"I still don't understand why we had to leave," Tori was saying, her voice reminding Jock of his wife's. That little girl was going to slay some men when she was older. And if she didn't, he had the impression that Ryan sure as hell would for her if any of them didn't treat her right.

"I said I'd explain later," Ryan said, a serious expression on his face. The door shut behind them and they hurried over to the built-in television, turning it on, the two of their heads together as they usually were.

Aiden was still grinning, "I can't help but notice you didn't answer, Brayden."

No comment from Brayden, who only glanced at Tori.

"Bray?" Gavin asked

"Our table's ready," Quinlan said, hanging up the phone.

"You need a woman, son," he said to Quinlan, still watching Brayden, who hadn't answered.

"Don't have time for one," Quinlan said.

Boy would never learn.

"Bray?" Gavin said.

Brayden sighed. "She wanted to wait until after the shower to say anything. We didn't want to take away from your and Taylor's day. And it's still early yet—"

Jock leaned back in his chair laughing.

"Daddy," Tori said, turning. "You weren't supposed to say anything. You promised Mom."

Ryan shook his head. "You think he could keep quiet about something like a baby? My dad couldn't."

"True," she answered, turning back to the television.

"You kids hungry?" Jock asked. Damn right. What man wouldn't want to shout to the world when learning he was a father?

He frowned as a memory, long buried, flinted through his mind.

Well, most of his family was happy. If he just had the chance to . . .

No point in that. He was happy with how God had blessed him. Four grandkids and two more on the way.

He smiled. He and Kaitie had succeeded with their kids.

All but one.

He rubbed a hand over his heart, feeling the tightening.

"Dad?" Aiden asked, concern etched in his face.

He shook him off and stood. "Let's go to Heather's. Quin just said they had our table ready. I hope Andre isn't cooking today, I really don't care for some of his dishes."

"Yeah!" Tori jumped up. "I want a burger with—" She stopped, watching Ryan.

Ryan watched someone outside. "He's here." He turned and hurried from the room, all but running out the door.

Tori hurried after him.

"Now where are they off to?" Gavin said, following. "I swear keeping up with those two is like keeping up with pet monkeys."

They all walked out of the conference room and he saw Tori catch up with Ryan at the end of the hallway.

It never failed. Every time he saw those two together, something around his heart squeezed. They all walked into the lobby and saw Ryan standing by a large potted palm near one of the seating areas. Tori was shaking her head and pulling on his arm.

Ryan jerked away and Tori turned to look at them, her face pale and worried.

Brayden hurried over and asked, "Honey, what is it?"

She only shook her head.

Ryan was looking toward a group of men at the front desk.

Jock scanned the crowd. Maybe he'd get the soup and salad. Kaitie would be proud of him and his aging body just didn't do food as well as it used to. He'd love a filet mignon and some potatoes, but he could just hear everyone if he ordered that.

"Ryan?" Gavin asked.

"It's him, isn't it?" Tori asked.

What were they talking about?

"I'll be damned," Aiden muttered.

Jock looked up. Ryan was pointing. "Dad," Ryan said to Gavin, "that's the man we told you about. The man who got us away from Nina."

That caught Jock's attention.

"Where?" Jock asked, scanning the crowd, interested in seeing the man who saved his grandkids.

"There, Pops."

All he saw was the back of a man holding a little girl, standing next to an exotically beautiful woman with light green eyes and a Mediterranean complexion.

"Are you certain?" Gavin asked.

Ryan nodded. "Yep, that's him. That's Rob Roy."

The man turned and Jock looked, studied him. Something . . . He turned more so that his profile showed.

Jock's pulse slowed, then sped.

Could it be? No. No, it wasn't. Or was it?

But then those eyes slammed into him like fists to his gut and he knew. Jock stumbled back.

Chapter 13

Ian turned from the front desk, wishing the older man behind the desk hadn't recognized him, but that's what life was about, he supposed. Of all the employees, he had to get the one that still worked here from when he'd been a kid. Fate loved to fuck with her minions. And he had used his name and come to the family hotel. He could have very well stayed at the Four Seasons down the road, but didn't. He always stayed in Kinncaid hotels if he could.

It had been so long since it mattered whether or not anyone recognized him, he wasn't certain what to do about it.

Ian Kinncaid. What kind of man was he that his own name took him a moment to recognize himself?

They had two adjoining suites. When the concierge had recognized him, old Thomas had tried to give Ian his penthouse apartment, but Ian declined. It was one thing to be recognized. One thing to stay in the family hotel. Another to walk in and assume you were home.

He had no home.

Not anymore. He'd done too many things, been gone too long to ever feel at home anywhere this normal. Place smelled like it always did. Not like many hotels he'd been in — that fake floral scent hiding the smell of bleach and disinfectant.

No, the Highland had always smelled like the outdoors to him. Somehow.

"Here's your rooms, Mr. Kinncaid. Though I still believe you'd much prefer the penthouse," Thomas said, sliding over the plastic cards.

"Thank you, Thomas, and one more thing. This is a quiet trip. I expect the same amount of discretion as any other guest."

The old man's gray brows beetled on a frown. "But you're not just any other guest, Mr. Kinncaid. You're a . . . well. You're a Kinncaid."

"Does the word 'mistake' float through that brain of yours now, boyo?" Rori asked to the side of him. He ignored her.

A tug on his leg had him glancing down. Ryan Kinncaid stood there in khaki pants, navy pullover, with a tentative smile. "Hi, Mr. Roy."

Bloody hell.

Mistake.

Ian ignored Rori's cough and mutter. He couldn't help it—he grinned into the kid's freckled face and summer blue eyes. "Hello, Ryan."

Ryan frowned. "I heard Mr. Thomas. You're a Kinncaid. I thought you were Mr. Roy."

Wonderful, just bloody marvelous. He glanced over his shoulder and saw his brothers and damn it all . . . Jock. He took a deep breath. Those dark eyes more lined, the face more haggard than he remembered, but still hard and fierce.

"I'm any number of things and people, kid."

Yes, this had been a mistake. But mistake or no, he could see they were all well and fine. He could let them know to be careful if nothing else. He glanced back at Ryan standing to his side. He hefted Darya up and turned, passing one of the keys to John and another to Rori.

"You have a penthouse apartment here?" she said with a raise of brow. "Wonders never cease. Mr. Rich boy turned—"

He merely held her stare, his own anger at the fact this was not going as planned—hell, the plan was shot out of the water—until she shook her head.

Her eyes moved slowly from him to his side. "Hello. Ryan, isn't it?" She looked back at him. "Looks as if your idea of just a few days and no contact isn't going to hold."

He stared past her to the men standing by the palm plants. Aiden was grinning, Gavin was shaking his head, as was Brayden, and Quinlan was walking back toward the ballroom.

Hell.

Roth slapped him on his shoulder.

Ian sighed, and said to John, "Johnno, check the security. I want to know every guard on duty, and a list of the employees."

John held up the keys. "We're still going to need these?"

Hell if he knew.

Aiden shook his head again and started forward. Two feet away he grinned, then stepped forward and wrapped Ian and Darya in a hug.

"'Bout time you came home, bro," Aiden said.

Ian felt Darya stiffen and burrow into him.

"Lyubimaya, ne volnooysya."

She only shook her head. He would make it all right.

Brayden was next to hug him and then Gavin. Jock stayed glued to the floor by the palm. No surprise there.

Old resentment started to worm its way through him.

Screw it. He had more important things to worry about. Jock Kinncaid was the most stubborn man Ian had ever met, and some things would simply never change.

"Who's this?" Aiden asked, looking at Rori and at Darya. Then his gaze landed on the other men.

Ian sighed. "Could we do this elsewhere? This is rather . . . open."

His eyes scanned the crowd again, noting two men in suits stood near the elevators. His gaze shifted to the front door. Two more men stood there looking at him.

Damn.

"Two at the doors," Rori said.

Roth slid up to one side of him. John stepped up closer to their back. He felt Rori start to bend down. She'd strapped an ankle holster and her clutch piece on in the car. Thanks to Roth.

"No," he said, grabbing her hand.

Without looking at Aiden he said, "We need a close secure location. Conference room still on the ground floor?"

"Uh, yeah."

"Johnno, call Pete."

They all stood there talking quietly, as if meeting up. Ryan and Tori were shoving back and forth, Gavin and Brayden watching them.

Ian tightened his hold on Darya. He glanced at the hallway back toward the ballroom, where Quinlan had disappeared to. Idiot probably went for Mom. That was all he needed, another person to cover.

John handed him the phone.

Pete Jones answered as he always did with a simple, "What?"

"What? Pete, tell me you put men on me."

A moment of silence passed before Pete's voice, as solemn as the man himself, said, "That would depend on your location."

"I don't care to give you that information."

Pete sighed. "We're working on the damn leak and this phone is secure. Are you stateside yet?"

"Affirmative."

The two near the front door shifted, one put his hand in his jacket.

Ian heard the faint swish of Roth pulling his gun.

"I've ordered men to watch the hotel, figuring you'd show up sooner or later."

Well, hell. "Have I gotten that predictable?"

Pete snorted. "More a hopeful hunch."

"Descriptions, ranks and names."

"Don't shoot them, for the love of God. You have any idea how hard it is to find half-ass decent agents these days?"

"Pete."

"Four. Evans, five-eight, blond, blue."

Man number one by the elevator.

"Becker, five-nine, brown, brown."

Elevator man number two.

"Callum and Fisher. Both six even, Callum lanky, brown and hazel. Fisher, linebacker, bald."

Match. "Callum and Fisher by the door," he said to Roth. "Check their IDs." To John he said, "Becker and Evans at the elevators, Evans is the arctic one."

John relayed the message to Snake and Snake and Roth moved off toward their targets.

"Let me know who and where or you might find a couple of agents with bullets in their brains." He clicked the phone shut, knowing Pete would now know where to get in touch with him. Fine.

The phone rang.

"What?" Ian asked in tandem with Pete's own verbosity.

"You still need to learn some manners," Pete's nonfluctuating voice said.

"I learned from you." He watched Roth and Snake talking to the guys and checking their IDs.

"True. How long you in town?"

"Don't know." He scanned the crowd again and stepped forward, jerking his head to Aiden who raised his brows and walked back across the foyer into a door marked *Private* and down the hallway.

"We need to meet."

Yes, they did.

He turned and saw Rori was directly behind him. "I want a name, Pete."

"I know that. We're working on it."

"Work harder."

With that he flicked the phone shut and handed it off to John as they walked down the hallway.

The receptionist frowned at them as they all trouped in and Aiden said, "Sally, we're ordering room service in the conference room. The ladies will be joining us shortly."

She nodded and picked up the phone. "Anything in particular?"

He shook his head. "I don't care. We'll let you know in a minute."

"Yes, sir."

The conference room had a faux fireplace in it, a long conference table that sat sixteen, a sitting area in front of the fireplace, and a built-in entertainment/conferencing area in one wall.

The door clicked shut behind them.

• • •

She watched all the people around them. They'd ridden on another plane and then in the car to this big building.

The man carried her like he always did, his voice gruff, reminding her of pebbles falling on stones.

Where were they? Maybe he was taking her to see Zoy?

Before, in the area out front, he'd become tense, his shoulders and arms like bands of steel, his voice low and cold. It reminded her of the night he'd taken her from the monster's den.

Her tummy rumbled and he looked at her and grinned, those hard features softening. "Are you hungry, pumpkin?"

She nodded and laid her head back on his shoulder. He smelled nice and funny. It was that stick he smoked. Aunt Sonya's man had smoked those. She didn't like them. Wrinkling her nose, she smelled the better scent on his lapel and his coat was soft against her face. Who were all these people?

She knew and understood the lady was Rori, and there was the man John and Roth and Tanner and Snake. He didn't look like a snake, but he had a snake on his bald head. She frowned. The last two were the last behind them, all walking down the hallway.

There were other men. Five. No. One. Two. Three. Four. And a boy and another girl.

She looked around as he turned with her in his arms, one of the other men saying something that made him grunt.

She leaned back and watched.

Ian said something in English to another dark-haired man. She looked from him to the man who held her. They both had dark hair, and the same blue eyes, the same eyebrows, but Ian had a streak through his eyebrow where no hair grew. She reached up and touched it. His gaze met hers and his eyes squinted at the edges when he smiled at her.

She looked around.

All the men. Her tummy tightened.

Maybe, maybe he was taking her back to the lady.

She stiffened.

Please, please, don't let the mean lady get her again.

He studied her, frowning. "What's wrong?" he asked her in Russian.

She darted looks around, saw the old man scowling at her, and tucked her face into Ian's neck.

That man looked mad.

Again, Ian pulled back. "What's wrong?"

She looked over her shoulder at the men behind them as the others started talking into those things in their hands. Voices coming from the strange boxes.

But the new men—they were all big. Tall and serious. Though two looked alike. They were brothers, she realized. Brothers who looked alike.

Like her and Zoy.

Zoy—she tucked her head down again.

"No one here will harm you," he whispered to her. "You're safe, Darya." His big hand rubbed her back like he did when she woke up thinking the monsters were after her.

He said she was safe, but what if there were monsters here?

At least she had Ian, who was nice, and Rori, and Mr. Bear. Mr. Bear would keep her safe. She knew it.

The big man with white and gray hair started talking, loud—he sounded like he was barking.

She could understand some of what Rori, Ian, and John said. She understood some English. But this man was angry. She could hear it in his tone, even if she didn't understand the words.

Ian's voice said something and the old man quieted.

He set her on the couch, but she didn't want to let him go. Her head hurt.

"You're safe here," he repeated in English and Russian.

She wanted to talk to him. To ask him where her sister was. But she wasn't ready yet to talk. She had to be quiet, quiet or the monsters would get her.

Rori watched as Ian tried to pull the small arms from his neck, but Darya was having none of that. He sat beside the little girl and Rori perched on the arm of the couch, running her hand along the cushions to rest it on his shoulder. Felt like a bleeding brick under her hand. She rubbed it, felt it stiffen even more, and watched as he glanced at her out of the corner of his eye.

For now, she'd play the wife bit.

Ryan—cute freckled kid—hurried over and sat on Ian's other side.

No one spoke.

Rori saw the old man's gaze harden as he looked at his son. What the hell was the man's problem?

Tall, still well built, his hair was gray and white, his face a bit tan and ruddy all at once. He had the same hardened angles that Ian possessed. The same dark eyes. That same unforgiving look about him.

Bet he was just jolly fun. And their scowls were identical she decided, looking from one to the other. Well, not identical. Ian was a frozen mask. No real anger behind it. One wouldn't know what the hell he was about. Or planning.

But the old man. Now, he simply looked angry.

Mr. Aiden—she was certain it was Aiden—was still grinning, and the twins were quiet.

The door opened and both Snake and Roth reached out to snatch it.

The other one—the youngest, Quinlan—walked in, raising a

brow at the two men beside the door as he gave them a once-over and said at the same time to the room at large, "Mom will be here in less than five minutes." Quinlan unclipped his cell phone and punched a button. "The shower was over."

"Shower?" Ian asked.

"You know, baby shower, gifts for the soon-to-be-parents," one of the twins—Brayden?—said. Then he smiled, walked to the couch, leaned down and gave Ian a hug. "Thanks. I never got a chance to thank you before."

She watched Ian stand and slap his brother's back. "Well, looks like Chris pulled through fine. Her family still doing well in New Orleans?"

Brayden's jaw worked a minute. "Yeah, they're doing fine. Her brother was up last week, in fact. She wants to go down there for the holidays."

Ian nodded, then shifted his gaze to the other twin. "Guess Taylor's about to pop. Would have figured you'd have started on the second one by now."

Gavin just shook his head and grinned.

The little boy jerked on Ian's sleeve again. "Mr. Roy—er . . . Mr. Kinncaid?"

Ian squatted down and ruffled Ryan's dark auburn hair. "Yes, Ryan?"

"What do I call you?" the boy asked, frowning.

Gavin, dressed in dark slacks and a pullover, placed his hands on his son's shoulders and said, "Why not Uncle Ian."

The boy's face split into a grin so wide his freckles looked like they'd leap off his face. "Cool. Uncle Ian." Then the face sobered. Those summer eyes looked for a long silent moment at Ian. He leaned forward and whispered something in Ian's ear, the gangly arms coming up around his uncle's neck.

This man and kids. He killed people as regularly as she did, yet the children flocked to him. But then she'd seen the fury he could unleash when a child was harmed. Maybe it was some instinct that they knew he'd keep them safe. Their own guardian angel.

The little boy pulled back, still grinning, yet it didn't reach his eyes. A muscle bunched in Ian's jaw, up near his ear.

"You're safe and happy now." Ian cleared his throat and looked up at his brother. "That's all that matters."

The gaggle of female chatter and giggles floated through the door seconds before it was opened. Again the guards stiffened.

Rori grinned. Yes, these women looked very dangerous. Then she looked closer and remembered what Ian had told her of them. These were no weak females. They fought when the need arose.

What a strange and motley crew, she thought. The gruff old man. His smiling, dimpled wife walked through the door, took one look around the room, and stumbled to a halt.

"Oh, my God!" she said, turning sheet-white.

Roth caught her before she hit the floor.

Chapter 14

Ian was at Roth's side before anyone moved. Jock, raking a hand through his white hair, said, "What? What the hell's wrong with her?"

They laid the woman, dressed in a copper-toned pantsuit, on the floor, her red hair curled and soft on the rug.

The men stood over her. Ian, Jock, Snake, and Gavin.

Gavin shoved Snake out of the way and said, "I'm a doctor."

Very calmly, Snake replied, "Medic."

"Really?" Gavin asked, taking his mother's wrist as Snake opened her eyes and checked their dilation. "For some reason that occupation never crossed my mind."

Rori hid a grin. She couldn't fault Gavin for his question to Snake, who looked liked a bouncer or gangbanger. Baldheaded and lanky, and a black and green snake slithered over the top of his head. Normally, he had the tattoo covered with a cap, hat, or do-rag. But not today.

Today he looked like a kick-ass bodyguard.

"Yeah, I get that a lot," Snake said.

"A trained medic?" Gavin asked, smiling.

"By the best in the Commonwealth of Virginia."

"Who cares," the big man boomed, all but looming over the prone woman. "Kaitie lass! Wake up, damn it. You're scaring the boys."

Like he wasn't just as worried.

"She only fainted, Mr. Kinncaid," Snake said. "We could put her on the couch."

"I'll get her." Ian moved in and easily scooped the woman up, as if she weighed nothing.

Rori quickly moved and reached over, picking up Darya.

When Ian laid her down, she saw his face pulled tight. First time home, his father doesn't speak to him, and his mother fainted.

She looked at John and raised a brow even as Gavin shouted for Mrs. Kinncaid to wake up.

John shook his head, slapped Ian on the shoulder and said, "Well, at least your brothers are happy to see you. Not all a complete waste."

"I'm happy to see him," Ryan said. "He saved Tori's life and mine."

John's lips twitched. "Right ya are, boyo."

Tori tilted her head and looked at John. "I remember you from Colorado. Aunt Jesslyn called you Mr. John Nolastname."

John bowed and offered his hands to the kids. "Glad someone is happy to see me, sweets. How about we wait over here out of the way." Tori took his hand and he led them over to the head of the conference table. She watched. Mr. Kinncaid knelt on the floor by his wife. Each son seemed to be joined by his wife, with the exception of the doctor and his obviously pregnant wife, who leaned back against a wall rubbing her enormous stomach. She smiled, showing dimples, her red hair pulled into a braid. Her eyes met Rori's. "Hi, I'm Taylor. Figured I'd be the one passing out. Woman's been stuffing water down me all day. All week, truth be known."

Rori took Darya's hand and led her over to the woman. "I'm Rori. This is Darya." She pointed to the woman's belly. "When's the big day?"

"In two weeks, which means anytime in the next month." Taylor Kinncaid had a slight Texas twang and was lovely.

Another one of the women joined them, blonde hair straight to her shoulders, sharp brown eyes, wearing a pantsuit. She was a bleeding little thing. Woman's head only came to Rori's chest, maybe her shoulder.

"I'm Jesslyn, Aiden's wife," she said, offering a hand. "Hi." Jesslyn's twang was so wide it made Taylor's seem almost nonexistent.

"Rori. And this is Darya."

The woman smiled. "A Brit. How refreshing. Are you John's wife?" She leaned in. "What's the man's last name? Annoys the hell out me."

Rori chuckled. "I'm not at liberty to say."

Jesslyn rolled her eyes. "I just knew you were going to say that."

A motion behind them made her turn. Kaitlyn Kinncaid, still a bit pale, sat up on the couch, muttering to her husband that she was fine, her hand to her forehead.

"You should go to the hospital. Might be your blood sugar," Mr. Kinncaid was saying. "Or maybe your blood pressure. You never know, Kaitie. Or it might—"

"For the love of God, Jock. Stop." She patted his hand. "I'm fine. Just fainted." Then she smiled and turned her head. For a long moment, she simply stared at Ian, who was kneeling in front of her. Her head slowly shook and she released her husband's hand to reach up and cup Ian's face.

His expression barely changed, but Rori saw the flicker of regret flash through his eyes—regret or something like it—but then he froze his expression. The man could mask easier than anyone else she knew.

"Hi, Mom."

Kaitlyn Kinncaid's shoulders jerked and then she pulled him to her, rocking. "Where have you been?" she strangled out, tears tracking down her face. "Where have you been?" Then she shook her head. "I don't care. You're home. You're home now. I've prayed for this for years. For so long and finally, finally I have my whole family back." She looked over at Jock, whose brows were beetled into an inverted V.

Man was just bark, no bite, Rori decided.

"Look, Jock. Look, he's home. He's finally home."

Jock only nodded and stood, sitting on the arm of the couch by his son. The feeling of seeing something she wasn't supposed to crawled over her.

Home. She shook her head. She personally had no idea what the hell that was other than her London flat with the two betas, who were probably dead if Nikko hadn't fed them.

Maybe she'd get a cat, and move to Ireland. Grow flowers or some such blarney.

John cleared his throat.

Ian heard John and looked up from his mother. "What?"

"Your Yanks say the place is clean, Tanner says the attendants haven't seen anything off, but he's checking the security tapes."

"What the hell is going on?" Jock asked, his voice reflecting the bafflement on his face as he noticed the number of people in the room.

Ian ignored him and kissed his mother on the check before standing and telling John, "Have them check the ballrooms, basement, and the family apartments upstairs. I want a list of all the staff members that have access to the family penthouses."

John merely raised a brow and stepped outside, leaving Tori and Ryan standing near the doorway.

Everyone was silent.

Aiden asked, "Who wants lunch?"

No one answered. Aiden took another tactic, his face losing its humor. "All right. Must be big. Why all the checks, what's with the entourage? And what happened to bring you back home as Ian Kinncaid and not as . . ." He stopped and cleared his throat.

Their mother pierced Aiden with a look Ian remembered all too well, yet there was hurt and the pain of betrayal in those beautiful green eyes. She shoved her red hair back. "You knew where he was?"

Aiden's expression slightly shifted. "Uhm—well . . ." Jesslyn coughed.

Mom was no longer pale, that faint telltale blush warned. "How dare you!"

"Mom," Ian tried.

"How could you . . ." Her eyes filled with tears again as she looked at Aiden. Then they shifted back to him. "Do you have any idea what it was like . . . what—what I thought? Worried? God, I was so worried. I—I pr-prayed for God to w-watch over you." Her tears trickled down those flawless cheeks, cutting straight to his heart. "Do you know . . ." She shook her head. Jock put his arm around her.

"Kaitie, calm down."

She shook her head. "I just . . ." Closing her eyes, she opened them again and stared at him.

Ian's heart hammered in his chest.

"Wow, darling," Rori said behind him. "And here you've always said how bloody wonderful your family was. Seems you left a couple of things out."

Damn. He'd forgotten about . . .

"Who are you?" Jock asked.

Kaitie elbowed Jock in the ribs. Wiping her eyes, she looked past him to Rori, and then to his side, where Darya had moved, silent as a shadow.

His mother narrowed her gaze at him. "Right now, I don't care. Not really. I'm just glad you're home. But later, my boy, we *will* discuss a few things." Her eyes flashed.

He couldn't help it, he grinned and nodded. "I love you, Mom."

She sniffed and looked back to Rori and Darya.

Everyone waited expectantly. Rori walked up to stand behind him. "Luv, they don't seem all that happy to see you."

Ian caught the sarcastic edge to her voice even as evenly as she'd spoken.

His mother frowned and stood, shaking his father off. "Of course we are. It's just a shock. I'd thought . . . I'd feared . . ." Her eyes drifted back to him and asked questions she wouldn't voice, and even if she did, he would lie.

He'd have to. As much as he didn't understand his father, he wasn't going to come between his parents.

"Mom," he said, taking Rori's hand, putting his hand on top of Darya's head. "This is Rori." He looked at her, and she cocked one perfect brow. She was without a doubt beautiful. He smiled and narrowed his gaze on her. "My wife."

Her eyes flashed even as she smiled at him. "Wondered if you even remembered what with all the hoobaloo going on."

Hoobaloo?

Ian glanced back at his parents.

His father's jaw dropped, his mother smiled, and he heard Jesslyn's, "Cool. A Brit in the fam."

"Jesslyn, shut up, honey, now's not the time," Aiden said.

"Well, I think it is. Entirely too serious when everyone should be celebrating." He looked at his short sister-in-law, who met his eyes straight on. "I know if I was ever given a second chance with the children that I'll never get back, I sure as hell wouldn't question the whys or how-comes. It's a time for celebration. More than one. Babies, pregnancies, and now marriages." Her head jerked to Darya. "And Darya . . ." She left the question open-ended.

Ian looked at Aiden. "Is she always like this?"

"Yes," his brother answered him, pulling his wife into his side and kissing the top of her head even as he put his hand over her mouth. She shrugged him off.

"I like her," Rori said, and then added, "little Darya is our daughter."

What the hell was the matter with him? He couldn't think. His chest felt tight as hell and he just wanted . . .

It was like an attack but not. He needed some air. He unbuttoned the top button of his shirt and took his coat off.

At his mother's gasp he realized his jacket had shifted and she saw the shoulder holster.

"Are you a cop?" Mom asked.

Snake coughed and Roth chuckled.

"Close enough."

"What the bloody hell does that mean?"

The phone rang and Aiden answered it. Then he held it out to him. "It's for you, some guy named Pete Jones."

Ian frowned. Grabbing the phone, he barked the one word they always greeted each other with. "What?"

"I've tried your phone and Brasher's and can't reach either of you. Have you seen the damn news? CIN. Christ."

Ian put the phone between his jaw and shoulder and looked over at the television on some documentary. "Where's the remote?"

Ryan said, "Here," and handed it to him.

"What's the channel?" he asked Pete.

"Fifty-four. Local. Are you alone?"

"Nope."

He grabbed the remote from his nephew and clicked on CIN.

". . . authorities are still investigating why a string of arsons are happening in Prague." Behind the news announcer flames and smoke shot up into the afternoon sky. "Luckily, no one was injured as the club was empty this time of day. This is the second club to be targeted since early this morning. Both clubs are reputed to have belonged to the late Viktor Hellinski, who was murdered here last week."

Ian leaned closer. Damn. Nero's.

Pete said, "And Hellinski's other club and . . ."

"Shh—" he told his boss.

"Investigators are also trying to learn if the fire in Prague's Lesser Quarter is related to this one. The apartment was empty as well. Reasons as to the motivations behind the fires are speculated to be related to the Czech underground."

Shit.

"Good thing we cleaned your flat out," Snake commented in a whisper, standing next to him.

Ian shot him a look.

"Pete, what else?" he asked.

Pete's sigh was warning enough. "Body of a young girl turned up in Monrovia. Tests are still being run, but looks like it might match the victim on the crime video you copied over." He stopped, took a deep breath and continued, "One of the safe houses in Paris, killed a guard and someone else we were watching. Another in Moscow. Technically belonging to one Yorin Balorsky."

Ian took a deep breath, his thoughts shifting. "What's the plan?"

"Dimitri Petrolov must be seen dead."

The camera scanned the area behind the news announcer to show the charred remains of the club. And there were two men he knew. Worked for one of the other bosses. Hoping for him, were they?

"And how do you plan to . . ." He remembered where he was and stopped. "We'll meet later today. Three here at the hotel."

"I'll get protection for your family."

Ian weighed his options. "I'll hire my own protection for my family. You've got a damn leak and I'm not about to gamble on their lives against an unknown traitor."

"How many do you have?" Pete asked.

He looked at Roth. "Get me Gar."

Roth raised a brow. "For what?"

Ian merely stared at him.

"Fine."

"Pete," Ian said back into the phone.

"Today at three. Goddamn mess you created."

"I created?"

"Wherever you go, people die, things blow up, I never the hell know. Just keep a fucking low profile. I don't need to be cleaning up crap this side of the Atlantic. We're scrambling here as it is."

"Who's behind the fires?"

Pete sighed again. Darya was clutching his leg and he looked down into those round blue eyes and ran his hand over her curls.

"Who knows. Hellinski's stuff is blowing up all over Eastern Europe. The odds are on the other families, who don't want his sister getting her hands on them. The other is that they are after you. I tend to think it's a bit of both. Why worry about two birds when you can take care of them together?"

"News just in . . ." the announcer was saying. "Another residence has been firebombed in the town of Kladno . . ." The picture clicked to another announcer.

"Damn." There sat the town house, windows blown out of it, fire licking up the side. Firemen were behind the gates.

"Bloody hell, they're hitting them all," Rori muttered.

Darya whimpered against him. He looked down and saw tears in her eyes. He looked back at the television. He shifted her, but she looked again and pointed to the TV, her mouth working but no sounds coming out.

"What? Sweetheart?" he asked.

Pete said, pulling his attention back to their conversation, "You see? You may be one of the best damn agents I have, but this . . . this . . ."

"This is the end, Pete. No more. I told you that. Today. Three." With that, he handed the phone back to Aiden, then picked Darya up and set her on the table.

John walked in and glanced at the television. His gaze shifted back to Ian. "Didn't take them long, did it?" He grabbed his phone and strode back out the door.

Darya stared at the television. Maybe she didn't recognize it.

But the pale face, the tears that tracked over her face . . .

She looked at him again, her brows furrowed, questions in her wet eyes.

"What?" he asked her in Russian. "What's the matter, pumpkin? You're safe." Gently he wiped the tears away.

She pointed back to the screen and whispered, "Zoy?"

He blinked. She talked.

"Zoy?" he asked.

Hurriedly she nodded and pointed back to the house. "Zoy."

"The sister," Rori muttered.

He closed his eyes and picked his daughter up. Looking at Aiden, he said, "We're going upstairs. Right now I have things to do."

"We've a few questions ourselves," Aiden said.

They all probably did, but they wouldn't be getting answers. He'd have to leave. Looking at his brothers, he said, "You told me if I ever needed anything . . ."

All three nodded. Aiden said, "Anything."

He kissed Darya's hair and looked at his brother without another word.

"Would someone please tell me what the hell is going on?" Jock barked.

Ian ignored him and finally said to Aiden, "I may need you to watch over my daughter."

Aiden's eyes shifted from him to the girl to Rori then back to him. "You're leaving?"

"Probably." He started to walk toward the door.

"Always things for you to do, to leave," Jock said.

Ian stopped, tightened his hold on his daughter, but didn't turn around. He took a deep breath. What did he care what the old man thought. Thoughts and emotions, what he needed to do, what he wanted to do, what he'd have to do all crashing together in his brain, disjointed and jagged.

"I see some things haven't changed. Is what you want always more important than your family?" Jock asked.

The tightness in his chest popped and Ian whirled, anger and rage at the man, at the things he couldn't control, at what he was, at the pain in Darya's eyes. "If I don't do this, I might not have a family." He pointed to the television screen. "You see that? Who do you think they're looking for?"

John walked in, took one look at the situation. "Well, since you're spouting off, I guess I might as well tell you that they hit the London safe house."

He closed his eyes, fury hot and heavy in his veins. "How many?"

"Luckily it was empty." John ran a hand through his hair. "They're only making a statement."

"What the hell do you do?" Jock asked. "They said the Czech underground. Are you some sort of criminal? I knew . . . I told you . . ." Jock trailed off, his eyes an angry blue.

"Never to come home?" Ian lashed out, no longer caring. "I didn't come home for you," he lied. "I needed to make certain Mom and my brothers were safe." He quickly scanned their faces. "You're all getting protection. Period. And if you fight me on this, I'll get it legally and have you moved to safe and secure locations. So no fucking remarks."

Rori stared at his father. "You really have no idea who your son is, do you?" She slipped her hand in his arm. As they walked out of the room she said, "They're like a dysfunctional Brody Bunch."

Even though he felt like hitting something, or shooting it, his lips twitched. "That's Brady Bunch, darling."

Jesslyn started laughing. "I do love it when Jock gets all irate over something and makes an ass out of himself."

Chapter 15

Ian sat with his back to the wall. Rori and John were upstairs watching Darya, the other kids, and his parents. The others were scattered around the hotel guarding whoever they were supposed to be.

Pete Jones, salt-and-pepper hair neatly combed in place, dressed in a suit, his two guards sitting to their right, stared at Ian.

The man had a long, apostolic face, clean-shaven and tired. Deep worry lines bracketed his mouth and etched his brows and eyes.

"You are in some very serious trouble," he said, tapping his fingers on the tabletop.

Ian scanned the crowd. "Pete, the point of the meeting."

Pete sat up. "You need to die."

Ian arched a brow. "Which 'you' would you be referring to?"

The left side of Pete's mouth lifted in what few would consider a smile. "Dimitri Petrolov. Who the hell else?"

Ian shrugged. "So take care of it."

"You need to be seen as close to the job as possible to increase the credibility."

Ian tilted his head, scanned the restaurant. Quinlan weaved through some of the customers, talking to one here, one there. Roth stood at the doorway shaking his head.

Why didn't his family take him seriously? They'd had a huge row upstairs. His mother's cold silence to his father could be felt across the room. He hadn't meant to snap out the truth of why he'd left, but damn it, the man could still push all his buttons. Hadn't he learned any control?

He rubbed his temple. What he wouldn't give for a beach, sand, a drink. Nothing but ocean breeze and the knowledge all was well and . . . Rori. Or maybe take her back to Scotland.

"Did you hear what I said?" Pete asked him.

Ian met his boss's hazel eyes. "I'm on the tired side. We caught the red-eye out of London last night, or would that be this morning." He sipped his coffee. "What?"

"Next week, or later this week, you fly to Amsterdam. It's being arranged."

"Sounds like fun."

"You'll go in, walk out the basement, the house will explode, and the body they find will match dentally with Dimitri Petrolov."

He smiled ruefully. "How convenient."

"Why'd you come back here?" Pete asked, leaning back as the waitress set a salad in front of each of them. "You easily could have sent someone."

"I could have, yes, but I wanted to assess the situation myself." Ian wasn't hungry. He rubbed his head.

"Headache?" Pete asked.

Undercover agents often went through debriefings, medical tests, and psychological tests to make certain they weren't too close to the edge.

Ian wasn't so certain he would pass as easily as he did the last time.

"Lack of sleep," he said.

Pete asked. "Why the woman?"

He looked at one of the only men who knew his true identity. Pete was the only person Ian ever contacted with information other than John.

"I needed the image of a family. A family doesn't leave a memory. A single father with a silent little girl is another matter."

Pete nodded. "True. Who is she?"

Ian debated and then figured that John had already told his boss, who had filled Pete in, or then maybe not. But Ian knew Pete already had a file sitting on his desk on one Rori Maitland—Kinncaid. She was Rori Kinncaid. Ian studied his boss. Who was the leak? Was it Pete? His kneejerk reaction was no. But what if he was wrong?

"Hired to kill me, I believe, but she said things were off, so she didn't. Saved my life, in fact. John said she used to work for MI6. Lenora."

Pete sniffed. "Lenora Maitland."

Tests. He hated fucking tests.

"Used to be MI6. Now supposedly she's a businesswoman. Mercenary is the word on the streets."

Assassin more like, but he wouldn't cut semantics when he was legit only because he worked for the U.S. government.

Leaning up, he said, "When do I leave? I want your word my family will be protected. I'll take John with me, but I'm leaving the rest of them, and I swear to you, Pete" — he looked straight into his boss's eyes — "you don't want anything happening to my family."

Pete only returned his stare. "After the way your family was in the news all last year? No, I don't want anything to happen to them. It's one thing to cover up an obscure, unknown death of a traveling businessman. It's another altogether when a well-known family is hit." He shook his head. "The media fallout alone would be the end of my career."

"You'd be worried about more than that," Ian muttered.

"Is that a threat?" Pete asked.

He sighed. "I want the leak, Pete. I want a name."

"I'm working on it." Pete tossed money on the table and said, "Get some rest. You need to come in for testing from the looks of things, and for the debriefing. We need some intel on the latest shipments."

"When this is over."

Pete raised a brow.

"The testing. When this is over." When this was over, he was done and wouldn't need testing, they both knew it.

"Eight a.m. I want a brief on my desk on shipments and any laundering, any fronting," Pete said.

Shipments of girls, drugs he knew about. And the whole reason for his cover to begin with. The fact that many Eastern European brothels and bosses were fronts to a deeper worry. Terrorists. Lots of field agents these days thanks to 9/11.

At least on the terrorism front, Hellinski had been clean — or mostly. He'd been low enough, yet involved enough on rare occasions that information flowed a bit more easily than it otherwise would have. Had Elianya been involved in something of that scale? Who the fuck knew.

He nodded.

When Pete started to stand, he said, "You get anything on Darya?"

Pete shook his head. "Not yet. But that doesn't mean anything. And you know that." Those shrewd hazel eyes bore into him. "What are you going to do with her if no one claims her?"

He returned the stare. "What do you think I'm going to do?"

Pete shook his head. "Just when I think most are too cynical, someone will do something that shocks me." The words were said so deadpan Ian knew sarcasm laced them.

Pete stood, then paused, straightening his jacket. "I'm keeping the detail on you and I want an itinerary."

"I'll think about it." Ian watched him walk away, weaving in and out of the people.

He heard a little girl laugh at a nearby table as she ate a chocolate confection piled high with whipped cream and strawberries.

Maybe Darya would like one of those. He motioned to the waitress to box one up for him.

• • •

Rori and John sat in the seating area of Mr. and Mrs. Kinncaid's penthouse apartment. The two older kids kept trying to draw Darya into their camaraderie. But she wasn't interested in the crayons or markers. She only looked at them when they got out a game. Finally, Ryan tilted his head and said, "You're very quiet."

"She doesn't speak English, Ryan," Rori told him.

Jock and Kaitlyn, who had been standing off by themselves, talking in hushed tones, turned at her words.

"What do you mean?" Jock asked, frowning.

The man always frowned. Personally, Rori thought he was an ass. He might have some good qualities, but she'd yet to see them.

"Exactly what I said, Mr. Kinncaid," she frosted her words. "Darya doesn't speak English, and in fact, this is the first we've heard her say anything at all."

"Ever?" Kaitlyn asked, coming over to sit with Rori at the table. "But she must be — what? — five?"

Rori shrugged. To hell with it. Ian left her up here alone with his family. She'd make up her own bloody story. "We honestly don't know."

Their eyes widened, before Kaitlyn frowned again.

"She's Ian's daughter, isn't she?" Kaitlyn asked.

"Maybe she's adopted," Ryan suggested.

Rori grinned at him. "Right on, boyo. We just adopted her last week." Rori motioned for Darya to come to her and the girl did. She still didn't know what to do with the girl, but she was becoming used to having her around. And knew, from experience, what it was to want a safe place.

Hell, had she ever truly known what a safe place was?

Darya climbed up into her lap and settled, still clutching the teddy bear.

"Where's she from?" Kaitlyn asked.

Jock reached out to touch the girl and Darya shied, burrowing into Rori.

She looked up at the man, not caring if he saw her dislike or not. "We're not certain of that either. Though Ian knows she speaks Russian."

John cleared his throat.

"What?" she asked him. "They asked, I answered. He doesn't want them to know, he should have said something before. I can't read the man's bloody mind."

John's lips twitched.

"How long have you two been married?" Mrs. Kinncaid asked.

Hell. How had she gotten to this point?

Was it all Darya? She brushed the girl's hair with her hand. No. She might tell him that. But it was also that smile she rarely saw, lightning quick, and made him more . . . real.

"Long enough to know he's difficult," she evaded.

John laughed. "That's our Ian."

Mrs. Kinncaid looked past her and Darya to John. "You've worked with my son a long time, haven't you?" She nodded. "Never mind. He'd never trust any of us with you if you weren't his friend. Thank you."

"My pleasure, Mrs. Kinncaid," John answered.

Ryan had come up. He put his hand out to Darya. "Would you like to watch TV with us?" He pointed to the television.

She buried her head against Rori, the soft fruity scent of her tickling Rori's nose.

Rori hugged her and smiled at Ryan. "Maybe later."

The door opened and Ian strode in, looking a bit tired. In his hands was a clear container, chocolate, whipped cream, and strawberries.

Darya lifted her head from Rori's shoulder and watched Ian walk to them, the smile on his face one of the real ones he seemed to reserve for Darya alone. The girl scrambled off her lap and hurried over to Ian, who scooped her up, his Russian throaty and deep as he spoke to her.

Darya smiled and nodded.

That smile swirled through the center of Rori. The child was beautiful when she smiled like that, her eyes sparkling with anticipation. And Ian . . .

His smile alone did more than swirl through the center of her.

He really could be her father. Same coloring and killer smiles. He set her down at the table and put the sugar mountain in front of her.

"Do you think she needs all of that?" Rori asked.

His eyes flashed his surprise and a remnant of his smile teased her. "Worried about her health, dear?"

She blinked. Damn man. What did she care? She shrugged. "I suppose so, yes. Shouldn't I be?"

His smile grew. "Depends."

"On what?" Mrs. Kinncaid asked. "Mothers try to keep the kids healthy and the fathers are stuck on spoiling them. You're as bad as your father."

His smile slid away, his eyes going cold. "I'm much worse, Mother."

With that, he walked into the kitchen and retrieved a fork.

Rori had wondered, why, if they had the entire hotel, a restaurant . . . probably several, and room service at their disposal—*why* would they need the large kitchen in their apartment, and she bet all the other penthouse apartments had the same layout.

"How'd the meeting go?" his mother asked.

The edge of his mouth lifted but his eyes, as they shifted to Rori, were serious. "Fine."

A single word, yet she understood they'd discuss it later. Wonder what his dear boss had thought of her.

She watched him open the container and scoop up a big bite for Darya. He said something to her in Russian as he fed her the enormous spoonful.

Darya nodded just before her eyes shifted to Rori.

She saw what he was doing and instinct had her tensing, ready to strike, but she waited, even as she knew.

His hand, quick as a snake, whipped up and bopped a dollop of chocolate-drizzled whipped cream on her nose.

His grin and Darya's were infectious. She smiled, wiped it off, licked part of it off. His eyes watched her, the blue darkening.

Her stomach tightened at the memory of their kiss, at the feel of his hands on her.

She knew his parents watched them, but didn't give a care.

Holding her finger out to him, she said, "I'm really not into sweets, but thank you."

His eyes flashed, but he drew her finger into his mouth. The swirl of his tongue on her finger did things in her gut she didn't want to think about.

Rori jerked her finger back and said, "I think I'll go to our room for a bit. I'm wiped."

She stood.

Mrs. Kinncaid said, "Ian Rohnan Kinncaid, you are coming home."

Rohnan? Rori cocked a brow at him and tried to hide her grin.

"Mother—"

Kaitlyn's green eyes flashed. "Don't you 'Mother' me." Her fist hit the table. "You owe me that at least."

His shoulders rose on his inhale and then he speared Rori with a look. He said something to Darya in Russian and locked his hand on Rori's arm, propelling her out of the apartments and into the hallway.

Down the hallway two doors, he shoved his key into the slot and all but kicked the door open.

When it shut, he whirled. "We're *not* going to my parents' house."

Somewhere in the back of her mind, she wondered if this was what married couples did.

Rori waited. He seemed a bit stressed to her, even if he appeared cool and calm. It was in the hard lines of his mouth, the way his eyes were narrowed. Then again, perhaps she was wrong.

He rubbed his forehead and muttered something. She vaguely wondered if he got headaches like she often did when suddenly the reality of things crashed down on her.

"You okay?"

He sighed. "What am I supposed to say to her?"

She walked to him and put her hands on his shoulders. They were hard as rocks under her hands, but still she squeezed and rubbed her thumbs in circular motions. "You need some rest."

He grunted and tilted his head to the side, giving her access to the tightened cords of his neck. They stood like that for several moments. "You ever get tired of what we do?" he asked softly.

Her motions paused for a moment. Then she dug her thumbs back in. She started to give a blithe remark, but sensed she didn't have to. "Sometimes, yes. I never really *like* what I do, but I also know it was and is necessary on more levels than the average person cares to reflect on."

"Ever think there's any redemption for us?"

"My, aren't we philosophical tonight." She sighed. "Would you sit on the couch?"

He didn't move. Soft and deep, he said, "I told my boss I was out. After this is over, I'm *out.*"

She nodded and continued to massage his shoulders.

He took a breath, as if to say something, then shook his head. "We can't go to my parents' house."

"Why not?"

He whirled on her, his eyes narrowed. "Why *not?*"

She crossed her arms and ran her gaze over him. He looked so bloody good in black she smiled.

"I find nothing amusing in this situation."

Rori waited and then said, "You hadn't *planned* on seeing them. They know you're here now. On some level you knew they might learn of your arrival, or you never would have briefed me on everyone. Secondly, if you don't go, it only raises more questions, especially if more find out about you. Three, if your cover is completely blown, do you think it matters if you're with your family or not?"

"By being too close to them, I make them targets."

"Simply being who you are makes them targets," she said with brutal honesty. His face hardened.

"I'm not putting them in danger. *Damn it!*" He shoved a hand through his hair and paced away from her, his hands fisted on his hips as he stopped near the window.

She wondered what it was like to worry about so many people.

The only person she worried about was Nikko, and she really needed to call him before he started his own search for her. She knew she had another day or so before he'd really start to worry.

"Ian," she said softly, standing her ground. "I don't know what it's like to have a family, let alone a large one that you feel you have to take care of and protect." She watched him, his jacket caught behind his wrists, the late afternoon light slanting through the windows. "You've done a marvelous job so far. Little Ryan seems to think you're a superhero."

He turned and the fire of those blue eyes burned her. "I'm not a goddamn hero."

He would never think so. In that moment, something shifted in her for him. She had no idea what, but she felt it. A man so bent on protection of those he loved.

"Do you have any idea how many men would have even looked for that little girl? Who, if they had found her, would take her with them like you have?" His eyes didn't move from her. "Not very many. Not all men are like you, or your brothers. You don't want to endanger them. Fine, I understand that. But do you honestly think it matters now?"

He didn't say a word.

She walked to him. "If they learn who you are, they will still target your family if for no other reason than to draw you out." Without a thought, she reached out and placed her hand on his chest, felt the beat of his heart. "If you're at their place, you can better keep an eye on them. You'll know what to look for. They won't."

His eyes didn't soften, but the fire banked. "I don't like it."

She nodded. "I know, and I don't like your father, so we'll both just have to live with it."

The intention flickered in his eyes as he leaned in and set his forehead against hers. "You know what I want?" he asked softly.

She licked her lips. "I'm not giving you *that*."

He grinned slow and sure. "We'll see, but I wasn't talking about *that*, though I do think about it." He paused and she wondered if he'd kiss her. Instead he continued. "I want a beach, little umbrella drinks. No worries."

"No hits?"

"That too. You like the beach?"

"Yes." Deciding to give him something else to think about, she added, "But I don't like tan lines."

Chapter 16

November 14, 10:42 p.m.

Ian brushed his finger over Darya's tear-stained cheek. She'd cried herself back to sleep. He'd been talking to Rori in the living area, planning tomorrow, when her whimpered cries and screams had brought them both running.

What did she see in her dreams? The nightmare she'd witnessed? More?

She hadn't said more than that one word since yesterday. Zoy. Her sister? Someone else?

He took a deep breath and left the light on. She laid on her side, her purple pajamas with cats on them contrasting against the white sheets. Her arm was thrown over her bear. He looked to the side, where a doll still sat in the box. She apparently just liked the bear.

Ian leaned over and kissed her on the cheek, breathing her scent deep. *"Dobroy nochi. Devochka moya."* Good night, my little girl.

And by God, she would be. She already was.

He had never thought of having kids, never thought of having a family. Families could be used against men like him for any number of things.

But here, with this lost child clutching tight to the bear he'd given her, to see her eyes crying from phantoms that stalked her, to feel those little arms wrap around his neck.

He wanted her. He wanted her to be his.

"Sweet dreams."

He stood, double-checked the windows, and silently walked out of the room. Rori stood in the doorway, her arms crossed over her chest as she leaned on the door frame.

Dressed in a white hotel robe, her long legs peeked at him where the terry cloth parted, one knee winking through. She seemed to be waiting on him.

Without a word, he walked to her, and pulled the door almost to, but left it cracked.

"She went to sleep easily enough," she said. She rubbed her arms and added, "You're really good with her, you know? She needs that right now."

Without a word, he wrapped his arms around her and ignored her stiffening. After a minute she sighed and wrapped her arms around him. "What the fuck are we doing?" she whispered against his neck, her breath warm.

Ian could only shake his head. If he wanted, he could forget, just for a second, that this wasn't real. That his wife, his daughter, his *life*, was just a façade. Like all the other times.

"I can't take her pain away, Rori," he muttered.

Her head shook against his neck and she squeezed him tighter. "Not immediately, no. But you will."

He tightened his arms for a minute then let her go, taking her hand in his and leading her back to the kitchen. For just a moment, he simply wished things were different.

Ian got them both water and handed her a bottle.

"Ready for tomorrow?" she asked, clearing her throat.

He grunted and watched her, watched as she closed her mouth over the top of the bottle and took a drink, the muscles in her throat working. He remembered what she tasted like just there beneath her jaw, how soft the skin on her neck.

"What?" she asked.

He shook his head, set the water bottle on the counter and grabbed her hand, jerking her to him.

Looking into those witch's eyes, he said, "There's a saying about temptations and once tasted."

"Is there?" she asked, cocking a brow. She relaxed and ran her hand up the front of his shirt.

"Yeah, there is." He kept his eyes open as he leaned in, licked her lips and watched her eyes widen.

Her tongue darted out to tangle his. Her arms slid up his chest, wrapped around his neck as she leaned into him.

Ian tilted his head and deepened the kiss, closing his eyes.

Her scent, spicy and exotic, engulfed him. He wrapped his arms around her, kissing her harder. Her teeth nipped his tongue, his lips, her laughter a faint vibration as he sighed.

"I've wanted to do this to you since I first laid eyes on you scoping me out."

"Luv, if I was scoping you, you'd be dead."

He grinned and pulled back, looking into her eyes. "Do you realize we know the other's darkest secrets and don't give a bloody damn?"

A shadow shifted in her eyes. "Darkest secrets are relative. What's bad to one isn't to another."

"What's that mean?" He started to lean back.

"You kill, I kill, we do our jobs and go on." She grabbed his head and kissed him, her teeth and lips coaxing his own. "I don't want to talk about our bleeding jobs right now."

He kissed her back, his hands unknotting the belt holding her robe together. She gasped as he simply spanned her waist, the muscles tight beneath his hands. He wanted more. He wanted all.

"What do you want to talk about?" he asked her, his hands gently squeezing on her hipbones.

She pulled her bottom lip into her mouth, her eyes on his. "I don't want to talk at all."

His eyes darkened, and he breathed deep.

Without another word, he picked her up and set her on the countertop.

He should probably ask her if . . .

She grabbed his head between her hands and jerked him to her. "Are you as good a lover as you are at everything else?"

He pulled the collar of her robe off one shoulder and bit the side of her neck. "Care to find out?"

She hissed when his other hand gently raked across her belly. "Are you going to talk all damn night? I'm not really a . . . aaahhhh."

He licked her ear, his hand reaching up to barely graze the undersides of her breasts with his thumb.

She leaned back and looked at him. "You know, Darya could wake up at any moment."

He looked at her. "True. But I want to enjoy this."

She hooked her heels in the small of his back, and he felt her heat even through his clothing and her robe. "You take too long to enjoy this and neither of us will even get to experience *this*."

Her eyes dared him.

He'd rarely passed up a dare. Grabbing her ass, her legs still hooked around him, he easily carried her into the bedroom. He'd slept out on the couch last night, but tonight . . .

He kicked the door shut and turned, trapping her against the side of it.

"Bloody hurry."

He kissed her hot and openmouthed. "I don't want to bloody hurry."

$$\bullet \quad \bullet \quad \bullet$$

Miami, Florida

Alla Gregary stood on the sidewalk of her hotel. The heels on her feet were killers, but they made her legs look even better than normal. Her short tight dress, the color of the sunset, only complimented her tan.

She ignored one man, smiled at another as she waited on a cab.

The doorman motioned with his finger just as another pulled to the curb.

Tonight she was going out. She'd kept a low profile thus far. Her beautiful house in Kladno had been bombed. Damn bosses. But then Alla Gregary wouldn't really worry about such things, would she? Elianya Hellinski would, but no one could find *her*.

Alla smiled. Changing identities was so easy. More easy than she would have thought.

One man whistled as he passed her.

She licked her lips and stared at him until the woman on his arm jerked his attention back around.

All men. She really had no use for men. She simply wanted to control them.

Climbing into the cab, she told the driver where she wanted to go.

She pulled her silver cell from her small black evening bag. She dialed the numbers and waited. Finally the voice on the other end answered.

"It's me," she said.

Her contact said, "Where are you?"

Alla laughed. "Like I would tell you that."

"I need to know. Things are going to hell faster than anyone can guess."

She purred, "Are they really? That's too bad. No?" She didn't care what was happening.

"I need—" the contact started.

Alla interrupted. "I *need*."

"Don't you always?" the voice snapped.

Alla laughed, throaty and husky as she always had, and noticed the driver glance at her and run his gaze to her advertised cleavage. Men were so easy.

"I want a name."

The silence on the other end went on so long she thought the contact had hung up.

"Are you still there?"

"Yes." A sigh. "What name?"

"Petrolov's."

The voice hissed, "I've given you his aliases."

"Exactly. I want his *name*."

No answer.

"If you don't, it'll only take one phone call and your life will come crashing down," she said into the phone.

"Fine. But he's being taken care of. The plan is for tomorrow."

Alla thought about it. She really wanted that bastard. He'd ruined everything for her and had always treated her with disdain. A saint who played the sinner.

"Just in case you . . . aren't successful, I want a name."

The driver was watching her too closely. She ran a finger down her breasts, down her torso.

His eyes widened and she laughed when he almost hit the car in front of them.

Another sigh.

"One call," she threatened.

"Fine. Ian. Kinncaid. His real name is Ian Kinncaid."

The line went dead.

Alla smiled.

• • •

Washington, D.C.

Rori took a deep breath. Please don't let him stop. She wasn't deluding herself. She knew this wasn't some big act of the *L* word on

166

his part. Or it was, but of lust.

His hands, those long-fingered hands . . .

Her head hit the door as she leaned back. His mouth nipped at her neck. He lifted her higher and licked a line on her breasts.

She took a deep breath and speared her fingers in his hair.

"We're mad, barking mad."

He chuckled, the gravelly sound vibrating against her chest.

When his mouth closed over her breast, she arched into him. God, the pull, straight to her gut, a lust-tipped bullet that rocketed her libido.

"Hurry," she said to him.

He lifted his eyes and she watched him as he licked at her. Then he trailed wet kisses over to her other breast, all the while watching her.

She licked her lips. "We don't have time to dilly-dally."

He chuckled again. "Oh, we're going to dilly-dally."

She rocked her hips against him.

He paused, frowning. "I don't have a condom."

No. She took a deep groaning breath then said, "I'm clean. Are you?"

He nodded. "Hell, yes. Where I worked, I was too selective."

"When was the last time you slept with anyone?" she asked him.

He thought, frowned. "Several months ago. Some college chick."

She laughed. "Tested?"

"Two months ago. I'm clean."

"Gor blimey, then just get on with it."

One corner of his mouth kicked up.

She started to unbutton his shirt. "Bugger this." She grabbed each side and ripped. Buttons flew and pinged across the room.

His grin grew. "You want me bad."

She leaned in and sucked on the side of his neck, marking him. He hissed.

His hands went back to her bare skin and pulled and jerked the robe away until it fell behind her, only hanging on to her shoulder and elbow.

"Are you on the pill?" he asked as his hands ran up her thighs.

"Children aren't an option for me. Can't have them. I'm sterile." His hand stopped and she opened her eyes, looking at him. He seemed angry.

"I'm not lying." Fuck, she didn't want to get into this now. "You want my bloody medical records?"

He blinked and shook his head. "Sorry. Someone lied to me once and tried to get me to marry them by lying about a pregnancy."

"Fine, I'll kill the bitch tomorrow, can we just get on with it?" Her breath shuddered out.

His fingers gripped the backs of her thighs, his arm muscles bunched. And still those eyes burned. She took his face in her hands. "I will never be able to have kids. No amount of medicine or technology will change that."

She kissed him. She didn't want to think about what she couldn't do, what was lost to her because of . . .

No.

She wanted to forget. Forget and just live in the moment. Too many reminders lately. Too many dark thoughts.

"Kiss me," she urged him. "Make love to me. Or I'll tie you to the bed."

He laughed, his features easing. "Promises, promises."

He grazed one finger so near, so near. She wiggled and he slapped her ass. "My way."

"Your way would take all bloody night."

"A man does have fantasies."

Then those fingers were skimming her, running the length of her. Her breath shuddered out.

"God, you're wet already."

His fingers pierced her and she arched, moaning as his teeth brought a nipple into his mouth. Wicked hands. They played her until she was writhing against the door, moaning.

"Please, please. Ian. Please." She looked into the blue depths of his eyes. The hardened features on his face.

He grinned, but it wasn't amused. She felt one of his hands leave her, felt him opening his pants.

"Hurry," she said again, rocking against him.

Ian looked into her eyes and wondered what madness possessed them. He wanted, just for now, to forget everything. Everything but her and what they pretended to be.

She was so damn responsive. Matching him in need, in wants, in his world where shadows met light and still were black. Where there was rarely any sanity.

Finally, he freed himself. She was there, her legs locked around him, her robe half hanging off of her, waiting.

For him.

He played her again with his fingers, dancing over the bundle of nerves that . . .

She gasped and arched. He grinned, fitted himself to her and surged inside.

God she was tight, wet, and felt . . .

Right.

He watched her eyes widen as she pulled back and slid back on him.

Without a word, he shook his head, hooked first one arm, then his other beneath her knees, keeping his hands on the wall. He slid even deeper and she moaned.

Her breathing quickened.

"My way," he said, keeping control of the pace, of her, of them.

Her head tilted back and the long line of her neck was beautiful in the low light of the bedroom, her skin dark and beckoning against his own.

He pushed against her.

"I've wanted this," he muttered, still watching her, watching the way he could make this woman who was so in control lose it.

Was there anything more alluring?

Her legs trembled. "Ian. Gawd. Ian."

He drove deeper, harder, faster. Sweat broke out on his forehead.

"I can do this to you," he whispered into her ear, just as he plunged again.

She gasped for breath, bit her bottom lip, and flew apart, her inner muscles vising around him.

He followed her over the peak, groaning into her neck.

His heart slammed against his chest, answered in the pound of hers, beat as one with a woman he wished was real.

Chapter 17

Rori grazed a finger over Ian's chest, her head resting on his shoulder. The sheets were twisted around their bodies; the room was dark now with the exception of the nightlights of D.C. permeating the room. The apartment was quiet, the only noise the faint hum of the heater kicking on.

His heart beat against her ear, his arm holding her and his fingers tracing patterns on her hipbone. His other arm was bent behind his head.

"What did you mean?" he asked, his voice gruff.

She frowned. "About what?"

"Not having kids. What happened?"

He would zero in on that, wouldn't he?

She started to roll away, but he didn't move, only tightened his hold on her.

"If you don't want to tell me, fine. Just stay where you are." He didn't lessen his hold on her.

She waited, tensed. She wasn't going into that tonight. Tonight had been too wonderful; she wasn't about to ruin it talking about *that*, let alone even *think* about it.

Rori took a deep breath and closed her eyes.

"That bad, huh?" He turned and kissed her forehead.

How could the man make her feel weak and strong all at the same time?

She waited. The night surrounded them.

Normally, this was where she got up and left. There were only three men she'd spent an entire night with, two of which she'd never questioned the next morning. Others were simply quick fucks.

She'd thought that Ian Kinncaid would be the latter.

But she knew, knew in the deepest part of her, this man holding her would be one of the former and maybe even something else.

She shied from the thought.

"If you're not going to tell me, at least stop thinking," he muttered against her forehead.

"You can go to sleep, ya know."

He grunted. "Not as loud as you're thinking."

She propped her head up on her hands and looked at him. They were in the shadows and she couldn't even make out his features, just the outline of his head, dark against the pillow.

"Well, since we're both awake, how 'bout another bang?" Rori leaned in and kissed him.

"Another bang? As in you want to play with my SIG?"

"Told you I knew how to handle a gun."

"A bang." She heard the grin in his voice. "I love it when you go Brit on me." His chuckle rumbled against her chest.

• • •

9:45 a.m.

Rori looked at the little girl sitting quietly on the couch. She was coloring on a sheet of white paper, blue lines and red squiggles. Rori had no freaking clue what she was supposed to do with the girl all day.

Ian had left early, telling her to go wherever, as long as she took one of the guards with her.

Like she couldn't guard one little girl?

Maybe they'd go shopping. Sounded like a plan to her. There were several shops downstairs.

She smiled as she rose and walked back to the bedroom. The sheets were twisted on the bed and she couldn't help but remember exactly *why* they were so twisted. Ian had merely screwed her against the door, they'd then gone to the bed and he'd shown her she could beg for just about anything.

She grinned and breathed deep. Like housekeeping wouldn't know what the hell had happened in here. But then, they were expected to be doing the deed, weren't they?

In the bathroom, she looked at her reflection. "What the bloody hell are you doing?"

She shook off the thoughts and quickly dressed in slacks, a button-down, and a jacket. She strapped her piece at her waist, the holster hidden at the small of her back. Technically, that was illegal. Policemen tended to frown on people carrying a concealed weapon, but she wasn't about to go out without one. If it came down to her and Darya and she couldn't avert their harm because she'd left her piece at home, well . . . that was simply unacceptable.

She turned and in the doorway stood Darya holding a picture. Hiding behind it, more like.

"'allo," Rori said, squatting down. She tilted her head and reached out, taking the picture.

There were three stick figures on it. A man, a woman, and a little girl. They all had big heads, but the hair color and eyes were all correct. She had to grin at the fact both she and clearly Ian held guns. Big guns.

Smiling, she looked at Darya and said, "Thank you." She clutched the picture to her and stood, holding her hand out.

Rori knew the girl probably couldn't understand her. But she set the drawing on the counter and asked if Darya wanted her to braid her hair. She motioned, then acted like she was doing it on the girl's head.

Darya frowned, then her expression cleared and she nodded.

Rori picked her up and set her on the counter, facing the mirror.

She picked up the detangling comb they used on the little girl. With her hair, tangles were inevitable. She grabbed the bottle of spritzy stuff one of the aunts had left yesterday. Maybe it was Taylor? Yeah, the redhead.

Rori carefully combed the little girl's hair. So soft, and an image popped into her head.

Sitting just like this, in one foster home, the lady carefully combing her own hair, laughing at something.

Mrs. Rittlebaum. Rori smiled at the memory. They'd been nice enough, but the husband had died unexpectedly and the kids had been put back in the system.

Not perfect by any means. Her next home had been hell.

Shaking off the thoughts, she focused on the hair in front of her.

It was too quiet in here. One thing, these Kinncaids knew how to keep guests happy. There were stereos in the bathrooms.

She clicked the radio on and found a country station. She loved country music and this was a George Strait.

Rori hummed along with the cowboy and then sang the song with him about a man bemoaning the fact his woman had left him.

She missed a word and her voice faltered. Darya giggled.

Rori smiled at her and parted her hair, braiding it. So soft. The girl had gorgeous hair, down past her shoulders and full of curls that so many women paid money for.

As she got to the end of the braid, smaller and smaller, she stopped and dug through the vanity draws until she found a band to put around it. She wondered where they'd come from, but since they'd been here, housekeeping and hotel staff, once cleared, had been in and out bringing packages, food, clothing, more stuff than she could keep track of.

Looking in the mirror, she wiped both palms along the sides of the girl's hair, smoothing the flyaways. Without thinking, she placed a kiss on top of the girl's head.

Darya frowned.

Rori frowned, then shook her head. Cute kid, nothing more.

She helped Darya off the counter and they went to the girl's room and chose an outfit to wear. In five minutes both were ready to go.

· · ·

5:04 p.m.

The sun was setting as they drove through the late afternoon traffic out of D.C. and into the suburbs. Concrete and rising buildings gave way to newer sprawling shopping complexes and discount stores. Homes and housing units.

He'd spent the day talking to Pete, going over intel report after intel report. Three raids were set up on brothels by several tasks forces thanks to what he knew. Maybe they'd free some girls without anyone getting killed.

Between what he'd seen and what he knew, what Pete knew, and then after lunch, when John joined them, they'd been able to see how large Elianya's operation really was. Or what they knew of it.

Right now, it seemed her newest operation was child porn hidden behind the innocent image of overseas adoptions.

It made him sick. They handed the tape they'd confiscated from the town house to Pete. He'd had to watch it again.

The big pale man, raping the young girl, finally squeezing the life out of her, and he knew Darya had seen that.

Those large male hands hurting that girl.

That girl.

Zoy. The image looked so much like Darya for several moments in the viewing room, he couldn't freaking breathe, felt the ice prickle over his skin, swallowed by the heat, and thought his head would explode.

God.

His hands tightened on the steering wheel as he glanced in the back and saw Darya sleeping against the side of the large car seat, her chin resting against the shoulder harness. She clutched the bear tightly in her hands. She hadn't had any more nightmares again last night. Just that first one. Thankfully the memories left her alone after that. It seemed the girl had nightmares every night.

He wanted to buy her more gifts. Clothes, toys. Most of all, he wanted to show her life could hold laughter.

Wasn't that ironic. He who never laughed wanted to teach the concept of happiness to a child.

God, he needed help.

Over an hour later, they were only minutes from his parents. His parents had gone home yesterday, finally. He loved his parents, really, but it had been so long since he'd had any contact with them, he found himself trying to read them. Read the questions in their eyes they weren't asking, or why they were asking, and tired of the endless questions they did ask of his past.

The boys had gone home with their wives, and their selective guards. John was watching Aiden and Jesslyn since he'd watched them before. Snake was with Gavin and Taylor, and both Tanner and Roth were with his parents at the family mansion. Since Brayden and Christian still lived there half the time along with Tori, he figured they could use two guards.

He and Rori drove the Mercedes. A dark unmarked car drove behind them with two more guards. Personally, he thought it was overdone, but Pete was stubborn.

Fine, so was he.

"Did she get anything today?" he asked into the silence.

Rori jerked and looked over at him, her profile tinged green from the dash lights. "Not at first. She put back everything I handed her."

She frowned. "I think I need to learn to speak Russian."

He grinned. "I'll teach you."

She muttered something under her breath. "But she finally picked out some drawing paper and crayons. I didn't know what to get so she's now set to draw whatever the hell she wants with any instrument known to children."

"Good." He patted his breast pocket and took out a cigarette, cracking the window.

"You know," she said. "You really shouldn't smoke. Secondhand smoke isn't healthy for her, and even if she doesn't directly breathe it, the allergens on your clothing can cause allergies later in her life."

He narrowed his eyes on the road. God, he wanted a damn cigarette. Fine.

He tossed the unlit cig out the window and crammed the rest of the pack under the seat, feeling the butt of the other gun he'd shoved there.

Pete had let him take a few other things with him as well, and they were in the backseat in the black duffel.

His cell phone rang. Grabbing it, he noted it was Aiden's home number.

"What?" he asked.

"You're always so cheerful when you answer the phone," Aiden said.

Ian took a deep breath. His family was going to take some getting used to. Like acclimating to a new location.

"What?" he asked again.

"Where are you?"

He glanced at the next mile marker and told Aiden, "About five minutes from your house."

"Good, then we'll leave. The mood Mom and Dad's been in, we really don't care to spend any more time with them than we have to."

"Add it to the list," he said, thinking of his screwups where his family was concerned.

"List?" Aiden asked.

"Never mind."

"See you at dinner."

"Aiden," he said and shifted lanes, "will everyone be there?"

"Far as I know. Gavin's already phoned, he's going to be late, but

Taylor and Ryan are already at Mom and Dad's. Brayden and Christian are not too far behind you."

Ian grunted and hung up the phone.

He drove on in silence and thought about the tension he was causing between his parents. He hadn't meant to. He'd never told anyone why he'd left. Never hinted to Aiden why he'd never come home, no matter how many times his brother asked him.

Well, nothing could be changed. He'd just have to live with it.

Rori leaned over and turned the radio on, flipping through the channels until she clicked on a country song.

"No, too hip-hop. Don't like them." She clicked on, seemingly going to a certain station as she passed over several he remembered listening to.

Slow, waltzing notes twanged through the car as the man sang of lost love. Rori smiled and settled back in her seat. She hummed the tune, one he'd never heard, but then he wasn't a big country fan, and then softly sang.

He listened more to her than he did the male vocalist. Learn something new . . .

She was a bit off-key. He looked at her and grinned.

"What?" she asked, her voice the normal clipped syllables.

He shook his head. "Nothing. Just enjoying listening to you."

She settled back and hummed again.

As they passed Aiden's turnoff, he saw headlights down the driveway heading toward the highway. How in the hell Aiden could live this close was beyond him. Never could he live right here next to Mom and Jock. It would drive him up the wall.

A few minutes later, he slowed and turned into the long drive. Lighted windows winked through the trees from the house. They passed through the gates and he realized he could get Pete to put some guards out here.

"I don't understand you when I see where you came from," she muttered.

"What's to understand? I'm still the same person I was when you met me." Their tires crunched along the drive as they slowly drove up to the house. The car's headlights behind them cut through the trees and something glinted. He looked but saw nothing. Something prickled along the back of his neck.

The turn slid his phone off the console and onto the floor at his feet. He slowed even more, almost to the circular drive, and reached down to get his phone.

His window shattered and something thunked into the dashboard.

"Jesus. Stay down," Rori said, pulling her gun free.

He grabbed the gun wedged between the seat and console. Another shot shattered the back window.

"Darya," he said, jerking the wheel, and floored the car toward the house.

He burst through the hedge, branches screeching down the side of the car, and hoped to hell no one stood in the yard. Rori scrambled over the front seat into the back and unbuckled Darya, covering her on the floorboard. He thought about driving around to the back. But Aiden . . . Who knew if there were more.

Checking his rearview mirror, he saw the car behind them blocked the driveway.

Another car pulled in behind that one, the headlights clearly belonging to an SUV.

Shit.

Aiden.

His phone rang.

"What the hell's going on?" John asked.

"Get them out of here. Get them out now — "

The windshield exploded.

"Goddamn it." He slid over the console onto the passenger's floorboard. "Rori! Is Darya hit? Is she all right?"

"No, I don't think she was hit."

He took a deep breath. He had to think. Who knew he was coming here? His family, their guards, and Pete.

Damn it.

"Rori, hand me the bag. Better yet, get me the damn goggles."

John was still yelling at him through the phone. He scanned the trees, but saw nothing.

Shots peppered across the hood. God, if they hit the gas tank.

"We're fucking sitting ducks," Rori muttered. "He'll go for the petrol tank next."

Weighing his options, he said, "Cover Darya and your ears."

He punched out the interior light above him and shot the one in the back.

"That was helpful," Rori muttered.

"What the hell was that?" John asked.

"Interior lights. We can't sit here. You know that."

Bastard was playing with them. Just waiting.

"Rifle shots. How many do you think?" Rori asked.

"Ian!" John yelled.

Fuck. "Where the hell are our guards? I've got to get Darya and Rori out of here!"

John was barking something in the background. "I've called Pete. I don't know what the bloody hell—thanks, Aiden."

"I told you to get them home."

"I will."

Damn it.

More shots ripped across the hood. Darya screamed.

"On three, I'm opening the door and we're going to try for the house," he said.

"All right."

"One. You've got my goggles?"

"Yeah, and the rest of the bag with the ammo."

"Good. Toss it here and get her."

She slid the bag to him. He slung it over his arm. "Two."

He took a deep breath.

"Three," they both said and shoved their doors open, scrambling out of the car. The lighted windows from the house slashed across the lawn.

Ian grabbed Rori's hand and ran. He felt her jerk, slip from his grasp.

He whirled to make certain they were both behind him.

He heard the impact of the bullet before the world exploded.

Chapter 18

Fire trucks and ambulances littered the driveway of the Kinncaid home in Seneca, Maryland.

Ian paced inside.

He remembered the explosion, but more, the gut-wrenching fear that he'd failed them.

Rori sat on the sofa holding Darya. As he walked to them one of the cops asked him another question.

"Why do you have bodyguards, Mr. Kinncaid?" one of the detectives asked.

He ignored the question as he had the others. He'd evaded answering the policeman's questions and the paramedics, the fire chief.

Until Pete Jones walked in—let that bastard clean up the mess.

Pain slashed ruthlessly through his head. Darya's hand sported a bandage, as did Rori's back, where a flying piece of metal scraped her. The paramedics wanted to take them all to the local hospital.

He wasn't that fucking stupid. They all declined medical attention.

The windows nearest the wreckage on the east lawn were gone. Luckily no one was in those rooms.

Everyone was now here, in the living room. Jesslyn clutched the toddler twins to her as if something would happen to them if she let them go.

He knew the feeling. He reached down and picked Darya up, closing his eyes as her arms came around him.

"I'm sorry," he whispered in her ear. God, those moments. He took a deep breath and gently set her back beside Rori.

The woman had to be in pain, he could see it in her eyes, but she refused to go upstairs. Not that he could blame her. He cupped her face and ran his thumb over her cheek. "You should be upstairs in the shower or lying down."

She snorted and grinned at him. "I've had worse. Besides, we both know this is going to be a bloody long night."

Too true.

Three of his men were out in the woods—Tanner, Roth, and

John—and the locals were not at all happy about that. Snake should be arriving with Gavin any minute.

What if the bastards had gone for the house? He looked again at Darya, who no longer had her bear. He'd have to get her another one. She picked on the blanket Rori tossed around her small shoulders. Her blue eyes met his.

God, what if . . .

Shaking off the thought, he turned and paced back to the window.

Everyone talked in hushed whispers.

The night rotated. Red. Blue. White. Red. Blue. White.

Where the hell was the bastard?

The woods beyond were dark, as they had been after arriving. He knew his three men wore night-vision goggles and were scouring the area for any sign of whoever it was that wanted them gone.

He looked over his shoulder, and for a moment his eyes met his father's, but then he moved on and zeroed in on Pete.

• • •

Jock looked across the living room. Kaitlyn was talking to Taylor, who looked ready to pop. Pregnant women didn't need this kind of excitement. Ryan stood beside her, more quiet than normal, his other hand holding Tori's. Those two were practically inseparable.

Both Brayden and Gavin had called, pissed because the road was blocked, but . . .

He looked into the entryway, where policemen gathered and talked to the men in suits who were quickly filing past.

Brayden, holding Christian's hand, and Gavin both shoved through the crowd, scanning the living room until they found who they wanted.

Jock knew he'd have that frantic look in his eyes as well if he'd been told something happened but had no idea what.

He hated, hated things like this. This was his home, and he still had not a fucking clue what the hell was going on.

They'd been in the back family room when an explosion had rocked the house, breaking glass.

When they'd hurried into the front entryway, it was to see Ian and his family scattered on the lawn, a car on fire, and men with guns firing into the trees and hurrying to them.

For a moment, his heart froze in his chest. That fear that there lay one of his children dead . . .

He took a deep breath and rubbed his chest. He never wanted to see that again.

Kaitlyn had come up behind him and then flown out the door, but their guards, Tanner and Roth, had jerked them back, not letting either him or his wife leave.

Tanner, brave lad, had picked Kaitlyn up and hurriedly got them both into the bathroom near the bottom of the stairs.

Tanner had stayed with them and Roth had run back out front, barking into some sort of radio device, a gun in his hand.

Up until that point, Jock had thought it was all on the dramatic side. Ian pulling some prank or stunt like he had as a boy.

But this . . .

He shook his head and watched his son. Arms crossed over his chest, he watched a man who stood talking to one of the policemen.

There was no boy before him in the man who stood at the window glaring across the way at a man with salt-and-pepper hair, a shoulder harness strapped to his muscled frame.

If Jock Kinncaid had met this Ian Kinncaid on the street, he would never have recognized him.

He wore more black clothing, a gun strapped in a holster crossing his back and shoulders. His features were chiseled and hard, unforgiving. And those blue eyes held no laughter, no mischievousness that Jock had always thought of through the years when thinking of Ian.

God, he'd made a mess of things.

What the hell had he pushed his son to? What had Ian become?

Would things have been different if only he had swallowed his misguided notions all those years ago?

He took another deep breath, pushed away from the wall, met Aiden's stare as the newcomer walked into the room and only said to Ian, "We need to talk."

"You've got that fucking right, Pete." A radio buzzed on Snake, who answered it.

But they all heard. The woods were clear.

Whoever had caused all the hell tonight was no longer here.

• • •

Ian followed Pete out of the room, ignoring everyone but the one man he wanted answers from. He led Pete down to what was once his father's office and saw that it still was. The smell was the same and memories wanted to flood him.

He didn't let them. He waited until Pete came in and then he slammed the door.

"Look, I know you're upset—"

"Upset?" he asked softly, shaking his head. "No, Pete, I'm not upset." He didn't move, tried to go past the pain in his head. "I'm past upset. I'm fucking pissed."

"I know—"

"No, you *don't* know," he hissed. "You have no friggin' clue, but you better by God get one." He walked behind his father's desk and stared at Pete. "You knew of my plans, my men knew of my plans, and my family."

Pete's hazel eyes watched him, sharpening. He sank down into one of the chairs facing the desk and steepled his fingers, his elbows resting on the arms of the chair.

Ian waited.

Pete waited.

Fuck it. He turned and looked out the window.

For a moment, neither said anything.

Then, Pete's voice asked, "Are you done?"

Ian rubbed the back of his neck, wishing the headache away. Headaches were bad, and whether this was a warning that he needed a break or from tonight, he didn't know, didn't want to even guess.

"You need to come in for a physical tomorrow." Pete sighed. "I've got people working on this, I've increased the number of guards and I want—"

"I want my family safe," Ian said.

"Yes. That's a given."

Ian waited but Pete didn't say anything else. Finally, he turned and faced his boss.

"You look like shit," Pete said.

He grunted, walked around the desk and sat in the other chair, leaning his head back. Closing his eyes, he asked, "Is it you, Pete? Have I become expendable?"

He waited, didn't open his eyes.

"I should be insulted, but I'm not." Pete cleared his throat and Ian heard his clothing shift as he moved in the chair. "I would come to the same conclusion if I were you. Without a doubt, the leak is in my office. We just have to find it."

No kidding.

"What do you want to do?" Pete asked him.

Ian opened his eyes and stared at the ceiling, still white, same wooden trim around the top as it had always been.

"Don't have a clue." God, he was so fucking tired. A log popped in the grate.

Neither spoke again.

Pete broke the silence. "You know, the local authorities are now going to be watching your family as well. I haven't figured out if this was a good thing or a bad thing."

"Local authorities knowing of our presence is never good."

Pete chuckled. "True."

"But the extra eyes will be a plus." Ian wondered if he could just pack up his family and move them elsewhere.

"I thought about just putting your entire family under protection and moving them to a secure location," Pete commented, standing. "But, considering, I don't know that it would do any good."

Ian thought about the firestorm that would cause. "Probably wouldn't do any good anyway. I don't know that any of them . . . Well, my brothers might, with their wives." His hand fisted. "My life, our lives are so fucked up compared to everyone else's, Pete. Ever thought of that?"

Pete cocked a brow at him. "I've always thought that everyone else simply lives in blissful ignorance."

"I don't know what that is."

Pete tilted his head. "You know, I honestly thought I could talk you into staying with us, give you time and another assignment. Maybe bring you in out of the field and into the office."

Ian was already shaking his head.

"But," Pete continued, "I can see I was wrong on that score. You really are ready to call it quits."

Ian sat up and rubbed a hand over his face. "Is there ever really such a thing as 'quits' for guys like us?"

"Sure" — Pete smiled, a full-fledged one — "when you're dead."

"Isn't that a cheery fucking thought."

"What are you going to tell your family?"

He shook his head. "Don't have a clue."

Pete leaned back. "We'll run the bullets the boys are getting from around the scene and see what we come up with."

Would it be for or against Pete? For or against him? Elianya? One of the other families that wanted him dead? Whoever the damn mole was.

• • •

Rori watched all the goings-on with a sort of detachment. She was part of this, and yet not. A feeling she was rather familiar with. Darya was tucked up to her side and she thought about taking the girl upstairs, but decided to wait to see what Ian wanted to do.

If it were her, she'd remove Darya to a safer place, make certain the girl at least was out of harm's way. Then again, knowing Ian, he'd want to make certain everyone was safe. Two or three people they could hide. A family this large — probably not.

Mrs. Kinncaid was walking around, asking people if they needed anything — the perfect host. It fit her. Jesslyn and Aiden were playing with their boys in the hallway just outside one of the doorways of the living room. Two of the other brothers were with their wives. She hadn't seen a sign of Quinlan yet, but figured Gar was with him, or someone. Had Ian thought of him?

Maybe she should ask Nikko to watch him.

And what the fuck did she really care? Was this her job? No. Was this her family?

No.

So why drag Nikko into the mix if she didn't have to. Nikko.

She looked at Snake and said, "Let me borrow your phone."

He unclipped it. "Why?"

"I need to call someone, and if I don't, they'll start to worry. Since my mobile is in little melted pieces, be a chap."

He handed it to her. "Who you calling?"

"Don't be a nosy parker, Snake." She took the phone, walked to a quiet corner so she could still keep an eye on Darya, who slid off the couch and addled up to her side. She rang Nikko.

He didn't answer.

She called again.

Then again.

Finally, he picked up. "Who the hell is this?"

"It's me."

His sigh was filled with relief and anger. She could tell. "Where the *bloody hell* are you?" he muttered in Italian. "Do you have a clue how long it's been since you checked in? You always check in."

She was tired. "I'm fine. Just busy."

"You quit."

"Not exactly," she said, and scanned the room. Snake still watched her, his thin black brow cocked.

"What does that mean?"

She sighed. "It means I'm doing a new gig now and things have become complicated. I'll ring you back later. I just wanted you to know things are fine."

"When you take the time to let me know things are fine, they rarely are, *cara*. What is going on?"

She sighed. "I can't get into it now. Just know I'm fine." She looked around this group of people Ian cared so much about, saw the worry on all their faces. "Nikko, have I ever told you thank you?"

"For what?"

She grinned. "Never mind. Take care, luv." She clicked the phone shut, and returned it to Snake. Picking Darya up, they sat back on the sofa.

Jock rubbed his chest again and walked toward her. He sat down on the other side of Darya.

"All right?" she asked him.

He nodded. No smile, no grimace, just a nod.

"I see where your son gets it."

He frowned. "Gets what?"

The man was worried, she could see it in his eyes, in the etched lines of his face. "Ian's attitude and inflexibility."

"I'm not inflexible," he scoffed.

She merely raised a brow. He lifted his hand to place on Darya's head, but faster than a blink, she scurried into Rori's lap, her thumb firmly in her mouth.

His frown deepened.

"Is she okay?" he asked.

"Do you honestly care?" Rori returned, leaning down to kiss Darya's forehead. The bear was nowhere to be found and it had become a security blanket.

"She's missing her bear," he mumbled.

Rori tried to hide her grin.

"I bet we can find another," he added, hefting his weight up and walking from the room. She watched him go and wondered where he was off to.

Kaitlyn joined her and took her husband's seat. "Has she said anything?"

Rori shook her head and Kaitlyn studied her.

"What?" Rori asked. Too damn many people around for her peace of mind.

Kaitlyn took a deep breath and closed her eyes. "I just thought . . ." She closed her mouth, looked down, and picked a nonexistent piece of lint off her pants. "When we got to the window. You and she were closer to us, Ian a bit away . . . And just for a moment, I thought . . ."

Damn.

Rori reached out and covered her hands. "Your son saved our lives."

Kaitlyn nodded and shoved a coppery curl behind her ear. She shook her head. "There's so much I want to ask him, so much I've missed, so much I want to know, and earlier none of that mattered. I just wanted him alive and you alive. I thought I'd kill that boy that picked me up and carried me to the bathroom."

Tanner as "that boy" brought a smile to Rori's face. "They were following Ian's orders. Their primary duty is to protect their charge."

"Why do we need protecting and who's after my son?" Those green eyes narrowed, sharpened to hard emeralds. "A car explodes on my front lawn, almost killing my son and his family, and by God, I've a right to know."

Rori tilted her head. Woman had a point. She squeezed Kaitlyn's hand, seeing again the plain gold band topped by a diamond anniversary band. "It's up to Ian to let you know. If you ask questions now, he won't tell you. After everyone clears out, he might." At the determined look on the woman's face, Rori added, "And I stress might more on the *probably not* side."

"Oh, he'll tell me, I'm his mother."

"Which is the reason he probably won't."

Kaitlyn's chuckle drew attention.

Jock strode up to their side and in his hand was a bear. An old blond and ragged bear looking as if he'd been in a battle or two. Kaitlyn's smile grew and turned tender as she looked at her husband. "I'm glad you thought of that."

Jock squatted down in front of them, his knees creaking and popping. Rori winced. That had to bloody hurt.

He held the bear out to Darya, who merely stared at him, not moving, barely even breathing.

"This was Ian's. Ian's, when he was a boy."

He held it aloft and still the girl didn't take it.

"He's yours now." He frowned, looked at the bear, then at Rori. "How do I say that in Russian?"

"I have no idea."

And then she felt him, directly behind her, only a second before his graveled voice said the words in a language no one but the little girl understood.

Darya didn't even turn to look at him.

Rori heard him sigh, but then Darya pulled her thumb from her mouth with a loud pop and tentatively reached for the bear.

Jock didn't move, let her take it.

She snatched the bear, then burrowed back into Rori.

Ian's hand rested on her shoulder. Jock looked at her for a long moment, then his eyes rose to look beyond and above her. "What happened to Darya, to make her so distrustful?"

Rori's stomach tightened and she cleared her throat.

Ian's voice hardened. "You don't want to know."

Chapter 19

Quiet like a mouse. She walked down the hallway, her fingers brushing the side of the wall, the paint cool, the carpets beneath her bare feet thick. She stopped, listened, and wiggled her toes.

It was so big here. Not like at the hotel where they stayed before. This was different. People in and out all the time. The same men she remembered from . . .

She shook her head. Here things were safe. She looked at the back of her hand, to the white bandage there, and remembered the pops, the shattering glass, the fire that backhanded them across the lawn.

The house was dark and quiet, for the most part. She heard a saw whirr to life near the back of the house.

No one moved up here. The others had left, she remembered the boy leaving with his parents. The other little girl was in bed asleep down the other hallway.

She'd had her bath. Rori and Ian's mother had given it to her. The lady with the red hair singing and squirting water while Rori washed her and talked.

Darya frowned. She had lain in bed, but something woke her up. She looked down at her other hand, where her new bear hung by one arm.

Ian's bear. She smiled and brought the bear up to her nose. He didn't smell like Mr. Bear. This one smelled dusty and she wanted to sneeze. But she liked him. He didn't have a name yet.

Maybe she'd call him . . . She didn't know. For now, he'd be Mr. K. They'd told her, her new name was Darya Kinncaid.

She didn't know why. She liked her old name. And if they changed her name, then what? But she didn't want Ian or Rori leaving her, or getting mad. What if she didn't like her name, so they gave her away like Aunt Sonya had?

Darya shook her head and clutched Mr. K to her. He needed a bath. She'd had a bath, she needed to give one to Mr. K.

A noise at the end of the hallway jerked her head up.

The old man with white hair stood there looking at her, his hands in his pockets, something under his arm.

He smiled, and his eyes wrinkled up. He said something to her, his voice deep and calm.

Not like it had been back at the hotel, sharp and angry. Slowly, he walked toward her.

Her heart beat fast and faster, and she looked over her shoulder, but no one was there.

Darya didn't move as he stopped in front of her. He said something again, that soft rumbling voice, like the sound of water filling the tub when she lay in the bottom and the water covered her ears.

He held his hand out to her and she only looked at it, then at him. Where was Ian? Where was Rori?

She frowned. His bushy white brows rose and he pointed back down the hallway, the way she'd come from. Again, he held his hand out.

He wouldn't hurt her. Not here with Ian. Ian would get him if he did. Taking a chance, she put her hand in his big one and walked with him down the hallway.

The room softly glowed from the lamp over on the side table. The bed was scrunched where she'd lay on it. The doors to the balcony were locked up high. She couldn't reach it, she'd tried. She wanted to open them and breathe the air.

He walked her to the bed and pulled the covers back. She looked up at him. Rori and Ian did it like that too. He wouldn't hurt her.

She climbed in bed and he pulled the blue cover up over her. She tucked it under her arms and stared at him.

He grinned back and looked around, then he looked back at her and wiggled his brows, saying something.

From under his other arm, he pulled out a book.

She tilted her head and watched him.

Ian had read her a story earlier, but she'd understood it. He sometimes talked like she did.

This man didn't. This book was different, with beautiful pictures. She sat up and looked as he opened it and held it on his lap. Darya ran her hand down the page the book was open to. A picture of a princess, the painting so real, she expected to see the lady in the dark red gown move, or see her long wavy hair blow. The edge of the page was all swirly gold and blue. It was the most beautiful thing she'd seen.

Smiling, she looked up at the old man.

He chuckled and pulled the book toward him and started to read.

She had no idea what he was saying, and she tried. Tried until her eyes grew tired and she leaned back against her pillows. His voice was gruff, but she almost felt as safe with him as she did with Ian. His voice rumbled over her, through her, lulling her back to sleep.

• • •

Jock looked at the little girl sleeping in his son's old twin bed. She was pale, her dark hair contrasting against the pristine white sheets.

So small, so . . . haunted. Yes, the girl was haunted.

He had no idea from what, Ian wouldn't say, but he could see it in little Darya's round blue eyes. Ryan had possessed that same look when Jock first met the boy over a year ago.

Since then, rarely, if ever, did he see it in the smiling, rambunctious boy Ryan had become.

Darya. He closed the book on his lap, glad he'd thought to get it from the library. He'd planned to check in on her and leave the book, not that he'd told anyone downstairs that. Kaitlyn had given him her "are you feeling all right, you should go to bed" look.

He was tired. Tired physically and emotionally, tired in soul like he hadn't been in a long long time.

"You're safe here, princess," he whispered, brushing a hair back off her forehead. "You're a Kinncaid now and I don't know if your daddy's told you, but we Kinncaids . . ."

A memory, razor-sharp, pierced him, robbing him of breath. Ian, angry and rightly so, standing in the entryway, betrayal and fury in those blue eyes. *"Fine. Disown me. Flesh and blood and the Kinncaid line of bullshit you always fed us, is just that, isn't it? Bullshit. Because when it comes right down to it, Jock Kinncaid doesn't stand with his own. Instead he believes the worst and disowns them. You're a goddamn hypocrite."*

Damn boy had it right then. Now?

He took a deep breath. He and Ian had never gotten along, not really, not like the other boys. Kaitie had always said it was because they were so much alike.

Now?

Now, he'd do whatever he had to, to keep Ian and his family in their lives.

Crow had never tasted good, and with everything he hadn't had time to apologize to his son. It was time he did.

His hips popped when he stood. Damned old age. He'd love to go to bed, but he wouldn't. At the door, he looked back.

Little girls needed to twirl and squeal, giggle and whisper — like Tori.

This granddaughter of his would as well if he had any say in it. Tomorrow he'd buy her a damn dolly. One of those ridiculous frilly ones.

Smiling, he pulled the door almost to and walked back down the hallway. He'd come up thinking to put the book in her room and just to check on her. But she'd stood just there, silent as a little ghost.

Forget the doll, he'd get her something else. He'd get her one of those little pink cars she could drive. He remembered Tori had one and chased anything that stood still and mowed down her grandmother's daffodils.

He chuckled.

Jock wondered if they still only came in pink. Maybe he could get her a purple one, or a blue one . . .

• • •

Ian sat in the living room, listening again as Roth gave him the rundown of the search.

Aiden and Jesslyn finally went home. Since they lived just down the road and he didn't want to find out tomorrow morning their house was hit, he'd made certain not only Pete's team had gone over it thoroughly, but also John. When the all-clear came, John drove up and then drove them back home. Pete had added another guard to everyone. Pete also had Gavin's place checked out, it too was clear.

Life was just fucking peachy.

He closed his eyes and leaned his head back against the couch, Rori snuggled up beside him, her head on his shoulder, listening.

Brayden and Christian had gone to bed earlier and Tori had been sent to bed after Ryan left. She had school tomorrow. Brayden wanted to take them to Louisiana earlier than Thanksgiving. Ian didn't blame them for wanting to leave. He blamed himself. Supporting Brayden, Ian had said he'd send Tanner or Roth and whoever Pete assigned.

Quinlan had never shown up, getting busy at the hotel, and then Pete sent a guard to keep him there. Quin wasn't happy and had called more times than Ian wanted to think about.

His stomach twisted and he took a deep breath. With the headache, and tonight's activities, he didn't dare eat.

Push past it. No matter what, things could get worse, and he didn't have time to wimp out now. Things could *always* get worse.

Someone cleared their throat.

"Sorry," Ian said, "could you repeat that?"

"We didn't find anything. John said he found nothing over at Aiden's place either," Roth said. "Well, unless you count the raccoon."

Ian shook his head and said, "You might as well all go to bed. Tomorrow is another day."

And he was leaving in three. He hadn't told Rori yet, and figured he'd just wait.

The sawing finally stopped from the other side of the house, and the hammering continued as the four men Pete hired got plywood up over the windows.

Fuck.

"It's not your fault," Rori whispered.

He grunted and kept his eyes closed. "How do you figure?"

"You didn't put that sniper in the tree."

He blew out a breath and sat up, Rori sitting up beside him. He linked his hands between his knees. "A fucking sniper. He could have taken any of them out. Walk by a window and boom. Gone."

His mother, his father, Ryan, Tori, whoever the man had wanted —

"Stop it!" Rori told him. "Quit thinking with your emotions. You will get them killed, you go down that road."

He turned his head and looked at her, sitting cross-legged on the couch. She was right and the look on her face said she knew it.

"I can't not think with my emotions when it's my family. He could have easily taken you out first. Darya."

Shit. He stood, raked his hands through his hair and paced to the fireplace and back.

"I never should have come back here, damn it."

His mother walked into the room, followed by Becky. Becky. She grinned at him and shook her head. "And to think I almost missed ye and yer pranks through the years, boyo." Her ample frame and dimpled cheeks almost pulled a smile from him.

He walked to her and wrapped her in a hug.

Her hands thumped him on the back. "'Bout time ye remembered me."

He pulled back, his hands at her shoulders. Why had he remembered her taller? He'd seen her last year when he'd come to help out Brayden, but he hadn't hugged her. And she still smelled like vanilla and spices. A warm kitchen.

"I've always remembered you, Beck."

She snorted. "Well, I've got some coffee and tea here." She motioned to the tray she'd set on the coffee table. "And some cookies."

He did grin. Snickerdoodles. "My favorite." Smiling at her, he leaned over and kissed her cheek. "Thank you, Becky. You have no idea how much I missed your Snickerdoodles."

"Aye, well. You don't eat them all. Some are for your wife and that little angel of yours."

With that, she picked up another glass and bustled out of the room. He watched her go, realizing how time went on. No matter the place, no matter the situation, the losses, the gains, time went on, and blinking, a person could miss more than they'd ever thought.

"Blow me, these are good," Rori said.

His mother choked and he turned, hurried to her and thumped her on the back. Tanner chuckled and grabbed a cookie. Tanner's eyes twinkled. "I will *not* say what I could."

Rori's eyes narrowed. "Gutter mind. That's not . . . You Yanks." She shook her head and took another bite, closing her eyes. "These I could live off of."

His mother smiled and then giggled. The sound was so refreshing he stopped what he was doing and just studied her.

"What?" his mother asked.

"Nothing."

"British expression will take some getting used to. Good thing your brothers weren't here or God only knows what one of them would have said."

Rori, eyes still closed, grinned as she finished off her cookie. He realized she had the same expression after he made love to her and she drifted off to sleep.

Outdone by a cookie?

Then again, he thought, shoving one into his mouth, they were *damn* good cookies. Thankfully, his stomach accepted them without too much rebelling.

He sat and Rori reached over and patted his thigh. "I know," she said.

He looked at her. "You know what."

She only grinned.

Jock walked into the room, drawing his attention. The old man paused, and a look of . . . confusion? . . . reluctance? crossed his face.

Tanner grabbed another cookie and said, "I'm off to bed. You know where to find me. I don't get some z's, I won't be alert."

"Thanks, Tan."

Tanner walked out without another look at them.

Roth pointed to his own eyes and then circled with a finger. He would check the house out. Ian nodded.

"None of you make a sound when you walk," his mother said. "I keep thinking I'll hear footfalls from them, but they're like shadows."

The living room was quiet with only the four of them in it. Jock finally strode across the room and sat beside his wife on the other couch, facing Ian and Rori. Ian's nerves twitched. He rubbed the back of his neck, taking a deep breath.

The air tightened, he could feel it. It was the same every time he got too close to Jock. He looked at the man and wondered what his problem was. He'd been with the worst criminals imaginable and none of them really affected him like this one man could.

Ian closed his eyes and Rori laid her hand on his, leaning over to whisper, "Relax. He's difficult, but not that bad."

He jerked his head and looked at her.

Jock cleared his throat again and said, "I'm getting Darya a gift."

Ian didn't say a word. Rori looked at him, squeezed his hand, then took the ball. "Thank you, Jock. What did you have in mind?"

Jock shifted on the couch. "Well, I thought a doll at first, but . . . oh, by the way, she was up."

"What?" Ian asked.

"Darya. I went upstairs to check on her and she was standing in the hallway. I coaxed her back to her room and read her a story."

He looked from Jock to his mother, whose brows rose.

To Jock, Ian said, "You don't speak Russian."

Jock shrugged. "She didn't seem to mind."

Ian stood. "I'll go check on her."

Jock waved him back down. "She's fine. Went to sleep before the end."

He looked to the door; he should probably go check on her.

"I left the door cracked," Jock said.

Ian looked back at his father, shoved his hands in his pockets and remembered times when Jock had read him and Aiden stories of Celtic warriors . . . Roman centurions. History lessons and bedtime all rolled into one.

Taking another deep breath, he sat back down.

Kaitlyn cleared her throat and set her coffee cup in its saucer with a faint clink. "What did you read her?"

Jock shifted again, then muttered. "*Sleeping Beauty.*"

Rori chuckled. "All this time I was trying to decide if you were just an ass or an oaf, but you're all bark and no bite, Mr. Kinncaid." She chuckled, then said, "Did she like it?"

Jock studied her for one long moment. Ian couldn't believe she'd said that.

"Don't blame you there, Rori," Jock said. Then his eyes shifted to Ian. "We need to talk."

"Those words make me cringe."

Rori punched his arm.

"In a bit, or tomorrow," his mother said. Her head tilted and looked at him. "Why did your car explode?"

"Mom, always straight to the point." To lie or . . . "It's being handled."

Her eyes hardened. She opened her mouth. Jock sat forward. "Your car exploded. Someone was shooting at you, and all you can say is, 'It's being handled'?" Jock took a deep breath and blew it out through his mouth, shaking his head. "We thought you were dead, boy. Do you have any idea . . ." He blew a breath out again and raked a hand over his white hair.

Darya . . .

Ian closed his eyes, licked his lips and stood. When he'd come to, it had thankfully been to Roth, and Ian had immediately come up swinging. He always reacted that way when coming to. Never a healthy thing, more than one medic and nurse had discovered. Darya had been crying, her wails slicing through his brain, and Rori was still lying over the top of her.

God.

He rubbed his hands over his face. "Yes. Believe me, I know what went through your minds." Walking to the windows he said, "I can't talk about it. Not all of it."

"What do you do?" his mother asked.

He chuckled and reached for his cigarettes. The breast pocket was empty.

"You're quitting," Rori reminded him.

Damn woman could read him like no one else.

"No one thing, Mother. Anything I'm told to do, go where they send me, and that's about all I can say," he finally said, looking out into the night. Nothing moved, and the moon wasn't even half yet. To hell with it. "I've been undercover for the last five years. Two weeks ago someone killed the man I was working for and blew my cover."

He waited. No one said a word.

"There's a leak and they're trying to find out who."

"If they don't?" Jock asked.

Ian ignored the question, or tried to. Looking over his shoulder, he studied his parents, both watching him with intense expressions, questions and worry in their eyes.

Rori, on the other hand, was eating another cookie.

If the mole wasn't found? He'd leave. He had to. He'd gambled thinking they'd use his family anyway, but it was clear to him now they were after him. Of course, if they couldn't find him, who knew what they'd do to draw him out.

"Did you know about this?" his mother asked her.

"What he does?" Rori nodded. "Yes."

"And it doesn't bother you?"

Rori slowly grinned. Looking from his mother, then to him, her green witch's eyes twinkling, she shook her head. "I'd be . . . lying if I said it did. He's who he is."

"And just who the hell is he?" Jock asked.

Rori tilted her head, the line of her neck lengthening. He didn't want to be here. He wanted to be upstairs making love to her, kissing her pulse in that little shadow of her jaw.

"He's someone who risks it all for those he loves. I thought you, as his father, would have known that, Mr. Kinncaid."

Ian opened his mouth to tell her that was enough.

A scream pierced the air.

Darya.

Chapter 20

Ian tore out the door, Rori right behind him. He jerked his gun free of the holster as the screams kept on and then abruptly stopped.

He raced up the stairs, heard people behind him and ran down the corridor.

Let her be all right. He should have come up here himself. He turned the corner. He should have . . .

He all but flew into the room, his gun held down near his thigh as he flipped the lights on.

The room was empty.

His heart slammed in his chest. Think. Pain beat behind his eyes. Think.

"She's here somewhere," Rori said.

He lifted his head and shot her one look. She stepped back, hands out, and he noticed she too held her gun.

Tanner and Roth both stood in the doorway. Roth stepped forward and looked at the balcony doors. "They're still locked." Roth frowned and jerked them open, looking out onto the balcony.

"Darya?" Ian said. "Darya!"

He checked the bathroom. Rori looked under the little bed. Nothing.

He took another deep breath. No way could they have gotten to her.

He could see Brayden in the hallway and heard Tanner talking to him. He shoved a hand through his hair, a Czech curse falling off his tongue as easily as English.

Rori stood and shook her head. "She's not under there."

"The bear's missing," Jock said.

Ian looked to his father, then back to the bed.

His brain flashed images over each other.

Empty beds. Beds of whores. Beds of young girls. Girls trying to breathe. Darya hiding . . . Empty beds.

He shook his head and focused.

The bear wasn't there. Which meant she took it with her.

Rori strode to the closet and pulled the door open, saying, "We'll find her." She looked over her shoulder at him. "Ian. You check the bathroom. We found her before. And this is a bloody mansion. Talk about hide and freaking seek."

He went back to the bathroom, checked the tub, the shower stall, under the sink, the middle linen closet. He noticed his hands trembled. God.

He jerked open the bottom double doors of the linen cabinet.

There she was, curled up atop the extra towels. Her eyes staring sightless, her thumb in her mouth.

Ian sat on the floor, relief flooding through him more than even the first time he'd found her. He shook his head and reached out. His heart fluttered and beat like a floundering bird against his chest.

Horrors so real, from sleep they chased one so small to hide.

Some parents told their children monsters weren't real.

Darya knew monsters existed, thundering and slinking through the darkness to prey on children.

"Oh, baby girl." He eased his hands under her and pulled her out, several towels following her and tumbling to the floor. He tucked her in his lap. As before she was clammy, limp.

He put her head on his shoulder and rocked her, shaking his head.

"If it's the last thing I ever do," he said softly to her in English, "I swear on all I hold dear I will find each and every one and kill them." He didn't look up when he felt someone behind him. Didn't turn around, just rocked the little girl in his arms. "You're safe. I promise I'll always keep you safe."

His heart hurt. He wanted to make it better for her, take all the pain away, but he didn't know how, and he knew he never really could. Not completely. Not like he wanted to.

At least she hadn't been raped, but what had happened to her? Those black thoughts pushed the rage through him faster and harder.

She tensed in his arms and still he rocked her. Finally, she pushed back from him and looked up. Those big round blue eyes, her curly hair a riot around her face. Confusion shifted as she blinked and glanced around.

"You had a bad dream, do you remember?" he asked her in Russian.

She frowned, then nodded.

"Do you remember getting out of bed and hiding?" he asked.

The lines between her little black brows grew. Then she shook her head.

Wanting to lighten the mood, he took a deep breath and said, "Yes, well, apparently you decided to play hide-and-seek in your sleep. You just about gave me a heart attack, pumpkin." Still holding her to him, he stood.

Ian kept her clasped against him and met his father's eyes. Rori stood there, with that look of compassion in her eyes that he'd seen in fleeting moments. Like she knew . . .

Jock moved out of the doorway as Ian stepped through. His mom stood to the side and opened her mouth to say something, but Jock put his hand on her shoulder.

Good. The last thing he wanted was questions, because right now, he might not keep his mouth shut about things he needed to keep his mouth shut about.

Ian gently laid her on the bed, her eyes still clouded with fear, but heavy with sleep. He saw the book on the nightstand and picked it up.

"You want to read this one?" She tucked the blankets under her arms and nodded, sniffing.

He reached out and wiped at a tear track with his thumb.

He didn't look as the others walked out, didn't turn to see if Rori stayed. He felt her. Ian opened the book and wondered if they'd always had it. Jock was a bit of a bibliophile. He might have collected it through the years. Not exactly the normal children's book.

Ian shook his head, read the words, then translated them into Russian for his daughter.

As he read he realized this was what he wanted. Things he'd never allowed himself to even hope for.

He looked over his shoulder to see Rori putting the towels back in the cupboard.

Ian kept reading.

Bedtime stories to a little girl who could easily pass as his, a wife who understood where he came from, why he often reacted the way he did, and accepted him anyway.

He shook his head. It was all just a ruse. A ruse until they learned who Darya really was, whom she belonged to and if she needed to go back.

Rori?

Time would tell on that.

For now, he had a death to fake — no, Dimitri Petrolov did — and a mole to find.

He felt something on the hand he had rested beside Darya. Her small one lay atop his as he read.

Something in him settled and smiled.

Tomorrow, he'd look again. If no yellow notices had still shown up, if no reports in the databases matched Darya's description, then screw it. The papers said she was his. And that would be the end of it. He'd made certain that the documents both for his marriage and the adoption of one Darya were in his legal name. As was Rori's.

He wondered if she'd even thought of it yet.

Somehow he didn't think so.

He kept reading and then realized Darya was back asleep. He gently closed the book and watched her sleep. He felt Rori's hands on his shoulders.

"We need to get one of those baby things."

He frowned and looked up at her.

"You know," she whispered. "Transmitters. We can hear her. Forget the cutesy ones. Don't you have any in your bag of tricks we managed to get out of the car?"

He grinned. "Yeah. We do."

Her brows rose. "It's late. I told your parents to go to bed. Why don't you stick one in here and then come to bed?" She continued to rub his shoulders.

He took a deep breath and nodded, rising and wondering why he hadn't thought of that sooner himself.

• • •

Rori washed the shampoo out of her eyes, the hot water stinging her back where whatever the hell it was had landed. She was bruised and sore and had an eight-inch-long burn down the middle of her back. At least it hadn't been Darya.

The stall door opened and she grinned.

He was really magnificent naked. Long lean lines of him, all hardened muscle. His chest had a swath of dark hair across the front, and a scar . . . several scars, she amended, wondering how he'd come by several of them. This was the first time she'd seen him in full light, she realized. Long-fingered hands that could kill as easily as most men signed their names, she knew, could also be as caressing as a gentle breeze.

A man so in control he was practically frozen. The more enraged, the softer, cooler he became.

She wanted him to lose that control.

Right now, he looked tired. No, more . . . weary, a headache in his eyes.

She took a deep breath. "I'd ask you to wash my back, but it's a bit sore yet."

He stepped in, pulled the door closed and said, "Turn around."

Her stomach fluttered. Bloody stupid is what it was.

She turned and gave him her back. He didn't touch her, but she could feel his eyes on her. Knew he was looking down her as she had him.

"You have a beautifully sexy back," he said, and she felt his fingers graze around the edges of the bruise and burn. "Why did you take the bandage off?"

"Don't care for them." She started to turn back around to him, but he put his hands on her hips and kissed the curve of her neck between her shoulder and jaw. "I've wanted to kiss your neck all damn evening. I'd look across the room at you and think I don't want all this to be going on. I wanted to be up here with you. Kissing you right here." He nudged her chin up and kissed just beneath the side of her jaw.

This man could make her feel.

She turned in his arms, and leaning up, she kissed him. "I want to make you feel better," she heard herself whisper. Not knowing where it came from, but knowing it was the truth. This would never last, but she would damn well enjoy the ride.

Water poured over his face as her mouth met his, the water sluicing over the both of them. She kissed him, nipped his lips, and when he reached for her, she locked his wrists in her hands. Of course, he could get out if he wanted to.

"What game are you playing?" he asked her softly.

She started to be cheeky, but kissed him again, saying against his mouth, looking into his eyes, "No game, Ian."

Rori kissed him with all that was in her. He saved everyone else, worried about everyone else, made certain they were all safe.

Who saved him?

The thought all but pierced her heart.

She leaned into him and rubbed her breasts against his chest, until he pulled out of the kiss, staring at her, his nostrils flaring. "I want to touch you."

She slowly shook her head. "No."

Then she stepped closer and rubbed her enter body against him. Her groin cradling his, his friction against her.

There was a tiled bench in the shower big enough to wash four people.

She nudged him backward, and without looking he stepped back until his knees hit the bench.

"I put the transmitter in Darya's room," he said as he sat down, his hands on her hips again, pulling her to him.

"I would assume so, yes. I'd never distract you otherwise." She ran her hands over his much shorter hair and wished that she'd been able to run her fingers through his long locks as he'd been Dimitri.

She leaned over and turned another faucet on, this one raining down directly from little showerheads all lined along one pipe directly above their heads. Rain showered down on them.

Ian looked at her. Not smiling, not frowning, the deep lines bracketing his mouth.

She ran her hands over his chest, stopping near his right nipple. "How'd you get this scar?" A long slash ran from there to his armpit.

"Knife."

"Hmmm . . ." Her hands swirled through his hair to his other pec. Many wanted a complete beefed bull. Not her. Men with too much muscle had never been her thing. Athletic, yes, muscled, yes, and Ian was . . . He was . . . "Bloody damn perfect," she muttered, leaning down and kissing him.

His hands ran down the backs of her thighs, pulling her closer to him.

"My way," she said, licking his lips.

"Rori," he mumbled.

She grinned and cradled his head in her palms, kissing him as deeply as she could, hoping he could read in that act what she couldn't put into words.

She ran her hands down his face, the water trailing her, down his corded neck. She gasped when she felt one of his hands playing near the back of her thighs, so close . . . so . . .

She moaned as his fingers slid deeper.

"M-m-my . . . way . . ." She leaned her head back, heard his chuckle gravel on the wet air between them.

His other hand ran up her stomach, her abdominal muscles tightening in his wake. He grazed his thumb over her breast.

With his arm around her, he all but jerked her forward.

She stared down at him. He looked up at her, through wet spiky lashes, and slowly leaned forward. She watched as he circled her breast with his tongue, then pulled the center into his mouth.

She gasped, and held his head.

She wanted to make him lose control, not her.

She shoved his head away and wiggled out of his arm. "You can put your hands on my hips, and only my hips, unless I tell you otherwise."

His grin was slow, but still she could see pain in his eyes. "And if I don't."

"It will be very bad for you, boyo."

He leaned back against the wall, his hands on her hips, and pulled her with him. She stepped up on the ledge and lowered to her knees.

His grin turned wicked.

She shook her head and slid off his lap, ran her hands down his thighs. They tightened under her fingers. She looked up at him as she ran her hands up the insides of his thighs until she cupped and fondled him.

Grinning herself, she leaned in and kissed him, licking him and finally taking him in her mouth.

He hissed, his hands holding her head.

"Rori."

She slowly licked her way back up to the tip of him, around and around, and then released him. "What? You don't like it?"

He jerked her to her feet. "Too damn much."

Shaking her head, she once again straddled him. "You know

what your problem is, Mr. Kinncaid?"

He watched her, reached between them, and those wicked fingers of his danced over her.

"No, Mrs. Kinncaid, what is my problem?"

She paused. Mrs. Kinncaid. Shaking off the stupid thrill that had shot through her, she mumbled-moaned, "You're too bleeding controlled."

He grunted.

She reached down and pulled his hand away. "My way. Or I'll get you just to the point and then go to bed."

His eyes narrowed. "You'd only do it once."

She leaned back to study him, even as she took him in her hand and slid herself slowly down on his erection. "Is that a threat?"

His eyes darkened, and his arms came up to hold her, but then he dropped them to his side. "It's a promise, babe."

She grinned. "One day when I don't want you so badly, I'll have to try it."

She closed her eyes, moving as gently on him as the water falling on them.

One day?

One day . . .

She had no idea how long they kissed, their hands running over wet skin as she made love to him in the shower, but soon, the tempo increased, his features hardening, a slight blush staining his cheeks. He reached between them and raked his fingers over that one spot that would shatter her.

"Come with me," he said, his other hand wrapping around her nape to pull her down for his kiss.

His fingers did a wicked dance, his tongue parried and forayed with hers, his thrusts hit deep within her . . . And through it all, she just wanted to hear him . . .

He groaned, thrusting again, his finger pressing her small bundle of nerves against him buried deep inside her.

She shattered, yelling out his name.

One day . . .

Chapter 21

Elianya, or rather Alla as she was calling herself, looked over the files she'd found. Mr. Dimitri Petrolov, with a dozen or more aliases, was no more than a rich boy.

His family owned high-class hotels all over the globe. She herself had stayed in several of their more exclusive resorts.

Ian Kinncaid.

What a little family man.

Four brothers, all but one married with families of their own. Two parents, still married, and a little great-grandmother in Ireland.

She grimaced. Alla simply did not work with the elderly. They terrified her with their eyes seeming to look either through you or all the way down to your soul.

Old people made her very nervous.

Alla wondered at Mr. Ian Kinncaid. What had made him leave the security of that home, that family, to become the person she knew as Dimitri Petrolov.

Did his family know he worked for his government in places the general public wanted to forget existed?

Probably not.

So how could she get to him?

She'd heard the attempt on him had failed.

Idiot. She'd thought the contact would be intelligent enough to handle this situation, but since that was not the case, Alla would handle it herself.

And have a hell of a time doing it.

So who could she get to? Any of them. She could become his mother's new best friend. Probably couldn't seduce the father. If he'd been married to the same woman that long, he might not be that easy. Then again, maybe he would. She'd keep her ideas open.

The brothers? The oldest was married to some writer and had twins. She pulled up their picture. Lovely happy little family. He might be doable. Handsome enough.

The next on her list was Gavin. A woman's doctor. She immediately nixed him. He might see through some of her lies. Then again, he might not. But a man who saw women's bodies as landmarks and made a living out of noticing deficiencies was not someone she wanted to bed.

The next . . . Brayden. Newly married as well within the last year. And what a lovely little girl he had.

Her business brain tallied what she might get for the girl on the market. Maybe that's the angle.

But then she remembered the girl had been kidnapped before with some cousin, which meant her parents probably kept a very close eye on her anyway. Maybe not. But she'd think about it.

The last brother's face flashed on-screen.

Wasn't he the changeling? He looked nothing like his other brothers, who were all black-haired and blue-eyed. This one, she checked his name — Quinlan — took after his mother. Green eyes, dark brown hair with tints of red. Handsome himself, just different from his brothers and just a bit . . . innocent-looking. She grinned. Oh, she could have fun with this one. Her source confirmed he lived in the D.C. hotel.

She still thought he was probably her best bet on getting an in with the family. He wasn't around the others much. And even if he had a guard, she didn't really look like Elianya Hellinski, with the different-colored contacts and new hair color and style.

"The things I will teach you," she muttered, tapping her long red nail on his picture on the computer screen.

She looked over at the file folder open to a photo of both Ian Kinncaid and Dimitri Petrolov. Even knowing they were the same man, they were so different, she might never have put them together.

Dimitri simply looked different to her. Harder, colder somehow. The Reaper.

Ian Kinncaid was the Saint.

She smiled. "Your time is coming, my friend."

No one rejected her, especially no man, and no one betrayed her the way he had. Taking a hit on her . . .

She shook her head and looked back at the computer screen. "Quinlan Kinncaid."

• • •

Ian sat in the chair he'd sat in years ago and looked at the man behind the desk. Jock sat, dressed in his normal chinos and a cable-knit sweater, his shoulders more stooped, his hands atop each other on the blotter, and those once leveling eyes seemed almost lost.

He shouldn't care.

But he did. Damn it.

"Is everyone all right this morning?" Jock asked.

Ian nodded and shifted, putting his ankle on his other knee.

A heavy silence thickened the air between them.

Ian sat, not saying a word and wishing he knew what to say. His skin itching, he stood and walked to the window, looking out at the back lawns. The workers had arrived already and were working on replacing windowpanes. Should keep them busy for an entire day.

The lawns were brown, dormant for the cold winter to come. The leaves that had vibrant shades of red, orange, and yellow only a month before were now a dull brown upon the ground beneath their bare-branched trees.

His mother's rosebushes were bare. He'd forgotten how she'd like to plant a new one every year.

"I've called all your brothers. Your mother wants her damn dinner tonight. Quin doesn't know if he can make it."

Ian smiled. "The workaholic wouldn't know what to do without a timetable."

Jock grunted and Ian looked over his shoulder at him.

"And you don't think family dinners are important?"

Ian closed his eyes and shook his head. "Jock, don't start."

Silence again. This time longer than before. Ian needed to call Johnno and check again to see if he'd learned anything else. He needed to get to the office and meet with Pete, there were things he needed to see to ahead of time.

A lawyer. He'd call his uncle Brody, see if he could draft up a new will. Never before did he care what happened to his stuff. He'd just left it all to Aiden.

Now?

Now he had someone to look after. Darya. And legally Rori . . . and then . . .

"Why is someone trying to kill you?" Jock broke the silence.

Ian sighed. "We've been over this, I can't talk about it." He didn't turn from the window.

"You said your cover was blown." A pause. "What cover?"

Ian finally turned from the window and walked back to sit in the chair. Steepling his fingers, he looked at his father. "Do you really want to know?" He held his father's stare. Not that he could tell him everything.

Jock stared at him, then blinked and finally shook his head. "I guess not."

Ian looked at his watch. "I don't mean to be rude, but I have meetings. Did you need something?"

Jock started to shake his head, then he tapped the top of his desk. Tilting his head, he said, "Do you remember when you were a boy?"

Where was this going? "Yeah."

A smile lifted one side of Jock's lips and a chuckle danced out. "You used to pull so many pranks I didn't know if I wanted to strangle you or if I wanted to laugh."

Ian laced his fingers over his stomach and listened, frowning.

"You were going to work side by side with Aiden. Always were since you two were little. I'd take you to the hotels with me. Your mother and I used to argue over what you'd do when you grew up. She wanted more kids in medicine. I said more hotels." Jock's smile turned nostalgic and he looked not at Ian, not at himself, but at some memory Ian couldn't see.

"You boys grew up on us. Faster than we ever imagined. Aiden went to the hotels and . . ."

Ian took a deep breath. "And I didn't." He grabbed the armrests, intent on standing.

"Sit down for a damn minute," Jock barked, his eyes their old sharp self.

Ian leaned back.

"I know you're busy. I know you haven't been back here in years, and when you do come home we don't have three words to say to each other." Jock frowned, and twirled the gold band on his finger. Taking a deep breath, he said, "I never meant . . . That is . . ." He raked his hand through his hair and stood. "Hell."

Ian waited.

"What made you come back now?" Jock asked, looking out the window Ian had vacated earlier.

Ian licked his lips and shifted. "I had to."

"Because of your job?" Jock looked at him.

Ian shook his head. "Partly. Mostly to make certain everyone was all right."

Jock nodded, looked down and ran his fingers along the windowsill. "Ryan said something the other day and I've heard him and Tori whispering."

Damn.

Those eyes pierced him to the chair. "This isn't the first time you've been back, is it?"

Ian thought about lying. He propped his elbow on the armchair and his temple on his fist. "No."

Jock nodded then shook his head, and his shoulders rose on a deep breath. His voice so quiet Ian had to lean forward to hear him, Jock said, "Did you really think I meant what I said that day?"

Ian didn't move, didn't speak. Another lie rose easily to his mind, but he shook it off. "No." He shrugged and sat up, rubbing the back of his neck. "I'd hoped not, but I wasn't about to test it."

Jock walked back and leaned against the desk. "You said some things that day that pissed me off."

Ian cocked a brow. "I remember it the other way around."

Jock crossed his arms and glanced down, then back up. "But what you said that day was right. I was wrong."

Ian blinked and stared at his father. Hell had frozen over and he'd missed it. Not because his father was wrong, but because the great Jock Kinncaid had *admitted* he was wrong. Ian took a deep breath and knew that was as close to an apology as it could get.

"None of the other boys ever knew, but your mother and I . . ." Jock shook his head and waved his hand, walking back around the desk.

"You and Mom what?" Ian asked.

"She figured out what happened and wheedled the rest out of me."

Damn. Ian stared at him, then grinned, then started to laugh. "I bet *that* was fun."

Jock didn't grin, but narrowed his gaze at him. "I don't remember it too fondly, as it's the only time in all our years of marriage she made me sleep somewhere else."

"Oh." What else did he say?

"Where'd you go when you left here?"

Ian leaned back as Jock sat in the chair beside him. "Around. I dropped the car off, checked my bank accounts, and had Aiden put anything I made from then on into stocks, since he's so good at that sort of thing."

"You never touched those accounts after one large withdrawal that first afternoon," Jock said.

Ian grinned. "Checked that, did you? Figured you would. I took out what I wanted to that first day and opened a Swiss account." He shrugged. "Between interest and work, I made enough."

"And after?"

"Joined the army. Became a Ranger."

His father pulled back a bit. "You were a Ranger?"

Ian nodded. "Yeah. For a while."

A slow smile started across his father's face. Some part of him had hoped to see it again, and another part had always said he didn't give a damn if he did or not—pride.

"And?" Jock asked, leaning closer. "I always wanted to do that. But your grandfather had no use for a soldier in the family." He waved his hand. "Things were different then. So I took the road paved for me and found your mother and the rest is history."

Ian had never known that. "You wanted to join the army?"

Jock shrugged. "I wanted to be a paratrooper like my father. Fought in World War Two. You'd have thought he wanted a son in the military. Grandfather was even against it. But to be fair to them, they'd both lost family members in both World Wars."

Ian tilted his head. "Learn something new every day."

"So you're a Ranger?" Jock asked again, shaking his head.

"Retired. Went to work for a different . . . branch," he supplied.

Jock frowned. "What does that mean?"

Ian chose his words carefully. "I do undercover work. That's all you need to know. And this is my last assignment."

"This?"

Ian waved the question away and sat up. He looked into Jock's eyes and said, "I have to go somewhere over the weekend."

"Rori and Darya going with you?"

Ian shook his head. "No."

A moment passed, then another and another. "And?"

Looking into the eyes so like his own, he said, "If I don't come back . . ."

Jock sat back, the lines of his mouth hardening, his eyes narrowing. He opened his mouth, then shut it again.

"If I don't come back, I want you to look out for Darya and Rori. They really don't have anyone else."

Which was in and of itself true enough. There was some other man, Nikko, he'd heard Rori talk of occasionally, but he didn't know who the man was, and he was looking.

A log popped in the fireplace and Ian knew he needed to go. The morning was growing.

"Where are you going?"

He really didn't think his father wanted to know that he was basically going to his death. And he couldn't explain a thing to Jock because it was all classified.

"I can't tell you."

"I guess I don't need to tell you to be careful?" Jock said ruefully.

Ian smiled. "I've been through worse."

Jock raised a brow. "It's usually the things we expect to be easy that turn out to be the hardest."

Ian frowned. "You're starting to sound like Mom."

Jock's laughter rang out and boomed off the walls. When he quieted, he asked, "If I wanted to go into town today to find something for Darya, what would it take?"

Ian shook his head. "I don't know. At least one guard. I'd really rather you wait until I had my meeting." If he left in the next few minutes, he'd be done by this afternoon with all the tests Pete would undoubtedly have all lined out for him and then be back here by dinnertime.

Jock hadn't answered him.

Ian looked from his watch to the man across from him in the other chair. "I need to get going. I am sorry this has disrupted all your lives. That wasn't my intention on coming back."

Jock nodded. "I do understand that much, even if I don't really understand what the hell is going on." Those eyes narrowed on him again. "You better be back in time for dinner, or you'll have to explain to your mom why you're not."

He nodded and stood, wondering if he should shake his father's hand or what, as Jock stood.

Ian turned away, but a hand on his shoulder stopped him. "I meant what I said earlier," Jock said.

"About?"

"Being wrong all those years ago. Brice was . . ." Jock took a deep breath.

"A liar?" Ian suggested.

Jock nodded. "Woman wasn't pregnant, or if she was it never came about."

Ian waited then said, "So you think the baby, if she had one, still could have been mine?"

Jock shook his head. "No. No, I don't. I didn't after I had a chance to calm down."

Why was it, when something was so long in coming, it was almost anticlimactic? He'd waited years to hear those words. And today, they seemed . . . not very important.

"Witch *did* abort Aiden's baby."

"Yes, I know." At his father's questioning look, Ian said, "Who do you think got him all the proof he needed? Medical records are rather sticky issues, you know."

Jock shook his head again. "Part of me wants to know every detail of your life for the last few years." Without warning, he leaned in and wrapped Ian in a hug. "And the other part of me is too damn scared to find out."

Ian stood awkwardly for a split second, then brought his arms up and wrapped them around . . .

His father.

When had the big man become so much older?

Ian took a deep breath and disengaged, smiling slightly. "I've got to go, or I'll miss dinner."

His father sniffed and nodded, his brows doing that damn V thing they did when he was trying not to cry.

Ian opened his mouth to say something, but nothing came to mind.

"Yeah, you better get going. With your mother worrying like she is, if anyone's late, they'll hear about it for weeks."

Chapter 22

Dinner was as strained as he knew it would be. Ian rubbed the back of his neck as he stood alone at the windows. Probably stupid to be standing in front of one, but he really didn't care at present. He hated debriefings with Pete. There was never enough.

More details, more info, more intel. Go over it all again and again and again.

Ian knew it was relevant, but he was just so damned tired. This weekend. This weekend was the last assignment he had.

Thank God.

His headache had been constant for two days. He just had to make it through this weekend.

Pete and the agency's team of docs had been concerned, but he told them to give him some damn pills and he'd deal with it. He could crash when it was all over. And he knew he would. Crashing was simply a side effect of what he did. He knew it and accepted it.

A cell phone chirped. Rori's new one he'd gotten her today. He glanced at her over his shoulder as she frowned and answered it.

Then a soft smile spread across those lips. Darya sat in the corner playing with a box of wooden blocks he'd decided to get her at the toy store before coming home. The glittering Barbie and accessories were opened, but sat untouched to the side. He watched as she stacked yet another block up, creating God only knew what. Other than her screams and that one time at the hotel, she still hadn't spoken again.

Pain flashed through his head.

"You okay?" his mother asked, coming up to stand beside him.

He bit down and nodded.

She frowned. "You look like you have a headache."

It felt that bad. No wonder people could see it. He took a deep breath and focused on his mother. Her green eyes were concerned and her hair was pulled back into some do. She wore brown woolen slacks and an off-white silk button-down.

"You look beautiful, Mom."

As he hoped, it distracted her. "Thank you, sweetie." She swept her hand over some imaginary spot on her shirtfront. "Did you eat enough? I noticed—"

"Yes, Mom," he interrupted. He needed a quiet place. Just him.

"Kaitie, leave the man alone," his father said.

"Nikko, luv, I've really got to go." Rori's laughter and words pulled his attention back to her. She stood over in the corner, talking softly.

His mother and father raised a brow.

Nikko.

"No," her voice sharpened. "Things are fine. Just . . ." Her gaze rose to his and locked. "Complicated." Then she shook her head. "No, Nikko, not like that. We're fine. Yes, yes, we're still looking for them." She nodded. "I need to go, Nikko. Yes, luv you as well. *Ciao!*"

Ian cocked a brow.

Johnno said, "Nikko?"

Rori's laughter was husky and deep as she flipped the phone shut. "You don't want to know, John." Her gaze rose to his. "You'd really rather be in ignorance on this one."

They walked out of the room together, John asking, "Is this the same Nikko you mentioned in passing before?"

"No, I've several men I call Nikko, luv. Doesn't everyone?"

Ian ignored that, he'd ask later. God, his head hurt.

"You let your wife call other men luv?" Jock asked him.

Ian only stared at him. "No one *lets* Rori do anything. She does whatever she wants to do."

Pain shot through his brain and he hissed. The edges of his vision were blurred.

"Ian?" someone asked.

Without a word to anyone, he walked out of the room. In the hallway, Johnno raised his brow, then frowned, said something to Rori and followed him.

Ian didn't care. He just needed to get somewhere and lie down. Chills danced over his skin.

Johnno's arm slipped around his shoulder. "That bad, is it?"

He started to bite out at his friend, but again the pain clawed inside him and all he could do was stop and take a breath, hoping he wouldn't be sick. "Fuck, Johnno."

"I know. Let's get you to bed."

Ian could feel his vision wavering. "Bad," he mumbled.

Johnno slung Ian's arm over his own shoulder.

"Well, this ought to give all the family something else to talk about."

Ian tried to smile. "They're currently wondering about Nikko."

"Aren't you?"

"Right now, I don't care."

"Yes, well, hopefully you'll still feel that way later."

He should probably try and figure out what the hell that statement meant, but God's truth. "I hate these."

"I know."

They were at Ian and Rori's room. Johnno paused to open the door.

"I'll get it," a new voice said. Gavin. Damn.

The room was thankfully dark.

Someone grabbed his wrist and Ian flung them off.

"You really don't want to be touching him, Gavin," John said.

"He's my brother."

"That may be—"

God, why the hell wouldn't they shut up?

He all but fell on the bed.

"Did you take anything?" Gavin asked.

Ian might have laughed if he'd had the energy or felt like it, but instead he didn't. He just wished for quiet oblivion.

He started to push himself up and grab the pill bottle he'd tossed on the dresser from Pete's doctor. But he hated pills.

"Stay the bloody hell there," Johnno's voice bounced off his eardrums. "This the bottle here on the dresser?"

He didn't even want to nod, just mumbled a yes.

Closing his eyes, he hoped this wasn't a trek into the dark realm, as he called it. A migraine was one thing. Even a prolonged migraine. A trek into the dark side wasn't what he liked to experience. It was soul draining. It was judgment on past crimes and punishment paid in pain. He called those times simply the Attacks.

Ian wasn't in the mood, even for his friend. He just wanted everyone out. Silence.

Rori looked at the man on the bed. She knew what he felt. The headaches that reached up and knifed through the skull so that all you wanted was to be left the hell alone.

She watched as Johnno gave him a glass of water and two white pills. Be lucky if he bloody kept it down and wasn't sick off of it.

He leaned up and took a drink, swallowing the meds and laying back on the bed. His brother reached again for his wrist and Ian muttered, "Leave me the hell alone, Gav. You can't fucking fix this."

Gavin cocked a brow and grabbed his brother's wrist anyway. "Be that as it may, you can either deal with me or you know Mom will be up here taking your vitals. So lay back and shut up."

"Paybacks are hell," Ian muttered, flinging his other arm up over his eyes. "My pulse is one thing, you try to look at my pupils and I'm liable to put a fucking bullet in you."

Gavin chuckled.

Johnno shook his head. "I don't know that he's joking."

"You get these migraines a lot?" Gavin asked, straightening. "How bad is it?"

"Ever been stabbed in the brain?"

Gavin's lips twitched. "No, and I'll warrant neither have you, lest you wouldn't be here."

Rori went to the bathroom and wet a washcloth. Coming back to the bed, she said, "I've always likened them to some medieval torture of hot pokers in my bloody brain."

Ian groaned. "Thank you, love."

She gently laid the cloth on his forehead. "You need anything?" she whispered.

"For everyone to get the hell out. And leave me alone. Yeah."

She asked John, "Has he always been such a compliant patient?"

"Rori," Ian warned.

"Let's go," John said, taking Gavin's arm. Gavin looked as if he wanted to ask more questions. She half-assed expected him to pull a stethoscope out at any minute.

Luckily John pulled him out of the room. At the doorway, John stopped and looked at her. He nodded to her and she mouthed "Darya." He nodded and left, closing the door softly behind him.

She didn't move. The silence became comfortable. Ian didn't move. She almost wondered if he was breathing.

"You get these too?" he asked, his voice low and gruff.

She started to reach out and run her fingers through his hair, but decided against it, as she didn't like anyone to touch her when her headaches were raging.

"Upon occasion."

"With analogies of hot pokers, I don't have to ask if they're bad."

Again, they lapsed into silence. She scooted up onto the bed, sitting beside his head. He lifted it and shifted so he lay on her lap.

"Our lives are screwed, Rori."

She chuckled and gently grazed her nails along the back of his neck. "Does that hurt?"

With his eyes still closed, he said, "No."

Barely touching him, she hoped she relieved some of his pain.

"You should be downstairs with Darya," he mumbled.

"She's fine. Safe and playing with the blocks you brought back for her. She noticed when you left and Jock went and sat on the floor with her, telling her he'd build her a house."

Ian still didn't open his eyes, just grunted. "Damn," he whispered.

His face taut with pain, the lines around his mouth deeper, harsher, the lines around his eyes more pronounced. The skin more pale than she was used to seeing on him. Black lashes lay in short spiky crescents against his skin. She lightly traced the crooked line of his nose, the outline of his M-ed hairline.

He was right, their lives were messed up.

"Who's Nikko?" he whispered.

Never opened his eyes. She'd hoped he'd been almost asleep. Instead of answering him she put her hand on his chest and leaned back against the headboard.

His other hand came up and laced with hers. "Nikko?" he pressed.

Rori shook her head. "What you are to Darya," she said, choosing her words. "That's what he is to me."

He opened his eyes, and she could see the pain clouding the blue irises and narrowing his lids. "I'd like to meet him then."

She grinned. "Oh, you will."

"Sounds like he's not very happy with me."

She chuckled again. "He's not. He's thinking of killing you. I had to explain you're just a job." Once the words were out of her mouth, she wished she could take them back.

His eyes bore into hers with an intensity she wanted to ignore and meet straight on.

"Just a job?" he asked quietly.

She leaned further over and gently kissed his lips, the edges almost white with pain. "Well, it was either that or tell him we were lovers."

That wicked grin of his was starting to mean way too much to her. "There is that."

Again she kissed him, just her lips brushing his, and then sat back. "He asked about Darya."

"Why?" he asked, frowning.

She shook her head. "I don't know. Because I'm involved. Because it's so bloody close to my own story, I don't know."

"What is your story?" he asked.

She took a deep breath, the snakes slithering through her gut. She looked at him and ran her fingers over his hair, barely touching. "You certainly are chatty for one who's in pain."

For one long moment, he stared at her, and for whatever reason, she actually thought about telling him. But why? It was none of his concern. None of his . . .

He closed his eyes, his fingers tightening on hers. "You know a husband really should know his wife."

She shook her head and ignored him. She watched the ceiling fan, studied the artwork on the walls. Rather impressive actually. They were probably just prints of van Gough and Mary Cassatt, but then with the Kinncaids, these could just as easily be some originals. She'd rather not find out.

She looked around. Just as she'd first thought. Someone could nick some really nice things from this house alone if someone were so inclined. She wasn't. She couldn't have cared less about such things. Just because people had nice things, the best of whatever . . . did not make them worthy of any respect in her book.

Actions, the people themselves made the impression on her, good or bad. Not what they owned or where they came from.

"So when will I meet him?" he asked, breaking the silence.

"You should rest," she whispered.

"I can't until you answer my questions." His eyes were again closed, his face pulled tight, but still she caught the edge of humor in his words.

She sighed. "Fine. Nikko is Nikko. He raised me."

"Where'd he get you from?" Ian whispered, not looking at her.

She remembered the fear, the blood, the man holding his head screaming at her as he hit her again and again.

She shook the thought off. Ian opened his eyes. "Who hurt you?"

She took a deep breath. "I don't know who my parents are. All I know is someone left me at an orphanage late one night. I was about one, they think." She shrugged and looked at his hair. "I was put in a foster home with these truly lovely people. The Rittlebaums. He worked at Cambridge as a mythology professor." She'd almost forgotten that. The way the man, with his whiskery beard, would come in and tell her good-night stories, bringing to life the story of Odysseus, and Agamemnon, Viking stories of angry gods punishing the hero. Someone was always being punished, tested. Always the hero, to make him stronger, bring him down and make him more thankful.

"You liked him," Ian said. "So what happened?"

On another deep breath, she figured to bloody hell with it. Just tell him. She'd told others. No different than when they asked in her psych evaluations. "He died coming home one day. Car accident on the icy roads."

A furrow appeared between his brows. "Sorry."

She smiled. "I am too. He was a sweet, kind man. Mrs. Rittlebaum's life was her home. She didn't have a job and suddenly there wasn't an income. They took us away."

"Us?"

"Oh. Yes, there were two others then." She frowned. "Both older, both boys."

"What happened to them?"

"I don't know, never really thought about it."

"Yes, you did."

Just like that. He knew.

"At first. I was seven when we were put back in foster care and they were the only siblings I'd ever known for the last four years." If she allowed herself she could still feel that fear, that horrible stomach-greasing fear of wanting her brothers and not knowing where they were. Hoping she'd see them at this next family and then the next . . . until the weeks went by and then the months. And never finding them. Then she had simply forgotten them altogether.

"So where does Nikko come in?"

"Not all homes are as secure as the Rittlebaums', or as safe as this one."

His eyes studied hers. "Who hurt you?"

She shook her head. "It was just me with them. I don't know how those people were able to take children into their home. She worked two shifts, he worked at the factory, and at first everything was fine, just different."

His thumb stroked the back of her hand. "Then his shift changed and he was home when I got in from school, then it changed again and he was home at nights while she worked."

His chest rose on an inhale, and just for a moment his thumb paused.

"We lived in this complex, paper-thin walls, people crying, parents screaming." She hated remembering that place. "I'd seen Nikko in the hallway a few times, this silent, dark-haired, olive-skinned man who called me Cara. I thought he didn't know my name, but it turns out he knew it, he's Italian and that was just his nickname for me." She grinned, remembering. "The people I was with told me to stay away from him and I got in trouble several times for not listening." She didn't want to go into the details and didn't need to with Ian.

"I still, after all this time, wonder how they were approved to sponsor and care for a child. He started abusing me on the nights his wife worked. One night I tried to hide in the coat closet. Which was a rather stupid thing to do. I don't know why I thought he wouldn't be able to find me." She slowed, the past like smoke, swirling through her brain, out and around. "I still remember that terror that doesn't let you think straight," she said, looking at the wall. "I could hear him slamming doors yelling for me. And I just kept thinking no more. There was a weight on the floor and I picked it up. When he grabbed me and dragged me out, I hit him with it."

Ian's hand ran up her arm. "Good for you, babe."

She shook her head. "Not so good. I wasn't very strong. Didn't do more than bust his head open. He was bloody furious. Started hitting me. I guess I was screaming, I don't remember." She frowned, trying to see it. "Nikko said I was, which was why he broke in. I just remember that suddenly Nikko was there. Just there telling me to come with him." She took a deep breath and let it slowly out. Looking down into Ian's eyes, she said, "I did. Went with him and never looked back. Was terrified he'd either turn on me or he'd leave me somewhere, but he didn't."

Ian's smile was tender. No pity, no horror. Just . . . understanding. Then he blinked and she saw it through the pain. Rage.

"Did Nikko kill him?"

"You would ask that."

"Did he?"

"Why?"

His eyes bore into hers.

She laughed. "I never asked . . ."

"Do."

"No."

"Why not?"

Choosing her words carefully, she said, "Nikko taught me everything I know. Everything."

He frowned. "Nikko." His voice was low, thoughtful.

"Leave it alone. Please, for me."

He closed his eyes. "Do you think I care what he taught you? Or who he really might be? One, he saved you. That's all that matters to me. Two, I'm the last man to point fingers at how a man chooses to live."

True.

"What were their names?"

"Who?"

"Your brothers."

She leaned over. "Go to sleep."

"What was the foster family's name."

"Go to sleep," she repeated

For a moment, he looked like he wanted to ask her more, press her for details, but then he sighed, barely shook his head and squeezed her hand. "You'll check on Darya?"

She shook her head. "Yes, after you go to sleep."

Chapter 23

Quinlan Kinncaid wove through the tables in the restaurant. There had been a slight problem earlier and he'd been notified. Nothing major, just a returning guest who demanded a table that was already taken. Their normal maitre d' was off tonight due to a family crisis and the replacement wasn't nearly as efficient. Quinlan stepped in to smooth things over.

He checked his watch. The dinner at home was probably over. Not that his brothers cared if he made it or not. Mom was pissed at him, and since she was, so was Dad. Quinlan had more important things to do than sit at a dinner table when he could just as easily eat here.

Aiden believed he needed to delegate more. Middlemen often screwed things.

"Evening, Mr. K.," one of the waiters — Harold — said.

"Evening, Harold. Thanks for pulling a double shift tonight."

Harold smiled. "No problem, Mr. K. I can use the money."

Quinlan nodded and moved on. Everything seemed to be going fine. At the bar, he decided he wanted a glass of water. As he waited, he thought of what he needed to get out of the way the next morning. Aiden was going to meet with the historical interior society or some such for the castle restoration via webcam at eight. Quinlan was meeting with their head of marketing to figure out how to get more people to shop in their boutiques in certain locations. Many of their in-hotel shops were incredibly successful and others would, under any other circumstances, be on the verge of bankruptcy.

He wanted all the shops to be trading at full capacity. Personally, he thought each shop needed more local specialization versus the normal generic —

"Hello," a woman's voice interrupted his thoughts.

He shook his head and looked at her. Beautiful, truth be known. Raven black hair was pulled back in a sleek yet sexy chignon at the back of her head. Her brows were perfectly arched, her makeup flawless over a perfect face — high broad cheekbones, a straight nose, full lush lips and eyes . . .

Startling deep green eyes that reminded him of a cat they'd had out at Seneca once upon a time. This woman's eyes were slanted just like that, a lazy appreciation framed by full lashes.

She smiled, slowly. "What's good here?"

"Here's your water, Mr. Kinncaid," the bartender said, setting the clear glass on the bar, the ice cubes tinkling.

"Thank you," he said absently, and focused back on the woman.

He took a deep breath and the smell of something floral and . . . something else floated on the air. Not cloying, not light, but subtle all the same.

Quinlan motioned to the bartender, yet never took his eyes off the woman at the bar. She wore a black pinstriped pantsuit, and from what he could see of her ample cleavage, he had to assume she didn't have a shirt on underneath. Which didn't bother him in the least.

Raising his gaze back to her eyes, he saw the smirk on her perfectly painted lips.

"What would you like to drink?"

Her brow rose. "Are you buying?" she asked, her voice husky and, he realized, European. German, Eastern Europe, Russian maybe. Her English was cultured, but still accented.

"Consider this drink and any others this evening on the house."

Her brow wrinkled as both brows rose. "Mr. Kinncaid? As in the owners of the hotel?"

And he could see the greed in her eyes. But he really didn't care either.

He tilted his head toward her, picked up his glass and drank.

Her bottom lip pouted out. "I can't very well enjoy a drink if all you're having is water."

He looked at his glass. He rarely drank, didn't like the fuzzy non-controlled feeling he always had when he drank. One drink usually relaxed him and two gave him a buzz. He smiled. "Coffee's more my poison."

"What a shame. Not even a glass of wine with me? Owner or not, I'll treat you to a dinner here. Or we could go out? D.C. has some lovely restaurants, I'm told."

"Our Heather's is rather well known," he offered, then set his water down and offered her his arm. "Shall I show you to a table?"

She smiled and slid off the bar stool, putting her hand on his arm. "What's your recommendation?"

He thought about it for a minute. To hell with it. He'd order them some wine. He leaned back over the bar and told the bartender to send a bottle of Gevrey-Chambertin Fonteny over to his table.

"Anything here is good."

"But you've already ordered the wine."

He grinned. "Yes, I did."

Minutes later they had both ordered and were talking of favorite places in Europe.

He realized he'd been too long without a woman when he started to imagine her with her jacket unbuttoned. Shaking his head, he asked her another question.

He knew women, watched them more than interacted with them. He wasn't like his brothers. He didn't charm to simply charm. He wasn't made that way.

"You're not the chattiest person, are you?" she asked, sipping her wine, her eyes narrowing slightly.

He shrugged. "Not everyone has something to say."

She smiled, and those lips made him think of . . . he shook his head.

"True enough, Mr. Kinncaid."

"Call me Quinlan," he said, sipping his own drink.

Her smile grew. He realized then he didn't know her name. "Then you must call me Alla."

Alla. Unusual. "What nationality is that?"

For a moment, she squinted, then said, "I've no idea, whatever my parents were studying at the time, I'm sure. They died when I was young. Professors of literature and humanities at the University in Munich."

"I'm sorry."

She took another drink, tilting her head. "Not your fault." She leaned up, her elbows on the table, her arms crossed, her breasts all but spilling from the V of her jacket.

"Can I ask you something, Mr. Quinlan Kinncaid?"

Her voice made him think of long, hot sultry nights of lovemaking.

"Depends."

She leaned even further over, and he couldn't miss her signals, unless he was blind or dead, and he was neither. Still, he only took a sip of wine, saw the guard look into the dining room again.

His mind shifted from the Helen across from him to the dark-haired man, who looked as much like a computer geek as Ian did. Gar. That was it. What kind of name was Gar? Details like that mattered. Was it an old family name? A nickname? In any case, Gar had Hollywood looks, an almost effeminate face, and he was built like a boxer. But his best quality, as far as Quinlan was concerned, was the fact he could crunch numbers, remember details with photographic detail, and still have humor to joke. He was a whiz with the computer and liked to hum Beatles tunes.

"Problem?" she asked, jerking him back to the present.

He shook his head. "No. No problem, I was just trying to figure something out."

She grinned and ran a finger, her nail long and a dark bloodred, down his tie. "What's our question?" A waiter dropped dishes, thankfully back in the galley and not in the dining room. Wiping his mouth, he said to his companion, "Please excuse me for a moment."

He walked away and wondered how he could go about getting the woman at his table into his bed.

• • •

She watched Mr. Quinlan Kinncaid walk toward the swinging doors. He was cute. And it had been a long damn time since she'd thought any man as cute. There was a seriousness about him she respected, she realized, but there was also an innocence. One she would use against him.

Leaning over, she pulled the vial from her pocket and shook out some of the powder.

She'd learned he didn't drink much, she knew he didn't do drugs.

It was in the control he had. Like herself. If one used chemicals of any kind, that was handing control over, and she'd never been one to do that. She could almost feel sorry for him.

She sighed, the smell of grilled meats and fish heavy on the air mixing with garlic, herbs, and hot breads. Her stomach grumbled.

She reached across and took a sip of his wine, which of course tasted exactly like hers. Under the guise of refilling his glass, she put the pinch of powder into his glass, added more wine, and then set it at his plate, just as he returned.

She licked her lips. "Thought I'd see if yours tasted differently."

He raised a brow and sat back down.

She wondered how quickly the drug would start to work.

She thought about being straightforward. Would he rather have a long flirtation? She really didn't have the time. Deciding to take a chance, she leaned forward and said, "I must be honest with you."

"What?" He set the wineglass down.

She leaned closer. "I want to go upstairs and see if you're as good as I keep thinking you will be."

A wicked smile peeked at the corner of his mouth. "Funny."

"What?"

"I was just thinking the same thing."

She ran a nail down his arm. "Do you have someplace to be tonight?"

This time he did smile. "Not anymore."

This was too simple.

She grinned.

He motioned to the waiter he'd talked to earlier. "Send our dishes up to my room in an hour."

He blinked, shook his head and stood.

She put her arm around his waist. "I'm going to show you things . . ." she whispered.

"Might show you a thing or two as well."

He was taller than she and built like his brother. She could feel the strength of his muscles through his jacket.

She saw a man walk up to them. The same man Quinlan was watching earlier.

His guard. Alla smiled slyly at him and knew he couldn't recognize her. She leaned into Quinlan, who started to stumble.

"Mr. Kinncaid?" the man asked.

He waved him away, looked at her and said to the guard, "Gar. Leave me the hell alone. You're not going to be present for tonight's activities."

With that, they walked out of Heather's and into the entryway. He took a plastic card out of his pocket, slid it into a security slot, and part of the black mirrored walls slid aside to reveal the private elevator behind it.

Stepping inside, he pulled her against his side and kissed her. Hard.

She laughed and ran her hands over him.

At least tonight's fuck would be enjoyable.

He stumbled again and said, "Damn."

She hoped she hadn't given him too much. Looking into his pupils, she shook her head and knew she hadn't.

When the doors pinged open, he kissed her and led her down the hall to another door. Once inside, he plastered her to the wall. For the first time in longer than she could remember, the man actually made her forget where she was. She enjoyed the feel of his mouth on hers, his hands on her, quickly undressing her. The way her blood began to hum . . . the way she wanted . . .

For a while she lost herself in the simple act of what they were doing, but then, as it always happened, she felt herself growing colder until she almost felt like a person outside herself. Watching, waiting . . .

She fisted her hands in his hair and said against his mouth, "Where's the bedroom."

• • •

Quinlan came to, a freight train screaming in his brain.

He didn't even open his eyes. He remembered the woman with the sleek hair, the dark green eyes, the body . . .

God, her body was a well-honed piece of art. Toned and muscular without being overly athletic. And her thighs . . .

He rolled over and winced.

The bed was empty.

He pushed himself up on his elbows and blinked.

This was why he never drank more than a glass of wine. He hated, hated feeling this way. He couldn't think and fog clouded out memories.

And he had no control over any of it.

He flopped back down and moaned again into the pillow. Shit.

Looking at the window, he saw it was still dark out. What the hell time was it? He tried to focus on the clock.

He remembered drinking two glasses of wine. It had been only two, hadn't it? He squinted and noticed it was almost six a.m. No, that couldn't be right. He checked his watch.

Shit.

Tossing the sheet back, he stood and reeled. God almighty. The freight train slammed into the sides of his skull. Putting a hand to his head, he sat back down. He was naked. The rug on the floor was littered with several condoms, their ripped foil packaging, and an empty bottle of champagne. Thank God. At least he'd had the sense to use protection. So much for only two glasses. He remembered now sharing the bottle of expensive bubbly with her, drinking it slowly off each other's bodies . . .

Who the hell was she? Alla. Just Alla.

Perfection and . . . controlling. Her husky laugh floated through his memory and disjointed bits of other thoughts.

Her riding him as he thrust into her, her head thrown back, her mouth smiling, her ample, tight breasts overflowing in his hands. Implants, but he hadn't cared.

Something was off. Way the hell off.

Her eyes. It had been her eyes.

One memory slashed through the others. Of her leaning over him, her lips void of any smile and her eyes cold and hard.

He tried to think, to remember more.

A phone, she'd had a phone in her hand and her words . . . he remembered they'd been garbled, as if she talked underwater.

Quinlan rubbed his hands over his face. He didn't have time for this now. He hadn't eaten and must have had more than he thought.

That was the *last* time he ever did that. He stumbled to the bathroom and didn't even bother to turn the light on. He reached into the shower stall and cranked the water at full blast.

Holy hell. Light or aspirin?

Pain pulsed in his head. Forget it, he'd figure it out later.

Hot water from the shower beat down on him until he felt sufficiently clean and couldn't smell Alla on him anymore.

Regardless of what he could and couldn't remember, he did know he hadn't had that good a lay in a long, *long* damn time. Maybe if he saw her again this week, he would just make certain they didn't have any alcohol. Woman made him forget his own head.

Just for punishment's sake — and the fact he really needed to get his brain to working — he cut off the hot water and stood under the icy spray. With a shiver, he stepped out of the dark shower and reached to the right, grabbing the thick terry robe. He pulled it on and grabbed a towel.

Time to start the day. He had progress reports to get up and a meeting with Aiden before eight. Marketing representatives to confer with.

And all he wanted to do was crawl back into bed. The last time he felt like this, or rather remotely like this, was last year when Christian had been hurt. He'd come back here after they knew she'd be fine and he'd gotten roaring drunk on a bottle of their best Scotch. Well, it hadn't been the whole bottle, just several shots.

Yeah, he'd felt this crappy then.

He walked into his room, opened his closet and removed a suit. That elusive and arousing scent of floral and something that tightened his gut, pulled on his lust, wafted in the room.

Damn. He'd have to make certain housekeeping did a complete sweep of the place.

Dressed in his normal attire of a dark suit, a dark green shirt and a black tie, he walked out the door and into the lighted living room. He squinted.

Gar sat at the kitchen table, his fingers clicking softly on his laptop. He looked up and raised a brow, muttered something under his breath.

Quinlan smelled coffee. "Thank God."

Filling a cup, he opened the top cabinet door beside the sink and took out his bottle of ibuprofen. Shaking out two pills, he tossed them back with the coffee, scalding his mouth and his esophagus.

"Must have been some woman," Gar commented. "She left about three."

Quinlan squinted at the tiled walls and turned to the man at his table. He looked like the normal computer geek, with the exception of his gun. That tended to bring things back.

"Yeah, well, not kissing and telling and all that." He frowned. "You been up all night?"

Gar continued working on the laptop. "Yes, well, someone had to look out for you." Those eyes cleared of whatever they saw on-screen and focused on him, hard. In that perfectly British voice that both John and Ian's wife, Rori, had, Gar said, "Regardless of common belief, killers are not limited to the male species."

"And since you've read everything on our family, I'm sure you know I'm aware of that fact."

Gar didn't say anything for a long minute. "What was her name?"

He didn't need this. Slamming his cup down, he grabbed his suit jacket and slipped it on. "Regardless of what my brother thinks, I don't answer to him."

Gar stood and slipped on his jacket, covering the gun. "No, but I do." His eyes met Quinlan's. "And I can tell you with certainty that I don't want to be on his shit list."

For some reason Gar, with his precise syllables, saying "shit list" pulled a grin from Quinlan.

Without another word, he walked out of his apartment, already thinking of the day ahead and wishing his headache away.

Who had the woman been?

Chapter 24

November 17, 6:22 a.m.

Alla put her espresso cup down and dialed on her cell phone. The little café near the Potomac was open at this hour. She'd left the Highland Hotel early this morning and took a cab to her actual hotel not far away.

"What?" the voice on the other end answered.

Alla sighed. "That's no way to greet a business partner."

The voice lowered. "Now isn't a good time."

"Too bad." Since her current business wasn't going as smoothly as it used to and she'd lost a huge profit over the last few weeks, she'd come up with another plan. Granted, her shipment of girls from Miami paid nicely, but she was used to more. "I want four million dollars transferred to a Swiss account. I'll let you know the account number later—"

"What the hell are you talking about?" the voice whispered.

"You heard me."

"I am *not* paying you four million in anything."

She laughed. "Oh, yes, my dear, you most certainly will."

"Just what makes you think that?"

Alla tapped her finger on the tabletop. "You don't want anyone to know your little secret, for one. What would people think? You don't want anyone to know we were lovers."

"But—"

"Two, you don't want anyone to know you sold confidential information to those who knew they could contact you and pay enough." Alla glanced around, noting it was safe to continue.

"I don't have—"

"Yes, you do. And if you didn't manage your money for any unseen eventuality, that really isn't my problem."

The contact took a shuddering breath. "But . . . I thought . . . I . . ."

Alla laughed. "You thought what? That just because we had some fun together that meant something. You have much to learn."

"This isn't my first game," the voice snapped. Silence from the other end. "I don't think I can."

She took a deep breath. "Then that's too bad. You didn't handle the problem two nights ago, and have brought even more attention to Mr. Kinncaid than either of us need. It's my turn and my way. Four million. Be ready for a transaction when I call you back in two days."

"But—"

"You disappoint me and your husband will find just exactly who the traitor is. The fact you married him for the sole purpose of selling confidential information should make him really happy."

With that Alla snapped her phone shut, laid it down next to her espresso and picked up the cup, sipping.

Today was looking brighter and brighter. And in several more she'd end the Kinncaid issue.

• • •

Ian Kinncaid cut through the water of the indoor pool. It was cold out this morning, and the water was warm, freeing against his skin. He reached the end of the pool and turned to swim another lap. He'd been swimming for about half an hour and knew he needed to swim another twenty minutes at the very least. He'd been lax lately in his workouts. Workouts kept him fit, on his toes, his muscles ready.

He turned his head, took a deep chlorinated breath and continued to swim, stroke after stroke.

The headache was gone and he sincerely hoped the swim would shove away any of the lingering heaviness he often experienced after those fucking migraines. He hated them. He knew they were a side effect of what he did. The psychologists on staff for Pete had run tests and confirmed what he already knew. Men who killed other men as part of their jobs had to, at some point in time, come to terms with what they did. And if they continued in a vein of denial, their psyche often reacted in various ways. Panic attacks, excruciating headaches, insomnia, some guys had delusions. Thank God he hadn't gone that far. At that point, he'd just tell John to shoot him.

All part of the job.

He didn't currently have time to "deal," as the doctor had warned him yesterday. The shrink had wanted him to take leave. Pete had backed him up, and he'd listened to his boss and the doctor argue for a good five minutes, until he'd finally just stood up and walked out.

Stroke after stroke. The water caressed him, washed away the remnants of nightmares, of terrors he didn't want or need to contemplate right now.

When it was all over. This weekend. Next week. Elianya.

The muscles in his shoulders and neck tightened.

He pushed off the side of the pool even harder and swam faster.

When he took another breath, he saw his father standing at the edge of the pool. Ian had no desire to talk to him. Keeping his rhythm, he kept swimming. Images flashed in his brain, and he tried to turn them off.

Black, white. Flash. People screaming, fires burning. Flash. Girls crying. Women dying. Flash.

Ian swam faster, faster and harder. The water would wash it away.

It had to.

Stroke, stroke, stroke.

• • •

Jock watched the boy cut through the water like a torpedo. Swimming as if the demons of hell were after him. He'd seen the shadows in his son's eyes, wondered and hadn't asked.

He'd heard Ryan and Tori talking. Knew Ian was the man who saved them. And something about him, something tickled the back of Jock's memory about the time when they'd had guards for Christian.

Had he been here then too?

And then it flashed. The bald man who'd grabbed Brayden as the congressman fell, his bloody hand locked on Brayden's shirt. The bald man who'd jerked Brayden back from falling as well. The bald man who'd shot the dangerous congressman as easily as if the gun was simply part of his hand.

The entire scene replayed in his mind.

Ryan worshiped him, thought of his Uncle Ian as some superhero. Had Ian taken care of Nina Fisher as well?

Jock frowned, wishing to hell he'd never latched on to the thoughts. They wormed their way into his brain and wouldn't leave.

What price did his son pay to keep them all safe from the shadows? And was Jock to blame for driving that boy to this point?

Last night Ian had appeared haunted, haggard. The boy wasn't but thirty-six and last night he could have passed for one of Jock's retired golfing buddies.

For a second, he thought about waiting until Ian was done and talking to his son. But he sensed Ian didn't want to talk. If he had, he would have stopped swimming and talked. Plain and simple.

Jock, towel in hand, walked out of the conservatory, the glass windows fogged from the heated pool and hidden behind masses of greenery. Shutting the door behind him, he took a deep breath, felt tears sting his eyes. Looking up, he prayed, "God, don't hold against him the sins I led him to. You know he's got a good heart." All this time, Jock had been angry, hurt, betrayed and wishing for his son, and Ian had been protecting them at a cost Jock didn't want to contemplate. What kind of father did that make him?

Swallowing, sniffing hard, he took another deep breath. He was tired. Maybe he'd go back upstairs.

In the hallway, he stopped outside of Darya's room. The sound of her giggles had him pushing the door open a bit more.

She stood in her swimsuit, Rori behind her in a robe, smiling.

They made a lovely family. Jock sensed things were still very new between them all and he longed, hoped with an intensity that his son found some peace in this woman and child.

Darya's grin grew and she skipped around.

Rori turned and met his eyes. "Are you going swimming as well, then?"

He shook his head. "No. But I know Ian's down there swimming a marathon."

A faint pull of brows marred her smooth forehead. He looked and really saw her. Tall and willowy, her skin bronzed, her eyes light, she was beautiful — exotic — and somehow he knew, perfect for Ian.

"What?" she asked. "Did I grow another head while I slept?"

"No, I was just thinking how lucky Ian is. You're beautiful, intelligent, and something tells me a perfect match for . . ." He shook his head. No, he wouldn't say matches. What did he know of spouses for his children. "I can easily see why my son married you, Rori."

For a moment she stared at him, then smiled, her cheeks dimpling. "Careful, Mr. Kinncaid, you'll ruin my image of you."

"You and Jesslyn," he muttered. "Call me Jock, for God's sake."

He turned to go, then turned back. Motioning to Darya, he said, "There are some kids' pool toys in the closet next to the table down there."

Her smile still in place, she nodded again, and grabbed a towel.

He turned and walked back to his room.

Ian might have only shown up to make certain they were all safe and well, but he'd come home. And five days later he was still here. Maybe, just maybe, they would stay.

Once in his room, Kaitie, sitting in bed, took one look at him and asked, "What?"

"I want all our kids and grandkids close."

Her laughter always managed to loosen the bands in his chest and calm him. "Jock, our children love us, but you've got to understand, they have their own lives."

He took off his robe and looked at her in her low-cut emerald gown. Crawling up onto the bed, he kissed her, pushing her back down. "Kaitie lass, don't pull that with me when I know you feel the same way."

Her grin was the same it had been since the day he'd met her, part sheepish, part seductive.

"Well . . ." She kissed him. "One of us has to think rationally."

He grinned, and whispered what he wanted to do. Her laughter rubbed the silk of her gown against him, and he decided to show her.

• • •

Darya skipped alongside Rori as they walked down the hallway. The carpet tickled her feet. A door opened and the other little girl came out, dressed to go somewhere. She said something to them and then raced down the hallway and stairs.

Darya looked up at Rori and wondered where the other girl was going.

She knew they were going swimming. She'd gone yesterday and seen the pool, and the other nice lady had given her this pretty suit. It was purple and had sparkles on it.

Down the stairs, to the back of the house, past the hallway that lead to the kitchen. She sniffed. Waffles. She loved waffles, and she even got them with strawberries here and lots of whipped cream.

They were going swimming. She knew how to swim. A fogged memory of her jumping to Papa in the water floated unattached through her.

She shook it off and hurried Rori along, pulling on her hand.

Rori shook her head, smiling, and said something, ". . . down."

Down? She thought of that word, tried to whisper it . . . d. duh. Duh-own. The door to the pool room was ahead.

She ran and tried to reach it.

Rori laughed and reached for her hand, but she darted free and ran across the tiles and jumped into the pool.

As the water closed over her head, she heard a yell.

• • •

Ian jerked his head up at the holler and saw a flash go into the pool.

Darya!

He took off across the pool. God.

His heart slammed in his chest. Rori dove into the pool.

Where the hell was she?

A dark head, slick as a seal, popped up right in front of him just as he reached her, and her grinning face met his. Water dripped off her nose.

A delighted laughter chimed out of her and bounced around the confined area.

His heart still slamming against his ribs, he grabbed her to him. "You can swim."

Rori broke the surface. "Ian!"

"I've got her."

Darya leaned back and wiggled out of his arms. He let her go, cautiously, and watched her swim to the side, dip under and flip. She popped up giggling.

The sight eased everything inside him.

Rori swam up to him. "She can bloody swim. That would have been nice to know before I died of a heart attack."

Smiling, he pulled her to him and kissed her, keeping one eye on Darya pulling herself out, only to turn back around and jump back into the water.

"Damn, I panicked," Rori muttered, shoving against him. "I never panic."

Laughing, he pulled her with him, wiping water out of his face. "Kids apparently are a different ball game."

"Wouldn't know."

He thought of what she'd told him last night. The fact she'd stayed with him. "I thought you'd be tired and still asleep."

She stood waist-deep in water, the one-piece swimsuit molding her like a leopard-print glove. His gut tightened and he stepped toward her.

She backed up. "No."

He grinned. "Where's your sense of adventure?"

"I left mine upstairs," she said, shoving water at him. "Which is precisely where you should have left yours."

He laughed, grabbed her wrists and jerked her to him. "I never leave my *sense of adventure* anywhere."

She wrapped her arms around him as they stood in the center of the pool. "Well, it better currently be left at *one* location."

"Jealous? That just warms my heart to hear you say."

Her eyes narrowed. "Why does your family have two pools?"

Trying to change the subject . . .

"Probably because one can't swim outside in the winter and they wanted an indoor pool bigger than the one outside. I have no idea. Don't care."

She shook her head and he reached up, running his hand over the short hair. "Your hair is shorter than mine. And it is just so bloody sexy."

Her eyes narrowed and then cleared.

Darya yelled to him. "Ian!"

He jerked around at the sound of his name from the child at the side. Slightly disjointed, not a smooth sound, but precious all the same.

"G'blimey, she speaks." Rori let go of him and he swam out deeper, standing in front of Darya, who stood on the side.

She grinned and he realized he hadn't ever seen her this happy. This total child exuberance over something as simple as jumping in the water. He wanted to see this excitement, this pleasure in her all the time.

She leaned down, bent her knees, and touched the pool edge on either side of her toes. Then she pushed off and dove cleanly into the water, swam to him, and popped up giggling again.

"Maybe I should put her in swimming and diving lessons," he thought aloud.

"Next you know," Rori said, from her perch on the side of the pool, her thighs wet from the water, "she'll be in ballet lessons or some such."

He shook his head and met Rori's gaze. "I was thinking more karate."

"Thank God. Ballet is beyond me." Then she shook her head. "I think tae kwon do would be better."

He looked at Darya smiling up at him and nodded. "You may be right. We could start teaching her now."

Rori nodded then frowned.

God, they sounded like . . .

Rori smiled, stood and dove in.

Ian shook his head and focused on Darya. He tossed her high and caught her, her giggles belly deep and heartening, even as they were alien to his ears. But he didn't care. He wanted to hear them again and again.

Ian held Darya in his arms as they swam in the indoor pool. He held her under her arms and swung her through the water in a circle around him, water spraying Rori, who splashed them back.

Her giggle tickled inside him and he wanted to hear it again. And again.

"You're going to make her sick you keep going in circles like that," Rori told him as she began her own lap across the pool.

"Get your workout out of the way and then you can play."

She glared at him and took off.

This time, Ian tossed Darya in the air, then caught her just as she hit the water, splashing water up above his head.

He was leaving in two days and knew right now he didn't care. Right now was about now.

A woman he was probably in love with swimming laps, a daughter who barely spoke English, brought to life hope in him he'd long ago forgot existed. This was what was real.

At least for the present.
He didn't want to think about tomorrow.

Chapter 25

The dinner was quiet. Brayden and his family were leaving in the morning for a trip to Louisiana to see Christian's family. He made certain they were taking Tanner with them. He and his brother had argued, but at the threat of just sticking them in a damn safe house, he'd finally won.

Aiden and Jesslyn were thinking of flying out to Colorado. He was trying to talk them into it. But then John needed to go and he needed John with him or maybe here when he left.

He still hadn't told anyone he was leaving.

The doorbell rang, and silverware clinked against china as everyone turned to the doorway.

Ian shook his head. Pete stood there, his expression grim. "I apologize for interrupting your dinner." He nodded to both of Ian's parents. Then those eyes zeroed in on him. "Something's come up."

Ian wiped his mouth, laid his napkin on the table and walked out of the room, meeting Rori's questioning look.

Again, they walked back to his father's study. When the door was shut, Pete wasted no time. "We need to move the date up a bit."

Ian walked around the desk and sat down. "Why? I thought it was all set for this weekend."

Pete nodded and shoved his hands in his pockets. "It was, but with the leak, I figured if we moved early, the chances of complications arising would be slim."

Ian frowned. True.

"When?"

"Tonight."

Ian sat forward. "Tonight?"

Pete nodded.

Ian's mind raced. There were still things to do, things to see to. Before he'd just packed up and left anytime he needed to. But now?

Now he had Rori, Darya . . .

The rest of his family.

He sighed and raked his hand through his hair. "What time?"

Pete paced, seemingly lost in thought.

"Pete."

"Oh, as soon as you're ready. Can you dress here? And how long will it take?"

"To become," he dropped his voice and added the accent back, "Dimitri Petrolov." He glanced at the clock on his father's desk. Almost seven. "At least an hour. I need to make my hair a bit longer." At least he hadn't shaved in two days. There was one bright side to his migraine. He would look more the part of the hired hit man.

"This is going to go smoothly," Pete said.

"Pete, things can always go wrong, my friend." How easily he could slide back into lives he wanted to leave behind. "You waiting?"

Pete nodded.

"Then go to the dining room and get something to eat. God knows there's enough." With that Ian hurried upstairs to his and Rori's room. He took the black bag down off the top shelf of the closet and walked to the bathroom.

Inside was a case. He opened it. To one side were pieces of hair. He hated hair extensions. They took too damn long. He could go with the wig. He glanced at his watch. He'd have to use the wig.

He pulled off his shirt, grabbed another from his closet and pulled it on. The tight black T-shirt would do.

He pulled on the dark wigcap, looking one way then the other to make certain it was straight. Next came the adhesive. He hated the stuff but was left with little choice unless he wanted to spend hours with the extensions. He'd rather use the water-soluble adhesive, but then he ran the risk of the wig coming off too soon.

He grabbed the wig and slid it on, straightening it as he needed to, careful not to get the longer strands of dark hair in the adhesive. That was always a bitch. Looking in the mirror, he straightened the wig and studied it.

It wasn't a perfect match. His natural hair had fallen differently. Taking the conditioning spritz, he sprayed the wig and tried to style it. The longer strands hung down to his chin.

In the harsh lights of the bathroom, he saw his image. Another face. Another person.

Self-loathing on a whole new level. Fuck.

He fisted his hands and leaned into the countertop, arms extended, his head hanging down. The need to punch something rose up in him, but he shoved it away.

The vacation was nice, but this was life.

Ian took a deep breath and shook his head. Didn't have time for this shit. Just get the damn job done.

He straightened and stood, being critical of the image in the mirror. Dimitri Petrolov.

Dimitri Petrolov.

He relaxed his jaw, pulled his brows a bit more.

Thinking of Elianya and Hellinski, letting his mind float to Nero's and things he'd been ordered to do, he watched as Ian Kinncaid slid further and further away and Petrolov started to take over.

"*Dobry den,*" he muttered into the mirror and rolled his shoulders. Shades. He needed his shades. Black. He'd borrow John's. They were the same brand Petrolov used.

"Dimitri Petrolov," he said again, the accent as natural to him as it had been a month ago.

He rubbed his jaw. Too bad he didn't have more of a shadow, but then in several hours his jawline would be even darker. He stared hard at the mirror. In the bedroom, he strapped on his firearm, pulled on a jacket and a long black coat.

Back in the bathroom, he packed up his bag, made certain there were other wigs in the bottom of his makeup case, adhesive removal. Another passport.

Extra gun, clip.

What was he forgetting?

He scanned the room. He crammed a change of clothing in his bag, and the zipper ripped across the quiet room. On the nightstand was a computer-printed photograph his mother had taken that morning. He was holding Darya after their swim and both of them were grinning from ear to ear. He should leave it, but . . . The slick paper was cool against his finger. He picked it up. To hell with it, he thought, and shoved it into his breast pocket.

He was ready.

As he picked the bag up, he glanced in the corner at the full-length mirror. There was a reason he'd always hated mirrors.

The Reaper was back.

The hallway was quiet, and as he passed Darya's doorway, he stopped. He pushed the door open, studying the lamp-lit room. He knew from something his mother had said today that this was now officially Darya's room. Mom had already hired someone to come in and paint it a periwinkle blue. She'd asked Rori, who had looked panicked at the talk of decorating. A smile caught him off guard.

God, he didn't want to leave. But if he left now, if he pulled this off—maybe, just maybe they wouldn't have to leave later. He wouldn't be running later, always looking over his shoulder in case one of Viktor Hellinski's men had found him. He wished he had something to leave for Darya, something that said she was his and he'd be back, but nothing came to mind.

Still holding his bag, he turned from the room and looked up.

Rori stood in the doorway, dressed in beige slacks and a dark brown curve-following sweater.

She stared at him for a long moment.

"Going somewhere?" she asked, stepping into the room and shutting the door.

He opened his mouth.

"How long have you known?" she asked him.

"Since Monday, Tuesday, sometime. The hit was supposed to go down this weekend, but with the leak, Pete moved it."

She nodded, her jaw moving slightly out, then in. "When were you going to tell me?" Her eyes flashed at him.

"When I needed to," he answered.

Rori looked at the man standing in front of her and wondered what the hell was going on.

Gone was the laughing man from this morning, gone was the fading vulnerable man she glimpsed last night, gone was the man who smiled at his mother so she didn't worry.

Here stood Dimitri Petrolov. Here stood the man she was hired to kill, who had killed just as she had, who had seen things and been part of things she could all too well imagine, the man who swore vengeance for the death of a young girl, and carried another from hell.

Bloody hell if she wasn't in love with the both of them.

They were one and the same, all rolled together.

And then she realized it was a mirror, the opposite sex of herself.

She looked down and took a breath, still angry at him, but not nearly as angry as she had been.

"When are you leaving?" she asked him, leaning back against the door.

He walked to her and dropped the bag. "ASAP."

"Where are you going? What are you doing? Dimitri Petrolov is not a man to be seen on the streets right now." The anger was quickly coming back. She flexed her fingers. "People are blowing up your places, men are out looking for you. Are you insane, then?" She shook her head and walked around him, pacing to the French door, the sheers obstructing her view of the dead gardens and leaf-laden outdoor pool.

"I'll be back in a couple of days," he said quietly behind her.

"I'm coming with you." She turned to him and dared him to disagree.

He did, shaking his head. "You can't."

"You can't stop me," she said, her heart thumping. "What the hell am I supposed to do, sit here and play nice with your family? What do I know about bleeding families?" She crossed her arms over her chest.

He took a deep breath and raked his hand through the long strands of hair.

"That's almost frightening," she heard herself say.

"What?" he asked, confusion in his face.

"Is that a wig?" Then she shook her head. "Like that would bloody matter. I honestly don't know how you do it. You don't just look different, you somehow become different." She studied him, watched the way his eyes darkened, hardened to dark stones.

"I'm just me," he said, his voice low and edged. Yet she could almost hear a plea in it.

She cupped his face. "Yes, you are, thank Gawd, just you." *And I think I might be falling for you.*

He turned his head, held her wrist and kissed her palm.

"You'll watch her until I get back."

She huffed out a breath. "I'm coming with you." The idea of him waltzing down the streets worried her.

He shook his head and let her hand drop. "No, Rori, you're not." He picked his bag up.

That order. That right there. Her anger returned in a rush. "Just who the bloody hell do you think you are? I'm not yours to order about." She stalked up to him just as he opened the door. "And you're not going alone."

His hand on the open door, he looked back at her over his shoulder, and again a shiver danced down her spine at his change. "You *will* stay here. And I'm not going alone."

She growled. She couldn't help it. Man made her barking mad. "Of course, how could I forget the esteemed Brasher." She looked at the end of the hallway, where said man had just topped the stairs. Upon seeing them, he simply turned around and headed back downstairs. Smart man.

"You don't order me about. They may think I'm your wife, but I'm not a damn lap dog that stays simply because you ordered it." She looked at him, noted the muscle ticked in his jaw.

He stepped back and slammed the door. He took two steps to her and grabbed both her arms. His face in hers, his teeth clenched, his voice low and cold as an ice storm, he said, "You are most definitely *mine*, Lenora Maitland Kinncaid. You might not think this marriage is real, but it is *legal* in every damn way that counts."

She blinked and tried to pull back, but his hands didn't let go. She crossed her wrists then shot her arms out, hitting his.

He didn't even flinch.

"Let me go."

He jerked her closer. "Not until we get a few things straight. You're independent, I admire that. I don't want a fucking lap dog, doormat, little miss, or whatever the hell other label you want to stick on it." Closer, his eyes blazed. "You might see this as just a cover, but legally it's not. Your country, my country, whatever fucking country we're in, you, Lenora Maitland, who signed said name to the marriage document with one Ian Rohnan Kinncaid. Both are legal names, the contract is legal and binding and that very much makes you *mine*."

She blinked and realized what he said was the truth. She'd never thought about it. What they'd done, they'd done quickly for Darya's sake. It was always for Darya's sake.

He nodded. "Yeah. And if anything happened to me, I wanted to know she'd be cared for. Not just by my family, but by you as well."

"Stop reading me. And you didn't know me."

His eyes still blazing, he said, "I knew enough." His hands manacled her upper arms.

"Let me go, Ian."

Still his eyes shot fire at her, his breath hot, his features hard. Having enough, she brought her foot down on his instep. He winced and let her go. She backed up and braced. For what, she didn't know. "I said to bloody take your hands off of me."

He stared for one long moment at her, shook his head, and turned, yanking the door open. Without a word, he picked his pack up in the hall and walked away.

She stood there for a split second, then ran after him.

"Ian, wait. Wait, bloody everlasting hell." She caught up with him at the top of the stairs, but he kept going. "You asked for it." She grabbed the banister and kicked out.

He ducked and whirled, reaching up and grabbing her ankle, yanking her to him.

She heard someone below yell. Heard John's "Christ."

Even as Ian turned and slammed her against the wall, bracing upward to keep their balance, and still he'd kept his arms around her so he didn't hurt her back.

His eyes didn't just blaze now, they engulfed. "If you ever try a stupid-ass stunt like that again, I won't be responsible for my actions," he gritted out.

She couldn't move. She tried to wiggle her arms free, but he had them pinned between him. The muscle ticked in his jaw. Taking him down on the stairs wasn't the brightest of her plans. "You were rude. I detest when someone is rude to me."

"Johnno's rude to you all the fucking time and I don't see you trying to kick his skull in." Still he didn't move.

"I didn't try to kick your skull in, Jesus, Mary and Joseph," she muttered. "I needed to get your attention." Jutting her chin out to his, she said, "Be glad I didn't reach for my gun."

His eyes narrowed, and if possible the cold voice froze even lower. "You and I wouldn't be having this conversation if you had."

"Why, you think you're that good?" He'd have shot her? Not that she really would have shot him. Gotten his bleeding attention, yes, which was all she wanted.

"I don't have to be. My boss would have shot you."

She took a deep breath. "You didn't listen to me," she tried.

"I heard all I needed to."

"I don't like being left out. Is that so bloody hard to understand?" she asked him, straining against the hold he had on her. She couldn't bleeding budge.

"And I need you here."

"Why are you going as Petrolov?" she asked.

He closed his eyes and sighed, whispering, "Rori, why do you think?" Opening his eyes, he looked at her, the anger not by any means gone, but banked. "What would make us safer?"

Us. Not me. Not Darya and me. *Us.*

She searched his eyes and saw he meant it. "Us?" she ventured.

"I knew exactly what I was doing for more reasons than one," he said ambiguously.

She sighed. "Why are you taking John?"

He leaned his forehead against hers and whispered, his breath hot against her mouth. She didn't know who all watched below, and frankly, she didn't care.

"I know you can handle yourself, but I couldn't handle anything happening to you. Rori, I need you here. I need to know you're safe. That our daughter is safe, and if, God forbid, I don't come back, someone here will know how to hide her." His lashes swept up as he looked straight into her eyes. "I need you." He kissed her, just a press of lips. "Please."

Something in her heart opened at those words. And he'd asked, not demanded, not ordered. Asked. Trusted. Wanted. Needed.

"No one's ever needed me before," she said, wiggling her arms.

He didn't ease his hold. "I do."

He kissed her hard, his body holding hers to the wall on the stairs, his gun pressing against her ribs, his mouth hot and demanding, yet giving and asking all at the same time.

He jerked away, then kissed her quickly again. Leaning back, he let her slide down until her feet were touching the stairs. He leaned down, picked up the bag and hurried down the rest of the stairs.

Mr. Jones stood below, glaring up at her, but with a smile on his face. He acknowledged her with a tilt of his salt-and-pepper hair. Ian's parents stood in the entryway gaping, John tapping his thigh, impatient as usual, and Darya stood pale, her eyes as wide as if she'd seen a ghost.

Rori shook off her wondering thoughts and hurried down the stairs. At the bottom, Ian garbed as Petrolov knelt in front of Darya. When he reached for her, she jerked back whimpering.

Ian's shoulders lifted on a deep breath and he asked the girl something. She shook her head, then shook it again. When he reached for her a second time, she glanced around and ran to Mr. and Mrs. Kinncaid, hiding behind Jock's legs.

Oh bloody hell.

Her little face peaked out from behind Jock's legs, tears sparkling in those blue eyes before tracking down her face.

Rori put her hand on Ian's shoulder as he stood, shaking his head. "She won't let me touch her." His eyes, hard before, looked at her, and for a moment the pain in them rocked her, but he quickly masked it.

Jock leaned down and picked up Darya, holding her against him. Ian raked a hand through the hair, then shoved it behind his ears, took off the coat and handed it, along with the bag, to Rori. He walked to his parents and took a photograph from his pocket. She heard him speaking Russian to Darya, who was frowning at him. A moment passed, then another, then her small arms reached out to Ian.

He took her, his shoulders relaxing. The little girl wrapped herself around him and wouldn't let go.

Rori could hear her talking softly; even as she couldn't understand the language itself, she could hear the questions in the tone. Ian's voice was soft and deep as he answered her. All Rori could do was watch. He showed her the photograph, waiting for her to take it. When she did, he kissed her on her forehead and tried to hand her off to Jock. But Darya clung to him, starting to whimper. His voice kept its low cadence, and finally he pulled her off him, handing her to his father. When he turned, the pain on his face was there for all to see.

Rori cupped his face. "She'll be all right."

He stared at her hard. "If . . ." Darya's crying got louder and he squeezed his eyes shut.

"We've got to go," Mr. Jones said. "I'm sorry."

Ian's eyes opened. "If I don't make it back —"

"You will," she interrupted him.

"If I don't, our old passports are upstairs in the dresser. Get to our house. Keep her safe for me." He opened his mouth to say something else. Grabbing the back of her neck, he kissed her again. "Be careful. I can't lose you."

With that, he turned, joined Johnno at the front door and walked out into the winter night.

His parents looked after them, and Darya's screaming grew frantic.

Rori grabbed Pete Jones's arm. "He's really that good, isn't he?"

Pete's eyes narrowed. "Yes."

She stared at him. "You make certain he comes home to us alive and well or you'll be answering to me and cleaning up a mess of those responsible."

He looked from her eyes to her hand on his arm, then met her gaze. "Is that a threat, Ms. Maitland?"

"It's Mrs. Kinncaid and that's a bloody promise." She let go of his arm. "You don't pull through and you'll find out just why the Raven was the one chosen to take out the Reaper."

She took Darya from the Kinncaids and walked to the front door, with the girl in her arms mumbling nonsensical words to her.

At the front door, they waved at the departing car.

Darya held the photograph he'd given her to her chest, her hiccups and shuddering breaths breaking the heart inside Rori that her husband had opened.

Chapter 26

Dimitri Petrolov climbed out of the cab, the Rosse Buurt, or red-light, district in full swing. The canal was crowded with some night revelers. He scanned the street. Oudezijds Achterburgwal was living up to its reputation. Women posed in the glass-front windows. Lingerie — almost there, almost nonexistent — adorned, or not, those that sat, lounged, or leaned in the windows offering wares.

To him red-light districts had always been just that, a blur of red lights, so even memories of the places kept that crimson glow.

He hated these places. He knew, without a doubt, that many of those women staring out would fuck more men in one night than many did their entire lives. While many didn't mind their profession, there were clubs where the women simply didn't have a choice.

At the not-so-gentle shove on his arm, he turned to John — currently known as Jean Tabeier, his bodyguard.

"We're just here to walk down that alley and into that abandoned shop."

The walk would undoubtedly take them right in front of one of the most notorious clubs in the district. Also run by one of the families who controlled holdings in Cheb, Prague, Berlin, and Moscow.

Near the entrance they did what they had rehearsed — arguing, drawing the attention of several people, including the two bouncers who were standing guard outside the door.

Petrolov saw the gun holsters beneath their jackets and the bulge of their guns.

He even recognized one bouncer, who had accompanied his boss on several occasions. The man's eyes widened and he immediately pulled out his cell phone and made a call.

Knowing his job was done, he took off across the street. Hopefully no one would get hurt in the explosion. The fact he was willingly walking into a rigged and wired building was not one he wanted to contemplate.

"You're such a likeable chap," John muttered. "We'll be lucky if his boss doesn't — bloody hell."

Dimitri looked over his shoulder and saw the guard start after them. They reached the building and pulled open the door. Darkness beckoned beyond.

Both of them had memorized the layout on the ten-hour-plus flight over here. They walked to the right ten steps, then opened the door, down the fourteen steps. Sixteen across the basement.

"I don't fucking like this, by the way," John muttered.

He ignored him and felt the wall. The door handle was just there.

"Shh," John said.

They heard the squeak of the door above and the groan of floorboard. The guard.

He cursed above them and asked a question. Dimitri currently didn't care. He felt the door on the wall, found the handle and wondered if they'd go up in flames if he pulled it.

"Wait."

John turned his small flashlight on. Wires ran around the perimeter of the room and plastic explosives sat in the center of the table.

"I'm ready to bloody leave now," John said.

They checked the door didn't see any rigs.

Both took a deep breath and he opened the door. Nothing happened.

They both exhaled, shut the door and hurried up the back-alley steps.

The shadows didn't move, but instead of heading back in the way they'd come, they walked across the alley to the other door and pulled it open.

"We need to hurry," he told John. Again they moved through a dark abandoned building and out a door leading into a different alleyway. No lights shone down on them.

They walked two more streets over, and Petrolov pulled off the wig and wigcap, running his fingers through his hair. John jerked off his own blond wig. When they reached the canal, they split.

Ian Kinncaid, traveling on business and enjoying an evening in Amsterdam, heard and saw an explosion as he stood waiting on a boat.

Dimitri Petrolov was dead.

• • •

Rori yawned and closed the door. She was tired. For the second night in a row Darya had awakened screaming bloody murder, bringing every adult within the house running. She leaned back against the door and closed her eyes. She wanted a drink of something.

She hadn't heard from Ian, didn't know if things had gone as planned or not. And it was driving her bonkers. She'd never been a worrier before and now she fretted. She hated to fret and brood.

His parents asked her if she'd heard from him. His brothers.

She cracked the door back open to check that Darya was still sleeping. The little girl lay on her side, the photo clutched in her hand, the teddy bear under her arm. They were starting to worry about her. Since dinner yesterday evening, she hadn't eaten a single bite. Darya gave a new meaning to the word "stubborn." She didn't want to go to bed, just sat on the bottom step and stared at the front door. Or she sat in the living room near the windows. She was always watching . . . waiting . . .

Rori didn't want to be gone long. She strode down the hallway and down the stairs. The house was quiet and dark, lit by the low-lit lamps sporadically placed. The hallway to the kitchen was lit with a nightlight near the floor.

The smell of cookies still hung in the air. Even Becky couldn't tempt Darya with a pumpkin cookie.

Roth sat at the kitchen table dunking cookies into a glass of milk. "These are really good."

She shook her head and walked to the industrial-sized refrigerator. The shelves were neatly organized and stocked full. She chose a bottle of protein juice and water.

Taking them both, she walked to the table, and sighing, plopped down in the chair next to Roth.

"You get her back asleep?" Roth asked.

She nodded. "Yes."

His gaze ran over her. "You look beat. You should get some sleep while you can."

She twisted the cap and drank the juice.

"Heard from Tanner?" she asked, setting the bottle back on the table.

He nodded. "Yeah, called and checked in from some Southern plantation. Said he felt like he was on the set of *Gone With the Wind* or some such."

Rori had seen the movie and had never understood the rave behind the bloody flick. But then that was her.

Roth stretched, his back popping. "At least Brayden and his family are safe."

"True." She studied him for a moment. "You have any luck yet on finding out where Darya came from?"

Roth grinned and rested his temple on his fisted hand. "If I did, I wouldn't tell you."

"Why not?" She snatched one of his cookies.

"Ian would have my ass."

"You don't tell me, and I'll have your ass."

Roth's eyes narrowed on her. "No, I haven't."

Not a big surprise. If someone wanted to get rid of a kid, they'd hardly advertise they were looking for them. Some did, but then those cases tended to be an altogether different issue.

"I see we weren't the only ones with midnight cravings," Jock said from the doorway.

Rori turned and smiled at them—Jock in a worn navy robe, the elbows faded and frayed, Kaitlyn in a silky ivory dressing gown. "Sit down, I'll put on some tea."

She stood and helped Kaitlyn set the kettle to boil.

Roth looked at her, then at them, and said, "I'm going to check in with the guys outside, then head to bed."

She nodded, and waited. She knew what was coming.

"Did you ever get Darya to eat anything?" Kaitlyn asked, sitting at the table.

Rori shook her head as she sat down in her chair. "No. She won't touch a bit of food."

"Maybe she's coming down with something," Jock said, frowning. He reached for the plate of cookies and grabbed three.

Kaitlyn slapped his hand. "One will suffice, dear."

He kept two.

Rori grinned.

Jock speared her with a look. "She had nightmares last night all damn night. She's already woken up screaming. What the hell's going on?"

And there it was.

Rori took another drink of her juice and wished she'd gone upstairs.

Some appliance started to hum and they both looked at her expectantly.

What the hell did she tell them? Nothing.

Kaitlyn looked down at her hands, then back up. "After the kids were kidnapped last year, they both had nightmares for weeks. Tori woke up crying for months."

Rori nodded.

"You said she was adopted, but the other night Ian acted as though something had happened to her."

And last night she'd been in the cupboard again.

Rori sighed and rested her head on her hand. "There's nothing you can do."

"Maybe not, but it would help if we understood," the woman said.

Rori looked from one to the other. "Sometimes people want to know things, then wished they didn't know them at all. Darya's story isn't a pretty one." She rolled the bottle between her palms.

"Just spit it out, damn it. Who the hell hurt our little girl?" Jock barked.

Rori looked at him. "I don't know, Mr. Kinncaid. We have no idea who she is. We found her on a child porn set hiding in a space we could barely get her out of." She shook her head.

"What?" Kaitlyn asked, leaning forward. "You mean to tell me . . . that poor girl . . . they . . . Did she . . ." She snapped her mouth shut and stood, hurrying to the stove.

Rori swallowed.

"What happened to her? Was she raped?" Kaitlyn asked from behind them.

Jock's face hardened, and in that instant she again saw where Ian got it. That hard, unforgiving expression.

"As far as we could tell, no. Thank God. Evidence from the house did show she'd been filmed in a new batch that thankfully never made it to the market."

"Poor, poor little girl," Kaitlyn said, sniffing. The kettle moaned then whistled. She slammed it down. "Bastards should be shot."

Instead of answering that they would be, she merely took another drink of her juice. The look in Jock's eyes said he knew what she wasn't saying.

Taking a deep breath, she decided to tell them all of it, at least as far as Darya was concerned. "There's more."

"More?" Jock asked. "What could be more?"

They didn't have a clue. "Her sister was brutally raped and murdered."

"Oh, God."

"Darya witnessed it, and when she ran, they tried to catch her."

Kaitlyn, her hand to her mouth, sat down hard in the chair, her eyes sparkling with tears. "Why?"

Rori shook her head. "There are some very evil people in this world, Mrs. Kinncaid. Darya was lucky she could run and hide. God only knows what they would have done with her." Though she had altogether too good an idea after seeing the room, the video, her own bloody memories.

Jock cleared his throat. "How old was her sister?"

Rori shrugged. "We have no idea. Probably thirteen is our best guess."

A tear slid down Kaitlyn's cheek. "I just can't fathom. I just . . ." She shook her head and stood up, pulling her hand from her husband's.

"So when we found her in the linen cupboard, that would be why," Rori said.

Kaitlyn slammed the cups down on the counter. Then she turned to Jock. "Well, Ian might not be home, but by God, that little girl is going to have some fun. Tomorrow we're going shopping."

Rori didn't think that was a very good idea. "Mrs. Kinncaid, with all due respect, I understand where you're coming from, but I really think it would be best if . . ."

She swung back to Rori. "I'm going and that's final. You and a contingent of guards can either come with us or stay here. But I'm taking my newest granddaughter shopping for clothes and toys. Period." Kaitlyn turned back to the cups.

Jock leaned over and patted Rori's hand. "It's no use arguing, trust me."

"Mrs. Kinncaid, it's simply easier to keep an eye on you here and it's not safe for Darya."

Kaitlyn whirled. "I want to show her, that . . . that . . ." Tears tracked down her face. Jock started to get up, but she waved him down and carried the tray over to the table.

She sat at the table and wiped her eyes. "Jock, I want to redo her room next week." Then she pierced Rori with a look. "And you will all still be here."

Rori's lips twitched. "Yes, ma'am. But about tomorrow. I won't allow you to put her in danger. Darya's safety is my first priority. When it's safer, you can take her to Schwarz if you want."

She looked like she was about to argue, but Jock put his hands on hers and squeezed.

$$\bullet \ \bullet \ \bullet$$

Jock squeezed his wife's hands and tried to let her know it would be all right.

Christ, his blood was boiling. If not for all his meds, he knew his blood pressure would be skyrocketing.

Rori stood, tossed her bottle into the glass bin and grabbed her water. "I should get back upstairs. I don't want to leave her too long."

Kaitie nodded. "Yes, of course. I'm sorry for going on so." She sniffed and wiped her eyes again. "Makes me so furious!"

"Well, Ian might not be happy I told you, but I figured you had a right to know what's going on with your granddaughter."

"Damn straight," Jock said, nodding.

She smiled at him. "Good night, then."

The phone shrilled and they all froze. He reached over and grabbed it just as it rang a second time.

"Hello?" His heart slammed in his chest. One a.m. phone calls were never a good sign.

"Dad?" Gavin asked.

He sighed, then straightened. "What? What's wrong? Is it Taylor? The baby? Ryan?"

Gavin laughed. "Taylor's in labor and we're on the way to the hospital. I just wanted to call and let you know."

He smiled and nodded. "Thanks. I'll let your mother know."

"Well, it's early yet and I've had her walking for several hours. Maybe you could stop by in the morning?"

Jock nodded. "All right. I'll let her know so she doesn't demand we come over there right now."

Gavin chuckled and Jock remembered that feeling of giddiness, of nervousness — the overall excitement of looming fatherhood.

"How's it feel to be on this side?" he asked his son.

"Different," Gavin answered.

Jock laughed. "Keep us updated or we'll be there as soon as we can."

"I know," Gavin said.

Jock heard the mumble of Taylor's voice in the background as he hung the phone up.

Kaitlyn was watching him. "Taylor?"

He nodded. "Gavin said to wait until the morning to go to the hospital."

He looked to the door and saw the slight disappointment shift across Rori's face. "I'm off to bed, then."

"Good night," he and Kaitie said at the same time.

They listened to her soft footfalls down the hallway. For a moment neither said a word, then Kaitlyn propped her chin in her hand and looked at him. "I like Rori."

He grinned. "I know, so do I."

Her russet brows furrowed. "I think she understands Ian."

"Yes."

"I don't. I don't know that man. Sometimes I glimpse our son, but . . ."

He brushed a strand of hair back from her face. "Time." He half expected her to still be angry at him, but she only looked at him.

"He found that child in hell, Jock. And I've heard Ryan and Tori talking. John was in Colorado. I know Ian sent him and I'm still so furious with Aiden for never saying a word. Not a single word in all this time." She took a deep breath and he stroked his thumb across the back of her hand.

"Kaitie. Time."

She nodded. "I know. I know." She grinned and that dimple he'd always loved winked at him. "I still want them to stay here." She sipped her tea. "No one's bought the Cooley place, have they? Maybe Ian would be interested in purchasing—"

"Kaitie, what did you just tell me this morning?"

She ignored him and sipped more tea.

He shared a smile with her.

"I want to get to know our granddaughter," she admitted.

"And our son?"

"And his wife."

Their grins grew. "I have a feeling Ian knows the Cooley place and I seriously doubt he'd want it."

Kaitie chewed on the inside of her bottom lip. "Maybe not. But the *entire* family knows what a great child's psychologist Dr. Petropolis is."

He chuckled. "Kaitie, you're hopeless."

"I know, and you still love me."

He leaned over and kissed her cheek. "That I most definitely do."

Chapter 27

Rori looked at the silent child, who still hadn't eaten since Ian had left two days ago. She still hadn't heard from him and she didn't want to worry.

She hated to worry.

The little girl was pale, but her eyes seemed overly bright.

"All right, Poppet?" She reached her hand out and felt the girl.

Darya was hot. Rori cupped her face in both her hands and Darya looked at her miserably.

"Oh, baby. You don't feel well, do you?"

No one was in the house. Roth had taken the Kinncaids to the hospital, where Taylor was still in labor. Rori had the fleeting thought that perhaps not being able to have children had some strong points — mainly avoiding hours upon hours of labor.

She picked Darya up and walked down the hallway with her. They had been in the living room, Darya playing with the blocks Ian had bought her, glancing out the window every few seconds. When she'd stopped playing, it drew Rori's attention. For Darya to be quiet was one thing, but she'd become withdrawn since Ian's departure and Rori so wanted to be able to communicate with the girl. No one had apparently thought of that fact. But they had gotten along well enough until now with only a couple of glitches. The nightmares and the fact she wouldn't eat. To get her to drink something, they gave her bright colored glasses with swirling straws — Mr. Kinncaid's idea.

But this . . . she was hot.

Fear thrummed through her. Probably just a fever. But what if it wasn't? What the hell was she to bloody do?

Becky was still here.

Rori carried Darya down the hallway and into the kitchen. The little girl put her head on Rori's shoulder, her arm slung over Rori's back. Becky was humming and rolling something on the center block.

"Becky?" she asked.

Becky turned and smiled. "Lonely, are you? Don't worry, they'll call. You should have gone to the hospital with them." Her grin grew. "Babies are such a joy."

"Becky," she said, walking up to the woman. "I think she's sick."

Becky's round face frowned. "What?" She wiped her floured hands on a dish towel.

"She feels warm to me."

Becky put her hand on Darya's face, then her arm, and shook her head. "No wonder. Child won't eat, doesn't sleep, she's bound to get sick sooner or later."

The panic fluttered anew. What did she bleeding know about sick kids. "Becky? What do I do?"

Becky's face softened. "Just hold her. I'll call Mrs. K. and see what we have to give her."

Rori pulled back and studied Darya. "Do you think we should take her to the doctor or something?"

Becky chuckled. "Oh, new parents." She patted Rori's arm. "You just go put her up in her bed and sit with her. I'll bring up some soup. Main thing is to keep liquids down her."

She nodded. "Anything else?"

Becky's smile was tender. "Just mother her, luv, like ye've been doing."

Rori turned and walked out of the kitchen. Well, she knew the girl had a fever, but what to do about it was another matter. Becky acted as if it was nothing out of the ordinary, but still . . .

She turned back and walked into the kitchen again. "Becky."

"Yes?"

"Mrs. Kinncaid was a doctor, wasn't she?"

"Yes. Doctored little ones, she did, still does from time to time."

"So she'll know what to do?"

Becky frowned. "We should take her temperature. Mrs. K. has one of the computer kind around here somewhere." She opened a drawer, then closed it, muttering. Next she checked the cabinet next to the sink. Aspirin, bandages, first aid supplies. "Ah, here it is, then." Becky pulled out a box with a coiled wire and thermometer on the end. She slid a plastic cover down over the thermometer and motioned Rori over.

Rori set Darya on the counter. The little girl blinked slowly. "Ian's going to be bloody furious," she muttered.

Becky humphed and picked Darya's arm up, sliding the thermometer under her arm. Five seconds and several beeps later, she said, "One-oh-two point three." She frowned at Darya and said to Rori, "Put her to bed and I'll call Mrs. K."

So relieved that something was being done, she leaned over and pressed a kiss to Becky's cheek. "Thank you so much."

She carried Darya out of the kitchen and upstairs. She opened Darya's door, the room cool to her. Maybe she should build up the fire. She sat her on the edge of the bed and undressed her, tossing her jeans and sweater to the side and putting some flannel pajamas on the girl. She at least knew enough to keep the girl warm.

She pulled the covers back and tucked Darya in. The entire time, the girl only stared, her hand clutching the photograph. She pulled the ragged teddy bear to her and lay down, her eyes closing.

"Please don't let her have any nightmares," Rori whispered, brushing the hair off Darya's forehead.

Maybe a cool cloth would be the thing to do. She hurried to the bathroom and wet a washcloth. Sitting on the bed, she put the folded linen on the girl, who opened her eyes and stared for a moment before closing them again.

God, what if they'd been wrong? What if she had been sexually molested or some such and had come down with something? It could be anything.

Rori chewed on her thumbnail and a memory flashed through her brain. Nikko nursing her after he'd rescued her from that hell of an apartment. They hadn't gone to his apartment on the same floor. Instead he'd taken her to a house, and then when she'd been better, they'd moved quite often until settling in Italy.

Nikko. God, her brain wasn't working.

"I'll be right back," she told Darya and hurried from the room into her and Ian's. There she grabbed her mobile, which she'd plugged in last night so it would charge.

She started to punch his number, but Becky came huffing up the stairs. "Mrs. K. said to give the poor dear a teaspoon of this, and in a few hours give her this other one." She held up two bottles of children's versions of pain and fever relief. "And we're to take her temperature every half an hour to make certain it's going down, and Mrs. K. said she'd be calling to check up on things."

Rori took the bottles and thermometer from Becky and said, "Thank you, Becky."

"Go give her the medicine. I'm going to put some chicken stock on for soup so perhaps she might eat something tonight."

"I hope she will." With that, she turned and walked back into Darya's room. The girl hadn't moved. Rori looked from one bottle to the other. Which one did she give first? Did it matter? Setting her phone down, she jogged out of the room and down the staircase, catching up with Becky in the hallway.

"Which do I give her first? You didn't bloody say."

Becky shook her head and muttered something. "Doesn't matter. Pink or purple, you choose."

That's it? She hurried back upstairs and measured out some of the pink bubble-gum-flavored fever reducer. Picking the girl up, she coaxed her to drink it all down.

Darya licked her lips, and lay back, staring at her picture.

She looked so lost.

Rori took the wet cool cloth and wiped Darya's face. "He'll be back."

Darya stared at the photo until her eyes slid closed.

Rori reached over on the nightstand, stood, and walked to the window ledge. Hitting the preprogrammed number, she waited for the phone on the other end to ring.

"It's about damn time you called. What the hell is going on?"

"Hello to you too, Nikko."

"*Cara,*" his voice warned. She caught the worry in it.

"How do you take care of a sick kid?"

For a minute he was silent and then he chuckled. "Oh, the things I miss!"

"Nikko, it's not bloody funny! She's sick, has a fever, and I haven't heard from Ian — have no bleeding clue where he is and she's running a fever. I gave her some bubble-gum fever reducer medicine," she rattled off, biting on her thumbnail.

"*Cara,* calm down."

She took a deep breath and watched the girl sleep on the bed.

"You haven't been sleeping," he commented.

"How do you know?"

"I know you. You ramble when you're tired. Why no sleep?"

She sighed. "Ian's been gone tying up some loose ends. Darya hasn't eaten or slept really since he's been gone. Not a bite in two days and nightmares every night." She ran a hand over her hair.

"It'll be fine. You were sick when you first came to live with me."

"What did you do?"

"Took care of you, same as you will do for little Darya."

Rori thought about how Nikko had a way of cutting through everything else. She sighed. "I don't know what the hell I'm doing anymore, Nikko," she admitted.

"How so, *cara*?"

She sat on the windowsill and thought about it. "This . . . this job is all fucked to hell."

He laughed.

"I don't find anything amusing."

"You know, I am as proud as any parent can be of their child. But do you know what I have always wanted, always prayed for you?"

"You pray?"

"I've returned to the flock. My priest is constantly giving me penances."

"Did you tell him what you've done?"

"I don't have that much time, *cara*. I'd be saying Hail Marys until I passed onto the next world. It's better to give it to him in small doses."

She laughed, trying to picture it.

"You."

"You," he answered.

"I miss you, Nikko."

"I know, *cara*." He sighed. "I want you to find happiness . . . peace . . ." He waited. "Does Mr. Kinncaid bring out those things."

She stared out over the sunlit dead grasses and bare trees. "Ian makes me feel. Period."

"Then that is a good thing. Now tell me, what loose ends must he tie up?"

"I can't talk about it."

Silence, then. "Perhaps you'd be interested to know the streets are alive with talk of Mr. Petrolov and his guard dying in an explosion in Amsterdam."

She hadn't known, damn the man. "That was the plan."

He humphed. "*Cara*, the man for you is not an average man. One, you are a very strong woman, you need someone who can meet you.

And you obviously have feelings for the girl."

She took a deep breath. "I think I did something stupid, Nikko."

"You never do anything stupid."

"I did this time. I signed my name to a marriage document."

"What?"

"The marriage to Kinncaid . . . it's um . . . real."

She expected silence, expected disappointment, even anger. What she didn't expect was laughter. "You, *cara*, have brought such joy to my life. Enjoy yours. As I said, you've never been stupid and you've read documents before."

So she had. "I just wasn't thinking," she tried.

He tsked. "No, this time you were finally thinking with your heart and not with that keen intelligence. Fate moves us in ways we should go if we're too stubborn to go there ourselves."

"Nikko, you're starting to annoy me."

"Denial is a terrible thing. Now, what are you going to do about Mr. Kinncaid?"

She shook her head. "I have no idea."

"He's keeping the girl?"

"Oh, yes."

"I like this man. If he hurts you, I'd have to kill him, but I think I like him. He makes you feel, truly feel, and that is much. Plus, he didn't have to take the child, but he did. That's a good man."

"He reminds me of you, I think." She rubbed her forehead and watched Darya shift to her back, still asleep.

"That is lovely. But love him for who he is, not because he reminds you of someone. I must go, *cara*. Take care and call me."

"I will."

"Oh, by the way, your two fish, Frank and Henry, or whatever their names were—"

"Frank and Fred."

"Yes, well, they are no more."

"It's sad, Nikko, when you've reached the point to kill fish."

He said something not very flattering. "*Ti amour, cara.*" And he hung up.

She realized he'd never answered her on where he was.

• • •

8:04 p.m.

Quinlan said good-bye to his mother and father and promised to be home tomorrow night for a family dinner. He set the vase of flowers on the shelf in the hospital and looked again at the newest little Kinncaid. Another girl. Seemed like there were girls everywhere. Miss Anna Marie was seven pounds and thirteen ounces and twenty inches long.

Everyone else oohed and ahhed over her, and though she was cute, he supposed, she looked like all babies looked to him. He'd already brought in a big pink chenille elephant and Gavin had only shaken his head. Ryan had been talking ninety miles an hour. He'd just missed Aiden, who was returning home, where Jesslyn was with the twins.

He had no idea Ian had even left until his mother mentioned it, and he was stupid enough to comment on his lack of knowledge. "If you'd come home more, interact more with your family than with the hotel guests, you might know what's going on."

For a moment, he'd thought she'd meant something altogether different. Then he shook his head and placated her by saying, "I'll come out to dinner tomorrow."

"And cancel at the last moment." She patted his hand.

"No, I won't." He would try not to.

"You know, Marylin Pladdock's daughter is staying with them for a bit. You remember the Pladdocks."

A shudder danced down his spine. "Mother, I have to go. If a date is required, I will find my own, thank you."

"At the hotel?"

Shaking his head, he slapped Gavin on the back again. Kissed Taylor's cheek. "Congratulations."

"Thank you, Quinlan."

"Isn't she just the coolest, Uncle Quin?" Ryan asked him.

"That she is, Ryan."

"Anne Marie." Ryan stood smiling beside his dad.

Jock was busy taking pictures with the digital camera. It was time for him to go.

"Tomorrow night," his mother reminded him.

"Yes, Mom."

He hurried from the hospital room before anyone else could grab him.

Once in his car, he breathed a sigh of relief and drove to the hotel.

A date. God, why couldn't Mom just leave well enough alone.

Back at the hotel, he walked to his office, checked his messages. No messages from Alla.

His stomach grumbled and he figured he'd go eat.

In the restaurant things were going smoothly for a Friday evening. The place was packed, people waited to be seated, but it was normal with no snags.

He glanced at the bar and saw her at once.

She sat again, dressed in a dark suit of plum, still sexy as hell, the dark V showing off something lacy and black. She stared at him, her slanted eyes promising delights that haunted him, her lips curved seductively in her come-and-get-me smile.

And why did he want to?

He remembered the feel of her on him, against him, under him. Her tight muscles, her beautiful breasts. The way she moved, tight as steel and fluid as water.

Hell. He sighed and shoved his hand through his hair. He'd been in meetings most of the day, spent the evening at the hospital and had planned to eat, and later work out on his treadmill.

Then again . . .

An image of her riding him, those lips of hers curved and demanding, her muscles squeezing, squeezing. Quinlan closed his eyes and shook his head. What the hell was with him? Women were nice, he enjoyed a good lay as well as the next guy, but this . . .

This was like a craving. A hum under his skin that itched to the surface.

She arched one brow.

Some inner voice said he should just turn around and walk away . . .

He walked toward her and figured why not enjoy that which was offered.

When he was even to her, he said, "You're back."

Her eyes ran the length of him, her nail raked down his tie, and he felt the tug straight to his groin.

He narrowed his gaze at her. "Staying the night?"

She licked her lips, grazing her teeth over the plump bottom lip. "Depends."

He leaned closer, smelled that enchanting swirl of floral and something he could never put his finger on. His hand on the small of her back, he whispered against her ear, "On what?"

Her lashes swept up as she stared at him. "You."

He grabbed her hand and pulled her behind him, her husky laughter floating out and tightening around his control as surely as her fist on his dick.

"I just so happen to have a room."

"I remember."

Tonight, so would he.

Chapter 28

Ian sat, the D.C. night glittering beyond the window of his boss's office. The Capitol building shone white, beckoning.

This was it.

"I can't believe you're actually leaving," Pete said yet again.

Ian turned from his study of the nightlife and looked across to the man he'd met so many years ago after he successfully completed a mission in the 75th. This man had found him and recruited him. His life was never the same.

"You regret it?" Pete asked, lighting a cigar.

He closed his eyes and took a deep breath. "You could offer me a departing cigar." He opened his eyes. "Like a celebration."

"Or a death." Pete didn't offer him the humidor. "Besides, you've quit. If you slid now, you'd have to start all over again."

Ian shook his head. "You always were a hard-ass."

Those hard lips flashed into a rare smile, or what could only pass as a smile on Pete Jones.

"If you ever need a job . . ." Pete left it open.

Ian shook his head. "No, thank you. I've had enough of shadows and games to last me way past this lifetime." He wanted to pace or tap his foot. He did neither.

Pete nodded and blew out a plume of smoke. "Well, you'll be delighted to know the remains of Dimitri Petrolov, his guard, Jean Tabeier, and another guard, belonging to a local club owner, were all identified."

"And?"

Pete shrugged. "The remains were cremated tonight."

Ian grunted. It was over . . . almost.

He scratched the side of his mouth with his index finger. "Guess I need to turn my gun in."

Pete raised a brow. "What gun?"

Ian waited a moment, then smiled. "Only one last loose end to tie up."

"Two," Pete corrected and leaned up, his maroon leather chair squeaking. He pursed his lips, tapped the desk and leaned back again. "About to become one."

"Really? Care to expound on that, Pete?"

Something shifted in his hazel eyes and he huffed a breath out. "Don't ever get married."

Ian frowned, wondering what the hell that had to do with anything. Pete had been married now for . . . well, several years to his second wife. Quiet woman who worked in an accounting firm.

"Pete, I want a name," he said, returning to the topic. "I want to know who blew my cover."

Pete stood and walked to the window, his hands shoved deep in his pockets, the shirtsleeves rolled up. "You'll get one, when I know for certain. Until then, you'll wait. You'll be notified if I find out anything for certain." He glanced at Ian, and those eyes were as hard as he'd ever seen. "I don't take the fact your cover, and others', was blown way the hell open any more lightly than you do. And probably a hell of a lot more serious than even you would imagine. It's not just you, we're learning. There were others, are others . . ." He rubbed his forehead. "Christ." Without looking at Ian, he said, "Go home to your family, Ian Kinncaid. Your work here is done."

Ian stood, slapped Pete on the back. "Why do I feel like you left off the 'until we need you' bit?"

Without waiting for a response, he walked out of the office. The secretary wasn't at her normal post.

An armed guard nodded to him and let him out the door. It shut and locked behind him.

John leaned against the wall by a bank of elevators, two carry-on bags at his feet. They walked through the lobby, across the Defense Intelligence Agency's seal, and out into the cold November night.

John waited as Ian flagged down a cab. As they stepped off the curb, John slapped him on the shoulder. "Feels different, doesn't it?" He grinned. "Ready to really get to work now, partner?"

• • •

10:34 p.m.

Ian Kinncaid shut the cab door. John climbed out the other side. "I'm so bloody jet-lagged," John complained.

"Could have stayed in London."

He raised a brow. "And miss all this? What do you take me for?"

Ian shoved some bills at the cabby and grabbed his bag. The paper on the cheap convenience-store flowers crinkled in his hand. He'd made the cabby stop and bought two bundles. He looked at them. One was rather a sad case of mums and lilies, the other colored daisies. Looking at his friend as they walked up the lighted walkway, he said, "Johnno, be honest. You just can't stand not being part of whatever shit I have going on."

"Oh, that's most definitely it."

They walked up the steps and Ian unlocked the door.

"You could ask your parents for a key instead of picking the bloody locks."

"Where," he asked, "is the fun in that?"

They'd left Amsterdam at ten a.m. and arrived in D.C. at six p.m. local time. The next two hours were meetings with Pete. The leak issue still bothered him on more levels than one.

Pete hadn't really answered him. Which was odd. He thought back over the conversation and wished he wasn't so damn tired. He'd asked about the leak, and Pete had mentioned marriage. Why?

He knew Pete was with his second wife. They'd been married for . . . six years? Wasn't it? At the time, back in Pete's office, Ian had assumed his boss had merely been trying to change the topic.

But something . . .

Unless . . .

No. Surely not.

Ian shook off the thoughts and stepped into the darkened hallway.

Forget it. He was tired. Pete said he'd call. Pete would call.

Ian, on the other hand, hadn't called Rori, and maybe he should have, but he wanted to surprise her too.

The house was dark and quiet.

"They turned in early tonight," Ian muttered, figuring someone would still be up.

"Did you let Roth know we were coming?" John asked him.

"No," said a voice from the shadows. Roth stepped out and holstered his firearm. "Idiots. I could have shot you."

Ian smiled. "You wouldn't have. You don't shoot first and ask questions later unless the situation warrants that. And this didn't."

Roth grunted. "Lucky for you."

"Where is everyone?"

Roth glared at him. "Trying to get some sleep."

"Why, what's been going on?"

Roth said, "First off, your brother and sister-in-law had their baby. Girl, get the details from your mother. Or your dad." Roth shook his head. "Never seen such a camera-happy man. Secondly, Darya's usually up several times a night screaming."

Ian didn't wait for the rest, but hurried up the stairs, the bag in one hand, the flowers in the other. At the top, he walked quickly down the hallway to his daughter's door. Pushing it gently open, he saw that the lamp on the dresser cast a soft glow on the room. Rori slept in a chair beside the bed, half lying on the bed, her hand on Darya's chest. On the nightstand stood bottles of medicine and tissues. A thermometer. Quietly, he set the bag down by the door, laid the flowers on top of it. He walked across the room and stood beside the bed looking down at his daughter, covered with the blue comforter.

Her cheeks were flushed, and in her hand, atop the cover, was clasped the photo he'd given her. From the crinkled edges, it appeared she'd never let go of the thing. He reached out and put his hand to her forehead. She was burning up. Worry thrummed through him.

Rori jerked.

"Easy," he whispered, laying his hand atop hers.

Rori's eyes opened and she sat up, stretching. "You're home."

Home . . .

He looked at her, sitting here exhausted beside their sick daughter.

He nodded. "Yeah, I'm home."

"Thank God. Everything went all right, then?" she asked, putting her hand to Darya's forehead and then checking her watch. "Another hour and we can give her something else."

"What the hell is going on?" he asked quietly, sitting on Darya's other side.

"Well, your daughter hasn't eaten a single bite since you left. We've managed to get some water in her and now meds, but she wouldn't eat. Hardly slept. Just kept watching for you."

He ran his hand over Darya's dark curls scattered over the white pillowcase. His daughter . . .

"I've been gone for over forty-eight hours. She was that sick?"

Rori chuckled. "We don't know if she was already coming down with something or if the combination of stress, her not eating, and not sleeping triggered the illness." She shrugged and brushed her hand down Darya's flannel-clad arm. "Your mother mentioned it could have been anything."

He frowned and felt Darya's face again. "She's too hot."

Rori nodded. "Yeah, goes up and down. Anywhere from ninety-nine to one-oh-three or four."

"What?" The worry turned to fear. "Did you take her to the doctor?"

Both her brows rose. "I called your mother, who did her doctor thing, called some antibiotics in this afternoon and told me what to do."

His mother. He relaxed slightly.

"I'm sorry," he muttered, worry still winding through his blood.

"S'all right. I just didn't know what the hell to do. Asked Becky, called your mom. Vented to Nikko and then to Roth." Her hands rubbed her short hair. "I didn't know what the bloody hell to do. I mean, she's so little, and what do I know of kids?"

He reached across the bed and pulled her to him, kissing her softly on the mouth. "You did fine. Go get some sleep. I'll watch her for a while."

Rori frowned. "You're jet-lagged. I can see it." She shook her head. "You rest. I'll give her the grape medicine in another forty-five minutes, and then when it goes back down, I'll catch a few z's."

Ian just watched her, noted her eyes were shadowed, the skin on her own cheeks a bit pale. "I slept on the plane. Fourteen hours and I was tired. I got at least six, which looks like more than you."

She looked exhausted, disgruntled, and adorable. He smiled.

"What?" she snapped, frowning.

"You look wonderful." And she did. "And I missed you."

Shaking her head, she stood, then walked around the bed, leaned down and kissed his cheek. "Wake me in four hours."

He nodded. "I will."

"Night."

"Night."

He looked at his daughter. Sitting on the bed, he pulled her into his lap and held her. Her hot face and head heated his neck and collarbone. He kissed the curls atop her head.

It was good to be home. And he'd make certain she got better as soon as possible.

"Hey, sweetie, Daddy's home."

Chapter 29

The next morning after breakfast, his phone rang. Ian answered. "Hello?"

"You wanted an update." Pete's voice, always devoid of emotion, seemed hollow, even for him.

"Just a minute." He nodded to Rori and walked out the double doors leading outside. "Okay."

"That loose end we discussed has just been cut."

Just like that. Anger and the fact he was denied justice licked through him, quick as a rattler. "You promised me a name." He raked his hands through his hair. "Damn it, Pete. I had a right to know."

"Yes, you did. And so did others."

"Pete."

"Ian."

"What?"

For a moment, the man didn't answer him, then he said, "I don't have time for this. I have a funeral to plan."

Ian blinked, shook his head. "What? I mean. Hell, I'm sorry, Pete. For wh-who?" Strange, they'd worked so long together, knew such dark things about the other, and yet knew so little.

Again the silence.

"The woman I trusted . . . my wife."

Ian frowned, then pulled back. The loose end . . . Pete's wife? Ian wasn't exactly surprised. Sometimes it was those closest, but still . . .

"Uh—Pete. I'm sorry."

"So am I."

"I would have . . ." *Helped* seemed the wrong word. Damn.

Pete cleared his throat. "It was a matter I had to see to personally."

With that, the man hung up.

Ian took a deep breath, a chill dancing down his back.

Just when he thought he was as far into the darkness as he could go, he was reminded there were shadows he still hadn't journeyed.

It was a matter I had to see to personally . . .

And those shadows Ian didn't want to visit. Ever.

Turning back around, he looked through the doors at Darya wrapped in a quilt on the couch, leaning against Rori.

Maybe, just maybe their lives could get on the right track now.

Whatever that track was. He didn't want to push it. Didn't know, suddenly, what the hell to do. What did he do?

About anything?

He had no orders. No one needed to be found right this moment . . .

Rori looked up at him and smiled.

And then he knew. Ian opened the door and walked into the living room just as his parents came in.

"You two simply have to go to the hospital," his mother said. "Have you gotten your brother and Taylor anything?" she asked.

Ian shook his head and shut the door behind him. "I thought I was supposed to get the baby something."

Rori didn't turn to look, but he caught her grin as she watched the television and stroked her hand over Darya's head.

His mother handed him a piece of paper. "Go take a shower, take your wife out. We'll watch Darya."

He looked at the paper and saw it was a list. "What is this?"

His mother shrugged. "Things Darya needs."

Dollhouse. Barbies. Books. Several stuffed animals. Bedding (something pink or purple – though blue or silver would work).

His mother tapped the bottom of the list. "If you don't want to pick out the bedding, that's fine. Rori and I can go sometime next week."

Ian shook his head. Rori jerked around and met his gaze. He caught the plea in her eyes.

He wiggled a brow at her and turned to his mother. "Well, you know us men. We're likely to choose the wrong fabric or color or something."

She nodded. "I know." His mother glanced over at the couch. "Rori and I will get what we need Monday or something." She put her hand on his arm. "Now go and get ready. I'd also like you to pick up some nice flowers before dinner tonight."

"We need more fever-reducer medicine . . . whatever it's called," Rori said, standing.

Darya was asleep on the couch. Ian shook his head. "I just got back. I don't want to go out again, Mother."

"Bah. Go see your brother and the baby. Aiden and Jesslyn went by, but Brayden's in Louisiana and you just got home."

"Quinlan?" he ventured. "You should let him know —"

Her green eyes narrowed on him. "He's been by. Last night. Promised to come tonight to dinner. He called earlier and said he was bringing a date."

Jock muttered something that sounded vaguely like *a hired woman.*

Ian hid his grin, leaned over and said, "Mother, I love you, but —"

"No buts, go see your brother. If you leave now" — she glanced over her shoulder at Darya and then back to him — "she'll be asleep most of the time you're gone." Her eyebrow rose. "You worried I can't take care of a sick child?"

He knew better than to argue that one. "I couldn't trust anyone more with her health, Mom."

Her eyes narrowed. "Some mothers might take issue with that wording. Considering the goings-on of late, I'll just leave it alone."

He laughed and pulled her close, kissing her on her forehead. "Well, I just learned the leak was found and taken care of, so the guards will be leaving."

"Thank God," his mother said, patting his chest and taking a deep breath.

"Who?" his father asked.

Ian looked at Rori as he said, "I don't know. They just let me know the matter was taken care of." Squeezing his mother, he added, "I decided to leave that alone and take it at face value."

No one said anything for a moment. Then his mother said, "So Roth will be leaving?"

He chuckled. "Not just yet."

Jock asked, "Why not? You said guards."

"Not my men."

At his parents' confused looks he added, "Tanner, Roth, and several others work for John and me. Or they do now."

"What?" his father asked.

Ian shook his head. "Never mind. Just know, Roth will be here a bit more. Tanner is staying with Brayden, Snake with Gav, and Gar with Quinlan."

"Why?" his mother asked.

He looked at Rori. "We should get going if we're going to go to town and get back before dinner."

They quickly walked out of the room before his parents bombarded them with more questions. To save time, they shared the shower, their bodies melding, sliding, holding and reaching until both moaned, peaked, and shuddered in the aftermath.

Ian stood in the bedroom, tucking his shirt in, and watched Rori — his wife — put lotion on. A simple thing that. Over-the-counter white lotion. She sat on the bed, her hands rubbing down her leg, gliding her knee, sliding over her thigh, grazing her belly before she squirted more and then rubbed it into one arm, then the other.

She glanced at him. "What?"

He shook his head. "Nothing."

She grinned. "Too bad we don't have all afternoon to ourselves."

He laughed and pulled her to him, kissing her again, feeling the cool lotion, her hot body molding against his.

"We don't have time," she said and pushed against him, and he let her go.

"Tonight."

She grinned over her shoulder, her naked back long and lean, graceful as a dancer's, her backside and thighs as tight as a Vegas line girl's. Damn.

• • •

5:06 p.m.

Quinlan Kinncaid drove the car. He kept rubbing his head. She watched him.

"Headache?" she asked, sliding her hand over the console and touching his arm.

He nodded. "Yeah, again." He blinked and shook his head.

"Why don't you let me drive?" she tried. This would be all she fucking needed. This damn close and he wrecks the car, all because he was a male and thus had to drive.

"We're almost there," he said, shaking his head again.

Alla shrugged and looked out the window. At least she'd taken care of the guard, Gar, while Quinlan had dressed for the evening. If anyone found the man, he might live, but the sedative dose had been high. She'd stuffed him in the spare room in Quinlan's penthouse.

Reaching down for her purse, she opened it partway, saw the 9-millimeter Glock inside, and smiled. Reaching past it, she pulled out her pill bottle. "I've got some aspirin. Would you like some?"

The man was so predictable. He shook his head.

Taking the female approach, she said, "Please, for me. I don't want to meet your family practically alone, and if you're nursing a killer headache, you'll look like you hired me to come along. I don't want your parents thinking I'm a whore." She held the white pills aloft in her hand.

They looked like aspirin. She had wanted them to, with the same initial coating so that they tasted the same — or rather had no taste at all.

But the ingredients were very different and practically tasteless, an accomplishment for her lab techs. Something the drug market and vice scene would love.

Ecstasy plus roofies. Basically. Bit of enhancement thrown in to keep things ready. The chemical makeup had to be altered a bit. But the feel-good of X with the disinhibiter of roofies and the ready-to-go of Viagra made for a wondrous little pill.

She could fuck someone all night long, and they wanted it. And the poor souls didn't really remember all the details the next morning.

The bright side? Supposedly the downer wasn't as bad as X. She should make a killing off this little creation.

But then her techs were still trying to perfect it. She wanted buyers, not diers.

He finally took the pills and glanced at her with a narrowed gaze, as if trying to decide, then tossed them back.

He'd already had two others half an hour ago in his coffee. Hopefully he wouldn't have a reaction. But if he did . . . then she'd deal with it.

She smiled at him and leaned over, the shoulder harness pulling on her, and kissed his cheek, then wiped her lipstick off. "Hope they help."

He nodded and stared at the road as he turned off. He shook his head again.

"Quinlan, quit being a man and just let me drive. You don't feel well, and if you pass out, we could both be injured." He nodded, slowed and put the car in park.

"Poor baby." She glanced either way down the driveway. A house sat back beyond the trees and no one was behind them.

She climbed out of the car and walked around. By the time she opened the driver's door, he was already half unconscious. Smiling, she leaned into the backseat and grabbed her shoulder bag with the lovely little bomb in it. Time to get to work before meeting the family . . .

• • •

Ian held on to the "oh shit" bar as Rori took another curve. "Damn it, slow down."

She laughed. "God, I miss driving. And I just have to say, this right side of the road is really off. You Yanks should have stayed with the left."

He shook his head.

She rounded another curve and the lights cut across the road.

"Oh, shit!" She swerved to miss the little eyes in the road and Ian felt the tires thump over whatever the hell it was.

Rori slammed on the brakes and looked in the rearview mirror.

"What the hell are you doing?" he asked, looking back behind them. No cars were coming. He looked in front of them as she pulled the car to the edge of the road.

"Rori?" he asked.

"What did I hit?" She looked at him, her face creased with . . . he had no clue, he'd never seen it.

She opened her door and the interior light popped on. He rolled his eyes, unbuckled his belt and climbed out.

She stood in the center of their lane dressed in her jeans, squared black high-heeled boots, and a black jacket, looking down at a dark spot in the road. Her hands were clasped to her chest.

"I killed it," she said brokenly.

Ian shook his head and stepped toward her, looking down. What was left of — a rabbit? — was a squashed area of brown fur, blood and guts.

"Uh, yeah, looks like you were successful there."

She choked a breath out and looked at him as if he'd lost his mind.

"What?" he asked, his hands rising, palms up. "What is with you?"

Her eyes filled with tears. "I just killed bloody Peter Rabbit."

Ian licked his lips. "Rori, it's a damn rabbit. Some farmer is glad the thing won't be eating his vegetables or some such."

"But I just mowed down a bunny!"

This from the woman hired to kill him. Sighing, he turned and said, "Rori, get in the damn car."

She stood for another minute and he turned, waited until she wiped her eyes. "I think you should drive."

He chuckled then quickly swallowed it as she shot him a look.

Without a word, he waited until she shut the passenger door. He looked back at the dead bunny and chuckled, shaking his head.

Ian climbed in, put the car in gear and continued on.

She was adorable. Completely adorable. The woman was one of the best assassins, and she freaked when she ran over a rabbit.

Smiling inwardly, Ian drove up to his parents' house near dark. Quinlan's Lexus sat in the driveway.

Rori hadn't said a word.

When she reached for the door handle, he grabbed her hand. "What are you thinking about?"

She took a deep breath. "Sorry I flipped back there. I've had a lot on my mind all afternoon and Mr. Rabbit just . . ." She huffed out a breath.

"What?" he asked again, running his thumb over the ring he'd placed there on her finger.

"You come from all this," she muttered. "Kinncaids are all about family."

And he wanted her to be a permanent part of it. "So?"

"So, I realize I don't know . . . that is . . ."

"What?" he asked, something in him tightening.

She took another deep breath. "Half the damn time I don't know what I'm bloody doing with Darya. I wonder if I'm doing it wrong, what it is, how to do it better, how to make her feel safe . . . And then other times . . ."

"Other times?" he prompted.

"I can see why people have kids. Like at the hospital. The baby was . . ." She frowned. "Well, different, all . . . little."

He chuckled, leaned over the console and kissed her. "They're supposed to be."

"I can't ever have one." Her voice wavered. "When the doctors told me, it didn't mean anything."

Her eyes filled with a pain he couldn't take away. But wanted to. God, he wanted to. He held her hands and waited. "Never thought about it. Never wondered until last year when I went in for my physical and my doctor started to run tests."

"Why?"

She shook her head. "I had a cyst. Nothing major, nothing he was worried about, but felt I should know I was sterile. From the rapes, or from an infection, he wasn't certain. But I won't have kids." She looked out the windshield. "And it never really bothered me until today." Then, looking at him with a sad smile, she asked, "Isn't that pathetic?"

He shook his head. "No. It's normal. We'll adopt more."

She blinked, then shook her head. "You come from this." She motioned to the yard and everything. "Kids and heirs and begetting and all that."

He grinned. "I never wanted kids, Rori. Never planned to get married."

She snorted.

He took her chin and turned her face to him, studying the angles, the long lines that showed more strength than any woman he knew, because some of her roads he'd traveled and others he could imagine only too well. "I never wanted to put someone in that kind of danger," he admitted softly.

"After being shot at, almost blown up, and left behind, I can appreciate that decision." She shook her head. "We are so fucked up, luv."

He laughed. "I love it when you say that."

"That we're fucked up?"

"No, *luv*, all British on me."

They climbed out of the car and walked up the driveway. At the door he paused, held her hand and rolled the wedding band on her finger. Looking at it, he said, "You know, I'm glad I got this when I saw it." The gold reflected in the soft outside lights. "It fits you. You. Us. Whatever." He held her hand, brought it to his lips and kissed the finger that held his mark. Ian leaned in and kissed her, held her face in his hands and tried to show her everything he couldn't put into words.

He finally reached behind her and opened the door. And the first thing he smelled was Elianya—a mixture of heavy, dark floral and musk.

He almost jerked back, but thankfully didn't. Still standing with Rori, his hand still on the doorknob, he scanned what he could and catalogued it as surely as he would any other hostile situation. He saw the coat, and glancing in the hall mirror caught a flash of a woman with a gun. God help them all.

Leaning closer, he whispered into Rori's ear, "Follow my lead. Get pissed, scream at me, call me names and then leave. Whatever you do, do *not* go in the house, don't even look in the house. Take the car, call John, and get your ass back here."

"Why?" she asked, tensing against him as he pressed the car keys into her hands.

"Tell John to call Pete. Elianya Hellinski is here with my family in the living room. From the gun in her hand, I'm pretty damn certain it's not a friendly sit-down. How the hell . . ."

"I'm not leaving you."

"Damn it!" he yelled, pushing her toward the yard. "I'm not asking you, Rori. I'm fucking telling you."

She took a deep breath, her eyes flashing. "This is so bloody like you! Everything is always Ian's way. On Ian's time. At Ian's convenience. Well, I'm tired of it! Sick and bloody tired!"

"Lower your voice," he said, still loud.

"I don't have to. I'm tired of this game. Tired of being at your bleeding beck and call. It's not my fault if you can't accept the truth."

"What truth?" He still didn't look behind him, but left the door open enough that anyone in the living room beyond could hear, if not all, at least enough to understand the disagreement.

"You don't listen!" she yelled. "I'm leaving!"

"No, you're not. Rori, come back here! Rori!" he yelled and hurried after her even as she jumped in the car, spitting gravel up into the air.

He prayed to God she got to Johnno. Taking a deep breath and making certain he had his extra gun in the small of his back, he turned and slammed the front door as hard as he could. "Damn it all to hell and back anyway," he said.

He strode past the living room, as if intent on going upstairs. And as he knew she would, her voice floated out.

"Ian, do join us."

He halted, stopped in the middle of unbuttoning the top button of his shirt, and slowly turned.

"Elianya." Her hair was jet black, styled shorter, her eyes a dark brown, thanks, no doubt, to colored contacts. Still, she shouldn't be here. There was no way she should have gotten past all the damn guards.

He glanced quickly around the room. His parents sat on the couch, Darya between them. Quinlan was tied to a chair, his head hanging. Was his brother alive? Where the hell were Gar and Roth?

To Elianya he said, "You've a new hairstyle and color, I see. The spa did a wonderful job." He nodded. "Not many can carry off that hair color."

Taking another deep breath, he stepped into the room. How much time did they have?

His heart thundered in his chest. One last mission. This one last job. Please, God, don't let this be his failure. He had way too much at stake.

Chapter 30

"Can you call Pete?" Rori asked into the phone, pulling to the side of the road and cutting the lights.

"Yeah, where are you?"

"At the end of the driveway, just off the highway." She cut the car off and knew they'd be going on foot.

"I'll be there in just a minute." John hung up and she waited.

Her hands shook. It had been so long since her hands shook because of a job; she could only stare at them. Hell. Leaning over, she checked the glove box. Empty. Console empty.

Under the seat. Ah. Extra gun. Thank God. She turned it. A SIG Sauer P222. Fit perfectly in her hand.

She got out, locked the car and waited. At least she'd worn black today and boots. Her fingers thrummed on her thigh.

She listened and heard John coming down the highway before his lights cut across the corner and he barreled to a stop by her car. He too was in black. Some habits were hard to break.

He pulled a bag from the back of the SUV he drove.

"You managed to keep Aiden at home."

He shrugged. "Didn't ask. Just took off and told him to stay by the phone and to let no one but Ian or me into the house."

John opened the case and took out a knife, shoved it down near his ankle. A gun into the small of his back, another in his waist. A coil of rope and duct tape.

"Cool, tape. Can I help?"

For a moment, he paused, then said, "Where did you get the car?"

"Ian. He took it from the garage this morning."

He nodded. "Hand me the keys. I can't take her in an SUV with car seats."

She didn't need to ask who, as she handed him the keys. "If she hurts them . . ."

He paused in shoving the keys into his pocket. "Elianya Hellinski is mine. She always has been. I've waited for too long for this."

Instead of arguing with him, she started off toward the house. He quickly passed her and she jogged alongside him through the woods back to the house.

"We'll go in by one of the back doors and try to sneak up on her."

"That's your plan?" she asked.

"Got a better one?"

"You take the back door. I'll take the upstairs. She'll either come out those French doors or she'll have to go through the entryway. If I'm anywhere else, she'll see because of that stupid hall mirror."

The dead leaves crunched under their boots.

John mumbled something to himself she didn't catch, then said, "Pete will be here in about half an hour. He said he was flying."

"Good."

He stopped, turned to her and put his hand on her arm. "I have to be gone with her by then."

"Why, John?"

With a voice as cold as the winter, he said, "She killed my family. My girls. My wife. I can't let her go this time. No matter what the cost."

"The explosion." Damn. Understanding, Rori nodded. "Let's rock and roll, mate."

Neither spoke as they made their way to the house and through the backyard. In one of the windows they could easily see in. The woman in a siren red pantsuit held a gun in one hand, a 9-millimeter from the looks of it, and something in her other hand, which she used to motion to Quinlan, still strapped to the chair. He had something taped to his chest.

"Bloody hell."

"Bitch." John took the phone out and she heard him softly telling whoever it was at the other end to get a bomb squad out here as well, explaining the situation.

Personally she thought the woman was stupid. Had she really thought she'd get away with it? Not that Rori wanted her to even *try*, but from what she'd read and learned of Elianya Hellinski in the last month, the woman should have really thought this one through a bit more.

Where the hell were their bodyguards?

There was no sign of Roth. Or she hadn't thought so until she saw his jean-clad legs near one of the doorways.

John motioned to the darkened French doors on the side of the house. She nodded and jogged down, climbing the ivy and trellis until she reached Darya's room. She kicked the doors in, then made her way through the room and quickly to the top curve of stairs, directly over the entryway.

. . .

"What do you want?" he asked Elianya, always keeping his eyes on her. One gun, one detonator. Anger pushed through him.

"Isn't it obvious?" she purred.

The 9-millimeter Glock was a concern, but it was the detonator she held in the other hand that worried him the most. He sat in the chair across from his brother, Roth's feet near him. He could see the pool of blood, the trickle out of the corner of his friend's mouth. Rage at that alone clawed through him.

His parents sat on the couch and he could see the mixture of fear and anger in their faces. His father was tapping his fingers on his knee. Mom's hands were white-knuckled. He couldn't blame them. Darya was staring at the woman, her face pale. If he'd ever wondered, ever had any lingering doubts on whether or not Darya had met Elianya, they were now gone. As clearly as if Darya had spoken to him, her eyes and expression, both angry and terrified, glared at Elianya.

He looked back at their captor. Think. Think. There had to be a way out. There was always a way out. "Let them go."

Elianya chuckled and leaned down the back of his chair, her breath hot on his ear. "Do they know who you really are?" she whispered.

His parents watched them, his father as angry as he'd ever seen him.

"What did you give my brother?" he asked, shifting his gaze to Quinlan.

"Little of this, little of that." Her laugh grated across his nerves. "A new Elianya creation."

Good God. Quinlan's head hung to his chest, and sweat dripped off his brow. Every now and then he'd twitch. Please let him be all right. She could have given him any cocktail. Hell, now his brother's heart could be giving out and . . . No! Pain hummed at the base of his skull.

Ian closed his eyes and took a deep breath. Focus. Anger wouldn't get anyone in this room out alive.

"Some do all right on my little creation, and other than the headaches, Quinlan's been doing fine."

"How long have you been giving it to Quinlan?" he asked. How the hell long had she been working to get to him?

She laughed again. "Since the night I met him." Again she leaned down. "Have to say, for brothers, you both do things marvelously similar and yet so differently."

He closed his eyes. "How much have you given him, Elianya?"

Her heels clicked as she walked around past him. "Enough, maybe too much. I've given him quite a bit tonight."

"What the hell did you give him, Elianya?"

She smiled, evil and catlike, and even with the colored contacts, he could see the madness that drove her, the depravity that lurked just beneath the polished exterior. "My newest money creation. A cross between X, Dimitri, and roofies, bit of enhancement. So technically he could fuck until he overheated himself, thus frying his brain. Probably die with a hard-on for me." Her laughter grated out again. "Think how many men will now die very, very happy. My creation has that same side effect as X and we can't ever seem to get rid of that one." She shrugged and straightened. Her laughter reminded him of nails on a chalkboard. She walked around the back of the couch and put her hand to Darya's head, watching him all the while.

He wanted to simply kill her.

Her grin grew.

Darya jerked her head up and glared over her shoulder at Elianya.

"You ruined so much, Dimitri. I worked long and hard to build up the business I did."

He nodded. "Child porn and child prostitution is a hard market to break into, is it?"

"Always playing the sinner," she said, "and all the while you're the saint."

She walked behind his mother and he fisted his hands. Leaning down, Elianya pointed toward him with the gun, and said close to his mother's head, "Do you know your son has killed people, Mrs.

Kinncaid?"

His mother's eyes locked with his, but he looked away.

"Like you?" his mother asked.

Ian closed his eyes and snapped in Czech to Elianya, hoping his parents would stay out of it.

"What? Don't want them to know how you carried out hits?" she asked him in turn. Then in English. "Killed for profit. Killed because he was ordered to and, I daresay, in some cases simply because he felt like it." Behind Darya she stopped again and put her hands, one with the gun, the other with the detonator, on his daughter's shoulders. "Did you kill my guard I left behind?"

He only stared at her.

She laughed. "Such the hero." Shaking her head, she said, "That was always your problem, Dimitri. Or should I call you Ian?"

He didn't answer and she continued, moving toward him.

"I wanted you. But you thought you were too good for me. No man rejects me. No man. And then you ruined it more by creating all that trouble for my business." She leaned down and kissed him, bit his lip until he bled. He pulled back and thought about hitting her. He could probably get the detonator away, but if he didn't . . .

Quinlan hadn't moved.

His mother kept looking from one to the other to the body on the floor.

"Let them go," he said.

Elianya shook her head. "No. And why would I?" Those dark eyes flashed. "I want you to suffer. So who goes first?" She stepped behind his brother and grinned, then his mother, tapping his mother's temple with the 9-millimeter, then his father.

"Time to choose. Come on, Ian. You were always so quick to make decisions." She strolled back toward Quinlan.

What the hell did he do in this situation? Disarm her? But there were too many possible casualties.

Without warning, she aimed and shot his brother in the thigh.

"No!"

His yell mixed with his mother's and his father's. Darya's scream stifled to a whimper.

The deranged woman merely quirked a brow at him. "So, which will it be? Who will go first?"

He would kill her.

"Or I can just play with them for a while?"

His brother hadn't even moved. Still he was slumped in the chair. What the fuck had she given him for a bullet wound to not even penetrate? He should know, bullets freaking hurt like a mother. From here he could see the blood soaking his brother's pants. Was it soaking too quickly? Had she hit an artery? Please, no.

Elianya pointed the gun at his parents again.

He could have sighed as she left Darya out.

Her husky laugh blacked the room. "Your *daughter* here will be coming back with me. I can make a *lot* of money off of her."

Something in him snapped and he simply stared at her. And stared. The edges of his vision cleared, sharpened, focused. He stared even as he felt the blessed coldness seeping over him, the ice that preceded the action. He calmed his breathing, felt his heart slow.

He didn't blink, didn't look away from the woman.

She blinked and took a step back. "Well . . ." She shook her head. "You should decide."

Ian took a deep breath and stood. She flinched. Good. And she took another step back, even better.

"You've taken my guns, Elianya," he said, his voice low and cold. "Surely you're not afraid of me."

Her chin jutted up. He wanted to get her away from them. Away from his parents, his brother, and sure as hell his daughter.

"I fear no man."

Staring at her another moment, he said, "You will."

She cocked a brow. "I doubt it."

He only smiled.

Elianya frowned, motioned with the gun to the people on the couch. "I haven't got all night. First? Well, it should be one of your parents since if I blow your brother . . ." She laughed again. "You see what I mean. Then it would be over for everyone."

• • •

Rori decided to hell with this. She quietly ran down the back stairs to the kitchen, where Becky hummed and slammed stuff into bowls. She took one look at Rori and startled. "What are you about, then?"

"Shh . . . and stay in here." She started out the door then turned back. "I mean it, Becky. Do *not* come out of this kitchen for any reason or you just might get someone killed."

Rori drew her gun and hurried toward the living room.

Outside the hall doorway, she saw John crouched low and holding his gun. He shook his head at her.

A bomb. A detonator. A gun. Five hostages.

But the woman didn't know who *she* was. She smiled at John, hurried back down the hallway and outside. At least she still had her coat on. She ran around the front of the house. She shoved her gun . . . coat pocket and shoot through it? Or leave it at her back and pull it?

Well, if back, it could be seen. Of course it would be hard to miss either way.

Bloody hell, she shoved it in her waist at the small of her back and pulled her shirt out.

She opened the door and slammed it, muttering, "Bloody-ass animals. Bambi would just *have* to run in front of me. First the rabbit, then the damn deer." She turned the corner and gasped. "What the bloody hell is going on, then?"

Ian glared at her.

"Ah, the little wife." She motioned with her 9-millimeter.

Well, damn. The woman should really try a different gun.

Rori stepped cautiously into the room. Play the stupid wife.

"What's going on? Ian?" She put a quiver in her voice.

Elianya Hellinski was beautiful, those large slanted eyes, jet-black hair, a body a centerfold would envy. She motioned with her gun for Rori to come closer. Detonator in one hand, gun in another.

Rori walked up to the woman, trying to act afraid. Not that it was too bloody hard. If they all made it out of here alive, she had several things to say to Ian. She and the woman stood on this side of the couch. Ian as well, but closer to Jock, who also stood now, but on the other side of the sofa.

"I'll give you any amount of money you want," the old man told her.

Elianya laughed. "Oh, dear man, I could buy out your entire operation. I don't need your money. What I want is your son to beg me."

Ian looked at her, his hands up as he tried to put himself between her and his family. "You want me to beg, Elianya. Then I'm begging. Please let them go. You don't need them. You want me."

She smiled. "Say it again."

He gritted his teeth, the muscle ticking in his jaw, his eyes as cold and merciless as Rori had ever seen them. "Please."

Elianya motioned with the gun. "On your knees."

His eyes met Rori's and in them she saw his anger, his fear, his love. He dropped to his knees.

Oh, God.

Rori stood closest to the door, Ian stood almost directly in front of his father, who thankfully remained on the other side of the couch. Elianya was between Rori and them. Kaitlyn and Darya were still on the couch and Quinlan moaned in the chair.

"Oh, my Gawd," Rori drawled, looking closer at Quinlan. His chin almost at his chest, sweat dripping off his forehead. Blood stained his thigh and his pants' leg. "What is the matter with him?"

It drew the woman's attention from Ian and she glanced at Rori, then back to Ian. "Is she really your wife? I didn't figure she was your type, darling."

Rori jerked. "Darling? You're calling my . . ." she said, stepping closer, ". . . my husband darling?"

First priority was the bomb. She'd leave the gun to Ian.

"Yes."

"*My* husband."

Elianya looked slyly at Ian. "You didn't tell her about us?"

She looked from one to the other. "Us? What the bloody hell is she talking about, Ian?"

Rori strode over to him, letting her anger at the woman boil over to Ian. "Us?"

Ian shrugged. "It's not what you think?"

"Not what I bloody think? Think?" She took a deep breath, braced her feet. Ian's eyes flashed and she whirled on Elianya. "Did you sleep with my husband?" She willed tears to her eyes.

Elianya shook her head and laughed. "Yes. Several times and several ways."

"You bitch!" Whirling back to Ian, she cried, "And you . . . you . . . how can I ever trust you to—" She kicked straight back, dead center at the woman's chest, and grabbed the woman's wrist, twisting it until Elianya dropped the detonator into Rori's hand. She tossed it over her shoulder to Ian.

As Elianya brought the gun up, Rori pivoted and kicked again, but the woman had turned. Elianya looked at Ian, then past him.

As Rori tried to kick her again, pulling her own gun free, Elianya leaned to the side, aimed and shot.

Rori heard Ian's shout, but didn't turn. She kicked the woman under the chin, Elianya's head snapping back, the gun shooting to the ceiling, even as she aimed her own at the fallen woman.

• • •

The sting of the bullet bit into Ian's shoulder. He slammed into his father, taking them both to the floor.

His eyes met Jock's and all he saw in his father's eyes was pain. God, no.

"Ian?" his dad whispered.

"It's okay, Dad. It'll be okay." He tried to roll off, but pain bit into his chest and his vision wavered.

"Ian? No. No. No." His father's voice sounded warbled.

The detonator. He felt the box in his hand and prayed to God he hadn't endangered them.

"Dad . . ." he hissed through the pain burning in his chest.

• • •

John ran into the room. "You're as bad as Ian is. Impulsive idiocy for lucky fools." He kicked the gun out of Elianya's hand. She was out cold.

Rori took a deep breath and turned. Kaitlyn was on her knees on the floor. Rori didn't see Jock or Ian. She hurried over and saw Ian lying atop his father, a hole in his back and Jock shaking his head, muttering, "No. No."

"Oh, Jesus."

Rori leapt over the couch, even as she heard the rip of tape from across the room.

"Ian hit?" John yelled.

Rori turned him over. No exit wound. Bloody hell. He moaned and glared up at her. "If you ever, ever do anything so fucking stupid again, I swear I will have your ass." He hissed an inhale through gritted teeth.

She was so relieved tears stung her eyes. "Stay still."

"Rori!" John yelled.

"Yeah, Ian's hit, but I don't think too bad." She prayed it wasn't lodged in his lung or worse. Bloody hell, she couldn't think.

The sound of a helicopter chopped through the air. Thank God.

"Detonator," Ian muttered.

She looked in his hand; he'd caught it and still held it cradled in his palm.

Jock pulled himself up and knelt over his son.

John came over and looked for himself. He helped roll Ian onto his back, felt his vitals.

Mrs. Kinncaid was looking at Rori from Quinlan's side, where'd she'd already tied off his wound with . . . a curtain cord?

Rori smiled slightly. "I think Ian'll be all right."

For a second, Kaitlyn's eyes dropped to Ian on the floor, before focusing on Quinlan again. Her hands slapped his face. "Come on, Quin! Damn it! Damn it! Someone get this damn thing off my son!"

"Mrs. Kinncaid," John said. "A bomb squad is coming. I'm not touching that until one arrives. I don't care for anything to go wrong. When help arrives, tell them Quinlan's overdosed on a type of ecstasy and roofies. A chemical blend of both. He's your more critical, especially since the bitch put a bullet in him as well." He slapped Ian's good arm. "This bloke here will be just fine." To Ian he said, "I won the bet."

"What bet?" Ian's mouth was white-lined and hard, his lips thinned.

"Which of us would get shot next." John looked at Elianya, his eyes hard. "Roth is bad. I think one of the bullets caught his lung." Leaning over Ian, he said, "I've got to go."

Ian nodded. "Call me."

Rori glanced over her shoulder to see Darya scamper off the couch and wedge her way to Ian. She put her hand on his and said, "Papa."

Chapter 31

Elianya Hellinski looked at the man who was slipping into a wet suit. He slung the scuba tanks onto his back.

"Let's talk about this."

He stopped and looked at her, his dark brown eyes devoid of mercy. "I've dreamed for years what I'd do to you. But I thought this was fitting. Unfortunately, I don't have time for more."

She pulled against her bound wrists, looked down at the bomb strapped to her chest. "I didn't mean—"

He whirled and leaned down low into her face. "You meant exactly that, Elianya. You murdered children. You've hidden that fact. You profit from their pain."

"You don't want to do this," she said, lowering her voice.

His eyes were hard and unforgiving, as she'd never seen them. "I've never wanted anything more."

Somehow she'd get out of this. Without another word, he walked out of the cabin and up the steps.

She had no idea where they were, only that they were on a boat. He'd told her she could scream all she wanted and no one would hear her.

Something banged on the deck and she wiggled again. She was not about to die. Not now.

She heard the splash.

God. Her heart slammed in her ribs. He wouldn't really do it. He wouldn't.

She didn't know how long she sat there. That was all it was. Just a terror tactic. Tell her it was a bomb and horrify her.

He'd loved her once too. He wouldn't kill her.

More time ticked away. Elianya strained against her bonds, but there was no give.

She took a deep breath.

The world exploded.

• • •

Jock paced the confines of the waiting room. Kaitlyn was down the hall lying down in one of the empty rooms. It was either that or he and the boys were going to have her admitted. She had been acting off all damn evening, not that he could blame her.

When Aiden said they wanted the nurse to check his blood pressure, Jock had said fine, worried himself. His blood pressure was fine, surprisingly. Kaitlyn's, on the other hand, was up. She was stressed and more upset than he'd ever seen her. The doctor finally just administered a sedative. Jock knew he and the boys would pay hell when she woke up in the morning. So be it. There was too much right now, he couldn't worry about her too. If she wasn't going to rest on her own, then they'd simply force her body to rest for her.

He raked his hands through his hair and checked the clock again. He had stayed in the room with Kaitlyn until he knew she was out, then he'd started to walk the halls.

It had been hours. *Hours* and still he didn't know for certain how either of his sons were doing. The doctors said they were both doing fine, but both were hooked to more machines and wires . . . Neither had awakened yet. Everyone was more worried about Quinlan. Without a doubt.

God. He sat in one of the chairs, glad no one else was around. The boys were somewhere, their wives . . . kids . . . Parents were supposed to protect their children.

His heart slammed in his chest.

Quinlan had coded when they'd reached the ER here. Jock's hands shook. Goddamn it! He swiped his eyes and took a deep breath. But they'd managed to bring him back and flushed his system. Jock didn't know how or care how, the fact his son was alive was all that mattered right now.

And Ian . . .

Jesus. When that bitch had come in and waved the gun around, the bomb strapped to Quin . . .

He propped his elbows on his knees and held his head in his hands. He knew that woman wouldn't have thought twice about shooting any of them, hadn't even blinked when she'd put a bullet in Quinlan and then Ian. Hell, she'd aimed at him. At *him*. Jock had seen the satisfaction in her demented eyes as she'd pulled the trigger and then . . .

Ian. Ian had slammed into him and he'd known, known the second that damn bullet hit his son, felt the thumping impact, heard Ian's hiss of breath.

And fear had sucked all the air from his own lungs, all the feeling from his fingers. For seconds he couldn't move. All he saw were those eyes he'd passed to his son, staring back into his own. All he could think of was Ian as a little boy and how he'd wasted so much time with his son because of pride.

Dad. Ian had called him Dad and it had been a long damn time since he'd heard that word from that boy.

It's okay, Dad. It'll be okay.

Well, it wasn't *okay*. Okay was *not* kids taking bullets for their parents.

He took a deep breath and wondered where he'd gone so wrong. Why couldn't his sons find happiness without pain and danger stalking them? He'd joked with Kaitlyn it was because of her grandmother's curse on their children. But honestly, he'd never put stock in the old woman's angry epithets. Though now he wondered if his children truly were cursed as she'd yelled all those years ago — that his and Kaitlyn's children would have to fight hard to find peace and happiness in love. Whether or not the woman affected them all, his children fought hard for what they had.

He didn't want them fighting this hard. God, not this hard. His fingers dug into his skull. One son shot trying to save him. And the other still unconscious.

Please, please, please, let them be all right, he prayed. *Please. Please.*

Jock startled at the touch on his wrist. He looked up and into Darya's blue, worried eyes.

She smiled, her cheeks dimpling, and patted his hand. She held up her teddy bear to him.

He sniffed, leaned up and patted his lap. "You want to sit here with me, princess?"

Her head cocked to the side, then she climbed up into his lap. She was so small, so little.

He took another deep breath and laid his head atop her black curls. He glanced up at the movement in the doorway and saw Rori. The look of relief on her face when she saw Darya told him she'd been looking for her. Without another word, she turned and walked back down the hall.

Darya snuggled up to him, holding the bear tight between both of them. The tick of the clock echoed in the still room.

He kissed the top of her head.

"Papa," she whispered.

He rocked her. "Yes, your papa is something else."

Darya closed her eyes as the big man rocked her. He smelled like candies and spices. She turned her head and breathed deep.

She realized he was like her new papa. This man often seemed mean, but he really was a helper. She wondered if he ever rescued little girls like her new papa. Had this man been nice to someone he hadn't needed to be nice to?

She frowned and stuck her thumb into her mouth. She wanted her papa. She hadn't seen her new papa since all the ambulance people came and took him away. But he'd had blood on his back and she didn't want him to die.

They told her he was fine.

So why couldn't she see him?

What if he went away too? What if the monsters took him away like they did Zoy? She knew, even as her heartbeat fluttered in her chest, that she'd never see Zoy again.

"Papa," she whispered, leaning back and looking at this big man who held her, another who would keep her safe.

He smiled down at her, reached over and picked up a book.

The pictures in this one weren't nearly as pretty as the one he read her at home, but it was still nice to listen to him talk, even if she couldn't understand him. The deep rumble from his chest lulled her to peace.

Please let her new papa be all right, she prayed.

She wanted her papa. She wanted to go swimming again with him.

Darya tried not to think of Papa or that he was behind that one big door where Rori kept going in and out of.

Instead she focused on the big man's voice, listened to the calming rumble and wondered what he was saying. When he sniffed again, she pulled back.

Tears glistened on his old weathered cheeks.

She frowned, reached up, and wiped them off. Maybe even big people got scared too.

• • •

The shrill notes of his cell phone woke him. He blinked and smelled the stringent smells of the hospital. He looked to his right and saw Rori and Pete.

He blinked, looked around, looked to the side of the bed and lifted his hand. God, how long had he been out?

"'Bout time you woke up."

He tried to lift his other hand and realized it was taped to his chest. A crackle against his chest between his fingers made him look down. A crinkled photograph lay there. He smiled.

"She left it," Rori said. "You want a drink?"

He licked his lips. God, he hated anesthesia. She held a cup and straw to his lips, her long fingers wrapped around it, the light glinting off her wedding ring. He closed his eyes.

Ian swallowed, shook his head, then settled back into the pillow. He looked at Pete. "What are you doing here?"

Pete glanced to Rori, who patted him, said something to Pete and walked out of the room. Pete stood by the bedside shaking his head. "Hell, I let you quit and still you cause trouble."

Ian waited, then remembered. "Quinlan?"

Pete frowned. "Holding his own. She'd OD'd him. He was crashing by the time we got him in, his brain so hot . . ." He shook his head. "Coded in the ER here. But they got him back. Still unconscious, had to do extensive surgery on his leg, bullet messed up his knee, but your mother and brother seem confident."

Fuck. "He's okay though?"

"Far as anyone can tell. They won't know the extent of any damage until he wakes up."

He looked around. "Where are we?"

"Naval hospital. Seemed the best way to keep it quiet."

Ian snorted. "Is Darya all right?" Images flashed in his brain. The shot, the pain, his father's eyes. "My father?"

Pete nodded. "Yeah. Both fine. Tired. Everyone seems worried about your mom. Had some dizzy spells and the doctors told her to lie down or they'd admit her. She didn't listen, they learned her blood pressure was up, so Gavin bribed one of the docs here to give her a sedative that first night and they poured her into one of the empty beds. She's still pissed. But she's better, pressure's down. Your dad is fine."

Ian took a deep breath and winced, the oxygen dry in his nose. He still hadn't asked about Roth. "Roth?"

"Roth is still in surgery. Took a bullet to the lung. Gar was unconscious at the penthouse, but the sedative she injected in him has worn off. He's outside still apologizing to your parents."

Ian closed his eyes. Damn. Thoughts and images, disjointed, jagged, sharp and blurred, danced endlessly through his brain.

Pete cleared his throat. "Thought you might be interested to know that all loose ends are now tied, knotted and snipped."

"When?" he asked, not bothering to open his eyes.

"I have no idea. But, considering Brasher's history, for him to call and tell me it was done was enough."

Ian felt Pete thump the railing on the bed. "Get better fast. The longer you're in here, the harder it is to keep things quiet."

He didn't open his eyes as he heard Pete leave, heard the door shut. The squeaks and rolling of a cart out in the hall carried into the room. God, he'd failed them. The entire situation . . .

He heard the door open, heard the whisper of voices and then felt the bed give.

The small hand on his face had him opening his eyes. Rori held Darya on the edge of the bed. "Hey, pumpkin," he said in Russian.

She leaned over and kissed his cheek.

He looked at Rori, noted the exhaustion in her eyes, the taut pull of her face. She was worried and he didn't like it. Smiling at her, he reached his good hand up and laid it on top of hers. "You make a damn good Kinncaid."

She smiled. "Your father said the same thing, then quoted some family motto or something." She shook her head, and tried to pull her hand free.

He didn't want to let her go. "No, stay. Both of you." He was tired. So tired.

"I want to take a trip," he said.

Her chuckle warmed him. "Another one?"

He opened his eyes and looked at her. "I was thinking something more family-oriented. Like the theme parks in Orlando, Florida."

Her grin grew. "Really? I've never been there."

He nodded and hoped. Hoped she wouldn't walk out of his life one day as unexpectedly as she'd strolled into it. "We could all practice being a family."

Darya leaned over, kissed his cheek, then squirmed off the bed and ran to the doorway. Jock stood on the other side staring in. He nodded to Ian and took Darya's hand, pulling the door closed again. Ian relaxed in the quiet, closed his eyes and just held Rori's hand.

Neither spoke for a while. The occasional beep of the IV machine pierced the quiet.

"I love you," she whispered.

He sighed, felt his heart relax, and grinned. "I love you too."

"There's just one thing we need to discuss," she said, her voice edged on a tease.

"What?"

"You ordering me about."

Still he didn't open his eyes. "Well, before we talk about it, I should go ahead and give you this one last order. Then we'll talk about it."

She sniffed.

"I think you make a great mom and you have to keep doing it." He opened his eyes. "I won't let you leave. You're mine. A Kinncaid, and by all that I hold dear, I'll keep you in my life. Period. You're my other half, the balance I've looked for, and I'll be damned if I have to live without that."

She didn't say anything for a long time, just stared at him. Finally, she scoffed. "Well, I think there are some unsettled issues there, at least with Darya. We need to close her past so we can all move forward."

He narrowed his eyes. "So you're staying with us?"

Her eyes narrowed back. "She's my bloody daughter as well, and why the bloody hell would I tell you I loved you, then turn around and walk away?" She took a deep breath, as if getting ready to battle. Then she exhaled, the breath hot in his face and faintly minty. "I'm going to write this off as your brain's still fogged from your injuries, boyo." She sniffed. "Now, as I was saying, before I was interrupted.

We need to *close* Darya's past."

He narrowed his eyes at her again and tightened his hold on her hand. "You're not going after them. They're mine."

She jutted her chin up. "I can if I want and she's *mine* as well, so I'll do as I please."

"No, you won't." He closed his eyes.

"You can't stop me if you're in bed, here in the hospital."

He shook his head. "Rori, wait until they release me, then we'll argue over which of us will or won't kill the bastards."

• • •

December 1, 3:45 p.m.

Ian sat beside his brother's hospital bed. He'd been here for two hours. Everyone else had something to do today, but he knew they'd all be by later.

Roth was released last week and had to go through rehab. The chest wound had not been nearly as severe as it could have been, thank goodness. He was on the mend and on paid leave, which the stubborn ass had argued about.

Ian leaned up and grabbed his brother's hand.

Quinlan had awakened from his semi-coma state earlier this week. But he still had long episodes of sleep, with only brief spurts of alertness.

Why, Ian didn't understand. Since she'd used a new combination of chemicals, no one really knew what the outcome would be.

But Quin, when awake, knew them all and spoke a bit. So that was a good sign.

He knew his brother wasn't awake now, but still he talked. He had to. The guilt was eating him up inside. No one blamed him.

But he did.

"Hey, buddy. You really should wake up. You know we've done this before when you were like what? Seven? Wasn't cool then. Isn't cool now." Nothing. "Your schedules and time sheets and what all are going all to hell." He waited, but Quin didn't wake up. "And I went by your office. Place is a wreck. With you gone this long, the whole place is just going to hell."

One corner of Quin's mouth kicked up under the oxygen hose

still in his nose.

"Your secretary quit," Ian said.

Quin opened his eyes. Licking his lips, he said, "She did not. She came by before you did."

Ian stared at his brother, bit down until pain shot up his jaw and began to hum at the base of his skull.

"You just like lying there?" he asked.

Quinlan snorted. "Real fun." He tried to shift.

"How are you feeling?"

Quinlan closed his eyes. "Ever been run over?"

"No."

"I think this is what it might feel like. Leg fucking hurts."

Silence settled between them. Quin's hand tightened on Ian's before his voice whispered, "I'm such a fucking idiot."

Ian shook his head. "No. I should have watched closer."

"As Mom had been preaching, if I'd come around more, I'd have known what was going on."

And if Ian had paid closer attention, things would have turned out differently.

"I'm sorry," Quin said.

"Don't."

He opened his eyes. "I will." He blinked slowly. "I let the viper into our family."

"No, you didn't. I did."

"You always had to have your way. I remember that now. Annoying as hell."

Ian smiled. "Yeah, well."

"What happened that night? No one will tell me." Quin's hand tightened even more on his and his eyes, so like their mother's, bore into him.

Ian took a deep breath. "You sure you want to know? I'm not going to tell you if you're only going to lie here, beat yourself up and feel sorry for yourself."

"Cold bastard."

Ian nodded. "I am that."

"Tell me."

"She drugged you, almost killed you, strapped a bomb to your chest, got you into the house under the guise you were sick. Shot

Roth, and then held everyone hostage . . ." He trailed off, the anger still fresh and hot.

"And?" Quinlan asked.

"Shot you too, if I didn't mention that. Why your leg hurts like a bitch. Messed your knee up, they replaced part of it, but the bullet did damage to your femur as well." He took a deep breath. "Yes, well, then my wife showed up and decided to take matters into her own hands." He was still pissed at her for that stupid stunt.

Quinlan took a deep breath, shook his head, and gave Ian a small smile. "You two are perfect for each other."

Ian grunted.

They lapsed back into silence.

Ian rubbed his forehead. "You need anything?"

Quinlan's eyes were closed again. "Yeah."

"What?"

Those eyes opened and were clearer than he'd seen them since Quin had first awakened. "Tell me where the bitch is."

Well, then. "Dead."

"Dead?"

"You want details? I don't have them, but I'm sure I can get them."

Quin shook his head. "Christ. I don't want to know, no. Just . . . just . . ." His hand fisted. "Damn it. I slept with the woman."

"Yeah, so did I."

Quin frowned. "Are you *trying* to make me feel better or worse?"

Ian chuckled. "If it's any consolation, I think she liked you better. She said you were marvelous."

"Fuck you." Quin closed his eyes and waved toward Ian. "Go away."

Ian waited a minute, then rose from the uncomfortable chair. "I am sorry, Quinlan. Sorrier than I can ever say, and just can't figure out a way to make it right."

"And people say I worry too damn much." He opened his eyes and still the clear brilliance shone through them, the sharp intelligence.

Just as Ian suspected. Quinlan was hiding.

"I don't blame you, Ian. And like a coward, I did try. I was pissed." He shook his head. "But I'm more pissed at myself. I'm so fucking mad I can't think straight. And I just don't know how to get around that."

Ian studied him a moment. "Quit feeling sorry for yourself for one. I'm an ass, I know that. But I won't let her win you over in any damn way, shape, or form. And if you blame yourself, feel sorry for yourself, hide behind a fake front, you let her win."

For a long moment, Quin's angry green eyes pierced him. Then he said, "When you can follow that advice you just gave me, let me know." He leaned back against the pillow and sighed.

Probably enough for one day. And damn it, if the kid wasn't right on that last shot.

Ian smiled as he left his brother's room. Quinlan would be all right.

And Ian wasn't going to let the darkness win any part of them. Some jobs were simply never done.

Epilogue

Christmas Eve

Ian, Rori, and Darya had returned the day before from an extended trip to Florida and the Caribbean.

They were home with Jock and Kaitlyn for the holidays and probably a while after — if Ian could find a way to live with that — until he and Rori found their own place.

He'd decided D.C. would be the best place for their American office of KB Securities.

His parents were in town picking up Quinlan and driving him out here. He knew what his brother must think of that.

As the quiet of the day settled around him, he wondered what Rori would think of her present. He'd debated over jewelry, even went so far as to buy and wrap a pair of ruby earrings. But then, he decided it just wasn't her. So he bought her a SIG P222. Of course, she'd have to then regale him with the fact it would never equal her Walther, but that made things interesting. He'd bought Darya anything that caught his eye from clothing, to toys, to ride-on outdoor equipment. He'd learned her real name was Ayrena Vacladova. Parents died in a plane accident. He was still trying to find the aunt who was guardian of little Ayrena, who was five, and her older sister, Zoy, fourteen. As yet, there was no sign of the aunt or her rumored boyfriend.

Just the thought brought the anger back, but he ignored it and sipped his coffee. All he needed was time, and he'd find them.

She was Darya now. A new life. A new beginning, leaving the pain and old memories behind, as much as she could. He and Rori were looking into child psychologists. Gavin gave him the name of the one Ryan saw. He'd have to check the woman out first before he let Darya see her.

Darya Lenora Kinncaid, so her adoption papers said. He'd contacted Uncle Brody to draw the papers up. Kinncaid, Kinncaid & Associates of New York were a very selective law firm. It helped that he was related to them. Also had them draw a will for him while he'd been at it. The firm already handled other legalities he needed and were handling his corporate side as well. Personally, he normally didn't give a damn if things were legal—guess that would have to change. He smiled out over the winter scene beyond the window, cold and gray, the clouds low, the trees bare.

Rori and Darya were around the house somewhere.

"Oh, there ye are," Becky's voice drew his attention from the window and his own musings.

"What can I do for you, Becky?" he asked, turning to see her walk into the room.

She tossed a package to him and he caught it one-handed. Becky muttered about cooking and mail service. He didn't quite catch it all as she left.

Across the front of the Express envelope was his name and this address.

Something prickled under his skin.

He took the package to his father's office to open it in private.

Damn good thing too. Glossy photos slid out and into his hands. Not what anyone wanted to see caught forever on a freeze-frame. The photographs were not for the faint of heart. There were four eliminations in all. Three males and one female. Two of the males matched those in the crime video they'd taken the night they'd found Darya. Two men who murdered her sister and went after her.

Eliminated.

The other male he didn't recognize, but the woman he did. Darya's aunt.

Ian shook the envelope and a paper fluttered out.

He sighed, pissed, and yet strangely enough, almost relieved. The note only read: *Take care of my daughter and granddaughter. —N*

The notorious Nikko, whom Ian suspected was none other than Nickolas Morano. British Italian who worked the cold war, only to drop off the scene to become more of a shadow than he was before when he was paid to not be seen. Morano had so many kills marked to him that Ian could safely say, in comparison, he was an amateur. He had yet to meet Nikko, though he'd talked to the man twice in the last month. Nikko was always cordial, polite, and yet warning at the same time. Ian rather liked him.

Great.

Hell.

He picked up the phone and dialed John.

"What?" Johnno asked.

"You know that search I wanted you to continue to work on?"

"Which particular search would you be referring to?"

"The one where I wanted you to find the men who killed Darya's sister and the people who sold her to begin with."

"Ah, yes."

He looked at the gruesome black-and-whites on the desk, picked them up and shoved them in the envelope. After he showed them to Rori, he'd destroy them. "Forget it."

"Do what?"

"It's a done issue. A wedding present."

"Who the hell from?"

"Rori's father."

A movement from the doorway drew his attention.

"What about my father?" she asked from the doorway.

He shut the phone, hanging up on Johnno, and turned to her. "He took care of our ongoing argument."

"Oh."

"That's all she says? Oh?" He pulled her to him and kissed her. He figured for them, this was as normal as it got.

Turn the page to read the fist chapter from the next book in the Kinncaid Brothers Series, **Deadly Secrets***!*

Prologue

He waited until the patient's breathing leveled out.

"This is insane," she whispered beside him.

His attention was settled on the woman on the operating table. No one would ever know. They never ever did. That was the beauty of it all, or part of the beauty of it all.

So fucking easy.

Her swollen stomach was already an orange brown from the Betadine. He watched the monitors, the computerized screen showing not only the mother's heartbeat but the baby's as well. He listened to the soft swishing to make sure the baby's heart rate stayed within a safe range.

"Is everything ready?" he asked, already thinking ahead to a phone call he needed to make and the happy parents-to-be.

"Of course." She sighed. "I don't like these."

He was tired of listening to her complain. A shrewd bitch, but too soft too often in his opinion. "These are never pleasant. Just don't think of it. Remember, this little one will bring in fifty thousand. And it's not like anyone will miss the bloody mother. If you could even call her that."

The woman next to him said nothing as she rearranged his tools. He heard her moving the instruments around on the metal tray.

The mother's heart rate was a little high, but that didn't concern him.

He picked up the scalpel, steadied it, and quickly made a lateral incision on the very pregnant belly. Blood welled in the wake of his sharp object.

Normally, he was obscenely careful in performing this operation, but it wasn't as if he had to worry about the outcome. The mother had become a liability. He gripped both sides of the incision, prying through fat tissue and muscles, feeling the tissues rip under his force. At the uterus, he slowed, took a deep breath and concentrated. He heard the mother's erratic heart acceleration. With a precision born of practice, he carefully cut through the extended womb. The babe within squirmed, shifting beneath the tissue. The infant's heart rate swished louder in the quiet room.

In seconds, he had the baby out of the confines of the uterus. A boy, which he'd already known. Quiet squeaks filled the air while he suctioned the mucus from the babe's mouth. Then the small eyes blinked open. The cord still pulsed.

He puffed out a relieved sigh. "He's a big one."

She looked at him over the top of her mask and he read the disapproval mixed with greed in her eyes. The greed always won, always.

She clamped off the cord, her surgical gloves squeaking on the instrument, and clipped it.

"What of her?" she asked, motioning toward the woman.

He ignored the question. "We don't need any more complications. Someone will come in and take care of her. Here, get the babe ready. We've three buyers to choose from."

The operating room was filled with the newborn's cries and mewls as she wiped him off and rubbed him gently, talking softly.

He took a deep breath and pulled the mask down. "Healthy little boy, aren't you then?" he asked, rubbing a finger down the small upturned nose.

He reached over and pressed an intercom button. "Send Kevin in."

She kept her attention centered on the babe; a head full of dark black hair topped the little pink head.

"Beautiful little guy, don't you think?"

She nodded. "He's healthy. Weighing in at . . . roughly eight pounds thirteen ounces."

Music still played; the slow strands of Handel waltzed around the room.

"Apgar's good," she muttered, noting and jotting down other details of the baby's health.

He nodded and reached for his cell phone. He hit the speed dial and waited. The voice on the other end picked up. "You better have come through for the amount on the table."

He smiled. "You worry too much. Pick a buyer. Healthy dark-haired boy."

There was a pause on the other end, then a sigh. "Good. No complications?"

He shook his head, part angered that the question was asked to begin with.

Who the hell did the guy think he was to question him? "No."

"What of the other matter?" the deep voice asked again.

He had no clue and he wasn't stupid enough to say that. "It's being handled."

"You better make damn certain of that. Do whatever you must to clean things up. I'm not going down because of a mess you dragged me into."

With that the line went dead.

Lawyers were always a pain in the ass, weren't they? Lawyers could always be replaced, and if the bastard became too much of a pain, they'd just find another one.

A knock at the door startled him. He opened it to Kevin dressed in green scrubs.

"You wanted me?"

He turned back to the gurney. She was still hooked up to the respirator, but he saw there was no need of that. She'd bled out. Her heart rate was too low. He sighed, walked over, covered her with a sheet and motioned to the body bag on the floor. "Get that and help me put her in it."

The babe still squalled over in the heated bassinet.

He had to get rid of the woman. She'd known too much, asked too many questions when she should have just ignored things, gone along with it all. He'd still have her baby in the end no matter what she wanted, but she'd have been alive.

He unhooked the IVs, the breathing tube, and waited while Kevin wrapped the woman's lower body. They lifted the bloody mess and awkwardly placed her in the black body bag.

The babe continued to cry.

He had another buyer.

And more waiting for precious little bundles.

• • •

Washington, D.C., October, the present

Where the hell was his wife?

He was married. Still.

Quinlan Kinncaid looked up at the ceiling in his darkened living room. The streetlights didn't glare into the window of his penthouse suite above the family hotel. He sighed and raked his hands through his hair.

What the hell was he doing? He'd left the rest of the family earlier. They'd all taken Mom out for her birthday, so hopefully the surprise party he and his siblings had planned for tomorrow night might actually work. Probably not. Mom knew everything.

Well, just about everything. Hell, his entire, interfering family knew just about all there was to know about the others — but that was the way it had always been in his family. Now, though, now he had a secret that none of them knew and he wasn't about to tell them.

Not that he didn't want to. He just didn't know how.

Two words, dumb ass. I'm married.

And chaos would undoubtedly ensue.

His phone rang, jerking him from his thoughts of his missing and estranged wife.

It rang for a third time before he finally wrestled it from his pocket, automatically sliding his thumb across the screen to answer the call before it went to voice mail. Figuring it was one of his brothers about last-minute details, he didn't bother looking at the caller ID before he answered.

"Hello."

Silence. He rubbed a hand over his face. He really didn't have time for this.

"Hello?"

A throat cleared. "Quinlan?"

He sat up, barely wincing at the pain in his thigh. "Ella?"

"Oh thank God. Thank God I got you. I know you probably don't want to hear from me and I'm sure you've already moved on and that's fine. Really." She paused in her rush of words. "But I've got to talk to you. I don't know who else to trust, who else to — "

"Ella?"

"Yes, it's me. I know, I know I walked away and I've never been sorrier for anything I've ever done, Quin. I'm sorry." Her voice stumbled. "I'd say I'm sorry a thousand times and I know you probably don't want to help me, but I don't know who else to trust, who else to — "

"Ella." He stood from his leather couch and walked to the window, looking over the D.C. night winking and spread out before him. "Calm down, take a deep breath."

She was always so . . . calm. Spirited, yes. Funny and quirky, smart-ass even, but always a level of calm. Nothing much rattled her. But this?

He'd never heard her this way. "You're not making a lot of sense."

"I'm scared, Quin." Her voice trembled over the phone. "I don't know what to do. I don't even know what's real anymore. I can't see past . . . I don't know. I just . . ." Her voice skipped for a moment.

"Ella, I can't hear you very well. Calm down, babe. Tell me what I can do to help."

For a moment there was silence on the phone. Then he heard her take a deep breath in and blow it out.

"I don't know how to tell you this. I called weeks ago and — never mind, that doesn't matter. Did you get my letters?"

He shook his head, then realized she couldn't see him. What the hell was she talking about?

"Letters?" he asked. "What letters? I haven't received any letters from you. Hell, I haven't received anything at all from you. Not even a text."

She made some sound, part groan, part laugh? "Oh God, that's just . . . perfect. Of course you don't know what letters. That doesn't matter, or it does. It really does, but not now." Again she was quiet. Again he waited, so glad to hear her voice, that smooth Southern drawl, even if he had no freaking clue what the hell she was talking about.

Ella cleared her throat. "Look, there's something you need to know. I just don't know . . . I don't know . . . Hell, I don't know how to tell you but I'm scared. I can't eat, I can't sleep and it's too late for me to fly out to you. I could take a bus or — "

"Why are you scared, Ella?" He fisted his hand on his hip, worried because he could hear the fear in her voice.

"God, Quin, where do I even start?" She laughed but it held no amusement to him. "They won't let me go. I know they won't. I thought I could help. Thought I was doing good. I bought into it all and that was so stupid. God, I was so stupid and naïve and . . . They want her, Quin, and I'm afraid, I'm so scared they're going to just take her and I won't be able to stop them. I won't be able to stop them. Can you come out here please? I know I don't have a right to ask you. I know I don't, not after throwing it all away and—"

He closed his eyes and pinched the bridge of his nose between his thumb and forefinger. "Honey. Stop. Just stop."

She did.

"Deep breath. Come on, I can hear you."

He heard her inhale, then exhale.

"Now, who is scaring you?"

For several seconds there wasn't anything other than her sniffle.

"Did someone hurt you?" he asked, straightening, anger flashing through him. "Ella?" he snapped.

"No. No, I don't think so. I can't remember," she said, her voice almost a whisper at the end.

He started to ask what she couldn't remember, but then shook it off and headed back to his bedroom.

"Okay, we'll talk about that later. Who's scaring you, baby? Tell me." And he'd damned well take care of them. In his room, he strode to the closet, grabbed a duffle and tossed it on the bed, along with a couple of pairs of jeans and shirts. "Where are you?"

"T-Taos. Taos, New Mexico. I'm still here."

"Okay, and what's your number?" He grabbed a pen off his nightstand and the pad beside it.

"Five seven five—" She cut out again.

"Ella. Ella, I can't hear you."

"Hang on. I need to plug in." He heard her rummaging on the other end of the phone.

"What's the number again?" This time he wrote down the entire number and read it back to her to make sure it was correct. "Is that right?"

"Yes."

Taking a deep breath, he asked, "What's your address?" When she told him, he wrote that down as well, then ripped the paper off and shoved it in his pocket. "So if I call you back in a bit, you'll answer?"

"Yes. God, Quin, I'm so stupid. Do you have any idea—" Her voice broke again before she continued, "how good it is just to hear your voice, Quinlan?"

At least she could call him; he hadn't had a number to reach her, but he didn't see the point in saying that. "Same goes. You're okay now?" he couldn't help asking. "Are you safe right now?"

She didn't answer him for a moment.

"Ella."

"I think so. I don't know."

"I'm coming out there," he said as he shoved his stuff into the bag and grabbed his small overnight off the counter in the bathroom.

"I could come to you. I can drive partway tonight and—"

"I'll be there in a matter of hours, Ella." He zipped the bag shut and hurried to the safe hidden in his office down the hallway. Punching in the combination, he quickly grabbed the papers he wanted, some cash, and shut it. "Now, who are you scared of?"

Taos. He was heading to Taos. He'd need a damned jacket. He grabbed his Marmot jacket and shoved it into the bag, then jerked on his black wool coat. As an afterthought, he grabbed his briefcase and hefted it over his shoulder as well. Bags, coat, cash. His cane. Glancing around, he saw it leaning against the side table in the living room where he'd been sitting when she called.

"Ella?" She still hadn't answered him.

Cane . . . anything else? He scanned the area. No. He was good.

"Ella, answer me."

"I don't—I don't know who it is exactly. I just know they want her, Quin. They want her! And I know, I *know* they'll take her from me, no matter what I've told them. I *know* it!"

He pulled his door shut and hurried to the elevators. "Who? Who will they take?" She wasn't making any sense and that worried him almost as much as the stark fear in her words, in her hurried speech.

Her quick breaths panted through the phone.

"Okay, someone, you're not sure who is going to take someone else? Who are they going to take?"

Again her phone cut out for a minute.

"Ella! Hello?" The elevator dinged but he didn't get in just yet. He held the private elevator with his hand. He'd lose the signal inside it.

"Who are they going to take?"

He heard her inhale. Exhale.

"The baby," she said quietly.

He froze.

"Whose baby?" he asked very carefully.

For a long moment there was nothing, just silence. He thought he'd lost her or she'd hung up, or her battery finally died. But then he heard her sniffle and inhale again.

"I'm sorry, Quinlan. I'm *so* sorry and I know I can never make it up to you. I *know* that."

Oh God, she *wouldn't* . . .

"Ella," he said, whether in plea or command he wasn't sure.

"She's yours, Quinlan. Ours."

He couldn't say anything . . . His? His baby? Their baby? *His?*

Shock. Then anger burst and flared. He opened his mouth. Bit down. Opened it again.

"How . . . When . . . How could you . . ." he managed past the tightness in his throat. Very softly. Very quietly.

"I'm *sorry*. God, I'm sorry. I was helping them, or thought I was. They asked me to help and they wouldn't let me tell you, said it could compromise things. But it's all lies. Women are missing, Quin. Dead. I know they killed her. They wanted her baby. And they just took it. I know they'll take mine too! I don't know any more who to trust. Except you. I'm not supposed to be calling you, but I don't care what I screw up for them anymore. Please, Quin. Help me."

He couldn't say anything. Hell, he couldn't see. He rubbed his eyes and blinked, but that didn't really help. Squeezing his eyes tight, he tried to understand, tried to make sense of the whole damned conversation.

But he couldn't.

All he heard was *baby. Yours.*

Her voice echoed through the pulse thundering against his ears. " . . . be mad at me. Hell, yell at me, be pissed at me, I wouldn't blame you."

"Well, that's great of you, Ella," he said.

"Look, hate me even. God knows I hate myself just knowing how this hurts you, how I've already hurt you. But please, *please*, Quinlan, I *need* you. *We* need you. If you can't come out here, I'm leaving. I have to get out of here—"

Her words tripped and rattled in his mind, broke his heart and made him wonder what the hell he'd been waiting for for the last few months. Did he even know this person? Nothing made sense.

"When . . ." He took another deep breath.

"Please," she begged. "Please, help me. You'll keep her safe."

His daughter? Hell yes he would.

He opened his mouth, pissed, confused, and knew the words hot on his tongue were probably not the ones he needed to say. Instead he closed his eyes, took another deep breath and another and counted very slowly to ten. A hundred would probably be better but he didn't have the patience for a hundred.

"Ella. Are you at home?"

"What? What has that—"

"Yes or no. That's really all I can handle right now."

A beat of silence. "Yes. I'm at home."

"Good, stay there and don't move until I get there." He took another deep breath as he bit down. "Then you and I, dear wife, are going to have one long conversation about many things."

"You're coming?" she asked quietly. "You're really coming?" Again her voice broke on the end and he heard her swallow.

"God, what kind of—" She was pregnant. Pregnant. The word kept rattling in his brain. Pregnant. He probably shouldn't yell at her. Probably, but damn it.

Very carefully he said, "Ella, I'm heading to the airport now." He checked his watch, calculated the time difference. "I'll be there in about five hours, probably less. I need to call the airport and have them fuel up the jet. I'll be landing in Taos and I'll call you."

"I can come pick you up."

He nodded. "Okay. Now, is there anyone you can call to stay with you until I get there?" She was scared. Terrified, to be honest, he could tell that much. He raked a trembling hand through his hair.

He heard something in the background.

"Someone's here," she told him suddenly.

He frowned.

He heard her sigh. "Oh, it's just a friend. I'll see if she can stay. Or I'll go stay with my neighbors the Richardsons after she leaves. Then you'll be here and it'll be okay."

A friend. He set his briefcase in the elevator and then tossed his duffle bag inside. He bit down. "Mrs. Kinncaid . . ." He shook his head. They'd get into that all later after he made certain she was safe. "Stay put. I'll be there soon."

• • •

New Mexico, October, the present

Can't die . . . can't die . . .

The lights. Too bright. Too dim. Everything in contrast. Where was she? She blinked and tried to focus.

The street blurred before her. She saw the dark river of asphalt. The tall, wavering streetlights. Flickers of lights zoomed to and fro farther down the way.

Where was she?

She stopped, the road cold beneath her bare feet. Her foot hurt. Her ankle hurt.

She raised her hands and saw there was blood on them. Blood and scabs on her mangled wrists. Her shoulders hurt. Her head throbbed. Hell, her whole body seemed to pulse with pain, almost distant and dull, but not quite enough.

The cold wind blew against her legs and she looked down. Something shimmered, dark and glossy, along the bottoms of her legs. Why couldn't she think?

Something important.

She put her hands on her stomach.

Important . . .

And remembered.

Her stomach.

The baby. The baby . . . *Her* baby.

The bump was different. Smaller, softer. She pressed her abdomen with her bloody hand splayed on her stomach.

No. No. No.

Images, disjointed and fractured, jumped in her brain.

A baby crying.

Red hair.

A room. A room where she'd been tied down.

They'd taken her baby. Taken it. Taken her sweet little girl.

No. No. No.

She stood there, shaking from cold, from shock. Ice in her veins.

"Ma'am?"

Bright. Too bright. Bright, bright lights.

"Ma'am?"

Slowly, she turned and blinked.

"Baby. My baby," she whispered.

Someone walked toward her, the image dark against the bright lights. A hand reached for her. "Ma'am . . . I'm . . . help . . ."

A man's voice, faded and loud, then silent against her eardrums.

"No, please," she whimpered.

"You're safe now. You're safe." The world tilted and she tried to make sense, but nothing did. Nothing solidified in her mind. Nothing congealed to a whole complete thought. Cold. So, so cold. Why was she so cold?

Quinlan. She wanted Quinlan. She'd called him. He was coming to help. Help her. Help them.

"Ma'am. Stay with me . . . stay . . ." A static of radio voices tunneled to her, swirling and merging, fading . . .

"Stay with me. Help is on the way," shouted down at her. " . . . name?"

The sky was dark, then bright. Red. Blue. Red. Blue. Dark. The darkness grew . . .

She tried to pull away. Tried to go. *Have to find her. Have to find her.*

"Ma'am, what's your name? Your name?"

A dog barked somewhere and kept barking, jerking her back to here, to now, away from the darkness for a moment. She could feel the darkness getting closer though, whispering to her. Sirens screamed louder and louder.

"Ma'am, calm down. Calm down." Hands held her and she blinked, finally focusing. A policeman. A cop.

She licked her lips. "Cop. Help. Please."

"What's your name?" he asked. Dark hair, dark eyes.

"Ella. Ella." She grabbed his shirt. "Help me. They took . . ." She tried to take a deep breath, but her chest felt funny, tired. So damned tired. "Baby. They took my baby. My . . . my . . . Please, I need him. Please. They took her."

"Him? . . . Ella! Stay with me! What's his name? Stay with me!"

"Quin." She licked her dry, cracked lips. Dry. So tired. *Have to find her. Have to find her baby* . . .

"Ella! What's his name?"

"Quinlan Kinncaid . . . D.C. . . . The baby. Took her. They took her. Please . . ." She wanted Quin. "He's my . . . my . . ." She tried to swallow; the world unfocused again in bright blues and reds as sirens screamed in her ear. "Husband."

She saw his lips move, knew he leaned over her, but the darkness grew, a terrible monster, and swallowed her whole.

About the Author

Jaycee never really grew up—she still enjoys playing with imaginary people on a daily basis. Sometimes those people are nice, sometimes they're not, but in the end the girl gets the guy, so all is well. Jaycee earned her degree in Elementary Education from Eastern New Mexico University. She lives in Texas with her family, who puts up with her when her characters demand more of her time and appreciates her weirdness—or so they claim. There are also the cats and the corgis, who, in truth, rule the family. When she's not chained to her keyboard, she's doubling as a parent, a teacher, a maid, a chef, a chauffeur, a therapist, and promoting her education in human development while finishing her masters in plant elimination.

You can learn more about Jaycee by visiting her website at www.jayceeclark.com or emailing her at jaycee@jayceeclark.com. Her newsletter and blog subscriptions can be found on her website, along with links to follow her on Twitter, Facebook, and various other sites.